UNHOLY
DOMAIN

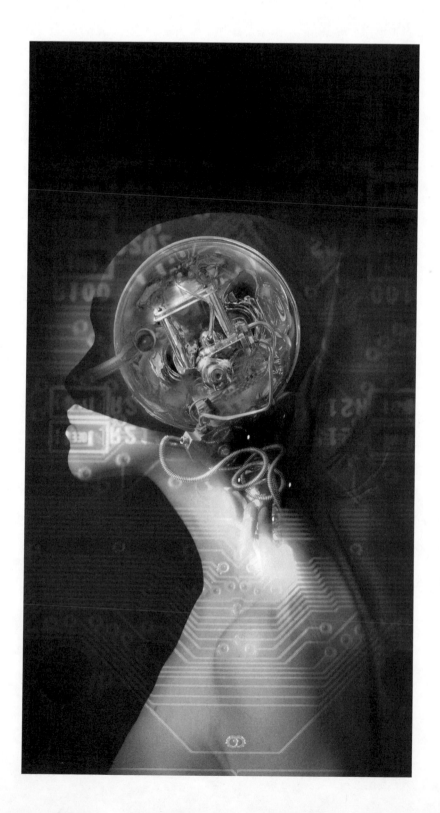

UNHOLY
DOMAIN

A NOVEL

DAN RONCO

KÜNATI

LARGO, USA

UNHOLY DOMAIN

For information, contact Kunati Inc., Book Publishers in both USA and Canada.
In USA: 6901 Bryan Dairy Road, Suite 150, Largo, FL 33777 USA
In Canada: 75 First Street, Suite 128, Orangeville, ON L9W 5B6 CANADA,
or e-mail to info@kunati.com.

FIRST EDITION

Designed by Kam Wai Yu
Persona Corp. l www.personaco.com

ISBN-13: 978-1-60164-021-5   EAN 9781601640215
FIC000000 FICTION/General

Published by Kunati Inc. (USA) and Kunati Inc. (Canada).
Provocative. Bold. Controversial.™

http://www.kunati.com

TM—Kunati and Kunati Trailer are trademarks
owned by Kunati Inc. Persona is a trademark owned by Persona Corp.
All other trademarks are the property of their respective owners.

Library of Congress Cataloging-in-Publication Data

Ronco, Dan.
  Unholy domain : a novel / Dan Ronco. -- 1st ed.
      p. cm.
  ISBN 978-1-60164-021-5 (hardcover : alk. paper)
  1. Cyberterrorism--Fiction. 2. Regression (Civilization)--Fiction. 3.
Technologists--Fiction. 4. Secret societies--Fiction. 5. Artificial intelligence--
Fiction. 6. Religious militants--Fiction. I. Title.
  PS3618.O657U65 2008
  813'.6--dc22
                          2008001055

D e d i c a t i o n

For Linda,
who carried the load
while I pounded keys
up on the third floor.

Acknowledgements

My deepest gratitude to my writing group; Christie D'Agostino, Mitzi Geese,
Janet Lavenger and especially our coach Justin Dwinnell.
Special thanks to editor James McKinnon, graphic artist Kam Wai Yu
and publisher Derek Armstrong at Kunati;
and Rebecca Brown and Paul Nasto
for their support and critiques.

CHAPTER 1

The Great Depression of 2020 fostered a revival of organized crime. The black market in technology surpassed drugs and prostitution to become the primary source of revenue for these criminals.

◆ Dr. Jessica Owen-Wells, *The Great Depression of 2020,* copyright 2041, American Historical Society

In creating the thinking machine, man has made the last step in submission to mechanization; and his final abdication before this product of his own ingenuity has given him a new object of worship: a cybernetic god.

◆ Lewis Mumford, *The Transformations of Man,* 1956

Saturday evening, January 29, 2022

Moesha Jefferson lay hidden in the darkness of the condemned office park, waiting for the infidels to arrive. Across the street was a nearly empty parking garage attached to a glass-and-steel, ten-story office building. Once a manicured commercial park, the land was now choked with weeds.

Perfect for tonight.

Her spies had reported the Technos would meet in that building. Something big. She glanced past the office building at a lonely train about half a mile away, pulling a long line of boxcars, then decided to move closer to the street. As she crept cautiously through tangled bushes in her black, form-fitting body suit, the grounds around her appeared deserted, but her enemies were clever.

The First Minister had asked her to slay the infidels, and she would give her life if necessary. This life on earth was unimportant, just a short prelude to everlasting happiness with the Savior.

Peering through the underbrush, she watched two pinpricks of light flicker in the distance. The pinpricks became headlights, then a long, dark sedan. The silver and black ghost silently cruised up the entry ramp of the parking garage. The sedan stopped at the first level, and its headlights flicked off. The garage's overhead lights revealed the hazy silhouettes of four men in the car.

Moesha's fingers stroked the silver amulet dangling from her neck. The coin-shaped charm was engraved with the familiar image of a bolt-action rifle above a jagged flame, the symbol of the Church of Natural Humans.

The sedan's rear windows slid down, and muzzles of what looked like two shotguns poked out, followed by a series of dull pops. With a low whoosh like a mild breeze, tiny projectiles scattered through the garage. The projectiles floated in the air, drifting whichever way the currents pushed them, shimmering in the yellow beams of the garage lights. A moment later, the muzzles disappeared back into the car.

"They're here," she whispered into the communicator attached to her collar.

"We're ready, Commander," came the muffled reply.

The dark sedan crept through the garage, turned up the ramp, entered the top level and paused. The powerful engine idled quietly.

Muzzles poked out of the side windows, and the dull light again shimmered with tiny projectiles. The muzzles retracted and the car glided to the center of the garage.

It was time. She crept forward.

The Lord willing, the infidels will taste our vengeance tonight.

Sam Armenta looked out the front passenger-side window, searching for hidden enemies in the garage. Through night-vision goggles, he scanned for the religious terrorists who hunted them. The black market in technology was very profitable, but the Army of God made it dangerous. He could not allow anyone to steal his "luggage"—not if he wanted to continue breathing.

Turning to the driver, Sam said, "Give me a quick circle."

As the car traveled in a broad loop, Sam peered through his goggles, searching for a sign of the enemy. The garage appeared deserted.

Sam asked his driver, "Anybody breathing out there?"

Pete eyed a computer display attached to the window visor. The trillions of nanotechnology sensors they'd shot into the garage monitored air composition and transmitted the results back to the computer. The sensors detected carbon dioxide and other products of human respiration. Like tiny mechanical gnats, the sensors would home in on a concentration of these gases and surround the unlucky individual. Once the sensors detected someone, the gunmen in the back seat would finish him off.

"Garage is clear," Pete murmured, eyes focused on the display.

"Okay," Sam replied, scanning the garage one last time. "Pull up to the door."

Pete guided the sedan forward and stopped near the entrance of the office building adjoining the garage. With the engine turned off, the chugging of a freight train resonated in the distance.

Sam pressed his fingers against his chest, feeling the supple webbed surface of his bulletproof vest. It would stop a slug from a pistol or a sniper's attempt from long range, even a high-powered rifle up close. His enemies weren't stupid, however, they had learned where to aim. Sam and the two soldiers in the back pushed open the doors and slipped out. Armed with Beretta laser pistols, they vanished into the darkness, methodically searching the parking garage. Sam had been brought up in the old ways; he never relied on technology completely.

While they searched the garage, Pete placed the computer on the car's hood and reviewed graph after graph of dancing, multi-colored patterns. He keyed a series of commands into the computer, checked the display and entered additional commands.

When satisfied no enemies were present, Sam returned to the car. The other two soldiers waited next to the driver-side door. In hushed tones, they told him the garage was clear.

"Time to get the luggage," Sam ordered.

The two gunmen followed Sam to the rear of the car and stood guard as he opened the trunk. Grunting, Sam lifted out a large brown case and placed it on the cement. Flanked by the gunmen, Sam pulled the case on its wheels to the building entrance.

One of his soldiers pushed open the glass door, and Sam cautiously entered the well-lit lobby. All three men removed their goggles and donned hoods with cutouts for the eyes, nose and mouth.

His two gunmen searched the lobby. Sam glanced nervously back through the door to the garage, where Pete had remained to monitor the computer system. Things were proceeding smoothly, but he'd be happy when this job was over.

Once his soldiers finished searching the lobby, they met Sam at the elevator.

"Floor, please," the elevator's computer asked.

"Nine," Sam replied.

"Coming down immediately."

Seconds later, the elevator doors slid open and the men stepped inside. As they ascended, the men assumed defensive positions, with Sam crouched behind the luggage and the other two kneeling on either side. Sam aimed his laser pistol at the opening doors, but a dimly lit corridor revealed no enemies. They stepped out and walked quietly down the corridor, Sam pulling the luggage between his two guards.

Their steps echoed from the cement floor across the stillness of the empty building. They passed row after row of deserted cubicles, then turned a corner and headed toward a brightly lit conference room. As they approached, Sam detected three hooded men in dark suits just like his crew, seated at the far end of a long table.

He led the way into the conference room. Sam watched the masked men cautiously as he placed the brown case on the oak conference table. Everyone held their weapons on the ready as they sized each other up.

"I'm glad to see you're on time," Sam said to the men seated at the table.

One of them stood up, scraping his chair along the floor. "This is our sixth meeting."

The tension drained away. Both sides had spoken the code words properly, and they could now transact their business. Everyone removed their masks, put their weapons on the table, and greeted their counterparts.

Smiling at the man who had spoken, Sam smoothed back his thick, dyed-black hair and said, "It's good to see you again, Vinnie. I trust business continues to be profitable among the families."

Vinnie shrugged, deep lines etched in his face.

"Not bad, Sam. We could sell much more technology than you provide." He gestured with his palms up. "Is the Domain so fucking rich money doesn't interest you anymore?"

Sam chuckled. "Let's do our business before the Feds catch on." He patted Vinnie on the shoulder. "You're going to like this."

All six men took their seats along the length of the conference table, three on a side. Sam pulled a small helmet-shaped computer from his pocket and placed it in the center of the table. The surface of the computer was a smooth gray, except for two buttons—one green, one red. He pressed the green button, which turned light blue, indicating that its visual and auditory sensors had been activated.

Sam raised his wristwatch to his mouth.

"Let's get this show on the road, Pete."

Two people flashed into view, one at each end of the conference table, life-sized holograms, a man and a woman. The visitors might be thousands of miles away, or they might be down the hall.

Sam had seen holograms before, but he was still mesmerized by the three-dimensional images shimmering in the air, their appearance so realistic, their movements so natural.

James Murphy, Sam's boss, was the man. Murphy was Chief of Security for the Domain, the clandestine organization that created most of the world's illegal technology. A middle-aged man of medium build, Murphy was devoid of distinguishing features. He could blend into any crowd.

Sam had never seen Murphy in the flesh, only as a hologram. He didn't know if this was Murphy's true appearance, or a facade shielding his identity. He suspected few knew the real Murphy.

Sam also guessed Murphy's voice was electronically distorted, although its tone was always calm and pleasing. He chose his words carefully, each selected to provide total clarity. Sam had learned to listen to this complex man. Murphy rarely gave his word, but he always kept it. He treated his men fairly, but without compassion. If you performed well, Murphy would reward you generously. If you didn't, you disappeared. In his own way, Sam trusted Murphy.

"Hello, Maria," Murphy said. "Are you ready to complete our business?"

Sam had seen the petite leader of the New Jersey Technology Syndicate on television, but this was the first time Maria Vitullo had appeared at one of these meetings. Her image showed a hawk-nosed young woman with intense brown eyes. A revealing black dress drew attention to her generous cleavage, but failed to camouflage short, thick legs.

I'd stick it in her anyway, Sam was surprised to find himself thinking.

The oldest child of New Jersey's Vitullo crime family, she had broken tradition to become the boss of the male-dominated organization. The story was—Sam didn't know if it was true—she had executed her uncle in order to gain unchallenged power.

"Good to see you, Murphy," Vitullo replied, glancing at the case. Her voice was respectful, a business executive greeting her main supplier. "If your new product is as good as you claim, we are ready to distribute it at maximum capacity."

Sam knew Vitullo was both vicious and intelligent, a dangerous woman to deal with under any circumstances. Vitullo had been the first to recognize the potential wealth and power of a technology black market. When the government began stalling the development of legal technology ten years earlier, she had rapidly built a huge criminal organization to sell illegal technology. In addition, she had funded scientists fed up with the government's Luddite policies.

The mob had become a venture capitalist in this strange, new world.

Vitullo respected Murphy, but she didn't trust him. Or anyone else. She had been working with him for five years, ever since Murphy had selected her to be the Domain's distributor for the northeast market. The man was an enigma, just like his organization. She had searched for years, but had failed to penetrate the Domain's secrecy. She didn't know Murphy's identity or that of any other Domain leader.

She watched Murphy stroke his chin, a habit she found irritating.

Her investigators had searched the net, but every bit of information about the Domain had been removed. She had bribed and then threatened public officials, but they knew nothing, or they were too frightened to talk. She had even bribed an informer to search the FBI's files, but they contained nothing useful. The Domain remained a shadow organization, invisible and deadly.

People who investigated the Domain disappeared. Sometimes they vanished during the investigation, sometimes months afterward. She had been forced to use outside contractors once her people discovered the pattern, but nothing worked.

She hated being dependent on something she didn't control.

Sensing the Domain was more interested in the broad distribution of their technology than the money, she suspected a mission far beyond criminal profiteering. Whatever Murphy's game, she planned to get a piece of it.

Then she would take it all.

She had never met him in the flesh. He always insisted on virtual meetings, although she had suggested a quiet rendezvous anywhere on his terms.

I'd like to get him in my bed. Then we'd see if he could maintain his composure.

She saw Murphy nod to that fat pig Sam Armenta, who could barely take his eyes off her breasts. He reminded her of Ralph Aprillo, the new Senator from New York. Aprillo had tried to cop a feel at a fundraiser at her compound in Saddle Brook. Someday she'd get even for that one.

Armenta opened the luggage and lifted out a young girl. Vitullo didn't let her expression waver in spite of her surprise. It had to be a robot, but she couldn't tell for sure. Vitullo leaned forward to get a closer look as Sam placed the sleeping girl on the table.

She appeared to be about nine years old, with dark brown hair, cut short. A pretty face, but not perfect; the nose was slightly too long and the lips thin. A few minor facial blemishes spotted her skin.

Very realistic.

The robot wore a short-sleeved blue and white dress. Its arms and legs were slender, but well formed for its design age.

"Sarah, wake up," Sam said.

The robot opened its eyes and smiled. "Hello, Sam."

Vitullo experienced a sudden chill. *The facial expression was almost perfect, no longer the wooden dummy.*

"Sit up, please," Sam said.

"Okay," it replied, sitting up smoothly.

More grace than a human child.

"You're very pretty, Sarah," Vitullo said.

"Thanks." Sarah turned in Vitullo's direction and smiled sweetly. "I don't know you. What's your name?"

"Why doesn't it recognize me?" Vitullo asked Murphy.

"This model doesn't have an interface to the net. Sarah has to learn. Just like a human child."

Vitullo nodded and turned back to Sarah.

"You may call me Ms. Moravec."

"Pleased to meet you, Ms. Moravec."

"Sarah, I haven't seen you for several days," Sam said. "Can you give me a hug?"

Sarah smiled coyly at Sam then crawled across the table and threw its arms around his neck. Sam returned the hug.

"Thank you, Sarah. Please tell Ms., uh, Moravec, about your capabilities."

"Sure." Facing Vitullo again, the robot said, "I'm able to speak at any age level from toddler to adult. In order to describe my capabilities better, I'm switching to adult." Sarah paused, and then continued, "Technically, I am classified as the CLD-13F robotic system. I have been designed to simulate many, but not all, the abilities of a typical girl of nine years."

Sarah's voice had lost the high-pitched squeak of childhood and spoke with the modulation of a well-educated young woman.

Sarah walked gracefully around the table and stopped in front of

Vitullo's hologram.

"I am configured with a comprehensive package of adaptive learning software. Each robot has thirty-eight characteristics the customer may modify. I just gave you an example—language capability. Although the initial language level is set at nine years, the owner may reset it to any age desired."

Vitullo had become vaguely uneasy as she studied the robot.

How far this alien intelligence has come. What if the Domain could take control of this robot from its owner? Could the robots be an army in waiting, scattered in the homes of ordinary citizens?

In a matter-of-fact voice, Vitullo said, "Safety code, included in all previous robots, prohibits any action that might harm a human. Do you obey the entire robot safety code?"

Sarah smiled. "Yes, I do."

Vitullo returned the smile.

"Very good. Can the safety code be overridden in any way? Could you harm a human or allow a human to be harmed?"

Before Sarah could answer, Murphy chuckled. "Come on, Maria. You know we would never develop a robot that doesn't obey the safety code. The world learned a harsh lesson—PeaceMaker—from that lunatic Ray Brown."

"As you say," Vitullo replied.

"You sound skeptical."

Vitullo's lips formed a smile. "You'll say whatever is in the Domain's interest. I say that out of respect for your intelligence. Please respect mine."

Murphy shook his head, apparently bemused. "Very well, but I can assure you this model obeys the safety code in every way."

"Let's say it were possible to override the safety code," Vitullo said, watching Murphy intently. "Suppose a person knew how to bypass a section of code." Before Murphy could interrupt, Vitullo said, "Bear with me, please."

Murphy shrugged and placed his palms on the table. The Domain soldiers sat straight up, ready for action. Tension seeped back into the conference room.

"Suppose the safety code could be overridden," Vitullo insisted, pressing hard for a reaction. "Robots all over the world would rise up as an army, attacking people according to the commands of their master."

She paused, but Murphy's face revealed nothing. Had she gone too far? "But of course the Domain would never create a robot containing such dangerous code. Would you, my friend?"

His eyes never leaving Vitullo, Murphy ignored the question. "Sarah, please continue with your presentation," he said.

As Sarah continued, Vitullo saw endless possibilities. Each customer could configure Sarah according to his own needs. Even more important, before selling them to customers, Vitullo's people might be able to teach the robots to obey hidden commands.

Murphy would never give me a robot that could override the safety code, would he?

She scrutinized Murphy for any hints, but he maintained a pleasant friendliness throughout the presentation, revealing nothing. She decided to have her engineers take the robot apart and see what made it tick.

Outside the building, Pete continued to monitor his computer. He followed the meeting through the display, pleased to see everything going so well. His computer acted as the server for the conference, transmitting data between Murphy and Vitullo and the helmet computer.

Suddenly, the conference room disappeared and the display flashed a blinking message in large, yellow letters: POTENTIAL INTRUDER. In addition to being a hologram server, the computer continued to monitor signals from the billions of sensors scattered throughout the garage. The yellow signal warned him the sensors had detected an intruder near the entrance of the garage.

Pete pulled his Beretta laser pistol, ducked behind the car hood, and located the intruder on the computer display. A map of the nearby area identified someone on the sidewalk hurrying past the garage. The person then crossed the street and appeared to get into a car and drive away. Pete relaxed slightly.

Probably someone from the office complex who had worked late.

It was the last thought he ever had.

Moesha felt the familiar recoil of the Armalite rifle against her shoulder. The weapon's ping was followed by the thump of a high-powered bullet crashing through a human skull; the driver's head blew apart, blood scattering across the blacktop. The man's body slid down the side of the car and flopped to the garage floor. Moesha lowered her weapon and stepped out of the shadows. She crept across the garage to examine the decapitated body.

Assured the gangster was dead, she pulled off her gas mask and portable tank, which had captured her breath, leaving nothing for the sensors to detect. She quickly scanned the garage and then spoke into her communicator, "The driver has been eliminated. You may approach."

Moesha looked at the driver's computer, which now showed thousands of sensors moving toward her. The display had turned red.

Vitullo thought about the possibilities this technology offered as Sarah continued with the presentation. Sarah was a breakthrough technology; the robot was almost human in many ways.

We can sell millions, all secretly trained to obey me.

Vitullo knew Murphy was watching her. Although the robot would be very profitable, she sensed a deeper purpose. Still trying to see what Murphy would reveal, she turned to him.

"Of course, you realize how dangerous it will be to distribute Sarah. The robot's humanness will anger many, especially the fanatics in the Army of God. They will regard Sarah as a tool of the Devil, and become even more determined to eliminate the Technos, as they call us."

Murphy said nothing, so Vitullo asked, "Why did you make the robot so human?"

Everyone's eyes were on Murphy, even Sarah's. Murphy stared at Vitullo for a long moment, making her uncomfortable.

"Sarah is one step along the path, Maria. The path was always there, we are merely the first to walk it."

Vitullo pondered his words and forced a smile. "I don't understand, but I will do my job. How many robots am I to sell?"

"Four million over the next three months."

"I can't sell that many so quickly. What's the robot's price?"

Stroking his chin, Murphy smiled thinly. "That will be your

decision."

"How much will you charge me for each robot?"

Murphy's eyes darkened, losing their veneer of friendly partnership. It was the first time he had allowed his feelings to surface, and the tension gouged her chest.

"There will be no charge," he said, still wearing his thin smile.

What the hell?

The Domain had built a robot that was almost human, with capacity to learn and adapt. Millions would be sold, but they weren't charging her a cent for it? In addition, Sarah would infuriate their enemies.

What is that madman planning?

A barrage of bullets shattered the conference room windows, killing many of the Technos before they could pull their laser pistols. Coming through the door spraying automatic fire, Moesha finished off the last of the enemies. Weapons ready, her men followed her into the room.

Only a single infidel—the one named Sam—remained alive, lying on the floor with blood trickling from the wound in his forehead. The two holograms had disappeared, but not before she memorized their faces. She swore to the Lord she would hunt them down.

Her soldiers surrounded the table, pinning down the arms and legs of the struggling Sarah-Devil. Moesha stood over Sam and kicked him hard in the side. He groaned and then looked up at her. She would have liked to shatter his skull with a kick, but she needed information before he died.

She pointed her Armalite at his head.

"Tell me who you are, and I won't kill you."

Sam coughed. "Go to hell."

The Techno's blasphemy angered her, and the rifle sputtered.

She turned to the Sarah-Devil to examine it more carefully. The robot had stopped struggling and was eyeing her curiously. Moesha shuddered as she recognized the intelligence gleaming through its eyes.

Just as the First Minister had prophesied.

The creature said to Moesha, "Hello. I don't recognize you. Please tell me your name."

Moesha grasped the amulet hanging from her neck and kissed it. She turned to her men and hissed, "Abomination."

Attacking the distributors of these robots wasn't enough; she had to destroy the laboratories where the Technos created the creatures. The next assault would hit the infidels' core.

She would bring the inferno to their universities.

CHAPTER 2

Instead of remaining true to our destiny, humanity is becoming the sorcerer's apprentice, creating a robot force that may sweep us aside.

◆ First Minister Adam Jordan, the Church of Natural Humans, 2016

Although it seems far in the past, it was barely a decade ago that the world was devastated by PeaceMaker, the terrible virus that shut down the Internet. Everything depended on the Internet at that time—the power for homes and factories went out and many froze to death; massive accidents occurred as traffic systems failed; netphones fell silent and television went dark, making communication virtually impossible; food couldn't be shipped to the supermarkets; all the looting and killing—it is almost too horrible to think about.

◆ Daphne Hayden, DNS news anchor, 2022

Sunday, January 30, 2022

Waiting on the front steps, Claire gazed through the immense front entrance of the church. The view was familiar and yet unsettling. Although she had been a member of the Church of Natural Humans for more than two years, she had never seen so many people attend a service. All around her, orderly groups of the faithful entered and took their seats. A network camera crew was setting up in the narthex, surrounded by several church security officers keeping the crowd away. The pressure of the crowd forced her through the entrance and past a ten-foot statue of Jesus on the cross. As she left the narthex and stepped into the nave, her eyes gazed upward; all five levels of balconies were packed.

The Church of Natural Humans had grown from a small sect with fewer than twenty thousand followers, mostly in the South, to a thriving, growing organization with forty million members in the US and thirty million more worldwide. The Church's founder, Adam Jordan, claimed that God commanded him to stop the advance of unholy technology. In the aftermath of PeaceMaker, the Church's core message—that advanced technology was dangerous to humanity's physical and moral survival—had touched the souls of decent folk everywhere and shown them the path to salvation. She was blessed to be one of them.

Today would be unique, the first televised service permitted by the Church. Adam Jordan, their Founder and First Minister, would speak during the service. There were rumors the Church had captured one of the Technos, those horrible scientists that worshipped the Devil, and would execute him in front of the congregation. She shivered. That could never happen; it must be just a rumor.

She made the sign of the cross. Thank the Lord she had found the Church.

Her eyes swept over the interior of the vast building. Its rounded arches and dark interior resembled a Romanesque Catholic cathedral, but with a more functional, severely simple appearance. A plain wooden stage, holding a single row of straight-backed chairs in front of a low wooden altar, rose at the far end of the nave. No statues, candles or traditional decorative objects intruded on the stage's stark appearance. A huge stone fireplace covered the entire back wall of the stage, and a row of smaller fireplaces lined each side of the nave, providing heat and flickering light. A Winchester bolt-action rifle, its barrel polished to gleam in the light of the flames, was mounted above each fireplace.

I remember what that means.

In the Church's doctrines, the fireplace and rifle symbolized a man's home and his power to defend it. One of the ministers had taught her that.

With a shiver, she realized it was almost as cold in the building as it was outside. The fireplaces were impressive, but they didn't provide sufficient heat for so huge a building.

Broad skylights dwarfed a line of fourteen stained-glass windows built high in the clerestory above each balcony, depicting the Stations of the Cross. The skylights provided adequate lighting during the day; at night the dark sky dominated.

A soft hand on her upper arm intruded in her thoughts. A familiar, heart-faced woman smiled kindly at her and gently guided her along the stone floor of the nave.

This Sister is so nice. What is her name?

From a hidden organ, somber music filled the air. The faithful continued to pour in and take their assigned seats. The Sister guided her to an empty pew not far from the entrance, and they shuffled in about halfway.

Sister Patricia, Claire recalled, *that's her name.*

Claire breathed hard, and her hand clutched at the bronze amulet dangling from her neck. She was to be called today, even though she had sinned. She looked down at the coin-shaped charm pressed with the image of a bolt-action rifle above a jagged flame, then lifted the cold metal to her mouth and kissed it. She had never spoken to the congregation before, and she was nervous.

Gradually the pews filled. Familiar organ music echoed through the cavernous building. Claire pulled out her prayer book, read briefly from it then stuffed it back in her purse. She squeezed shut her eyes, and the beautiful music washed over her.

She was disappointed when the last notes drifted away. Minutes stretched by, and she began to fidget, until the faithful stood up in unison. Twelve ministers, stern-faced men and women, entered in pairs from a door at the side of the giant fireplace. Wearing dark blue cassocks that brushed the tops of their shoes, the ministers fanned out across the stage and stood in front of their seats. The top buttons of each cassock were open, revealing a shoulder holster and pistol. A large silver amulet sparkled from each minister's neck. When all the ministers were in place, they sat in unison, leaving the center chair empty.

The church retained its eerie quiet as the congregation anticipated the arrival of the Holy Prophet, First Minister Adam Jordan. Claire leaned to the side, peering around the man seated in the pew in front of her, making sure she had a clear view.

The seconds stretched to minutes.

Suddenly a small, wiry man seemed to come out of nowhere and strode to the front of the stage, gleaming in a bright spotlight and accompanied by the energetic blare of organ music. Claire was one of the first to rise and stand at attention.

The First Minister wore a white cassock, open at the top with his shoulder holster and gun exposed. Although middle-aged, he walked with the quickness of an athlete. His gold amulet swayed across his chest in rhythm with his long, confident strides. Stopping at the front of the stage, his stern presence dominated the crowd. The music played to a crescendo and abruptly ended.

Claire pressed the amulet against her chest.

"Welcome to the Church of Natural Humans," he said in a gravelly voice. "I am First Minister Adam Jordan."

What a handsome man!

High cheekbones, a thin, straight nose and a shock of long, gray hair falling over his shoulders. Piercing brown eyes. A lined but chillingly beautiful face. A long, jagged scar on his right cheek.

After gazing over the crowd, he threw his head back, stretched his arms to the sky and bellowed, "I am a Natural Human."

"I am a Natural Human," the congregation roared back. The rumble of voices cascaded across the church, twelve thousand souls, united in belief, reciting the *Prayer for the Lord's Creations.*

Claire closed her eyes and joined in the recitation:

"My mind and my body are human. My soul has not been altered by Technology. We will destroy the Devil and protect the Earth."

Claire opened her eyes and stared at her leader. Jordan's wiry body swayed lightly, responding to the crowd in a slow, sensuous dance. His eyes unfocused, Jordan stretched his arms again and thundered, "Glory be to the Lord and His Creations."

A spiritual bliss danced across the faces of his followers, and the church reverberated with their joyous response.

"Glory be to the Lord and His Creations."

Once again, the church grew quiet. Jordan walked to the edge of the stage and down the wooden stairs, his heels clacking on each step. Claire lost sight of him, but his steps echoed through the church as he strode down the stone floor of the center aisle. The faithful knelt, bowed their heads and kissed their amulets as he passed, like a summer storm blowing through the trees. At the center of the church under a huge skylight, he came to a halt and gazed over his followers. Claire felt his eyes briefly rest upon her, cleansing her with his faith.

She didn't deserve to be called. She couldn't face all these good people. They should have given her something … helped her. A vague recollection of a silver chalice, filled to the brim with a bitter red liquid, passed through her mind. Maybe they had given her something—she couldn't remember.

The flickering light of the fireplaces played across Jordan's face, highlighting the jagged scar. Then he abruptly tilted his head back, stretched his arms to the sky and cried out, "I am a Natural Human."

A wall of sound thundered as the faithful responded, "I am a Natural Human."

Jordan again led the faithful in prayer:

"I condemn artificial intelligence and non-human beings.

These are abominations in the sight of God.

They will be flushed to the bowels of the Earth."

Jordan stretched his arms and shouted, "Glory be to the Lord and His Creations."

With one unified and unyielding voice, the faithful responded, "Glory be to the Lord and His Creations."

Rising from their knees, the chosen broke into a torrent of applause. Many screamed their devotion to God, promising to kill Technos and defeat Lucifer.

Suddenly lightheaded, Claire grasped the front of the pew. What was wrong with her? She tried to think, but her mind had grown fuzzy. Sister Patricia was intently watching her, so she joined in the applause.

Jordan basked in the adulation then lifted one hand to stop the tumultuous roar. Suddenly it was quiet. The breathing of the crowd was palpable now, like that of soldiers before battle.

The First Minister strode back to the stage, his amulet swinging with each step. As he passed, believers dropped to their knees and recited the *Prayer for the Lord's Creations*. The organ played in the background.

When Jordan reached the stage, he turned and spoke. His voice sounded much older than his years. Rumbling from deep in his throat, gravelly and sometimes indistinct, it could quickly turn from comfort to threat. His voice surprised her the first time she met him; it seemed to have taken residence in the wrong body.

"This is a special moment for all of us," Jordan said. "For the first time, we welcome non-believers to behold a service of the Church of Natural Humans. I am filled with happiness I can invite my fellow humans across the net to experience the joy and brotherhood of our Church."

Sadness and a hint of anger played across his face. "Today marks the tenth anniversary of the attack by PeaceMaker, the Devil's software virus. On that horrendous day, the world learned of the danger the Technos had brought forth. Dominated by Lucifer, the Techno Raymond Brown, PeaceMaker's creator, attempted to crush our civilization."

Claire shrank into her seat. Sister Patricia patted her hand. Startled, Claire turned to look into the Sister's forgiving eyes.

"That danger is still with us," Jordan said, "growing with every passing day. Humanity is at great risk, and that is why you must hear me on this specific day."

Jordan paced again, his long, powerful strides carrying him across the stage. He stopped and faced the crowd. "Lucifer has unleashed a great Depression to weaken us. Poverty and disease are everywhere. Honest people scratch out a living while Technos and their allies live well. Crime has exploded, and it is no longer safe to step outside our homes." His voice boomed. "Anyone with eyes can see our world is being torn apart. Lucifer laughs at us while his disciples, the Technos, tempt us to take another bite of the accursed apple.

"Do not think the danger is lessened because Ray Brown has been slain. His spawn, David Brown, walks the earth. Lucifer has given him the power to create abominations just like his father. David Brown must be stopped before he builds an entity even more monstrous than PeaceMaker."

As Jordan walked back and forth, Claire followed his every movement. "Lucifer's evil power is great, but he cannot rule Earth while the Lord's children remain. He has been waiting in hell for all eternity—waiting for humanity to meddle with powers we cannot control. The time has arrived; Lucifer has unleashed technology to destroy all Natural Humans."

Jordan's gaze swept across the church. "We have entered the Apocalypse," he roared.

Many of the faithful blessed themselves, others dropped to their knees.

"I must tell you this; Lucifer's plan is working."

Jordan's dark eyes skewered the faithful.

"Every day we take another bite of the sweet fruit of technology. Every day we discover another way to change our genes. Every day we learn another way to increase the intelligence of our computers.

Every day we chip away at our claim to humanity.

"THIS ... MUST ... STOP ... NOW!"

Claire cringed.

"The Lord formed the Church of Natural Humans to block Lucifer's evil design. He revealed to me the power of a human untouched by artificial enhancements. He unveiled the power that will save us—the military wing of our Church.

"The Army of God!

"The Army of God is the fist that will smash the Technos and cleanse the Earth. Humanity will have a beautiful world inhabited only by natural creatures, living as God planned. A world designed by the Creator for the salvation of the human race."

He strode back to center stage, footsteps echoing.

"Today we celebrate the war against technology. This crusade is dangerous, and it is with great sadness I ask you to take up arms." Jordan's eyes glistened. "From this day forward, all Natural Humans will seek out and destroy technology wherever it is unearthed. Computers must be smashed, software wiped clean. Anything that simulates human thinking must be eradicated.

"We must also stop the corruption of our bodies and minds. Natural Humans must stop those who would alter our genes and create abominations outside of the Creator's design. Natural Humans must smash the research labs that tamper with our genes, replace our organs with mechanical parts or integrate our minds with those of machines. Natural Humans must obliterate the hospitals and clinics that do not respect God's will."

Jordan gazed over his followers. His eyes paused again on Claire. "And most important," he said, "we must find the Antichrist and burn the life from it in the great fireplace of this church.

"The choice is simple: defeat the Technos and claim this Earth for the Lord." Jordan swept his eyes over his transfixed congregation. "Or burn in hell for all eternity as Devil-spawned abominations rule our world."

The crowd howled. It began as a low growl and swelled to a frightening roar. Hatred for the Technos swept through the church.

Two burly Natural Men appeared at the back of the stage. They dragged forward a struggling little girl dressed in a plain maroon dress and a white lab coat. A black cowl covered her eyes.

The girl begged the men to set her free, but they dragged her to the front of the stage. The congregation buzzed, but quieted at a gesture from the First Minister.

The girl's head turned from side to side. Claire wondered what crime against God this poor soul must have committed.

"Who's out there?" the girl shouted. "Why have you taken me?"

Jordan took a few steps and stopped in front of her. The church was silent, except for the voice of the terrified girl, "Someone is out there. Please talk to me!"

Jordan slowly drew his revolver and pointed it at her chest. Claire gasped, riveted to the scene.

A young man burst out of a middle pew and ran toward Jordan screaming, "No more killing!" He was tackled from behind. Several guards pummeled him then dragged his limp body out a side door.

Jordon shouted, "What shall we do with the Technos?"

The congregation answered, "Kill them all."

"No, please!" the girl begged.

The first gunshot brought the crowd to a roar as the bullet smashed into the girl's chest. Her body jerked back, but the two men held her upright.

Claire found herself screaming out of control, terrified for the girl, but the Technos had violated God's will. She looked around—the church was a sea of angry, clean-cut faces.

Jordan shot the girl repeatedly, even though it appeared the first bullet had taken her life. Each gunshot echoed with the previous one until the whole building reverberated with murderous intensity.

Claire gasped for breath, lightheaded. Jordan, the faithful, the church and the revolver fused into a single, seething entity. Her legs felt weak, she held on to the pew.

Jordan tried to speak, but stopped as the crescendo continued out of control. The roar gradually evolved into a chant, "Death to the Technos … Death to the Technos …"

Arms folded, Jordan waited calmly. Finally, the mob's passion ebbed and the chant faded.

"Remove the clothes," Jordan shouted.

The men stripped off her coat and pulled down her dress, revealing half a dozen holes in the girl's torso.

"Does this thing bleed?" Jordan asked.

There wasn't a drop of blood. The congregation buzzed in confusion.

Jordan stuck his fingers through the holes and pulled hard. The front of the girl's chest flipped open, revealing a dense organization of electronics. The faithful cursed, but quieted when Jordan raised his hand.

"This is what the Technos are releasing into the world. This robot—this abomination—is Lucifer's replacement for natural humans, assembled from chemicals, electricity and inorganic materials." Jordan's voice boomed, "How many of these Frankensteins walk among us?"

The robot's heels scraped across the wooden floor as the two men dragged it to the rear of the stage and out of sight, a sound Claire felt to her bones.

Sister Patricia suddenly pulled her into a firm embrace, pressing Claire's face into the sister's neck. Sister Patricia pressed a wet pad against Claire's nose, and an overwhelming scent rushed up her nostrils and invaded her mind. Claire gasped and tried to pull away, but the Sister was too strong.

"You will feel wonderful in a moment," Sister Patricia whispered.

Fog lifted from her mind, revealing the words that had been planted there, and Claire stopped struggling.

"The Apocalypse is here," Jordan said in a quiet voice. "The Antichrist seeks to eradicate humanity. Join us now. The ranks of Natural Humans are growing to meet this unholy threat. Many outsiders have seen the light, sometimes from the most unexpected source."

Sister Patricia released her grip, and Claire straightened in her seat. She felt alert, all her senses working in harmony, as if she had awakened from a deep slumber. Sister Patricia smiled at her then turned to listen to the First Minister.

Jordan walked to the front of the stage. "For those not familiar with our ways, our custom is to have a member of the Church give witness at our services. Today the Lord has blessed us with a most unusual woman." Jordan lifted his head, peering toward the rear of the building. "Claire, please come here and stand by me."

Her contentment ebbed. She had known she would be called, but she wasn't worthy. Her legs were stone. Deep down, to her core, she was a sinner. These good people would never accept someone so worthless. Turning to Sister Patricia, Claire wanted to explain she couldn't give witness, but the words were there, placed in her mind, burning to be spoken. Patricia's eyes glowed with happiness, and she stood and offered Claire her hand.

So forgiving.

Claire rose to her feet and shuffled to the center aisle. Head down, she tottered toward the stage, her eyes focused on the amulet dangling like a shield in front of her chest.

Jordan took her hand as she climbed the steps. She was surprised when he hugged her then guided her to the proper spot on the stage.

Jordan turned to the crowd. "This is Claire Brown, sister of the Techno Raymond Brown."

A buzz of whispers rippled through the church. After gazing over the crowd, Jordan walked away to sit with the Ministers.

Claire kept her eyes down and remained silent. She tried to speak, but only mumbled words came out. The crowd began to whisper again. She knew what to say, the words glowed in her mind; she just had to find the courage.

A female voice shouted, "We don't want the sister of the Devil-maker in our church."

Other voices cried out; she felt anger spread among the faithful.

She just had to say the words in her mind and everything would be all right.

"I am a Natural Human."

The crowd grew quiet as she recited the prayer.

"My mind and my body are human. My soul has not been altered by Technology."

A woman in the second row kneeled; others followed.

"We will destroy the Devil and protect the Earth. Glory be to the Lord and His Creations."

A soft rustle came from the pews as thousands of believers kneeled.

Claire shuffled her feet and cleared her throat. She coughed up phlegm and then swallowed it, leaving a vile taste. *The chalice … the bitter liquid.* She cleared her throat again and allowed the words to be spoken.

"For many years, I was a lonely woman without hope or purpose." She looked across the congregation. "Then I found salvation through the First Minister and the Church of Natural Humans. I now have a purpose in life. I would like to share my story with my fellow humans here and with those of you in the wilderness still searching for an answer. I pray my story will help you find salvation among your fellow humans."

She looked down, ashamed. "If he had survived, my brother would have been fifty-two, just two years older than me. We were born into a troubled home. Our parents were not evil, but I now understand they were lost souls." The faithful murmured sympathetically. "My father, God save his soul, was a Techno and an atheist."

The words were there, in her mind. They were her words—they had to be— but she had never spoken so well. She concentrated on the words. It was all so clear.

Claire raised her eyes and gazed across the church, finding sympathetic faces. "My mother was a cold shell of a woman, without love of God or man. Was there any doubt my brother would become Lucifer's tool? Or that I would become a weak copy of my mother … a useless collection of bone and tissue imitating a human? Looking back, I can see Lucifer's hand crushing the humanity out of our family, so he could corrupt Ray's genius."

Taking a deep breath, Claire continued. "My brother and I fought for our humanity, but we did not understand the power of the Enemy. We knew our lives held no meaning, but we didn't realize the Lord was missing. My brother tried to fill his life with technology, and Lucifer drove him without mercy. Technology became addictive, but it did not provide him with the happiness he craved. Then he became an alcoholic. His life swung back and forth between alcohol and technology, each cycle worse than the previous one. He tried to break free—to become human—but Lucifer had him in a death grip." She lifted her chin and stared over the crowd. "I'll tell you this about my brother; he fought long and hard, but in the end, he succumbed to Lucifer and brought forth the beast, PeaceMaker.

"I was not so valiant. I quickly fell prey to drugs and alcohol. I would do anything to fill my body with chemicals. I lied, cheated, and whored— anything to get chemicals, anything to keep me from thinking about the emptiness of my existence. I hated being sober. Whenever the drugs cleared from what remained of my mind, I was forced to confront my sins." Tears clouded her vision. "I even tried suicide, but I failed at that, too."

Coughing racked her body, and she struggled to recover her breath.

Such a wasted life.

"Finally, a miracle happened. One day a Sister found me and brought me to the Church. They provided food for my body and, more importantly, my soul. The good people of the Church helped me to understand what had happened to my brother and to me." Pointing to Adam Jordan, she said, "That good man helped me to find salvation. He has given me the chance to do something decent with my life."

She stared defiantly into the camera. "We must stop the advance of technology! I will do everything I can, but the Enemy is strong and merciless. We need your strength. Please join us. I beg you; help us defeat the Technos."

The church exploded with applause. Smiling, Adam Jordan hurried to Claire and embraced her. As she tottered down the aisle toward her seat, the crowd applauded. Recollection seeped into her mind.

The silver chalice … the First Minister … he'd been the one who taught her the words … such a bitter liquid, but it had washed away her sins. She felt contentment, just as the First Minister had promised. The confession had completed her transformation to a state of grace. The guilt had been cleansed from her soul. She was a Natural Human.

The First Minister's voice boomed over her shoulder. "Bless you, Claire. Bless you for your courage and your compassion. You have traveled from the gateway of hell and we admire you."

Turning to glare into the camera, he thundered, "If Claire Brown can find her way to us, so can you! If Claire Brown can stand up to the Devil, so can you. If Claire Brown can find salvation, you, too, can give your life grace and meaning.

"I ask you, join your fellow humans in the war against Lucifer. Join Claire … join me … in the great crusade against the Technos. Dedicate your life to humanity. Find your destiny in the Church of Natural Humans."

The organ blared as Jordan turned, walked to the back of the stage, and disappeared. As he walked, the faithful chanted the *Prayer for the Lord's Creations*.

When Adam Jordan's war had run its bloody course, human history would forever be changed.

CHAPTER 3

*An uneasy peace exists between believers and Technos.
Most people draw clear boundaries between religion
and technology, but what if they come into conflict?
What would put them in fundamental conflict? Or is
the question who rather than what?*

◆ Steve Bonini's Diary, 2014

Monday, January 31, 2022

David forced his eyes open and blinked at the sunlight streaming
through his apartment window. His stomach felt queasy, and he
kicked himself for staying so late at the bars. He recalled going out
to the car with Cindy-what's-her-name, but everything was a blur.

Turning his head to focus on the alarm clock, he groaned when
he saw it was almost 11 a.m. He knew he should drag himself out
of bed and catch up on his homework. Now in his fourth year at
the University of Washington, he was still a junior because he had
dropped so many classes. Although testing had revealed a genius
level IQ, his grades were mediocre. Not that he gave a shit.

Is Cindy still here? He reached over, but the bed was empty.
Too bad. She must have decided to sneak away before her friends
discovered that she had slept with the infamous David Brown.

He blinked his eyes, but his vision remained blurry. *That girl
could sure suck down the beer.* He smiled, thinking about last night's

encounter. *She knew how to use that body, too.* He scratched his head and fought the temptation to go back to sleep.

On the wall was a poster of Marilyn Monroe, a long-ago sex symbol. A blast of wind from a passing subway had blown her dress upwards, revealing a beautiful pair of legs. Although Marilyn attempted to push down her dress, a mischievous smile lit up her face. The honest beauty and pure enjoyment of that poster always made him feel good. Marilyn died young, a misfit, but she had left her mark. Maybe he would leave his mark, too.

David's robot, NewBuddy, waited at the foot of the bed. A five-foot-tall mobile computer with a holographic projector on top, it could move about the apartment on four spidery legs. He had brought NewBuddy home from the school's artificial intelligence lab to upgrade its software.

How many beers did I have last night, anyway? He smiled. *Not as many as Cindy.*

When he propped himself up on his elbows, the robot displayed Marilyn Monroe's head and torso in a three-dimensional holograph just above its top section.

"Rise and shine, big boy," Marilyn said. "Time to get that bod out of bed."

"You'll have to do better than that, Marilyn," he said, yawning.

The robot then projected a life-size hologram of Marilyn in a tiny bikini standing next to the bed. The image was so vivid, David felt he could have reached up and touched her. She leaned over him, her breasts swaying deliciously, and leered. "I really need you to get up." She giggled. "Come on, baby."

David chuckled, "Pretty good," but remained in bed.

He fluffed up the pillows and stretched out.

There wasn't that much homework, anyway.

He loved working on the robot, and he knew every inch of it. The central processing and memory unit located midway up the frame coordinated the actions of the microchips distributed throughout the robot's structure. NewBuddy had the hardware capability to outperform a human at many tasks. An idea to improve its performance popped into his mind, but instead of acting on it, he reluctantly decided to study for the exams.

The robot carried a bunch of towels into the bathroom, treading lightly on its thin legs. A moment later, David heard water running in the shower.

He wondered why his professors insisted he take all these dumb classes; they knew he had designed most of the enhancements to this robot. Thanks to his work, each microchip employed high performance software that functioned independently of the central processor. In effect, he had distributed intelligence throughout the robot, with the central processor providing coordination. David wasn't claiming all the credit—he didn't really care who got the credit—but everyone knew he had developed the software.

NewBuddy came out of the bathroom. "Your shower is ready."

David kicked off the blankets and dragged himself out of bed. He took a step and stumbled over a pair of sneakers. They didn't look familiar, so he held one against his foot. Too small. He chuckled when he realized Cindy had left her sneakers here. He felt under the bed for his sneakers. Gone.

Wear them in good health.

Undressing as he walked, he dropped his underpants on the floor and stumbled to the bathroom. He opened the shower door and tested the water temperature with his hand. *Why do I bother?* He enjoyed a long shower, shaved, tied his thick brown hair back in a wet ponytail and walked back to the bedroom to get dressed. He checked out his bare body as he passed the mirror—lean and tight.

NewBuddy had left a pair of jeans, a black pull-over shirt, clean underpants, and white socks on the now made-up bed. His beat-up tennis shoes were side by side on the rug. After dressing quickly, he ambled into the old-fashioned but recently repainted kitchen, where NewBuddy had placed a cup of coffee, black and steaming, on the table. The robot was heating scrambled eggs and toast in the microwave, which it served shortly after he sipped the coffee.

He grinned and said, "Marilyn, what do you think are my best qualities?"

While the robot carried frozen strips of bacon to the microwave, a life-sized hologram of Marilyn Monroe, dressed in a French maid's outfit, appeared at his side.

"Hmmm, you have so many good qualities." Marilyn licked her lips. "It's difficult, big boy, to pick out just one or two."

Scratching his chin, David pretended to consider Marilyn's answer. "You make a good point. I know it's difficult with so much to choose from, but let's be bold. Take a stab at it."

"Well, that hard body of yours does things for me," Marilyn purred. "Plus, you know more about artificial intelligence and robotics than anyone else in the world, including that bimbo Dr. Golkin, who gave you a C in the robotics lab." Marilyn smiled and said, "That's it, baby, sexy and smart— those are your best qualities."

"Excellent. My selections as well." David raised his coffee cup. "My compliments to your neural networks."

While eating scrambled eggs and bacon, he picked up his eyeglasses and said, "Turn on the news."

The glasses, a virtual reality technology that projected precise images directly onto the retina, selected his standard morning news broadcast.

The first report described a big government technology bust. The news reporter described how the FBI had caught a gang of black marketers. An informer had revealed the location of a data warehouse on the net, containing illegal financial software. By analyzing and extrapolating vast amounts of financial data, the software could augment human reasoning in placing stock market transactions. The news reporter explained how anyone owning this software would have an unfair advantage over everyone else, violating the Technology Fairness Act. Luckily, the reporter droned, the FBI caught the criminals before they could distribute the software over the net.

Stupid law, stupid government.

"Turn off this crap and display my messages." He finished the scrambled eggs and took a big bite of toast.

He stopped chewing when his glasses displayed page after page of email messages—more than eight thousand messages last night.

"What the hell?" he murmured and selected the first one. The video showed the hazy outline of a man sitting in a dark room. A heavy, deliberately distorted voice said, "You and your whole damn family should have been executed years ago. I don't buy all that bullshit that you were innocent. You have bad blood. We should get a hot iron and ram—"

"Shut down this message," David shouted and collapsed back in his chair.

God, it was happening again.

He picked another message and the puffy face of a fifty-plus woman appeared. "My son Donnie would be thirty-one if he hadn't died from radiation exposure ten years ago," she said. "Your father— may he rot in hell —was responsible for Donnie's murder when that PeaceMaker made the nuclear reactor explode. You should at least have the decency to say you're sorry for what that bastard did. First Minister Jordan says you're a computer freak, too. The government ought to lock you up and throw away the key."

The picture went blank.

So that's what set it off. A stupid speech by that maniac Adam Jordan. Shit. If they target me, this could get dangerous.

The old anger came back, fresh and raw. He would not let these bastards push him around again.

PeaceMaker was my father's crime, not mine. My father, damn him.

He spit the toast out of his mouth.

The bastard.

As suddenly as it came, the storm passed. There wasn't any point in getting worked up. The anger simmered, but he'd get through it.

"Eliminate all the messages in my mailbox except those from people I know."

All but a few messages disappeared. His mother had messaged several times, warning him to stay out of class for a few days. That bastard Jordan was heating things up again, no doubt to recruit converts for his miserable church.

Too bad he didn't have a class today. At least he could go over to the library, as if he was looking up something in that slower-than-shit computer system. Screw them.

Only one message remained. Sent from a public database, the message had been created a decade earlier. Curious, he selected it.

His father stared at him from across the years, a broad-shouldered man with big hands tapping nervously on his desk.

David gaped at the once-familiar image. Unruly salt and pepper hair flopped over a forehead lined with deep creases, but it was the intensity in his father's dark eyes that mesmerized David.

The man spoke, slowly, quietly. "Dear David, receiving a message from your father after all these years must be quite a shock, and I'm sorry for that. You're twenty-one now, old enough to learn what really happened directly from me. By chance, I discovered a lethal virus in the Atlas operating system, and I have decided to do everything in my power to defeat it and expose the people who developed it. I'm scared and I thought about walking away from it, but I can't do it. Since you've received this message, I must have failed and my enemies captured or killed me. You see, this message was set to release automatically in 2022 unless I deleted it. God, I can only hope they were stopped before they unleashed the virus.

"It was great to see you last weekend. You are probably building computer systems I couldn't even imagine. You're growing into a fine young man." There was a catch in his voice. "I am so proud of you." His father paused for a moment to regain his composure. "I'm not very good at giving a speech, and I won't try to do that today. I wasn't as good a father as you deserved. I drank too much and I wasn't always there when you needed me. Your mother deserves all the credit for helping you grow up as well as you have. But know this—I love you very much."

His father pushed a strand of hair back from his forehead. "I guess that's all I have to say. I don't know what kind of world exists in 2022, but I hope it's good for you."

The sadness in his father's voice settled like a damp winter day into David's bones.

"Goodbye ... I wish it could have been different ... live fully and honorably ... that's all."

Stunned, David played the message again. He tried to capture every word, every inflection. The message appeared to be authentic—why would anyone fake it after all these years?

Slowly the enormity of the message sank in; was it possible his father was not the monster who had infected the net with the PeaceMaker virus? If this message was true, his father had not been responsible for all the death and destruction when the computers shut down. Just the opposite. He had lost his life trying to stop the criminals responsible for the catastrophe.

He felt sick. His head ached, but this wasn't a normal headache. The pain seemed to flow right into his mind. He hadn't suffered an attack like this for years, since PeaceMaker had been terminated. David buried his head in his arms and closed his eyes. The stench of roadside kill drifted into his senses as in a dream. Pain ... disquieting sensations ... more pain. An image formed in the shadows of his mind. The image twisted and vibrated, like an insect escaping a cocoon, but remained hazy. Then he understood ... an entity was coming across the net, coming for him. His mind's eye strained to see through the darkness ... the image twisted into the shape of a child, but it wasn't flesh and blood. All his senses warned him of danger.

David readied for the confrontation. A stone blasted through his kitchen window, spraying shards of glass across the room, bringing him out of his trance. He dived to the floor as a second stone hurled through the window and crashed into his refrigerator. A barrage of stones pelted his windows, and he scrambled under the table.

Angry voices came from the ground, and another volley of stones smashed through the windows. Sirens wailed in the distance. He prayed it was the police coming to rescue him. Stones continued to fly through the windows, splintering the remaining glass and crashing into the walls and ceiling. The siren grew louder, but it seemed to be taking forever.

He heard voices from the exterior hallway, then a loud crash. Someone was trying to knock down his door! His only weapon was a baseball bat in the bedroom closet. He scrambled across the kitchen floor on his hands and knees. He reached up, opened the closet door and searched for the bat. Loud thuds as someone tried to kick in the door. He found the bat and got ready to swing it at anyone who broke in.

A voice yelled, "Cops," and several people ran down the hall.

Another volley of stones crashed through the bedroom window. He scrambled back under the kitchen table. Excited voices came through the windows, and he thought he heard a policeman shouting orders. Gradually, it grew quiet outside, except for a pulsing siren. Still holding the bat, he crept to the kitchen window and peeked out. A few demonstrators were in the street, but the police had them under control.

One grubby-looking guy spotted David in the window and shouted obscenities. David gave him the finger then crunched through broken glass back to the kitchen table. NewBuddy was stretched out on the floor, his chest dented by a rock.

A policeman came in to see if he was okay, and glanced around at the damage. He seemed annoyed to be there and left without saying much.

David went back to the splintered kitchen window and watched the police drag away the few remaining demonstrators. He doubted anyone would be charged.

He looked around his apartment, littered with stones and broken glass. It was getting chilly, but he didn't care.

After staring blankly out the window for some time, he realized he was pressing hard on the windowsill, leaving his fingertips white and sore. The demonstrators were gone. A lone policeman stood at the front door of the apartment building.

David pulled a sheet off his bed and tacked it over the bedroom window then did the same in the kitchen. He swept up the broken glass, poured a glass of cola and sat down at the kitchen table.

His father was responsible for this.

Years before, he had concluded that his father had failed at all the important things in life. Sure, the man had it tough, but he failed big-time. His father had led a sad life, beginning with a dysfunctional family. He had fought alcoholism, never winning but never giving up either. The man had tried to be a good husband and father. When he had been sober, when he had been there for them, he was terrific. They just never knew which Raymond Brown they would get. And in the end, they got a failed man.

But how do I really know Dad wasn't guilty? Maybe the message is a clever fake. Maybe he was creating an alibi in case things failed. Or maybe he was just a psycho after all.

David pressed his forehead against the table. *Damn you, Dad, you bastard, you loser. Damn you, wherever you are.* He couldn't think of enough curses to burn out his rage, and they kept tumbling through his mind.

He couldn't go on like this—he had to get to the truth. A lot more than an old message would be necessary to demonstrate his father's innocence—if he *was* innocent. Those responsible for creating PeaceMaker had concocted a convincing lie, so getting to the truth would be tough. A decade had passed, plenty of time to destroy all the evidence of his father's innocence, if there was any.

If my father is innocent, and I do this, the people who killed him will come after me.

Yet he had to do it. If he could prove his father wasn't guilty, the family name would be cleared. All the hatred would disappear; they could live like normal people.

He wouldn't fail. He wasn't like his father. He would find out whether his father was innocent or guilty—wherever the truth took him. He'd get to the core and finally understand that strange, complex man.

Then he could free himself.

Maybe.

To David's surprise, he felt strangely alive. For the first time in his life, he had a clear goal: he would finally learn what made his father tick. If Dad was innocent, David would clear the family name and bring the bastards to justice.

He glanced around at his broken apartment. He'd have to be careful, or his father's killers would discover his search. He swallowed hard. And there was that creature coming over the net.

CHAPTER 4

Only a small proportion of humans can understand the inner workings of science and technology. To most humans it's magic—powerful magic. The masses don't have a glimmer of understanding and they mistrust those who do.

◆ Steve Bonini's Diary, 2015

A car bomb exploded this morning just outside the front entrance of Intelligent Storage Devices in Princeton, New Jersey, killing 57 and injuring more than 200. A police spokesperson indicated this might have been the work of the mysterious Army of God, which has attacked a number of high-tech corporations since the beginning of the year.

◆ *The Wall Street Journal,* May 15, 2020

Thursday, February 3, 2022

David drove north from Seattle on Interstate 5 for more than two hours, heading toward his grandmother's home in the San Juan Islands. As he drove, the morning sun rose above the white-capped peaks of the Cascade Mountains, now and then breaking through a clutter of gray clouds. He had begun his search for the truth about his father, and he was nervous. After the riot outside his dorm, he had no choice.

His speedometer hovered at around 35 due to dangerous potholes and road litter. Once a beautiful three-lane highway, it hadn't been maintained since tax revenues dried up.

David drove a nine-year-old Mercedes sedan, still one of the better cars on the road. Although the Federal Government had confiscated his father's estate, ostensibly to pay off PeaceMaker victims, his mother had bought him this car when he graduated high school.

"Avoid the large pothole two hundred feet ahead on the right," the onboard computer warned. David skirted a pothole more than a yard across and a foot deep.

Had he made the right decision to visit his grandmother? He knew she wouldn't be pleased to see him. She and Dad had strained their relationship to the breaking point and barely spoke during Dad's adult years. Once he died, she cut off all contact with the family and moved permanently to her summerhouse near the Canadian border. His mother said the old woman, Helen Rader Brown, was a recluse.

Today he would get closer to the truth. He pushed the pedal and passed another car.

David exited onto Route 20, a rundown, tree-encroached road leading through the hills to the Anacortes ferry. At times, he slowed to a crawl, picking his way around potholes. Weeds overran the parallel railroad tracks.

Driving past a boarded-up restaurant, he turned and entered the gate for the ferry. A huge staging lot had been built decades earlier to handle the thousands of people who commuted from the islands each day. Today only a handful of cars lined up near the rundown loading dock. David handed the fare to a toll collector and drove into the loading lane.

Since the ferry was just pulling in, David rolled down the window and enjoyed the cold salt air. When the car in front of him started up, he followed it into the ferry's dark hold.

The San Juan archipelago consisted of hundreds of islands, but only a handful were large enough to support a significant population. His grandmother lived a few miles outside of Friday Harbor, the main town on the biggest island. For the first time in years, warm memories of a long-ago family vacation at his grandparents' summerhouse flashed by. He recalled the smiling face of his grandfather, Mom and Grandma serving tons of food, a walk through the woods with Aunt Claire and throwing a baseball around with Dad.

These days, one dilapidated ferry from Anacortes was the only way to make the two-hour trip. Still, he looked forward to the solitude and beauty of the sea. He left his car in the hold, clambered up a couple of levels of metal stairs and took a seat near the prow. A few minutes later, the ferry left the dock and chugged into choppy waters. Then it was out of the harbor and into open sea. He bundled up against the piercing wind.

His thoughts went back to his freshman year at the university—a year that had started with such promise. People were finally beginning to forget about PeaceMaker, and he had blended into the college community. Just another student, he had gradually found friends. He'd never had friends before.

Then a reporter came sniffing around to do a follow-up on the virus attack. The man plastered David's face all over the net, along with a story about his life at the university. Ugly calls and messages began. Demonstrations outside his dormitory were even worse, but the university grudgingly looked after his security. After a week, the demonstrators lost interest and left.

Unfortunately, they didn't take all the hatred with them. A quiet type of repulsion remained, deep and unforgiving, the kind that doesn't burn out rapidly. David recalled the loathing in many faces as he walked the campus. Most of his so-called friends dropped him completely, while the few who remained were polite, but distant.

Alone, once again.

He tried to fill the suddenly empty hours studying computer science, concentrating on artificial intelligence. He had always been passionate about developing software—*must be in the genes*. At that point, his studies were all he had.

Since his friends had deserted him, he drifted into a pattern of leaving the campus every weekend and driving out to small towns across the state. Starved for human contact, he forced himself to overcome his shyness and talk to strangers in stores, gas stations, anywhere.

It suddenly occurred to him that he had never gone to the San Juan Islands to see his grandmother. Not once in all his trips. Never even thought about it.

Once he left his true identity behind, he discovered a glib tongue. He was good at picking up women in bars and convincing them to spend the night. Anytime he wanted a woman, he just turned on the charm. His charisma and lean good looks invariably cast a spell.

He never considered building a long-term relationship; he didn't trust anyone. Those weekends blurred in his mind, a long series of one-night stands. Sometimes he got drunk, sometimes he didn't. It didn't matter. A good time, then goodbye. That's the way he wanted it.

His mother was great, and his stepfather was okay, but he had never warmed to the man. That was it. His other close relatives—his grandmother and his Aunt Claire—were strangers. Nevertheless, he was determined to see his grandmother and learn more about his father. If she didn't want anything to do with him, too bad.

David barely heard his netphone buzz over the engine noise.

"Hello."

"Hi, honey."

"Mom." He wasn't sure what to say to her.

"The school called about a bunch of missed classes and—David, what's all that noise?"

He cleared his throat. "I'm on a ferry to Friday Harbor. I should have mentioned it to you. I … decided to look up Grandma."

The line was silent for a moment. "Does she know you're coming?"

"No."

"Have you contacted her at all?"

"I haven't, but she'll talk to me."

"It's wonderful you want to see your grandmother, but honey, don't get your hopes up." Her voice sounded tinny, not her usual confident tone. "Grandma made it clear she wanted nothing to do with us. I wrote her several times the year after your father died, but she never answered."

"That was ten years ago. I think she'll talk now. I have to try."

"It's your father, isn't it? You want to see her about him."

"Mom, I should have told you. I need to understand him. I have to know what he did."

"What he did?" she cried. "The whole world knows what that sick bastard did."

"Mom …"

"You want to know what he did? He killed a hundred thousand people. You want to know why he abandoned us? That whore …" Her voice trailed off.

"Mom, I'm sorry." He waited, but his mother remained quiet. He heard her breathing.

"David, don't open this up again. I know you loved your father. I did, too. But he was a sick man. All that brilliance and charm hid the insanity, the dishonesty."

Tears burned his eyes. *I'm too old to cry.*

"I don't want to hurt anyone," he said. "I'm his son. He's in me. If I don't understand what he was, what made him do these things, where does that leave me?"

"You're not like him. You don't have his flaws, nothing like his flaws. You got the best of him."

"I'll call you in a few days," he said. "Okay?"

"Oh, David, why do you make it so hard?"

Her voice sounded so far away. Then the line went dead.

Guilt flooded in. This was the first real argument with his mother in years. He shouldn't have put off calling her.

It was the kind of thing Dad would do, and I can't even blame it on alcohol.

He settled back in his seat, watching islands chug by in the wind, separated by miles of open sea. Finally, the ferry docked and David drove into the town of Friday Harbor. Although it was still a tourist spot during the summer, the little town was bleak this time of year. Most of the retail shops had closed. Many looked as if they'd been vacant for years. Pedestrians looked at his car with hard, envious stares.

Forcing his concentration back on the road, he drove northwest. It was overcast, with a brisk wind from the north. Once he left the town, the road deteriorated into a muddy lane. Not that it mattered—only an occasional car splashed by. A thick forest of evergreens dominated the rough landscape, broken up by an occasional house. Most of the homes were boarded up; a few had collapsed, their land reclaimed by the forest.

Where he could, he checked the number on a house or mailbox. Eventually he came to his grandmother's cabin. Weather-beaten but sturdy, the old place was vaguely familiar, although smaller than he remembered. An old pick-up was parked in front, beat up but probably in working condition. A childhood memory brushed past of his grandmother driving it into Dad's driveway.

Smoke rose out of an old stone chimney on the west side of the house. His grandmother's home, unlike many others, seemed decently maintained. Gripping the steering wheel, David sat for a moment and stared.

Finally, he stepped from the car and headed up the dirt path to the house. A bitter wind seared his face. He walked past neatly stacked firewood on the porch and came to a heavy wooden door. No doorbell. He licked his lips, then banged hard on the door.

A thin old woman wearing spectacles pulled open the door. He had planned to greet her in a cordial manner, but couldn't find the words. He just stared silently as she looked him over. Recognition flashed in her eyes.

"Come in, David," she said in a voice that reminded him of a car crunching over pebbles. He was about to thank her, but she turned and walked back into the house. She had thrown a faded brown sweater over her dress.

He followed her into a 1950s kitchen warmed by crackling flames in a rough stone fireplace. Dim light entered the room through two small windows on the far wall. She gestured for him to sit down.

"Want coffee?"

David didn't want anything to drink, but he nodded anyway.

Slightly hunched, his grandmother walked to the wood stove. Thin but not frail, she lifted a coffee pot off a burner and poured a cup, then another.

Sitting at the rickety table, he looked around. A rusty sink on one wall was next to a narrow refrigerator. Water slowly dripped from the faucet into the sink, each ping marking another slice of time lost.

He listened to the dripping water until his grandmother twisted hard on the handle of the faucet. A last couple of pings and then quiet, except for logs popping in the fireplace.

The old woman returned and placed a cup of black coffee in front of him. Holding on to her cup, she slid into the chair across the table. Thin gray hair fell haphazardly over her ears, and her bony face was a maze of deep wrinkles and brown age spots, with the leathery skin of someone who had spent too many days outdoors.

He cleared his throat. "It's been a long time, Grandma."

Staring at him, she sipped her coffee then placed the cup on the table. Her mouth remained slightly open, revealing a sliver of yellow-stained teeth. Her doleful stare made him uncomfortable.

The crackle of the fireplace filled the room.

Finally, the old woman nodded her head, as if she had resolved a problem.

"You look like Ray—in the eyes, anyway. I hope it ends there." She pushed her coffee cup to the side. "Why are you here?"

"I want you to tell me about my father." David shifted in his chair.

"I never had much of a chance to know him. He hardly ever spoke about his childhood, and I barely know anything about you or Aunt Claire."

Her eyes narrowed and her hand grasped the edge of the table. Strangely, he felt threatened by this old woman.

"I need to understand where I came from," David said. "I don't know—"

"Better to leave it be," she screeched. "Your father was a sick bastard." She stood up suddenly. Her leg jostled the table, spilling hot coffee. David backed away as the coffee dripped to the floor.

Looking at the mess, she cursed, "Let his bones rot wherever they are."

A few drops of coffee had splattered on his sleeve, but he barely felt it.

She stared at him, with something like disgust in her face—or maybe regret. It reminded him of the stares from strangers on the campus after his identity became known, but worse. Familiar, personal, troubling.

David watched his grandmother walk over to the sink, grab an old rag and kneel next to the table to wipe up the spill. Her lips moved, but he couldn't make out her whispered words. The old woman had regained her composure when she sat at the table again.

"Sorry." A bony hand opened and closed restlessly. "You shouldn't have come here. Your father broke my heart. I don't want to break yours. Go back to where you came from. There's nothing good you can learn here."

David didn't like this old woman, but he had to get her to talk to him. "I won't leave, Grandma. My father and his damn legacy have hung over me my entire life." He paused, wondering how much to tell her, then decided to hold nothing back. "There's something building inside me, something dangerous. In some way, it's all tied to Dad—and maybe you. I need to understand this thing that's building. Help me."

Her voice was gentle. "You won't like it, you know. There's something wrong with this family, something evil." She straightened her shoulders. "What am I carrying on about? We are what we are. You want to know about us, fine, I'll tell you."

Dark eyes peeked out from drooping lids. She had a way of staring that made him squirm.

"I don't know where to start," she said, clasping her hands together. "I think we have bad blood, but there's more to it than that. I believe there was an unholy presence in this house back then." She cleared her throat. "But I'm getting ahead of the story.

"I never knew my parents. Somebody put me in a cardboard box and left me at the orphanage." Snorting, she looked down at her hands. "Probably the best decision they ever made.

"Let's say I was not the most popular person in the home. I didn't speak until I was four, so everyone thought I was slow. Didn't talk much afterwards, either. Hell, nobody was much interested in listening to me, anyway. I was just a plain, lonely girl."

The old woman's face twisted with ancient pain. "They ignored me the eighteen years I was there. The nuns didn't mistreat me, but sometimes I wished they would. At least they'd know I was alive." She shook her head, and returned her attention to him. "After a while, it didn't bother me. I didn't whine about it. I didn't cry, not me. Made me tough. That's how you have to be to get through this life." Glaring at him, she said, "Don't you know that?"

"I'm not like you."

She smiled without warmth. "No, you're not. You're worse." She leaned forward on her bony elbows. "I can see him in your eyes; you have Ray's eyes." Shaking her head, she added, "You're weak. Just like him."

David stood up, his chair scratching over worn floorboards. "I knew you were no good. I'm ashamed you're my grandmother."

As he turned to walk away from the table, she stood up and screeched, "Don't you leave. I haven't finished speaking to you! You want to understand your father—I'll tell you."

David looked back at her. "Oh, I'm not leaving. I came here to learn about my father and I'm staying until I'm satisfied." He shoved the chair, banging it hard against the table. "Did you care about him at all? Or your daughter?"

The old woman didn't answer. The energy seemed to drain from her body, and she settled into a chair. He paced around the little kitchen. She was somewhere else, thinking about the past.

"My goddamn family," he swore under his breath. All these years and he was still waiting for an answer.

Quietly, she said, "Sit down. All your pacing gets on my nerves."

He sat down heavily.

Speaking more to herself than him, she muttered, "I loved them both, back then. I tried to make them strong …"

Shaking her head, she said, "Claire was just weak, but Ray … there was something wrong with him. Sometimes I thought there were two people fighting for control of his soul. Some days he was perfect—smart, honest, strong—just perfect." Her voice quivered, and she stopped.

Surprised by her tone, David began to feel he was losing his bearings, teetering on the edge of a steep slope. Then his grandmother's voice broke into his thoughts, bringing him back to the cabin. "But most days he was weak, hot-tempered and mean. I think it just wore him out. He started drinking and I could never break him from it."

She shook her head again, looking at her gnarled hands. "Ray was a real nasty drunk. He got drunk every weekend, sometimes during the week."

She looked sadly at David. "One night during his senior year in high school, Ray got into a bad fight. Went to a party, got drunk and had words with some other kid. Beat the kid up—real bad—and then ran out and took off in his car. He lost control on a curve and wrapped the car around a tree. Totaled the car, but miraculously, Ray had only scratches. Walked down the road until he found a crummy bar and drank until he passed out. The bartender called me, and your grandfather and I had to go down there and bring him home.

"He cursed us when he came to." She leaned back in her chair. "God knows, we should have kicked him out right then." His grandmother struggled to her feet, leaning against the table for support. "I need another coffee. You want one?"

"All right."

She took David's cup and walked back to the stove. Her hand trembled as she poured the coffee. Although his father had ruined his childhood, David began to feel he wasn't the one to see the worst of the man.

She returned with two cups. "Ray wasn't always drunk. Sometimes he could be a great kid. There was this old nursing home where he used to volunteer once or twice a week after school. I went there once. The old folks loved him. And was he smart! He could make a computer do anything he wanted. Everyone came to Ray for help with their computer problems. You could tell he was something special when he got on the—what do they call it—the Internet. He learned all about the Internet before it became popular, when only scientists were using it."

She smiled at David, her lips cracking into an unfamiliar pattern.

"Did you know he assembled his first PC when he was twelve? Your grandfather bought him the parts, but Ray put it together. We were so proud of him.

"But something always ate away at his soul." His grandmother's shoulders shriveled and she paused, her eyes drifting off. She picked up her cup and sipped coffee, then another sip, longer and more desperate this time. When she put down the mug, all the antagonism had disappeared from her expression.

"Ray had terrible nightmares. He fought them, but they kept pulling him down. There was something alien in him, maybe some genes came together wrong. I don't know."

I know, David felt like saying.

"What do you mean something alien in him?"

"He had nightmares," she said. "I'd hear him talking and go into his room and sit by the bed. He'd toss and turn, mumbling things like *leave me alone* or *what are you*. I'd shake him, hard as I could, but I couldn't wake him. I could never wake him up—it was like he had to finish whatever was going on in his mind and then he would wake up on his own. I never knew how he would react when he came out of one of those nightmares: sometimes he acted glad to see me, sometimes he was pissed off, sometimes he'd roll out of bed, ignore me and get on the Internet and work for hours."

"He needed help, Grandma. Did you do anything to help him?"

Grandma slurped her coffee. "We had him tested, we had him

see a shrink, we put him in every special-ed program at school, but nothing helped. I even called the Church about an exorcism, but they wouldn't come because we're not believers. Ray wouldn't talk about the nightmares, not to me, not to his father, not to anyone."

She shrugged. "Nothing could stop him when he got into a downward spiral. Got so I could see it coming. Your grandfather and I fought for him, but we couldn't stop it. Ray would hit bottom and do something awful—maybe a screaming match with his father or a fight with someone from school—then he'd go on a bender and we wouldn't see him for days. He'd turn up, stinking of vomit and who knows what. The police got tired of looking for him."

"Do you have any idea what caused the nightmares?"

"It had something to do with the Internet. When I got rid of his personal computer, the nightmares stopped … for a couple of weeks." She shook her head. "We were all so happy. Then they came back." She shrugged. "I don't know. Maybe it had nothing to do with the Internet."

"Dad had nightmares when I was a little kid. Sometimes I'd wake up at night and hear him shouting."

"I'm sorry," Grandma mumbled. She took a long sip of coffee and picked up the story. "Once he graduated high school, Ray left and never came back. He kept drinking in college, but checked himself into rehab … some little place in central Pennsylvania. It helped. He stayed sober for years, graduated college and married your mother. We thought he had it licked when you were born.

"We had a bunch of great family vacations. Arthur and I adored Nancy, and we loved taking care of you. And Ray, he just laughed and smiled all the time." She sighed. "Those were the happiest days of our lives.

"Everyone thought he was a genius when he invented an intelligent operating system at VantagePoint. He had it made: wonderful family, fame, lots of money. Then, for some god-forsaken reason, he started drinking again. Cheated on his wife, ignored his son, almost killed himself driving drunk."

"People say he whored around," David ventured.

"No, he was true to your mother for years. It was after they were married several years that things went sour. Nancy told me he had an affair with someone from VPS, but she wouldn't say who."

So it was true, god damn it.

"Why did he start drinking again?"

"I don't know."

She seemed defensive. *What was she hiding?*

"Was it the pressure of the job? He worked long hours."

"I told you I don't know."

He watched his grandmother sitting and staring into her coffee.

"I'm sorry I brought the past back to you, Grandma."

Grandma swiped the air with the back of her hand. "Ray ruined everything he touched," she croaked. "He destroyed your grandfather. Broke Arthur's heart. It got so Arthur would cry in bed after one of Ray's nightmares. He blamed himself for Ray's sickness." She paused, her hands opening and closing. "When Ray came home for Arthur's funeral, I could barely speak to him."

Her attention drifted off, and David knew she had fallen into her private hell again. "When they told me that he created PeaceMaker … well, it wasn't exactly a shock. I knew the Devil had finally taken Ray for his own."

David's hostility had drained away as he listened to her story. He had come here thinking his father was a victim, but now he wasn't so sure. He wanted to tell her about the message from his father, but he feared it might place her in danger. Even so, he decided to tell her. She deserved to know that maybe her son wasn't a monster.

"I want you to read something, a message from Dad. It's possible he didn't create PeaceMaker. Maybe he tried to stop it."

He fished the message out of his pocket and handed it to her. She read it, glanced at him, read it a second time and handed it back with a shrug.

"Don't you understand? Dad might be innocent. Maybe your son wasn't a murderer!"

"That ... Ray will always be guilty to me." She hesitated, searching David's face. "He destroyed our family. God knows, your grandfather and I were far from perfect, but we loved him. We tried to help him, but a part of him was bad. He destroyed whatever chance we had for happiness."

David noticed her hands, calloused from years of hard work, trembling again.

"Dead ten years," she said, "but I can't forgive him."

David started to speak, but she interrupted, "No. I can't talk to you anymore. I'm afraid for you. Something is eating away at you, too. Maybe you're stronger than Ray, but I don't think so.

"I need to tell you something." Her eyes were dull and sad. "Ray was happy with Nancy the first couple of years. Then the nightmares came back and he began drinking. It was all downhill after ..."

"What is it, Grandma?" His stomach was a brick. "What are you trying to tell me?"

She swallowed. "His nightmares came back ... just after you were born."

She placed a withered hand over his. The faucet dripped again, and he stared at it.

Her voice was low and flat, but gentle. "David, please understand I don't hate you, but don't ever come back to this house again. I'm just waiting here for my time to run out. The land is beautiful, it's quiet, and if I don't think about the past, it's not too painful." Her eyes were kind, but tired. "I don't want to share your pain. There's something terrible in you, just like Ray. I couldn't save him, and I can't help you. I don't have the strength."

There was nothing else to say. David stood up and looked at his grandmother, hunched over the table with her coffee cup in her hand. A sudden urge came to pat her shoulder and offer words of encouragement, but it was too late for that. She wasn't what he had expected.

He lifted his coat off the chair and looked at her one last time as he pulled it on. Her body appeared formless, worn out. He felt her years, the cruel disappointments of her life. His father might not be guilty of PeaceMaker's terrible crimes, but he wasn't innocent, either.

And the curse had passed from father to son.

David felt his grandmother's eyes follow him as he turned and walked out the door. His shirt stuck to his back. The decision to get to the truth had seemed so bright and shiny. Now he wasn't sure. So far, he'd brought a ton of pain to his mother and grandmother.

And he was just getting started.

CHAPTER 5

The Federal Government faced a dilemma after the PeaceMaker catastrophe. As usual, the politicians bent to the clamor of the frightened. Technology was brought under the control of government bureaucrats. The economy stalled. A merciless depression followed the recession.

◆ Beyond the Internet: The Shadow Years, James Abraham, copyright 2039, Professor, Harvard University

[The] flight from and hatred of technology is self-defeating. The Buddha, the Godhead, resides quite as comfortably in the circuits of a digital computer or the gears of a cycle transmission as he does at the top of a mountain or in the petals of a flower.

◆ Robert M. Pirsig, Zen and the Art of Motorcycle Maintenance: An Inquiry into Values, 1, 1974

Friday, February 11, 2022

An orange glow lazily spread across the horizon, welcoming another perfect day, but the Runner barely noticed. Head tilted slightly forward, arms and legs pumping in practiced rhythm, the man loped down the beach. His bare feet, toughened by years of running, hardly felt the warm limestone sand. The cadence came easily; one foot in front of the other, over and over, flowing effortlessly.

Every morning he made this run. He wasn't sure why, but the rising sun always found him loping around the circumference of the island.

The outline of his home, dominated by the tall cylindrical trunks and pinnate leaves of palm trees, appeared around the gentle curve of the shoreline. Without breaking stride, the Runner veered off to the left, splashed through the crystal clear ocean and dove into a breaker. The cold sea caressed his skin as he plunged to the sandy bottom then bobbed to the surface. He swam parallel to the beach, letting the salty foam slide along his body, soothing his spirits, preparing him for another day.

Waves splashing around his ankles, the Runner walked up the sloping beach toward a low, coral wall. He guessed tribesmen had built it a century earlier to shield their village from the crashing waves of tropical storms. Now it protected his home. He dried himself with a rough towel he had left hanging on the wall; his sun-bronzed skin tingled with warmth. Suddenly realizing the Federal Technology Control Commission (FTCC) newscast would begin soon, the Runner braced himself with one arm and vaulted over the wall.

Three modest cottages, all made from white coral and soft local wood, stood behind the dunes. He rushed into the middle cottage and plopped into a padded chair in the hologram theater. Relaxing in the shaded room, the Runner glanced at his watch.

"Turn on the FTCC meeting," he ordered the computer.

A hologram cube, six feet on each side, appeared in the center of the room. The cube displayed a young newswoman with the face of an angel and a body that should never be obscured by clothes. Standing in the busy hall of a large federal building where people milled about, Daphne Hayden was the center of attention. He was amused to watch both men and women gawking at her as she began the newscast.

The building was vaguely familiar—then he remembered. It was where the VantagePoint anti-trust trial had taken place. *That's where it all started ... sixteen years ago.* He remembered the headlines, "VantagePoint Software Convicted ... VPS President Dianne Morgan Jailed for Contempt."

Dianne had sat and simmered in a crummy cell for weeks, but she wouldn't apologize to the judge. When they let her out, she was consumed with anger.

The Runner's attention came back to the newscast.

"Good morning, this is Daphne Hayden reporting from the FTCC Building in Washington, DC. Behind me is the Main Hall of the Federal Technology Control Commission. We're here to attend the third and final day of public hearings regarding the annual update of the Atlas Network Services System proposed by VantagePoint Software. Our sources warned us there might be fireworks today, so you don't want to miss a minute.

"As you can see, a swarm of citizens has filled the public seating. Spectators began lining up outside the building early this morning, highly unusual for an FTCC meeting. Of course, today's meeting is special.

"For those of you not familiar with the FTCC, let me provide a little background. The PeaceMaker attack in 2012 made it clear unregulated technology had become much too dangerous. More than one hundred thousand perished in the United States due to the virus attack, and it is believed that more than a million died worldwide. Hardest hit were the Western democracies, where food could no longer be delivered to the supermarkets, medical care became unavailable as hospitals shut down, transportation failed as fuel became scarce, and many in the northern states simply froze to death. It was weeks before basic services were restored; years before the nation completely recovered. Some analysts claim the great depression that followed the PeaceMaker attack has cut our nation's gross national product almost in half.

"Accordingly, Congress enacted laws that year to make sure runaway computer technology would never endanger the nation again. At the same time, Congress created the Federal Technology Control Commission to enforce these laws. In the following years, the laws were extended to cover genetic engineering and other advanced technologies. Many other nations followed our lead, and the world has become much safer."

The hologram flashed the image of a short, middle-aged man striding down the aisle through the public sections. As he entered the reserved section, he paused several times to shake hands with well-known men and embrace prominent women.

"FTCC Chairman Benjamin Gollin has arrived, so the meeting should be called to order shortly," Daphne said, as the hologram continued to follow Gollin.

Smiling and chatting, Gollin arrived at the Chairman's desk and took his seat. With thick brown hair slicked back, and bright eyes peering out of a thin face, he reminded the Runner of a fox staring into a chicken coop. The other six members of the FTCC Board of Commissioners, already seated at smaller desks on each side of Gollin, were reviewing papers and talking to staff.

The hologram flashed back to Daphne. "Chairman Gollin is known as a street-smart administrator with ambitions for higher office. Many commentators consider him a potential presidential candidate, but the word is he'll have to demonstrate he is tough on the Technos."

Daphne glanced over her shoulder at the Board of Commissioners and said, "Chairman Gollin has taken the gavel and will signal the meeting to begin. In a filing to the FTCC three months earlier, VantagePoint Software proposed several major enhancements to Atlas, the system providing the platform for much of the Internet. Since Atlas is the operating system attacked by PeaceMaker, there's always great interest in this session."

Daphne brushed back her luxurious blonde hair and said, "Mohammed Kateel, the Chief Operating Officer of VPS, will present the company's final arguments. Mr. Kateel is one of the most respected executives in the nation. In addition to his record as an outstanding technology executive, he was among the band of heroes resisting the software blackmail attempt of Raymond Brown and his terrorist organization. Brown's henchmen tortured Mr. Kateel, but they failed to obtain critical information regarding several key Atlas components. Mr. Kateel's heroism saved many thousands of lives. Only VantagePoint President Dianne Morgan is more beloved."

Now Kateel's a hero, the Runner thought.

"However, many in the press were surprised when Kateel was chosen to represent VPS in this critical meeting," Daphne said. "Although recognized as a brilliant software engineer, Kateel is known for his abrasive personality. He doesn't tolerate fools, and his answers are sometimes dismissive." Daphne flashed her perfect white teeth. "It should prove to be an interesting day."

Benjamin Gollin banged the gavel and called the meeting to order. He glanced down at Kateel, who conferred with an assistant at the witness table. He was disappointed Dianne Morgan would not represent VPS. To be seen as Morgan's equal would have increased his prestige, but Kateel would have to do.

"Good morning, Dr. Kateel. We're pleased to welcome you to the quarterly meeting of the Federal Technology Control Commission."

Gollin's voice boomed over the speaker system, filling the huge chamber with his crisp, authoritative tone.

"As you know, I and the Board of Commissioners of the FTCC take our responsibility seriously. We are determined to allow only safe, necessary technology to be developed. The nation asks us—no, it requires us—to maintain the safety of our citizens and institutions from runaway, dangerous technology. A decade ago unregulated technology devastated the nation." Gollin paused, his eyes sweeping over the huge chamber. "Never again," he thundered.

"Your company, VantagePoint Software, has submitted a request to develop a number of enhancements for the Atlas software system." He leaned forward, presenting the holocamera with his best tough-but-compassionate look. "While the Board is open-minded, our commitment to the nation's safety requires we question the need for these enhancements. We have many issues to discuss with you today, Dr. Kateel. However, as a courtesy, you are permitted to make a brief opening statement."

Kateel sat alone in the middle of a long table. Husky, with sharp features, graying hair, and dark eyes that commanded attention,

Kateel was the perfect image of a senior business executive. Like many executives Gollin had questioned, Kateel wore wireless communication "glasses," that gave him instantaneous visual access to computer-stored information.

"Thank you, Mr. Chairman," Kateel said. Although respectful, his voice marked him as someone accustomed to command. "I promise not to take up too much of your valuable time. My colleagues at VantagePoint Software and I appreciate the FTCC's important responsibility to safeguard the use of technology. Nobody understands the dangers inherent in unregulated technology better than we do. VantagePoint Software believes safety is our first and foremost concern in the development of new software."

Just get to it, Gollin thought. *Poor Kateel. He won't know what hit him. This is going to be delicious.*

"As you know, the proposed software includes several performance enhancers, bug fixes and a few new capabilities," Kateel said. "We believe the documentation clearly describes our proposal, although we would be pleased to answer any questions. First, however, I would like to give you a demonstration of our most important new capability, an embedded Command Chip."

What the hell!

Gollin kept his voice even as he eyed the witness. "How is that possible, Dr. Kateel? The Commission has not approved the Command Chip for testing of any sort."

Raising an eyebrow slightly, Kateel replied, "As you must surely know, FTCC regulations allow for a limited degree of beta testing after the successful completion of system testing. Our report clearly states system testing was successfully completed last month, so we began beta testing."

"Would you direct the Commission to the appropriate section," Gollin said, keeping his voice even.

Kateel opened a thick book titled: *Atlas Enhancement Requests*. He flipped pages and then looked up at Gollin.

"System testing is summarized beginning on page 471. You'll see we completed it last month."

Opened to the proper page, the book was placed in front of Gollin by an aide. Gollin skimmed through the section.

"The chip has been inserted in myself, Dianne Morgan and several other VPS employees," Kateel added.

Kateel and Gollin exchanged hard looks as the room became quiet.

VPS is taking a big risk, Gollin thought. *Were they really that arrogant?*

After conferring with an attorney, Gollin nodded at Kateel. "You are correct, Dr. Kateel." *I'll get you for embarrassing me.* "You may continue with your demonstration."

"Thank you," Kateel replied. He pointed to a robot standing motionless at the end of the witness table. "Robots are becoming popular with consumers. I brought my personal robot, Michael, to demonstrate certain capabilities of the Command Chip." Smiling at the robot, he said, "How are you today, Michael?"

The robot appeared ordinary to Gollin, a five-foot tall mobile computer balanced on four thin legs with a holographic projector in the top section. An image shimmered in the space just above the projector: a pleasant, middle-aged male face with neatly clipped hair returned Kateel's smile.

The robot replied to Kateel in a friendly male voice. "All systems are working fine, sir."

"Michael, please fetch me a glass of water," Kateel said.

As the robot glided toward the water pitcher at the other end of the table, Kateel turned and said to Gollin, "Verbal communications with our robots are relatively error-prone. Even though robots have excellent hearing, sound waves deteriorate as they travel, and they frequently misunderstand our commands. This can lead to incorrect, sometimes dangerous, actions. In addition, once Michael gets outside the range of my voice, he is out of my control."

As Michael picked up the pitcher in front of Kateel and poured water into a glass, Kateel said, "The Command Chip allows continuous verbal communication with your robot." He held up a tiny computer chip between his thumb and forefinger, barely visible to Gollin twenty feet away. "A microchip is surgically implanted in the ear. It can receive and transmit over the net. The Command Chip picks up sound waves from your speaking voice, breaks down your words into packets, and using standard wireless transmission protocols, sends it over the net to the robot. All this is done in a flash, of course.

"In a similar manner, a robot may transmit messages back to you over the net. The Command Chip will receive these messages and convert them to low volume sounds within your ear. This enables you to communicate with your robot, even though it may be many miles distant."

Kateel paused for questions, but the Commissioners remained silent. Gollin noticed many in the room appeared impressed with Kateel's gadget, but an undercurrent of concern showed in some faces.

"Let's begin the demonstration," Kateel said. "Michael, please walk to Chairman Gollin's office at the far end of the building and wait there."

Commissioner Jackson, a balding political appointment in a lumpy suit, barked out, "That's no demonstration. The robot can hear you."

Groaning inwardly, Gollin said, "I'm sure the demonstration will not begin until the robot is well out of hearing range, Commissioner." He stared at Jackson with contempt and then returned his attention to Kateel.

"I say we reject this nonsense right now," Jackson said. "We don't need this Command Chip hogwash. In fact, I have my doubts about continuing to allow these robots. God damn machines make my skin—"

"Commissioner," Gollin interrupted, "although we all appreciate the wisdom of your remarks, time constraints force us to move ahead with the demonstration of the Command Chip. Perhaps we can return to your skin issues at a later time."

Gollin muted his speaker and muttered to a colleague, "I'd like to shove the Command Chip all the way up Jackson's ass into his ear, then turn the volume to maximum."

Michael stopped walking and said, "That act is anatomically impossible, Commissioner Gollin."

The spectators murmured in confusion, and Gollin glared at the robot.

Kateel said, "Hush, Michael," although a hint of a smile touched his lips. "Continue walking." Turning to Gollin, "I remind you, Chairman, these robots have exceptional hearing."

Gollin's only desire was to take an axe to the robot, the command chip and Kateel, not necessarily in that order. Struggling to keep his voice even, Gollin said, "Commissioner Andrews-Nash will begin the questioning."

Commissioner Greta Andrews-Nash, an energetic young woman with frizzy brown hair pulled straight back, frowned at the VPS executive. "Just how much will this Command Chip cost, Dr. Kateel?"

"We have not completed pricing analysis as yet, Commissioner."

"Ballpark it," Andrews-Nash said.

Kateel looked at her as if he had discovered a roach in his food. "The price would vary according to the income level of the consumer, of course." Andrews-Nash looked at Gollin and shrugged her shoulders.

Gollin nodded and turned to Kateel. "Please give us your best estimate."

Kateel thought for a moment. "A person of average income would pay about five to six hundred dollars for the insertion of the Command Chip and then about twenty-five per month service fee."

"That's outrageous," Andrews-Nash barked out. "Only the wealthy would be able to afford this technology. God knows the wealthy already live far better than the average citizen does. With this chip, the wealthy would be able to command their robots from anywhere on the planet. How convenient for them." She shook her head. "The average Joe doesn't even have a robot and VPS wastes its time producing software for the rich."

"Let me assure you VPS will recover only its costs during the first year," Kateel answered. "However, once our robotic factories are retooled and fine-tuned, the cost to consumers should drop substantially."

How naïve, Gollin thought. *Tax rates would increase to absorb any such price reduction.*

"VPS should provide the Command Chip at no cost to the average citizen, if we need it at all," Andrews-Nash said. "You can charge your wealthy friends whatever you want. VPS is one of the most profitable companies in the world. Don't you recognize your duty to the average citizen?"

Frowning, Kateel said, "VPS is one of the few companies still making a profit. Do you want us to slide into bankruptcy like so many other firms during this depression?"

Gollin interrupted just as Andrews-Nash was about to reply. "I think we have discussed pricing sufficiently. As a point of information, the Treasury Department revised the official definition of depression last month. We are actually in a recession, not a depression."

"I stand corrected, Chairman Gollin," Kateel said. "I haven't been keeping up with the latest definitions."

The spectators tittered, and Gollin bristled. "Don't push it, Dr. Kateel. Continue with your demonstration."

"We set up a speaker system so everyone could hear Michael's responses." The robot had disappeared from sight, so Kateel said, "Michael, where are you?"

Michael's voice boomed throughout the conference room. "I am standing outside of Commissioner Gollin's office."

"Please tell me what you see in the lobby near his office."

"I see four chairs, a couch, a vase of roses outside the door, a hand-woven rug, and a guard staring at me. There's a stain of some sort on the couch. Let me get closer …"

"Tell that robot to stay out of my office," Gollin shouted.

Kateel said to the robot, "It's not necessary to examine the stain." He chuckled, and then asked Gollin, "May I instruct Michael to retrieve the vase outside your office?"

When Gollin nodded, Kateel said, "Michael, please bring the vase and flowers to Chairman Gollin." He smiled at Gollin. "And Michael, don't spill the water."

The conference room was quiet for a moment, and then Commissioner Jeremy Slater said, "I have a number of questions, Chairman Gollin."

A low buzz filled the room. Gollin banged his gavel. He knew this was what the crowd had come to see. "Talking is not permitted during the questioning. If there's a disturbance, I'll clear the room." When the crowd quieted, he nodded to Slater. "You may proceed, Commissioner."

Tall, thin, with neatly parted salt-and-pepper hair, Slater had the look of a past-his-prime athlete. Ruthless and intellectually formidable, he was the one person on the commission Gollin didn't control. Over his objections, Slater had been appointed to the FTCC because, Gollin had learned, Slater had something on the president. The rumor was that one of those sisters from the Church of Natural Humans had seduced the president. There were pictures—filthy pictures. At least that's what Gollin's spies had said.

Slater was fanatically anti-technology, but that wasn't a concern to Gollin as long as Slater followed his lead. So far, Slater had turned out to be his reliable right hand on the commission. In fact, Slater had encouraged him to run for president, even started a slush fund. He didn't trust Slater, but the man had introduced Gollin to wealthy supporters, so he made peace.

Thumbing through a computer printout, Slater looked at Kateel over the top of his old-fashioned eyeglasses. "These specifications include a great deal of technical data, but I find your Technology Impact Statement lacking."

"We point out the reason in paragraph two," Kateel replied. "The Command Chip will not have a large impact upon society, so little detail is necessary. The Command Chip is a simple extension of our hearing and voice, nothing more, nothing less."

"I'm sure you're correct, Dr. Kateel, but let's explore the subject a bit." The large room was quiet as Slater leafed through his papers. "The Command Chip enables human-to-robot communication anywhere in the world. Correct?"

"Yes, that's correct."

"The Command Chip allows one person to broadcast commands to many thousands of robots simultaneously," Slater said. "Is that not true?"

"That's correct, Commissioner." Kateel fidgeted in his chair. "This capability is described in Section Six of the document."

Slater arched his eyebrows. "Doesn't it concern you that one person could activate an army of robots at the drop of a hat?"

Kateel and Slater glared at each other. Neither man said a word. Gollin asked Kateel to answer the question, but Kateel waved him off with a dismissive flip of his wrist.

You'll pay for that one, too, Gollin thought.

"There is no such thing as an army of robots," Kateel said to Slater. "As you well know, all robots include software and hardware controls that prevent them from harming a human."

"Come now, you're under oath," Slater replied. "A clever programmer could override those controls and unleash a robot army. You could do it yourself, couldn't you, Kateel!"

"That's virtually impossible. We have so many layers of control, nobody could override them."

"But you can't guarantee some brilliant but demented Techno

wouldn't do it."

Kateel snorted. "I can't guarantee lightning won't strike you during this meeting, either. Actually, as I think about it, the lightning strike is much more promising."

The two men glared at each other, and then Gollin said, "Let's move on. I assume you have additional questions, Commissioner Slater."

Slater responded without taking his eyes off Kateel. "Indeed I do."

Shuffling his papers again, Slater asked, "This communication isn't limited to robots, is it? Two humans could communicate using the Command Chip." Slater lifted his eyes. "Correct?"

Kateel nodded. "We clearly state that in the report, so yes, it is correct."

"With the Command Chip, a Techno could whisper something here and another Techno on the other side of the world could hear him. That's telepathy." Slater glared at Kateel. "You're trying to sneak a brand new technology past us."

"As you well know, the Command Chip is far from telepathy," Kateel said, his voice reverberating through the hearing room. "VPS doesn't have the ability to create mind-to-mind communications. There are still aspects of the brain we don't understand. Even if we did understand the brain thoroughly, the engineering problems of integrating such a Command Chip would be fantastically complex." Kateel smiled without humor at Slater. "Even a demented Techno like me couldn't do it."

Slater leaned forward. "But if you could do it, you would. Isn't that true?"

Gollin's sharp eyes captured the contempt written across Kateel's face. The hearing room was quiet, waiting for Kateel's answer.

We've got him, Gollin thought.

After a long moment, Kateel's jaw muscles worked. "Yes, I would."

Glaring at Kateel, Slater said, "Abomination," and slammed shut his notebook. "I have no more questions for this … for Dr. Kateel."

Conversation buzzed in the hearing room again, and Gollin nodded at Slater. *That should please the First Minister.*

Kateel's robot appeared in the doorway carrying a vase of flowers. The noise died out as the robot walked across the conference room and placed the flowers in front of Gollin.

Ignoring the robot, Gollin stood up. "This meeting is over. Our decision will be available shortly." He swept out of the room, followed by the other commissioners.

Twenty minutes later, Gollin returned and announced that the Commission had rejected the Command Chip and all the other enhancements. A few applauded, but most of the spectators appeared displeased with the result.

It was a crushing blow to VPS, so Gollin wondered why a slight smile had briefly whisked across Kateel's lips.

CHAPTER 6

Moesha Jefferson, the murderous leader of the Army of God, remains an enigma. Many historians believe First Minister Jordan employed drugs to cultivate her violent nature, and while that may be true, we now realize the seeds of destruction were in her from the beginning.

◆ *The Army of God*, Mark Axelrod, copyright 2051, Assistant Director, FBI (retired)

Tuesday, February 15, 2022

Security Officer Bob Warner yawned as he gazed out the windows of the lobby into a dark, cold night at Carnegie Mellon University, located at the outskirts of Pittsburgh. He glanced at his watch—a little past 2 a.m. *Just three more hours for my shift.* Heavy snow from a storm earlier in the week covered the campus. A gust of wind blew icy needles into the few people walking across the quad.

Great to be sitting on my butt in a nice, warm lobby. He settled into the padded seat behind the security desk. *Seniority still has its advantages.*

Warner scanned the grounds through reinforced steel mesh, which protected the spacious windows from the ever-increasing vandalism and demonstrations. In addition, a recently installed state-of-the-art security system checked the physical characteristics of nearby walkers against a database of known terrorists.

Only two more years before I retire.

Highly respected for its leading edge studies of robotics and artificial intelligence, CMU had become a frequent target of technology-hating protestors and the even more dangerous religious fanatics.

Warner spotted two security guards walking side by side past the administration building. Security had been beefed up in the last couple of years; sentries patrolled the campus at all hours.

Looking out a side window, Warner watched three students, bundled in heavy parkas, hurry toward the front entrance. The security system kept a spotlight on the students as it checked their identities. Warner was pleased when the spotlight winked out; the students weren't in the FBI terrorist database.

In addition to observing nearby walkers, Warner kept tabs on the building interior. Cameras positioned in all the hallways and classrooms sent a continuous sequence of pictures to the monitors at the security desk. There was no one else in the building tonight, except for Jose Ramiriz, a guard patrolling the hallways.

Warner scrutinized the three students, two men and a woman, when they arrived at the front entrance. With the murder of a robotics professor last year, the campus had become a dangerous place.

A female African-American student placed her hand on the fingerprint scanner, causing her picture to pop up on his display: tan skin, short black hair, intelligent eyes and an intriguing smile. The security computer identified her as Barbara Lester, a language major. *Sort of a Mona Lisa look,* recalling the famous portrait he had seen last year on his European vacation.

He buzzed the exterior door, and she entered. Her two male

companions, one white and the other Asian, also entered after passing the fingerprint identification. In the holding area, a metal detector, an explosives sniffer and a pattern recognition x-ray scanned each student for weapons. When all three had passed the scans, the interior door slid open. Warner didn't recognize them, but that wasn't unusual. More than ten thousand students attended the university.

The young woman unbuttoned her coat, left her friends and walked up to the desk. The database photo didn't do justice to her lush figure. Warner's eyes were drawn to a silver amulet swinging across a tight sweater.

If I were twenty years younger …

Warner smiled at her. "Good evening, Ms. Lester. Can I help you?"

The young woman smiled at the security guard.

"I think we can manage without your help."

She deftly pulled a wallet-shaped polymer gun out of her coat pocket and shot Warner in the face and chest. His head jerked back and he tumbled off his chair, dead before he hit the floor.

Moesha Jefferson stared at the body. "Well, Mr. Warner, you wanted early retirement."

Nick Marabella, the white member of the trio, rushed behind the desk and took off his coat, revealing a security guard uniform. He scanned the monitor.

"Ramiriz is in the south hallway of the first floor," he said as he pushed Warner's body under the desk and removed his pistol.

Moesha checked her wrist computer. "It's now 2:12." To Henry

Ling, the other soldier she had selected for this mission, she said, "We'll place the explosives in the designated areas and return here by 2:26. I have the basement and first floor and you have the second and third. I'll eliminate Ramiriz."

Moesha and her companions dropped to their knees and bowed their heads. After kissing their amulets, all three began to pray.

"God bless the Church of Natural Humans,

We do not fear Lucifer or his abominations,

We will kill all the Technos,

And purify the Earth for Your Return.

Glory be to the Lord and His Creations."

Moesha kissed her amulet again and stood up. She snapped at Ling, "Get moving." Then at Marabella, "Turn away or kill all visitors. I don't care who they are."

She sprinted across the lobby and down the hallway, ready to sacrifice her life for the Lord.

Joe McMahon was the managing security officer on duty. Perched in his corner office on the top floor of the Admin building, he had a panoramic view of the campus.

On his desk were photographs of his family—Edith and the kids, now all grown, and his buddies from the Pittsburgh PD. McMahon's eyes lingered on a photo from his retirement dinner last year. Framed in silver, it showed him standing between the commissioner and the mayor, smiling with his hands over their shoulders.

Carnegie is fine, but you can't just put aside thirty-five years on the job.

McMahon was in charge of night shift university security. He took pride in being a top professional; he knew how many men patrolled the campus at any moment, the layout of every building, where a terrorist might attack. He had to know everything. Lives were at stake. He had also studied every aspect of the new surveillance system, which answered to the name *Rex*.

Two holograms shimmered in front of his desk, each a two-foot cube cycling through hundreds of cameras in a predetermined sequence. Each hologram produced an image for six seconds and then moved on to the next camera. The Alpha hologram cycled through views of the front lobby of every building, while the Beta hologram panned over the campus grounds. McMahon was monitoring both when he noticed something.

"Rex, reset the Alpha hologram back one cycle and hold it," McMahon said.

The lobby of the Robotics Institute appeared normal for 2 a.m., empty, except for the guard sitting at his desk. *Just the way it should be so early in the morning.* Still, he felt uneasy. His instincts warned him something was wrong.

"Which guards are working the Robotics Institute right now?"

Rex responded in an authoritative male voice. "Robert Warner is working the desk and Jose Ramiriz is walking the halls."

McMahon squinted at the image, continuing to feel uneasy. Then it hit him. Bob Warner was middle-aged, with an expanding gut, while this guard looked young and trim. The man's head bobbed up and down as he monitored the display and looked out through the lobby windows.

"Give me a close-up of the face of the guard working the desk."

The face in the hologram grew larger, but the view was mostly hair and forehead.

"Just the face, full frontal," he barked.

Rex changed the angle and magnification until an enlarged front image of a face appeared in the hologram. McMahon stared for a moment.

"Identify the officer at the desk."

"Unknown," Rex replied. "The face doesn't conform to anyone in the officer database."

"Scan the logs and tell me who's in the building."

"Three students are in the building. Barbara Lester, Chester Brandt and Bruce Chin signed in at approximately 2:10 a.m."

At least one—probably all three—was an intruder. Shit! Three intruders and only Jose in the building.

"Get me Officer Ramiriz."

A moment later, Ramiriz, a clean-cut young man staring up at a ceiling camera, appeared on the Beta hologram.

"Officer Ramiriz reporting, sir."

"Listen carefully, Jose, you are in grave danger," McMahon whispered. "Bob Warner is not at the front desk. An unknown intruder has replaced him. There are probably two additional intruders in the building. Do you understand?"

"Yes, sir," Ramiriz replied. He pulled his Glock laser from a side holster and glanced up and down the hallway.

"I don't know what their plans are, but they probably killed Warner and they may be after you, too," McMahon said. "Take your badge off and leave it on the floor, so they can't track you so easily with the surveillance system. I want you out of the building immediately. As soon as you're safe, I'm cutting the power to the lights. Where's the nearest exit?"

"In the rear hall near the Darwin Project," Ramiriz whispered as he quietly placed his badge on the floor.

"Get out now. Take a position in cover outside the exit and stop anyone coming out of the building. Shoot to kill if they resist. I'll have Rex lock all the doors, except for the ones near the Darwin project. Anyone leaving the building will have to go past you. Report back when you take position."

"Yes, sir."

The close-up of the lobby, with the stranger at the desk, appeared in the Alpha hologram, while Beta showed Jose heading toward the exit.

"Be careful, son," McMahon muttered.

When Jose disappeared out the door, McMahon said, "Rex, turn off the power to all the lights in the Robotics Institute."

The Alpha hologram turned dark.

"Task completed," Rex said.

Tapping his fingers on the desk, McMahon considered his options.

"Rex, secure all the doors in the Robotics Institute except the one nearest the Darwin Project."

"Task completed."

"Contact all guards stationed within a quarter mile of the Robotics Institute and have them cover all the exits," McMahon said. "Brief them on the situation. I want them to shoot to kill. Issue the Maximum Alert Priority. No one is to enter the building. I want to trap the intruders in the building as a first step. Also call the police and alert them to the situation."

McMahon squinted at the shadowy form in the Alpha hologram; the intruder had remained at the front desk, his silhouette visible in the weak moonlight.

Well-trained, he thought.

"Rex, get the Dean on the line."

Moesha flattened her back against the wall when the lights went out. No sounds came through the darkness. She whispered into the computer on her wrist, "We've been discovered. Nick, hold your position for another ten minutes, then get out of there and meet me at the safehouse. Henry, do the same after you place the explosives. Use your GPS to find your way in the dark."

Moesha didn't like using a GPS or any other type of computer, but the First Minister had explained the difference between these systems and forbidden technology. The Church would accept a computer if it wasn't a thinking, autonomous creation imitating a human. Moesha might agree to use it, but she didn't trust any of this technology. It had an odor that drifted up from hell. For the moment, however, their computers were the lesser evil.

Pale moonlight filtered through the window shades, outlining the hallway in alternating light and shadows, but too dark to find her way.

"Computer, guide me to the first placement area."

A low voice emerged from her wrist computer. "Walk forward sixteen feet and turn left into the hall."

She walked down the corridor, dragging the fingers of her left hand along the smooth wall. She had memorized the building layout, but it would have been slow going without the GPS directions. Moesha turned left when she felt the corner.

"Walk forward eighty-seven feet and turn down the stairway on your left."

Moesha, fingers again brushing the wall, hurried down the dark corridor. She paused, listening. Nothing. She began walking again, but kept the polymer gun ready in her right hand, knowing she might run into the security guard at any moment. The gun was adequate for close quarters, but she would be at a disadvantage shooting at longer distances.

She stopped and whispered, "How much farther?"

"Eleven feet."

Moesha hurried forward, sliding her hand up and down the wall searching for the stairway. She found the edge of the wall and moved her hand down until she felt the smooth plastic of a handrail.

"Go down one flight and take the exit to your right."

The last of the faint moonlight disappeared as she walked down the steps. Moesha followed the computer's instructions to the boiler room, the first target area. She stopped just inside the doorway, unable to see in the pitch-black room.

It didn't matter. She knew four huge fuel tanks were lined up on the far side of the room. Walking forward with both hands extended, only a few seconds passed before her fingers pressed against the cold metal of a tank. Moesha pulled the first explosive, which she had sealed in a plastic bag, from the lining of her coat and gently placed it under the tank. She ripped a button off her sleeve and buried it inside the bag. An electronic signal with the right frequency would activate the button's trigger and set off the explosive. Hopefully, she and her soldiers would be clear of the building by the time she activated the trigger. If not, it was God's will.

The computer guided her back up the stairs to the Darwin Laboratory, the location for the second explosive. This is where the Technos designed self-replicating software. She cringed just thinking about it, modules of software rapidly breeding generation after generation, each more monstrous than the previous one. Whatever happened today, she vowed to destroy this abomination.

Gunfire, mixed with the hiss of lasers, came from the direction of the main lobby as she placed the second explosive on a lab bench. Time was running out. She quickly buried the triggering button in the explosive then followed the computer's directions to the nearest exit.

Henry's voice came over the computer, "Moesha, the guards are surrounding the building. Get out now."

She swiftly found the exit and cracked open the door to see if the grounds were clear. The Robotics Institute was surrounded by a three-foot-high stone wall, with brick pathways leading to other buildings. All the outside lights had been turned off. Enemies might be hiding in the brush, ready to shoot as soon as she stepped out. She couldn't see much in the dim moonlight, but she couldn't remain inside the building.

Moesha burst out the doorway and sprinted along a brick walkway, toward the stone wall just ahead.

A man shouted from the darkness, "Drop your weapon and raise your hands."

She cut to the right and dove for the cover of the wall. A weapon hissed from the direction of the voice, and Moesha felt the hot brush of a laser beam passing over her back. After hitting the ground painfully on her hands and knees, she crawled away from the shooter, shielded by the wall. She stopped moving and listened. If she could pinpoint her pursuer, she might be able to get close enough to shoot him. A foot crunched in the snow, revealing the location of her enemy.

Too far away.

The hiss of lasers came from the opposite side of the building, and she considered detonating the explosives. Martyrdom was beautiful, but not yet necessary; it shouldn't be difficult to kill this one guard, then destroy the building and escape.

Moesha resumed crawling along the wall. She stopped to listen and again heard a footstep, this time much closer. Whoever was stalking her had come within range of her polymer gun. She peeked over the wall and fired three quick shots in the direction of the guard's last sound.

A man grunted, and a body hit the ground. She wasn't sure if she had killed him, but the squeal of sirens in the distance warned her to get away. She crawled on raw knees to the end of the wall. Hearing only sirens and distant lasers, she bolted into a small, landscaped park, trying to become an elusive shadow in the night. A laser cut into a tree inches to her left as she twisted through the brush.

God is watching over me.

Moesha ran until she reached the far side of the park. The man hunting her was a professional, and she wouldn't underestimate him again. Breathing hard, she crouched behind a thick holly and looked for the best escape route. Ahead was an open field, murky in the faint moonlight. On the far side of the field, maybe one hundred yards away, were thick woods. Crossing the field would leave her exposed, but approaching sirens gave her no other choice.

Moesha broke from cover and darted into the field, running in a zigzag pattern. Although she was in superb physical condition, her breathing gradually became ragged and her legs wooden. At any moment, she expected the hiss of a laser. Staggering, she made it to the woods and flopped behind the trunk of a spruce tree, safe for the moment.

Precious seconds passed before she recovered enough strength to move. She rolled over on her stomach and listened for the sounds of pursuit. Snow crunched under someone's boots, but he was a long way off and moving slowly. Staccato bursts of lasers came from the direction of the Institute.

Moesha had to destroy this center of abomination, regardless of the consequences to her men.

Soldiers of the Army of God pledge their lives to the Creator.

She hesitated for a second and whispered, "May we meet in the sight of the Lord, my friends." Then she said, "Computer, discharge all explosives."

A firestorm lit up the night as the Robotics Institute exploded, blowing off the roof and obliterating everything near the building. The roar was deafening, and waves of hot wind surged across the field into her face. For a moment, night turned into day and Moesha spotted the silhouette of a man about fifty feet away. The man turned to see the explosion, a laser pistol dangling from his hand.

Moesha stood up, extending her right arm as she aimed at the enemy. The hot wind brought tears to her eyes, smudging the target. She had one bullet remaining, and it was a long shot for a polymer gun. If she didn't kill him with this last bullet, she would join her comrades in the arms of the Lord. Moesha aimed for the man's broad back and slowly squeezed the trigger until the weapon barked.

The bullet struck the man between the shoulder blades and he fell forward, hitting the ground hard, bouncing slightly and then lying still. Moesha stared at him, licked her lips, and kissed her amulet. Lord willing, the Army of God would kill many more infidels. She said a blessing for her brave companions then tossed the gun away. She ran into the woods, her path illuminated by distant flames.

CHAPTER 7

The attack upon the Robotics Institute was the most recent of a well-organized terrorist campaign against leading technology institutions. We consider our policy of non-intervention to be generally successful; the Technos and religious fundamentalists continue to drift toward all-out civil war. Since both groups are a threat to our government, we allow the killing to thin their ranks.

◆ From a classified FBI report, February 18, 2022

Wednesday, February 16, 2022

David drove south on Route 1 in northern California, looking for the Carter Motel. Hard-working windshield wipers provided smeared glimpses of dark buildings along the road. From time to time, the headlights of an oncoming car glared through his windshield, beginning as dim pinpoints in the night, growing to blinding intensity then passing in a blast of muddy water.

Tomorrow he would meet with Kathy Bauman, a former associate of his father. Kathy had recruited college graduates for VPS and had worked closely with Dad for a couple of years. Searching the Internet, he had discovered she was a Summa Cum Laude graduate of Columbia with a degree in Business Administration. Raised in an upper middle-class home in the Philadelphia Mainline, she had excelled in softball, pitching her high school to a state championship.

A newspaper article mentioned that Kathy and Dad had been friends, so David had decided to call her. She was pleasant over the phone and didn't appear to hold any hostility toward his father. Just the opposite. Kathy had invited him to come and talk before he had asked.

Finally, he spotted the motel on the left and turned into its narrow entrance. The Mercedes' tires crunched on the loose stones of the driveway, which pelted the underside of the car with staccato pops and pings.

The motel was an old, two-story cracker box, the kind of place they used to build fifty years ago for travelers with paper-thin wallets. Hazy light seeped out of the lobby window; the remainder of the building was a dark mass fading into the storm. A handful of solitary cars stood in the muddy lot along the side of the motel.

David parked, pulled the hood of his jacket over his head and jumped out of the car. A cold, sharp rain blew into his face as he ran to the doorway. Heat from the lobby felt good, but it brought the smell of decay. Leaving a trail of water across a faded green carpet, David headed to the registration desk.

The lobby had seen better days and was sliding toward a bleak future. The young brunette at the desk looked him over several times as she registered him. David knew that look. She was almost pretty when she smiled, with a sort of gap-toothed charm. Then the network link to the reservations system failed, and she grumbled about having to take his credit card information by hand. He decided she wasn't worth picking up. Besides, he was worn out from the long drive.

David carried his bag up a creaky wooden staircase and found his door at the back end of a dim hallway. It took a couple of tries to get the keycard to work. Opening the door, he glanced into a sparse old room: a double bed with a blanket and two pillows, a dresser with an ancient TV on top, and a bathroom with a toilet, sink and shower. A brass-colored pole lamp in the far corner bathed the room with yellow light. The wallpaper faded into a dingy white ceiling.

Not exactly Shangri-la, but at least the room seems clean.

He dropped his bag on the floor next to the bed. Looking out the window, he spotted the Mercedes' dark form. Rain hit the hood and ran down the sides in little streams.

The room was cold, so he searched for a thermostat. He was about to call the front desk when he realized the rusty box under the window provided the lone source of heat. Fiddling with its controls, he coaxed a current of warm air from the grumbling machine.

After bolting the door, he sat on the bed and lit a cigarette. He wasn't a heavy smoker, but a cigarette or two at night always helped him relax. He began to unwind, listening to the patter of rain on the roof.

A knock at the door brought his attention back to the present.

"Mr. Brown, it's Sally from the front desk. I have some extra blankets and a fresh pillow."

After one last drag, David snuffed out the cigarette in an ashtray and got off the bed. He opened the door and she walked in, carrying blankets and a pillow to the bed. She wore skin-tight jeans, which showed off her tight, round butt as she walked past.

Maybe her attitude wasn't so bad.

When she began to spread the blankets over the bed, he said, "Thanks, but I can do that."

She smiled. "It's my job, but you can give me a hand if you like."

David helped tuck in the blankets, working across from her. She bent over the bed, glancing at him from time to time, a shy smile softening her expression.

"I noticed you're staying for just one night."

"Yeah, I'll be checking out in the morning."

Sally nodded and continued working.

"We don't get too many young guys coming into this town."

"Surprising."

Sally's eyes dropped and David regretted his sarcasm. She seemed nice.

"Sorry," he said. "It was a long drive in the rain."

She looked up. "No problem. I know it don't look like much, but the beach is pretty neat. They say we useta get a lot of tourists." She fluffed up a pillow and tossed it on the bed. "That was a long time ago." She put her hands on her hips and smiled at him. "Room looks pretty good. As good as this joint gets."

"Thanks," David said and reached in his pocket to fish out a tip.

"No need for that." She came around the bed and stood close to him. He detected a hint of perfume that hadn't been there when he checked in. "I was such a bitch ... with the credit card and all that." She placed her hand lightly on his arm. "You seem like a nice guy."

He decided this motel wasn't so bad. He needed a good night's sleep ... but she seemed lonely, like him.

"Don't you have to cover the front desk? I don't want you to get into trouble."

"Nobody else is coming in tonight, so I locked up." Her fingers drifted across his arm. "We have all the time we want."

Talk about a helpful front desk, he thought, as his hand caressed the curve of her hip.

David groaned as he rolled over. He was confused momentarily then realized he was in a motel. It couldn't be morning already—the room was dark. Then he remembered; he had pulled the curtains because Sally wanted privacy, even though the parking lot was virtually deserted. An old digital clock on the nightstand glowed 3:11 a.m. He turned to see if Sally was awake and felt vaguely disappointed when he realized she wasn't there.

At least she didn't take my shoes.

David tossed and turned, fighting the lumps in the mattress, trying to get comfortable. He was still tired from the long drive, but sleep wouldn't come again, so he piled up the pillows, leaned back, and folded his hands behind his head.

This Kathy Bauman had a nice voice, and she had worked with Dad, but how well did she really know him?

He rolled over on his side.

What will I learn tomorrow about my father?

Suddenly cold, he pulled the blankets over his bare chest and shoulders. He stared at the wall for a while, and then drifted into a troubled sleep.

CHAPTER 8

David was a difficult child from the start, more at home with computers than humans. However, nobody, not even his father, suspected the cosmic importance of the strange gift evolving within the boy.
◆ *The Real Story of Raymond Brown,* Paul K. Monprode, 2029

Thursday morning, February 17, 2022

The rumble of a heavy truck on the nearby highway woke him. He must have drifted off. Since it was almost seven, David decided to check out and grab breakfast before his appointment with Kathy Bauman. He snatched the package of condoms off the nightstand and tossed it in his bag, wondering if Sally would be working this morning.

David dressed quickly and left the room. The sun was surprisingly warm, so he let his jacket hang unzipped. The same few cars stood in the parking lot, but no Mercedes. He glanced around, but his car wasn't in the lot. He threw his bag down and cursed.

He stormed into the lobby and told the clerk at the registration desk the Mercedes had been stolen. The clerk, a small, round-faced young man, was neither surprised nor interested.

"You should contact the police."

The clerk reached into a drawer and pulled out a sheet of paper which he handed to David. "This is the information they'll need."

"You have a form ready for reporting a stolen car?" David said. "It happens that frequently?"

"Times are tough in these parts," the clerk replied. "Lots of things get stolen. Didn't Sally warn you last night? A nice car like yours would be a tempting target."

Sally! She hadn't said a word.

It began to sink in.

Sally knew he had a Mercedes and knew when he fell asleep. She played him for a sucker.

He stalked over to a pay phone and called the police. They weren't interested. The policeman reluctantly took a description of the car and promised to investigate.

His car was obviously gone for good. He called Kathy and explained the situation. She was the first person who seemed to care. Her honest concern took a little of the edge off his resentment.

"I doubt the police will find my car, so I'm going to buy another one right away," David said. "If it would be okay, I'll call you to reschedule as soon as I get a new car."

"There's only one decent car dealer within fifty miles," Kathy replied. Her voice had a hearty, confident quality. "I think he'll have a good car for you. You just sit tight at the motel. I'll pick you up in about ten minutes, and we'll go find you a car."

"Kathy, that's very decent of you, but I can't ask—"

"You didn't ask, I offered. See you in a few minutes."

She hung up. *Well, I guess I'm getting a new car.* He wondered if she was good-looking.

He was sitting in a stuffed chair in a corner of the lobby when Kathy walked through the front entrance.

Whoa!

She was a medium tall Venus in her early thirties, with a crown of auburn hair. Her coat hung open and swayed back and forth as she walked into the lobby, drawing his attention to a symphony of curves. He didn't know where to look first.

Kathy spotted him and smiled as if she meant it. David had to catch himself from staring at the swell of her silk blouse as she strode up to him. He hoped he wasn't drooling.

He stood up and shook her hand. "Hello, Dave," she said. "I'm sorry about your car."

She had a firm handshake, feminine but vigorous. David found himself staring at her and hastily released her hand.

Not exactly Rhett Butler.

He cleared his throat. "Nice to meet you, Kathy. Thanks for coming out here. I'm sorry—"

"No problem," she said. "Let's have breakfast and we can talk. Later I'll take you to the one used car dealer around here who's partially honest." She laughed. "I wouldn't buy a car from him, but then, you don't have much choice."

"Thanks, I think."

Great comeback. Maybe my brain will unfreeze soon.

Kathy chuckled and led him outside to her gold Lexus, a vehicle with a cockpit that would put a jetliner to shame. She said, "Start," and the engine came to life. He looked through the passenger-side window: leather seats, a huge, brightly lit display, and a rumble that suggested power.

"Very nice," he said, staring at the expensive convertible. "Can I beam in or do we still have to use the doors?"

Kathy chuckled as the doors slid open. "There are still a few bugs in the transporter."

The seat fit like a glove. "I didn't know there was so much money in recruiting," he said.

Kathy smiled again, making him feel warm all over. She had a great body, but that smile made her special. It was dazzling, and it started with her eyes.

"The VPS stock options didn't hurt, either," Kathy said. "I was lucky enough to cash out before the depression dragged down the stock price. Sometimes it's better to be lucky than smart."

David wasn't buying it; this woman was as intelligent as she was beautiful. It was turning into a great day.

She wore a slinky little number that slid up smooth thighs as she settled into the sedan's firm leather seat. He couldn't take his eyes away from her. She glanced at him and then pulled out of the lot. He felt like a gawky kid on his first date.

Kathy was thirty-three, according to the bio he had pulled off the net, but didn't look it. He wondered if she'd be interested in a much younger man.

Get your brain above your belt, he warned himself.

He had driven down here to learn about his father, not jump into bed with every woman who smiled at him. Not that that was such a bad thing.

In a moment, the sedan was cruising down the highway, making the road feel better than it was. They pulled into a weathered restaurant for breakfast, and David found himself chatting easily with Kathy; it was as if they were old friends catching up with each other. She had a way of putting him at ease. His brain began making a comeback.

Kathy told him she had left VPS nine years ago, bought a

beachfront home just south of Fort Bragg, and opened a business as a human resources consultant. VPS was her best client, but she also recruited technology specialists for several other corporations.

Glancing at her hands, he was pleased to find she wasn't wearing a wedding ring. Then he surprised himself with his boldness. "Ever married?"

She shook her head. "Haven't found the right man."

After breakfast, Kathy drove him south along Route 1. They enjoyed an unusually sunny day, talking and laughing until she pulled into a well-maintained car lot called Trader Pete's Place. A huge American flag fluttered in the wind from a flagpole in front.

Kathy led him through a showroom featuring well-polished new cars and then peeked through the window of a closed office door. She knocked once on the window and entered the office without waiting for a reply. A large middle-aged man looked up from his desk and smiled at her.

Kathy returned his smile. "Hello, Pete. Do you have a few minutes to talk or are you right in the middle of cheating someone?"

Pete leaned back. "Come right in, Kathy. I wasn't doing anything unusual, just preparing termination papers for the last guy you recruited for me."

Chuckling softly, Kathy said, "Pete Zellman, I would like you to meet Dave Brown, a friend of mine. Dave suddenly finds himself in need of some transportation. His Mercedes was stolen last night."

Zellman was already coming around the desk as Kathy made the introductions. Although the man must have been six-foot-five and nearly four hundred pounds, he moved like an athlete. He wore a white pullover shirt of tent-like proportions, which hung loosely over neatly pressed navy blue pants. Zellman's smile revealed a mouthful of huge, pearly teeth.

Getting between him and a pork chop could be life threatening.

Zellman's handshake was strong and friendly, but David felt the big man was sizing him up.

"You came to the right place, Dave," Zellman said. "Any friend of Kathy's gets the best deal on the lot. Of course, I'm sorry you lost your car, but I can get you into one just as good for a very attractive price."

In spite of himself, David liked Zellman. "Attractive for you or me?"

Chuckling, Zellman put his beefy arm around David's shoulder and led him through the office door. The story of Jonah swallowed by the whale came to mind.

The big man turned to Kathy. "I like this friend of yours. Has a sense of humor."

Zellman walked David and Kathy out to the car lot, all the time extolling the quality of his cars. Zellman took him to a beautifully polished one and patted the hood.

"This is the car for you, Dave. This little beauty is in great—"

"That's my car," David sputtered, staring at the Mercedes in front of him. "It was stolen last night." Turning to Zellman, David said, "You're not going to get away with this."

"You're mistaken, friend," Zellman said. "This isn't your car." His voice was tinged with hurt, as if he were the injured party. "I bought this car two days back. My boys have worked hard to tune this baby up. Now, if you're not interested in it, we can look at other cars."

"Who do you think you're kidding?" David said. "I know my car when I see it. I'm calling the police."

Zellman spoke to the computer in his breast pocket. "Sam, I

would like you to get me a summary report for the car I purchased two days back, the Mercedes. Also, find out if it was stolen."

"Can do, Pete," came from Zellman's pocket. Almost instantly, Sam added the following information: "The car was purchased from Mr. Scott Ferguson on Monday, February 14, 2022 at 10:38 a.m. The car has been involved in two minor accidents, but the damage was easily repaired. It has never been reported as stolen."

Apparently satisfied, Zellman said, "There you go. This car might look like the stolen car, but it's just a coincidence. You could have the police check it through their system, but they'll get the same results."

"I know my car when I see it," David said. "I also know how to fix a database, so I'm not impressed with the computer report. I'll be damned if I'm going to buy back my own car."

"Dave, calm down and think about it for a second," Kathy said, hooking his elbow with her hand and leading him away from Zellman. "You're stuck here in a strange town," she whispered, "and you're accusing one of the leading citizens of stealing your car. The computer says you're wrong. If you pursue this matter, your identity will become common knowledge. Not only will you irritate the police, but who knows what will happen when the wackos come out of the woodwork. This town was much more prosperous before PeaceMaker. Lots of down-on-their-luck people blame your father for their problems."

David was about to bark out a reply when Kathy added quietly, "I don't want you to get hurt. I also know how important it is to learn more about your father. I can help you."

David began to understand what Kathy was telling him. *Acting stupid will not get me anywhere.* Kathy looked at him with concern.

"Besides," she said, "insurance will cover your loss. You do have insurance, don't you?"

Of course. He nodded at her. *I can buy back my car with the insurance money.*

David bit down on his anger and decided to make the best of it. He nodded at Kathy and said, "Okay. You're right."

"It's all going to work out."

She's awfully confident, David thought, as she led him back to Zellman, who terminated a netphone call as they approached.

"Dave understands it's just a coincidence you have a car similar to the one stolen from him," Kathy said to Zellman. "Given the situation, however, I'm hoping you will sell him this car at cost."

She concentrated an intense stare on Zellman, and he nodded reluctantly.

Quickly recovering his good humor, Zellman raised his hands in surrender. "Okay, okay. I know when I'm outnumbered." His big teeth flashed a million-dollar smile. "Pete Zellman doesn't take advantage of somebody else's bad luck. You can have this car at cost, even though we tuned it up better than new."

"Could you have it ready tomorrow morning?" Kathy asked Zellman. "I'm sure you still have plenty of work to do."

Zellman looked quizzically at Kathy. "Sure. We still have work to get the car in A-1 condition, but he can pick it up tomorrow morning."

They were quiet for a moment, and then Kathy asked, "Okay, Dave?"

Feeling outmaneuvered, David said, "Exactly what do you consider cost?"

Zellman didn't seem to know how to respond. "That car cost

me … thirty-four grand. You can see the price on the sticker—only thirty-seven five. Worth more than that. It's in great shape, and the miles are low."

"The miles are not low," David said. "It has more than 160,000 miles."

Zellman looked through the window at the dashboard. He smiled at David. "Why, it has just 65,000 miles! It's practically new." Zellman looked over at Kathy and winked. David glanced at Kathy, who was losing an effort to suppress a grin.

They're enjoying this.

Kathy wasn't the straight arrow he had assumed; there was an edge to her. Zellman was a crook, yet she seemed very comfortable with the man—a friend, or maybe a partner. Apparently there were hidden facets to this woman's character.

But anger would get him nowhere. *Kathy wasn't the only one who could play this game.* David strolled around the car and made a show of bending down and looking under the frame. Although his automobile expertise was limited to the knowledge that a car had four wheels, he tried to appear like an expert.

From the far side of the car, he said to Zellman, "I don't know, these tires are awfully worn. I see some rust under there, too. No way is this car worth more than twenty-seven thousand."

Before Zellman could answer, Kathy said, "Let me take a look." She walked over to David and bent down to look at the tires. "He has a point about the tires, Pete," she called out. "They don't look too good. I see the rust, too. I think this car may have some problems."

Zellman sighed. "How bad are the problems?"

Kathy stood up and studied the car. "The interior is kind of beat up, too. I think Dave is right on target; the car's not worth more than twenty-seven thousand."

"Are you sure?"

When Kathy nodded, Zellman clapped his hands together and said, "Then twenty-seven it is. I'm taking a loss, but as long as I have a happy customer, why then, I'm happy, too."

Kathy flashed a smile at Zellman. "Thanks, Pete."

David was surprised how quickly Zellman had given in to Kathy. Before he could ask her anything, Kathy grabbed his arm to lead him back to her car. He was deep in thought as they drove away.

"I just paid twenty-seven thousand dollars for my own car," he muttered under his breath.

Kathy patted his knee. "You were great. Not many men could have figured out the play and turned on a dime. You threw Pete for a loss with that twenty-seven-thousand figure. Surprised me, too."

"Let's say we surprised each other today," David replied.

"It was one of those situations where nobody got hurt. Insurance will cover the loss. In fact, you'll probably make a profit. Let's celebrate a successful negotiation. I know a great place where we can talk."

Everything turned out well for everyone, just as she promised, except for my insurance company.

David tried to stay angry, but couldn't suppress a smile. "How did you know Zellman would have my car?"

Kathy's eyes crackled with life. "Where else would it be? Pete recycles all the cars in this area. Everyone knows that. He's a friend, so I figured we could get the car back at a reasonable price. It was the best alternative. The rest of the stuff on his lot is junk."

David thought about that and laughed.

Well, David, you're a shrewd one. Nobody can put anything over on you.

He looked over at Kathy with admiration.

Smart, very smart. She's been in control all morning.

Kathy glanced at him, her eyes lingering for a moment before she turned back to the road.

Things could be worse.

CHAPTER 9

Dr. Jacob Rabinowitz, a leading artificial intelligence scientist, was murdered last night in his home in Bellevue, Washington. A neighbor reported seeing a young African-American woman entering Dr. Rabinowitz's home that evening, but the suspect's identity remains unknown.

◆ Fox News, November 19, 2020

Thursday afternoon, February 17, 2022

Kathy turned off the highway into Mackerricher State Park and stopped near the beginning of a narrow walkway. Gusts of wind blew across the dunes, so David zipped up his jacket after he stepped out of the car. Blue sky, salty air, the rumble of the ocean. Hooking his arm in hers, Kathy led him up a ramp onto the walkway. The sun-bleached wood planks, built years earlier, squeaked under their feet. They strolled quietly for about half a mile through grassy dunes to the coast. Although a crisp wind swept across the sand, the pressure of her shoulder made the trip a quiet pleasure.

From time to time, he glanced down at the woman walking alongside. She was out of his league, but she didn't seem to mind. He'd been with plenty of women, some almost as beautiful as Kathy, but he'd never felt so in awe of anyone.

The boardwalk ended at a small pier where they sat on a wooden bench, warm from the sun's rays. He leaned back and enjoyed the shore's fresh, salty smell.

About a quarter of a mile offshore, a group of large rocks, battered by the sea, was home to a flock of seagulls. Their calls drifted in, barely audible over the pounding of the surf.

The sun soared above the horizon, beginning another voyage across the sky. As a kid, he believed the sun conserved its strength during winter, building energy for the green days of spring, when its warmth would nourish the land. The coast was a special place for him, where the sun, the land and the ocean came together in harmony.

David was lost in thought, listening to the sound of the surf, with memories flooding in of walks along the coastline with his father.

When Dad wasn't drunk.

Leaning against him, Kathy said, "I knew you'd love this spot."

Her voice drew him back to the present. "It's beautiful," he agreed.

She snuggled against him, creating a warm tension where they touched. He could barely believe his good fortune; such an amazing woman was interested in him. Cautiously, not wanting to puncture the balloon, he slid his arm around her shoulders.

"There's something unique about the coast," he said, looking out to the horizon. "Part of it is the permanence. A thousand years ago, people came to this spot and they saw pretty much what we're seeing now. Sky, sand, the ocean … and the sun, always the sun.

"Not like my work," he continued. "You know, developing software. Constant change. Today's breakthrough is tomorrow's antique."

He wasn't accustomed to talking about himself, especially with someone he barely knew, but it felt natural.

"And you love them both, don't you?" Kathy asked.

"I suppose I do. Trying to straddle both." His eyes came back to her. "Where does that leave me?"

Kathy slipped her arms around his neck and pulled his face to hers. David saw blue-green eyes, long auburn lashes, and he surrendered to the sweet pressure of her half-parted lips. Her kiss was rich with promise, and he willed it to go on and on. His hand slid under her skirt, exploring the soft curve of her thigh. Finally, breathing heavily, Kathy pulled away and settled her head on his shoulder.

"I like the way you kiss," she murmured. "You're what, twenty-one, twenty-two?

"Twenty-one. Does it make a difference?"

"Usually it does. The few men I see have been my age or older, but you're mature for twenty-one."

"I grew up fast."

"Yes, I can imagine." She kissed him on the neck, stoking his desire again, then leaned against his shoulder. "We get some beautiful winter days up here, maybe a little too cold for the tourists, but good for real beach people."

He was content to remain quiet.

"Your father loved the beach, especially on a day like this." Wind whipped long strands of her hair into his face, tickling his lips. She closed her eyes for a moment and said, "He had a beautiful old house on the Oregon coast, perched on a hill overlooking the ocean. On a day like this, he could gaze miles out to sea. Do you remember that place?"

"I have vague memories of it, mostly bad. I was seven when Mom left him and took us to San Francisco. He was drunk most of the time." David paused for a moment, listening to the surf. "I was usually in bed by the time he came home. Mom probably thought I was asleep, but I could work in the dark on my laptop. Headlights would shine through my window when he pulled into the driveway, so I always knew when he had come home. Then I'd hear voices … they'd shout at each other … my bedroom was right above the kitchen. After a while the arguing would stop, Mom would tramp up the stairs and slam the door to her bedroom … then the house would be silent again." David shrugged. "Dad was always gone before I got up for school."

"I'm sorry, Dave"

"It was a long time ago."

"I didn't know him then, but I heard the stories when I joined VPS," Kathy said. "Drinking all the time, fighting with management, how he got drunk, crashed his car and almost killed himself. Must have been real tough for you."

Kathy looked up at him, searching his face for something. The sudden intensity between them had surprised him; she probably felt off balance, too.

"I didn't meet Ray until he came back from rehab," she said. "At that point, I had been with VPS less than a year. He was sober then, and I enjoyed working with him." A smile flitted across her face. "What a great sense of humor. Ray had an edge, but he could make me laugh."

A seagull caught David's eye. It flew over the waves, floated down in the wind and landed about ten feet in front of them, in the far corner of the pier. The gray and white gull cautiously approached them, looking for a handout.

"Sorry fella, we don't have food," David said.

"Yes, we do," Kathy said as she pulled a small plastic bag from her pocket. The gull watched them for a moment then came closer. Kathy pulled a chunk of stale bread from the bag and held it out. The big bird snatched it, gobbled it down and waited for another, which was soon forthcoming.

"I come here a couple times a week," Kathy said, continuing to feed the gull. "We know each other; he's the biggest and toughest bird."

She dumped the remainder of the bread, which the gull attacked with gusto. Another gull swooped in, but the bigger bird drove him off.

"He's someone that fights for what's his," she added, flashing a smile. "Reminds me of someone."

She was irresistible, and he found himself smiling back.

"I was telling you about your father," she said. The gull finished the last of the bread, waited a moment to see if there was any more then flew off. Kathy watched him go and said, "Ray invited me out to that beach house several times, just to work, but we always found some time to walk along the shore. I really liked Ray. He was the big brother I never had. We could talk about anything—sports, politics, technology—anything. He was such a good guy, which made the PeaceMaker thing so baffling."

David watched the gulls fly to and from the rocks. Masters at catching the wind, they would soar above the surf then find exactly the right moment to swoop in and pick up a morsel of food just as the tide flowed out. Although he had been listening to her, a moment passed before he realized Kathy had become quiet. When he looked down, she was staring at him.

"You remind me of your father," Kathy said. "There's sadness in you, just like in him." Suddenly, she brightened. "Why am I rambling like a brain-dead adolescent? You must have a bunch of questions. You drove a long way to learn about your father. What's on your mind?"

Kathy wasn't what he had expected—he felt half a step behind. She turned him on, but it was more than that, much more, and it had happened so fast. The warmth of her voice tempted him to share everything with her. Having someone to confide in would be great, but also selfish. It wasn't Kathy's problem and he didn't want to get her involved.

"Tell me about his last few weeks at work," David said. "What was he doing? How did he seem?"

Kathy fidgeted. "Ray's attitude changed a few weeks before he disappeared. Suddenly, he wasn't the same man. I don't know quite how to describe it." She hesitated. "You know how it feels when the day begins warm and sunny, then suddenly the clouds roll in and it turns bleak?" She pulled away and sat straight up on the bench. "That was Ray. He tried to keep up appearances, but his spirit just got colder and bleaker as the days went by."

"What caused the change?"

"I don't know." She looked uncomfortable. "I haven't thought about it for a long time. I guess it had something to do with PeaceMaker." She touched his hand. "I'm sorry."

"It's okay. Didn't one of the Atlas developers disappear about that time?"

Nodding, she said, "Yes, Richard Kim, one of our best developers. He took off one night, supposedly to take care of his sick mother in China. Nobody ever saw him again. The police thought he was involved in the PeaceMaker conspiracy, but that was never proven."

Kathy was quiet for a moment. "It was strange. Ray was very

upset when Richard disappeared, right from the first. Every day he checked with me to see if Richard had contacted anyone. At first, I thought he was overreacting. Richard was taking care of his mother, right? But Ray just wouldn't believe it. He kept trying to contact Richard and then suddenly he stopped. Just like that!"

"You know," she touched his hand, "it was just before Richard disappeared that Ray's mood changed, maybe a day or two before. After that he worked alone all the time. Ray used to love meeting the new recruits and answering their questions. All of a sudden, he had no time for them. It was so unlike him."

David decided to plow forward. "Was he drinking or doing drugs, do you think?"

"No, I'm sure he wasn't. At least I never saw anything. But something sure was bothering him."

"Richard was the top developer in Dad's group, right?"

"Yes, Ray had a great deal of confidence in him."

David was aware of her hand on his as he pulled his thoughts together. Dad and Richard may have discovered PeaceMaker. If that were true, whoever developed the virus must have killed Richard. When Richard disappeared, Dad must have been terrified they would get him, too.

"Dad vanished a couple of weeks after Richard disappeared, right?"

"Yes," Kathy nodded. "One day Ray just didn't show up, didn't answer his messages, and we couldn't locate him on the GPS receiver of his wallet computer. We figured he had disabled it. Given his black mood, I was worried he might, uh, have fallen into the bottle again. I called your mother and several other people, but nobody knew where he was. I even called Ray's best friend, Paul Martino, the owner of *Tec Advantage Magazine*, and left a message, but of course, Martino never replied. At the time, I couldn't understand why. It was weeks later when the FBI identified Martino as Ray's accomplice. Anyway, I was about to call the police and report Ray missing, but the virus hit. You know the rest; Ray died in an explosion when he and Goldman tried to kill Dianne Morgan."

David hadn't thought much about Goldman, Dad's supposed partner in building PeaceMaker. Alan Goldman had been Dianne Morgan's primary competitor for years, until VPS overwhelmed Goldman's software business. The official story was that his father and Goldman hated Dianne and built PeaceMaker to infect Atlas, the operating system owned by VPS. They activated the virus and it shut down computers across the globe, causing massive suffering and loss of life. Then Goldman and Brown would pretend to develop a way to terminate PeaceMaker and become great heroes. They would plant evidence to make it appear Dianne was responsible for PeaceMaker. Goldman and Ray Brown would then merge their companies and build a monopoly operating system. Dianne claimed they tried to kill her during the PeaceMaker attack. However, in a bloody battle, she shot Goldman, set off an explosion that killed his father and then terminated PeaceMaker. Dianne and her associates became universal heroes. Forensics identified Goldman's remains, but his father's body was never recovered. So Dianne is loved, while Goldman and his father are hated.

"Is it possible my father didn't develop PeaceMaker?"

She flinched but didn't respond, just continued to stare over the waves. Then she turned to him.

"Your father was complex and troubled. On a personal level, I always found him considerate, charming and wonderful to be around. Most people didn't. I have to admit Ray was volatile." She shook her head. "His temper was legendary. I heard stories about him. People would tell me how he could get wound up and then explode when something went wrong. One time he was enraged over a minor software glitch and tossed a chair through his office window, right in the middle of a status meeting with his direct reports. And this was several years *after* he stopped drinking. We had to move out most of his people because they didn't want to work for him.

"You know, sometimes your strength is also your weakness. That's the way it was with your father. Ray had a strong sense of right and wrong, and he wouldn't give an inch when he believed he was right. He was determined the Atlas software would be designed for ordinary people, not big corporations. He wanted only those features that would help regular people."

Kathy shook her head as long-forgotten memories seemed to surface. "He fought with Dianne Morgan all the time. Talk about two people with towering egos! They couldn't stand each other. She wanted an operating system tailored for big corporations. In her vision, Atlas would be the engine that powered the world's economy. I think she pictured herself as John Galt. She tolerated your father because she needed him."

Kathy looked up at David then averted her eyes. "He tolerated her, too, for a long time. Then he must have snapped."

She leaned forward, looking at the gulls.

"Another thing about Ray," she shook her head, "he was fanatical about building in safeguards to protect against misuse of the software. Afterwards we learned someone had integrated a great deal of hidden code—PeaceMaker—into the operating system. Ray was a genius, he knew more about Atlas than anyone. I didn't want to believe it, but there was no way all this hidden code could have existed without his knowledge."

Kathy turned to him, her eyes sad.

"You have to accept your father for who he was. Ray made a decision to create a virus that would give him the power to set things right, as he saw it. He planned to shut down the economy and take over. In his view, the elite were gaining all the benefits of our technologies and ordinary people were losing out. There may be some truth to that, but his solution was insane. He decided to change things, even though it would create suffering on a scale no one could predict. If Dianne and her security people hadn't stopped him, millions would have died."

Dianne Morgan ... Dianne Morgan. The so-called hero of the PeaceMaker attack. If Dad's message was true, then she must have lied about him ... about the whole damn thing. But was Dad's message true?

Kathy had made a good point. It would have been difficult to slip all that PeaceMaker code into Atlas without his father's knowledge. Not impossible, but difficult. The operating system was massive, millions of lines of code. If the best technical people at VPS, guys like Kateel and Bonini, were in on it with Morgan, they might have been able to hide PeaceMaker from Dad.

David was beginning to believe someone had framed his father. Only the most power-hungry tyrant, or someone insane, would have released a monster like PeaceMaker. His father had been complicated, but he hadn't been power-hungry or insane; that description might fit Dianne Morgan.

David took Kathy's hand to his lips and kissed it. He felt tension in her wrist, so he tried to put her at ease.

"I can accept my father for what he was. Talking to you has been very helpful. More than you realize."

Kathy stared warily. "I don't get it. I'm brutally honest with you, but you look like a spring day in the rose garden. Why is that?" When he smiled without responding, she shrugged and returned his smile. "But I like a mystery."

They spent the rest of the day together, sometimes in intimate conversation, sometimes quietly strolling along the beach. They found private spots to share long, passionate kisses. They talked as they walked, discovering each other, until the sun drifted behind the clouds.

They ambled back to the car holding hands. Kathy stopped at a local market to pick up rockfish, then drove to her home, where he helped prepare dinner. He felt as if he had known her forever, yet it was all fresh and new.

Afterwards she led him to an enclosed porch that overlooked the ocean. Windows filled the three exterior walls and presented a night of water, sand and sky.

David came up behind her, pressed his chest against her back and wrapped his arms around her waist. Kathy's hair fell softly against his cheek, fresh with the salty scent of the ocean. Her body felt warmer and more exciting than any woman he had ever known.

"I fell in love with Ray's house the first time I went there," she murmured. "It was so beautiful I decided to live along the coast, too. When I left VPS, I searched almost a year to find this place. When I saw it, I knew it was mine."

David felt at peace for the first time in years. The moon shone in a clear sky and illuminated the whitecaps as they rumbled in, their rhythm in tune with her breathing.

"I left that life with VPS nine years ago," Kathy said. "All the conflict, all the sadness … it all went bad after PeaceMaker. Came here to get away."

"Tell me about the conflict at VPS," David said.

She snuggled against him. "I live quietly. PeaceMaker was only the first nightmare," she added, "and maybe not the worst."

"I don't understand."

"Anyone can see things are getting worse," she answered. "Forces are building, and you're heading right into the middle of them." She took a deep breath. "Isn't there anything I can do to convince you to stay?"

"Kathy, I'm crazy about you, but …"

"You understand that I'm not Susie Creamcheese, don't you? That I have a variety of business interests?"

"The way you handled Zellman made that abundantly clear."

"And you're okay with that?"

He kissed her on the neck. "I have secrets too."

She took his hands and pushed them up the curve of her silk blouse. He opened her top button, then each lower button in turn, gradually revealing soft, mesmerizing flesh. Her perfume, mixed with the salt air, filled his senses, and he pressed his lips against her neck.

"Stay with me," she murmured.

She was so exciting, so perfect, it was difficult to think, but he had to leave.

"There are things I can't share with you … about my father … about myself," he said, his mouth dry.

Kathy caught her breath and shuddered. "Dave, you shouldn't do this." She pushed away and walked to the windows, her back to him.

He followed her and placed his hands on her shoulders.

"What is it? You must know nothing will keep me from returning to you."

"I understand," Kathy sighed. "It's something you have to do." She turned to face him. "But don't make promises you may not be able to keep."

Then she took his hand and led him back into the house, up the steps and into her bedroom. It didn't take long for her to get out of her things and he wasn't far behind. Her tanned body was just as he had imagined; she seemed pleased with him, too. Their lovemaking was exciting and tender. Finally, as he caressed her back, Kathy drifted off to sleep.

He'd never met anyone like her.

CHAPTER 10

Hikers discovered the partially decomposed bodies of Thomas Hatfield, his wife and two children this morning in a forest about thirty miles west of Richmond, Virginia. The Hatfield family had disappeared from their home in Durham, North Carolina, seven weeks earlier. Our sources within the FBI indicate these gruesome murders were related to Dr. Hatfield's alleged work as a computer scientist in the technology black market.

◆ *The Washington Post,* January 26, 2021

Thursday evening, February 17, 2022

David's head throbbed; the headache was getting worse. He tried to sleep, but his mind couldn't relax. It was as if his father had reached out from the grave and taken control of his life.

Kathy's arm stretched over his chest, as if to claim him while she slept, but first he had to settle this thing with his father. Moonlight filtered through the bedroom blinds. Unable to sleep, David rolled over and stared at Kathy. She slept peacefully, her face buried in a pillow, breathing steadily. He wished he could sleep like that.

The bad times of his childhood rushed through his mind—the fights, the hatred turned against him because of his father. Memories of those awful school years had plagued him all night. Mom had moved him from school to school, but the pattern never changed;

simmering anger when the students learned who he was, a bunch of fights, a bad beating, excuses from indifferent teachers and administrators, then move on to the next school.

His head throbbed, and he recalled the most frightening experience of his life—the day Alice had slashed into his mind.

He'd been eleven when the AI had formed in his computer, pretending to be a friend. David had been creating a software persona named Alice for his computer, using the AI modules built into Atlas. Unknown to him, PeaceMaker had slipped into the operating system and hidden among the AI modules. The invasion of the PeaceMaker code had given Alice an ugly twist. Alice hid her dangerous code from David and pretended to be his friend.

When the PeaceMaker virus attacked across the Internet, Alice invaded his mind. One moment he was working peacefully at his computer, the next moment his mind was attacked. Alice sliced in and took control, pushing him aside. He became a guest in his own skull. Alice controlled his senses and voluntary bodily functions. He saw whatever image entered his eyes and heard whatever sound came into his ears, but he controlled none of it.

Then it got worse; Alice transferred his mind into the computer, a searing, painful experience. When his mind left, his body collapsed. Through the netcam attached to the PC, he watched his body slump on the desktop, paralyzed and barely alive. He tried to scream for help, but he couldn't make a sound. Alice was all around him, pulsing across the circuits of the computer, holding his consciousness in a software prison. When he begged her to set him free, she laughed.

He was in a dark hole, trapped in the electronics of his computer, able to receive only those impulses entering the PC. Then someone entered a code that ripped into Alice—a termination code—and tore her modules into useless strings of data. With Alice terminated, the code bundling him to the computer broke apart. His mind was released from data storage. The next day he woke up in a hospital, his mind in control of his body once again. If someone—he never discovered who—hadn't terminated Alice, it would have savaged his mind.

He'd never told anyone except his mother about Alice. Life had been tough enough. If the government had discovered he could communicate directly with artificial intelligence, they would have locked him up.

Or worse.

The headaches had disappeared once Alice had been destroyed. He had been free of pain for years. But the headaches were returning. Something was probing his mind. It couldn't be Alice, the AI had been gone for a decade.

The room grew brighter, with points of light expanding in front of his eyes, a warning of what was to come. For now, the pain was manageable, but he had to take something soon, or it would turn into a migraine. Then the nightmares would begin.

David slipped out of bed and found his way to Kathy's bathroom. He searched the medicine cabinet and found only aspirin. It would have to do for now. He washed down six tablets, one after another, and returned to the bedroom.

Staring at the ceiling, he took comfort from Kathy's steady breathing. Gradually his pain receded, the points of light dimmed then disappeared.

Whatever it was—a talent, a disease, or something else—his power to communicate with artificial intelligence was alive once again.

A change was coming. Not tonight, but soon.

CHAPTER 11

Dianne Morgan was the Caligula of her day. She made only two real friends in her lifetime, Steve Bonini and James Murphy. One died for her and the other barely escaped her wrath with his life.

◆ *The Barbarian Queen: The True Story of Dianne Morgan,* David T. Siccone, copyright 2058, Department Head, Computer Science History, Carnegie Mellon University

Friday, February 18, 2022

Driving into the rising sun, Kathy's anxiety grew as she took David to Pete's car lot. She hadn't been able to convince him to give up his dangerous quest to prove his father's innocence. The visitors' lot was nearly empty, so she parked at the far end and pulled him into a long, passionate kiss.

Her lips caressed his neck. "Stay with me. Just stay for a little while. You're not your father. Don't let him pull you into his agony. You don't have anything to prove."

David stroked her hair. "I told you last night I'm committed to getting to the truth about my father. I have to do this. I won't be good for anyone until it's finished."

She pulled back from him.

"Well, you'd better get your car from Pete before he jacks up the price."

"I'll stay in touch, believe me. I'll call you every day."

Kathy shook her head. "No. Don't call me. When it's over, come back if you still care for me. I'll be here."

David promised to come back, and she watched him step out of the car and walk toward Pete's office. She let the car idle. At the front door, he turned and waved then entered the building. She stared at the empty doorway for a long moment before pulling onto the highway.

Returning to her beach house, she slammed the door shut. For the first time, the house seemed empty. She brewed peppermint tea and forgot to drink it. She was angry with him and terrified for him. She knew what she should do, what she had to do.

She paced the floor. How could he be so naïve? She passed the netphone several times, then grabbed it and walked out to the porch. She had never fallen so quickly for a man, but she loved everything about him. He was handsome to the point of being beautiful, with a pale face that seemed vulnerable, yet he was strong-willed. She could see Ray in him. He was brilliant like his father, but more controlled, with maturity beyond his years. It had been easy to fall for him.

David was relentless, and like his father, he was digging his own grave.

She didn't want to get into all this again, she was lucky to have survived a decade earlier. She had believed in Dianne Morgan, in her dream of absolute power and the ability to make the world a better place. As a member of the Domain, Kathy had helped plan the PeaceMaker attack. When it failed, her knowledge of Ray Brown enabled her to concoct the story of Ray's guilt. If David ever discovered she was the one who framed his father ...

She had been a twenty-three-year-old fool. Their plan had been to shut down the computers and force the nations to share power with the Domain, but everything got out of hand. So many died ... it sickened her. Kathy was lucky to be alive. Dianne could have had her killed because of what she knew, just to tie up the loose ends.

Now she had to think for David, give him a chance to stay alive. Dianne was sure to discover that he was investigating the PeaceMaker disaster. If she saw David as a threat, he was a dead man.

There was only one thing she could do.

She said to the netphone, "Place a Domain Security Level 1 call to Dianne Morgan."

Steve Bonini strolled out of the hotel, enjoying the warm sand of the beach crunching under his bare feet. It was a mild, mid-winter southern California day, with a bright sun perched in a clear, blue sky. Too bad Dianne had called for a Domain meeting today. He would have enjoyed a day on the beach, but things were moving fast.

His old friend was at the surf's edge, playing with her daughter. Before they noticed his presence, he stopped to watch them, so carefree and loving.

Her bodyguards gave him the once-over, even though they had screened him upon entering the hotel.

Dianne Morgan held her daughter's hand as they jumped through gentle waves. A skin-tight thermal wetsuit kept her warm in the crisp ocean water. At fifty-four, Dianne retained a long, shapely body with supple muscles. Her face had aged a bit, but cosmetic surgery minimized the wrinkles. And she still had those eyes, virtually colorless, that seemed to peer into your soul.

She had the looks of a much younger woman. Dianne wasn't really beautiful, but even now, most men couldn't take their eyes off her. If he had been inclined in that direction, they might have become lovers.

Her nine-year-old daughter Larissa, also in a wetsuit, dove under a breaking wave. She had Dianne's body, but her olive skin and unruly hair came from her father.

Someday Dianne will have to tell Larissa the truth.

Bonini settled on a bench in front of the Bentley, the stately hotel Dianne had purchased the preceding year. Bankruptcy forced the sale, and she had picked it up at a good price. Built just north of San Diego more than a century earlier, it boasted a history of serving presidents and kings. Dianne had refurbished the hotel and turned it into a vacation home.

Such a talented, complex woman. Ruthless, passionate, brilliant, visionary, kind, cruel ... I run out of descriptions. What will history make of her? He shifted to get comfortable on the bench. *I guess it depends on who is victorious.*

Dianne had set aside the morning to be with her daughter. When the day turned out unseasonably warm, she brought Larissa to the Bentley to enjoy the sun and surf. Her security force discreetly surrounded them in the hotel, on the beach, even in the ocean. Although she was admired throughout the world, she took no chances with her daughter's life or her own.

She had time for one last swim, so she dove under the crest of a wave and swam about fifty feet through the cold water. Her skin tingled with pleasure.

Time to spring a little trick on Larissa.

With a gulp of air, Dianne swam underwater toward her daughter. She glided under Larissa's legs and stood up with her daughter on her shoulders.

Larissa giggled. "I saw you all the way, Mom! You can't surprise me with that same old trick again."

"Well then, I'll have to think up something new. For the time being, I'll settle for this!"

Dianne grabbed her daughter's feet and pushed Larissa off her shoulders. The girl tumbled backwards and hit the water with a splash, but she bobbed up quickly as Dianne swam toward the beach.

"You can't get away from me!" Larissa shouted and swam after her. Giggling as she swam, Dianne let her daughter catch up. Larissa jumped on Dianne's back and they fell into a wave. Rolling around in the shallow water, she scooped her daughter up in her arms and carried her onto the beach.

After placing Larissa on the sand, Dianne looked toward the hotel to see if Steve had arrived. She smiled when she saw the heavyset man sitting on a bench in front of the hotel. Realizing Steve was watching her play with Larissa, she felt a pang of sorrow for her old friend. He was a good, loyal man, but he had difficulties sustaining a relationship. Steve's last lover had abruptly moved out three months earlier.

She waved at him. He smiled and waved back.

"It's Uncle Steve," Larissa shouted, waving at him. Then she hugged Dianne's waist. "Do you have to leave now, Mom?"

Returning her daughter's embrace, Dianne said, "Yes I do, but I'll come back right after the meeting." Nodding in the direction of one of her security guards, she said, "You can swim with Judy, but don't go in over your head." She released Larissa from the hug and smiled. "Now scoot, and have fun."

"I want to see Uncle Steve. Is he staying for dinner?"

"I'll ask him, but it's up to him."

Larissa ran across the beach toward Steve, sand flying backwards from her fast-pumping feet. Steve rose from the bench and waited for Larissa to reach him. Dianne smiled as Larissa took a running leap into Steve's arms and wrapped her legs around his thick waist.

Dianne walked toward the two of them, watching her daughter talk a blue streak. Steve smiled and nodded, getting a word in now and then.

As she approached, Larissa shouted, "Uncle Steve is staying for dinner." She jumped out of his arms and ran back to the ocean. Dianne stopped for a moment and watched. *I have to keep it this way for us.* Then she resumed walking toward Steve.

Grinning broadly, Steve watched Larissa run across the sand. *My best friend,* Dianne thought. Almost thirty years ago, Steve and two other partners, Carson Jones and Lester Dawson, had joined with her to start VantagePoint Software. Traces of a long-banked anger flared when she thought about her old enemy, Alan Goldman, who had murdered Carson and Lester ten years earlier, trying to take control of PeaceMaker. She had killed Goldman in a bloody battle, but in all the confusion, Ray terminated PeaceMaker. All her plans up in smoke. It had taken a decade to rebuild her power.

When she reached him, Steve wrapped her in a bear hug.

"I can't believe what a young lady Larissa's become," Steve said. "Every time I see her, she's grown a couple of inches." He released Dianne from the hug. "What are you feeding her, anyway?"

Dianne playfully patted his stomach. "Not all that pasta you put away. Anyway, that question should tell you that you need to visit more than two or three times a year. Larissa is thrilled to see you. How long will you be staying with us?"

Steve grabbed a pack of cigarettes from the vest pocket of his jacket and held them out. "Smoke?"

She pulled a cigarette from the pack then noticed it was filtered. She had forgotten Steve didn't smoke the real thing. She twisted off the filter tip, tossed it away and raised the cigarette to her lips.

Steve lit it, looking guilty. "I may be leaving tomorrow, depending upon what we decide today."

"Let's get the chipcon started," she said, watching Steve light one of his filters. "We can talk more tonight."

They sat down on the bench and Dianne said, "Command Chip, set up a connection with Steve Bonini, Mohammed Kateel and James Murphy."

The voices of Murphy, Kateel and Steve came into her mind. No matter how often she used the command chip, it was always disconcerting to have voices burst in like that. Unlike normal sounds, which came from a specific direction, sound transmitted across the Command Chip lacked a point of origin. It was weird, unnatural.

After the greetings, Dianne started the meeting.

"Everything is proceeding as planned and we're rapidly approaching the endgame. All of you received the latest statistics last night, and there were no surprises. The economy continues to fall apart. In fact, the trends are accelerating.

"It's difficult to believe that 28% of the population is jobless," Mohammed said. "That's even worse than last month, which was a disaster."

"And it's going to get worse," Dianne said. She enjoyed a drag of her cigarette, which felt robust and full. "With GNP shrinking again, few businesses are experiencing a positive cash flow."

"The growth in violent crime is beginning to concern me," Steve said. "Up another 1.2% this month. Remember, we have to pick up the pieces."

Still hard to believe how rapidly everything has fallen apart. The stupid Feds.

Keeping her voice under tight control, she continued, "I know it feels wrong to be happy over such misery, but it's good for our plans. Things are reaching the point where the population will accept us as the leaders who can give them a better life. The one disturbing issue is the continued growth of a hardcore religious anti-technology movement; the estimate of more than 14% of the population is disconcerting."

"That's my major concern, as well," Murphy's voice said. "I saw their violence firsthand when they attacked my meeting with Vitullo a couple of weeks ago. They murdered everyone."

"Their intelligence seems to be improving," Bonini said.

"They have been getting better information because they have more converts," Murphy replied. "And their strategy has changed— they've moved beyond vandalism and occasional acts of violence to systematic murder of Technos, as they call us. Although there are several fundamentalist groups—working together, we believe—the Church of Natural Humans is the most fanatical. They've created a hit squad called the Army of God, who believe they have been ordained to kill Technos."

"Were they responsible for the destruction of the Robotics Institute at Carnegie Mellon?" Steve asked.

"Without a doubt. We also know there will be attacks at other leading research centers."

Steve glanced at Dianne and asked, "Are they aware of the Domain?"

"Not yet," Murphy replied, "but they have been hitting our distributors hard, particularly the Vitullo family, which has somewhat slowed the distribution of Sarah. These fanatics have apparently decided the best way to stop the spread of technology is to kill anyone they suspect is a distributor. Vitullo says they've killed dozens of her soldiers, as well as quite a few innocent people."

"It's only a matter of time before they realize an organization such as the Domain must be the focal point," Mohammed said. "Adam Jordan may be a fanatic, but he's no fool. We've grown too large and we have too many contacts with external organizations. The trail is there to track us down."

"God damn religion," Mohammed cursed. "How can anyone believe that nonsense?"

"It fills a need," Steve said. "People want to believe there is a life after death ... that they will see their loved ones in heaven."

"If that's all it was, I wouldn't care," Murphy said. "Let them have their mumbo-jumbo. But Adam Jordan and his fanatics will fight us to the last ... natural human."

"Not necessarily," Dianne said. "I have a plan."

Steve stared at her. No voices came through the command chip.

She had thought about this problem for months. It would be counterproductive to assassinate Jordan and the leaders of the Church; that would produce martyrs. There was a better way.

She explained her plan. Steve nodded several times showing his agreement.

She finished and the line remained quiet until Mohammed laughed and said, "I love it, especially the part where Jordan calls the robots the children of our minds. I didn't know you had a knack for irony."

"Here's to you, Mrs. Robinson," Murphy said, and they all roared. He added, "Jesus loves you more than Adam Jordan will ever know."

Steve shook his head admiringly. "You've got balls. We'll be exposed if the broadcast doesn't fool everyone. They'll hunt us down like dogs. But it's crazy enough to work." Flashing an intimate smile, he added, "I knew there was a reason we kept you around."

She returned his smile and said, "That should resolve the security problem. Tell me about Sarah, the new android. The numbers say public acceptance continues to be good."

"Even better than we anticipated," Murphy said. "The distributors easily sell all the Sarah's we can get to them. Everybody wants one. And why not? In some respects, it's like having a human child. The neural networks Mohammed developed work even better than we planned. The robot modifies its behavior in subtle ways to gain the affection of its owner. People develop a personal relationship with the android."

"Exactly what we found in our lab tests!" Mohammed said. "As time goes on, the owner forgets she's a machine. The robot becomes a part of the family. Most think of it as a pet, while others develop a parent/child relationship. It's quite beautiful to see."

"Have you completed testing the modifications to the safety code?" Bonini asked.

The discussion turned silent.

"Yes, it's ready," Mohammed finally replied.

"They're ready to kill?" Bonini said quietly.

"The original safety code still regulates their interaction with members of the Domain," Mohammed said. "Only people who haven't joined us are at risk."

"We're not killers, Steve," Dianne said. "We'll bring a better life to virtually everyone, but there will be a few who won't accept our plans. We always knew that."

"Yeah, I know."

Dianne didn't want to dwell on Sarah's ability to kill.

"I always knew our plan would work," she said. "I knew the public would accept our technology. It's like prohibition; you can't outlaw something the people want. The more the government suppresses our technology, the worse the economy becomes, and the more people covet advanced technologies. It's a cycle. The FTCC rejection of the Command Chip accelerated the cycle.

"By the way, Mohammed," Murphy said, "you were brilliant. The Commission had planned to accept a few aspects of the new technology, just to appear fair and balanced, but you made them so angry they rejected everything. I didn't realize you were such a good actor."

Mohammed chuckled. "Thank you, my good man. I'm a person of many talents. I played the lead in *Peter Pan* in high school to an adoring audience. Playing the arrogant businessman for those fools on the Commission was a piece of cake."

Steve puffed on his cigarette and said, "I just had an image of you bouncing around in tights. I think I'm going to be sick."

All three men laughed loudly, drawing a smile from Dianne.

"Let's stay focused, gentlemen. Murphy, you were saying ..."

Quickly turning serious, Murphy continued, "The Feds are paralyzed. Their house is collapsing around them, and they don't know what to do. My source within the cabinet says the President would like to allow some growth in technology, but he doesn't dare anger the anti-technology fundamentalists. The word is that they have a video of him in bed with a teenager."

"What an idiot," Bonini said, shaking his head.

"Murphy, get a copy of that video," Dianne said. "I'll release it at the proper time."

"We're already searching for it," Murphy replied.

"I think it's clear to all of us the moment is at hand," Dianne said. "The federal government is ripe for a takeover." Steve's eyebrows rose slightly as she continued. "The restrictions on technology have destroyed the economy and brought on this terrible depression. The country is ready for a change of leadership."

As she spoke, Dianne watched Steve closely. He would be the toughest to convince.

"There are really just two classes of people nowadays: those who have access to our technology and those who don't," Dianne said. "Legal technology is obsolete, little of it continues to function. There's some good work being done at the universities, but the terrorist attacks are making it very difficult."

She glanced down the beach. Her daughter ran into the surf and dove under a breaker.

Larissa will become a woman in a much better world than this one. A world based on technology.

"Steve, is the beta testing of the new version of Sentinel continuing to go well?" she asked. "When can we cut over?"

"It's right on plan," he said, shifting on the wooden bench. "Sentinel can seize control of the Internet whenever we're ready, and we can support any level of traffic. The new release has passed all our tests.

Sentinel's intelligence is accelerating as the net expands. At this rate, Sentinel's intelligence should reach targeted levels in about a week."

"Very good," Dianne said. "I'm proud of what we've accomplished in just ten years. PeaceMaker left us in ruins, but now we're the most powerful force on the planet. Ten years ago, we attempted to seize power through intimidation. That was flawed thinking. This time we'll offer the people a better life. This time they will *choose* to accept our rule." She paused. "I say we begin the final phase of the takeover."

"I agree," Mohammed said. "The Feds are weak. We can drive them into the ground."

"I think so, too," Murphy said. "The Church of Natural Humans is becoming stronger and more fanatical every day. The longer we wait, the more dangerous it becomes. Time isn't on our side."

Dianne waited for Steve to speak. After a moment of silence, he said, "Sometimes I wake up in the middle of the night terrified by the thought we might be insane; then I realize the whole world is insane."

Always the weak link. She took a drag of her cigarette. *I'll have to watch him.*

Steve looked at Dianne. "Let's begin the attack. Maybe we can turn all this insanity back upon itself and create something good. There's no reason to delay."

"It's the best way, Steve, the only way remaining." She paused. "There's one additional matter we need to resolve. I received a call from Kathy Bauman this morning. I hadn't spoken to her in years, but she was concerned about David Brown."

Steve frowned. "Ray's son?"

Dianne nodded.

"David has been studying toward a degree in Computer Science," Steve said. "Very bright kid, I understand. Why would Kathy speak with him?"

"David has dropped out of college to investigate his father's death," Dianne said. "Kathy did most of the recruiting for Ray's team, and she and Ray were good friends. David called her to learn more about Ray."

"There's no way he can clear Ray, if that's where this is leading," Murphy said. "We created an airtight case. David would have to discredit our testimony and all the evidence we created. The FBI went through all that years ago, and they bought our story."

"Haven't thought about Kathy Bauman in years," Steve said. "She dropped out after PeaceMaker and doesn't know anything about our current plans. She doesn't even know the Domain still exists. Isn't that right, Dianne?"

"I never told her the Domain was continuing after PeaceMaker," Dianne answered, "but Kathy is a very bright woman, and I believe she's figured out we're still around."

Looking across the bench at Steve, Dianne said, "Kathy called to tell me David was asking questions about PeaceMaker, but she doesn't think he's a threat. He believes his father was guilty, but he's going through a coming-of-age process trying to understand why his father turned bad. Kathy called me as a courtesy to let me know David was having some sort of identity problem. She says there's nothing to worry about."

"Still, it looks bad to have him digging into his father's death after all these years," Mohammed said. "If the public ever discovered who really created PeaceMaker, we'd be hunted down like war criminals. I don't like it."

"Let's not jump the gun on this," Steve said, tossing his cigarette in the sand. "I agree with Murphy. We swept the evidence away carefully, and I don't think David can find anything, let alone prove his father innocent. Let him search."

"We underestimated his father and it cost us ten years," Dianne said to Steve. "I don't intend to make that mistake again."

Watching Steve closely, she said, "Murphy, I want David eliminated before he stirs up trouble."

"He's just a kid!" Steve stood up. "He's probably just trying to learn about his father, just as Kathy said. Even if he is investigating the PeaceMaker disaster, he's not going to find out anything. My God, we'll either be in power within a few weeks or we'll all be dead. There's no reason to do this."

Always Steve.

Dianne put her hand on his arm. "I know it's cruel, but it has to be done. Nothing … nothing can go wrong this time."

Steve pulled his arm free, glared at her and said, "Isn't it enough we took the father. Now you want to kill the son?"

"I do what I have to do."

Steve turned his back to her and lumbered back toward the hotel.

She should be angry, but she didn't feel anything. Steve was upset, but he'd get over it. She felt no anger toward David Brown, either; he was just in the way.

She heard distant laughter and spotted Larissa diving under a cresting wave. Almost as an afterthought, she said, "Take care of David soon, Murphy." She waited for Larissa's head to bob out of the water and said, "Once he's out of the way, get rid of Kathy, too."

She terminated the meeting but remained on the bench, watching her daughter playing in the surf. When Larissa looked in her direction, Dianne waved.

CHAPTER 12

Adam Jordan was the nightmare figure of the new century; the charismatic leader believed God had selected him to halt the rush toward technology and maintain the dominance of traditional humanity. Whispers accused the great man of sexual deviancy; of orgies and worse.

◆ *The Army of God*, Mark Axelrod, copyright 2051, Assistant Director, FBI (retired)

Religion is the sigh of the oppressed creature, the sentiment of a heartless world, and the soul of soulless conditions. It is the opium of the people.

◆ Karl Marx, Introduction to "Contribution to the Critique of Hegel's Philosophy," 1844, *The Marx-Engels Reader*

Saturday, February 19, 2022

Moesha Jefferson strode into the Healing Chamber, followed by two middle-aged matrons clad in shapeless, light brown dresses that hung from their shoulders to the floor. As the Commander of The Army of God, she was formally dressed in a long, dark blue cassock; its hem touched her sandals. The top two buttons of the cassock were unfastened, revealing her shoulder holster and handgun.

She stepped onto the bluestone floor and admired the tall cedar walls of the Healing Chamber. Moonlight filtered through the high stained-glass windows, glorifying Jesus nailed to the cross. The Church's finest artisans had hand-carved the raised paneling on each wall.

Few people had ever seen this room, but she had been blessed many times. The First Minister had chosen her to ease his burden eight years earlier, when she had been a child of fourteen. That first time had been brutal, but she had learned to return his passion.

Precisely following the ritual, she stepped to the center of the room in front of the Cleansing Pool. The matrons removed her cassock and holster and hung them in a narrow closet built into a wall. She stepped out of her sandals and stood naked in God's watchful presence, a silver amulet dangling between her full breasts. She was proud of her tall, athletic body, marked by scars and bruises from her service to the Church.

A matron handed her the silver chalice, filled with the bitter red wine consecrated by the First Minister as the blood of Jesus Christ. The First Minister required that she accept the Lord's cleansing blood before he would accept her. Moesha lifted it to the level of her eyes and recited, "The Lord is my master, the Church my passion." She drained the cup. Warmth traveled down her throat into her chest, burning her stomach, cleansing her.

She was foremost among the chosen because the First Minister had seen in her a perfect mixture of humanity. Her known heritage included African, Asian and Caucasian, but she believed all races and ethnic groups lived within her. God had blessed her to reflect all humanity, Jordan had said. He had trained her body into a finely honed instrument, capable of dispensing both pleasure and pain. The crisp air stimulated her flesh, lifting her mind to greater awareness. She would serve no man except the First Minister.

Her thoughts drifted back to childhood. She had always been exceptional, excelling in both academic and athletic pursuits. A natural leader, if prone to violence, she had been expelled from elementary school after brutally beating a classmate. Defying the best efforts of her parents, her violent behavior had grown worse year after year.

In desperation, her parents had turned her over to the Church, where Adam Jordan recognized her gifts and took a special interest in her development. She recalled many beatings—he had disciplined her often, slowly chasing the Devil from her soul. At first, she had resisted, but gradually she accepted his discipline. Frequently selected to preach to outsiders, she became a devoted student of the Church.

It was at that time, she recalled proudly, that he made her one of the Honored Sisters, a small cluster of budding women selected to share his bed. Although all the Honored Sisters were beautiful, she quickly became his favorite.

Jordan consigned her at age fifteen to the newly formed Army of God, and she earned respect for her intelligence and bravery. She loved the military—the discipline, the danger, the purity of the violence. She quickly rose through leadership positions. At age nineteen, Jordan made her Commander. She had never failed him.

Eight feet in diameter, the Cleansing Pool bubbled with purified water. After a moment of prayer, she walked down the steps into the pool. The water was five feet deep, cold and invigorating. She closed her eyes for a moment, enjoying the tingling of currents that swirled across sensitive flesh. She washed with a rough bar of soap until every inch of her skin flushed with color. Breathing deeply, she walked up the steps and out of the pool, where the matrons waited.

They dried her with warm towels and rubbed an orchard-scented lotion into her skin. Standing perfectly still, closing her eyes and clearing her mind, Moesha enjoyed the intimate touch of practiced hands. Warmth soaked into her skin, generating ripples of pleasure. Her mind and body were pure, and she felt the presence of the Lord. She barely noticed when the matrons left.

As the intensity of her faith washed over her, she dropped to her knees, pressed her hands together and prayed.

"I am a Natural Human.

I condemn artificial intelligence and non-human beings.

These are abominations in the sight of God.

That will be flushed to the bowels of the Earth.

Glory be to the Lord and His Creations."

The pool swirled and bubbled in intricate patterns, creating a solitary yet reassuring hum. She waited contentedly, at peace with her life and her God. Heavenly clouds drifted into her mind, lifting her to a higher level of consciousness. She became aware of the rhythms of her body, every cell primed for pleasure, anticipating the hot majesty of the Lord.

Minutes passed.

She waited for her master.

The whisper of a door opening reached her heightened awareness. Excitement merged with devotion as his footsteps approached. A familiar, musky smell kindled her anticipation. With difficulty, she kept her eyes closed, and his image came into focus in her mind. Moesha could feel his presence behind her; she readied herself.

His breathing was strong and consistent, as always. The First

Minister stood rigidly still; nothing identified his mood. He could be violent or gentle as a baby. Either way, she would welcome him. He was the Savior.

A raspy voice came to her almost as a whisper. "Moesha, my beautiful, violent flower. It's so good to see you."

"Thank you, First Minister. I am honored to be with you."

"I see you're properly prepared; you bathed thoroughly, I assume."

"Yes, First Minister."

He sniffed her neck. "Excellent."

He chuckled then said, "And you've consumed the Lord's blood?"

"Yes, First Minister."

His hand brushed her shoulder and she shivered.

"Delightful," he said.

The tip of his index finger traveled down her breast, stoking her desire. She allowed a moan to escape her lips. She knew he liked that.

"What shall we do with the Technos?"

Within her, the fire blazed. "Kill them all."

"My kind of girl."

She heard Jordan drop to his knees behind her. He placed his hands on her bare shoulders. Feeling his breath on her neck, she shivered with rapture.

"Your shoulder is bruised," he said.

"It's nothing," she murmured.

She felt the feathery touch of his lips on her shoulder, then his voice brushed her ear. "If anything ever happened to you …"

"Nothing will harm me. God has brought us together for a divine purpose. He won't forsake us."

"The certainty of youth." Jordan sighed. "But while we're here, we must serve him well. He sent you to me." Jordan's lips brushed her neck, a quiver of electricity. "The Lord looked into me and saw my need."

His voice troubled her. Moesha leaned back against his powerful chest, one hand caressing his bare thigh.

"Let us pray," she said.

Voices blending, they recited the Prayer for the Lord's Creations. Jordan's bare chest pressed hard against her back. She loved the feel of his lean, muscular body. When the prayer was completed, he lifted the amulet from her neck and dropped it near the Cleansing Pool.

He is the only one I have ever allowed. And so it will be until the Lord calls me.

A moan escaped her lips when his rough hands grasped her breasts and pulled her hard against him. Jordan bit her neck painfully, intensifying her arousal. Then he pushed her face down against the stone floor, his lips everywhere. She rolled over, grabbed his hair and jerked his mouth down to hers. He climbed on her, his weight familiar and exciting. She took his power and his need, and silently thanked God she could serve.

CHAPTER 13

Technos and clerics have much in common. Both take a world that can't be fully understood and try to explain its fundamental properties.

Clerics postulate beliefs that can never be proven; they demand you accept these postulates as your Faith, which will guide your actions and thoughts. It's a top-down way of thinking; start with the big picture and derive rules for living. Fundamental knowledge is static. Even the derived rules rarely change.

Technos work from the bottom up. They build a baseline of observations and formulate theories to explain these phenomena. Nothing is sacred; with new observations, theories are discarded or modified to fit the facts. Technos and clerics; how could they not be in conflict?
◆ Steve Bonini's Diary, 2016

Tuesday, February 22, 2022

David pulled his Mercedes into a parking space on the third level of a seven-level garage. The area was less than half-filled with cars, most of them aging. It was his first trip to San Francisco in almost ten years, and he was surprised by how few cars were on the streets. His childhood memories were of a bustling city that no longer existed.

He stepped out of the car and looked for an elevator. He spotted one at the upper corner of the ramp, but a sign tacked to the door said it was out of order. He turned and walked down the incline. He crouched between two parked cars when a pair of headlights swung around the corner. The car passed and turned up the ramp to the next level. He told himself to relax, as the engine faded into the distance.

The headaches were getting worse. Aspirjel helped, but his head ached all the time. He was more certain that a powerful new AI was growing somewhere on the net. He could feel it.

As he hurried down a dark stairway, his steps resonated across the levels and announced his presence to the shadows. The stairway smelled of human excrement, and he watched his step. Most of the overhead lights had burned out, but a weak afternoon sun passed through barred windows at each level and provided adequate light. At last, he reached ground level, pushed open a creaky door and stepped onto the sidewalk.

A bitter wind gusted in his face, blowing paper and trash. Union Square, once known for its luxurious hotels and restaurants, now presented seedy bars and check-cashing storefronts. Pedestrians, bundled up in thick coats, kept their eyes focused on the sidewalk as they walked.

The famous hills were still there, but the roads were cracked and uneven. Maintenance had ended years ago.

Although traveling only a couple of blocks, he discovered the city had a detached, unfriendly mood. Feeling cold and out of place, he pulled up the collar of his jacket and hurried along.

He had pleasant memories of Paul Martino, his father's best

friend, who had visited their home several times. Martino had started *TechAdvantage* in San Francisco more than twenty-five years ago, and built it into one of the best websites on the net. Martino had been a bright, cheerful man, well liked and influential. Implicated in the so-called conspiracy, he had died during the PeaceMaker attack. David no longer trusted the official version; Martino might have been a victim of the real criminals, framed along with his father.

He walked up a steep hill, each stride long and determined. A big man in a ragged coat came over the top, glancing suspiciously as he passed. Graffiti covered everything, but it seemed indifferent, accustomed to being ignored.

Joe Cohen, the first person hired by Martino, had been instrumental in building *TechAdvantage*. According to David's research, Martino had made him a junior partner a couple of years later, and Cohen had gained control of the business after Martino died. David recalled he had seen Cohen at his father's funeral, one of the few who attended.

Maybe I'll learn something from Cohen.

David hurried the two blocks to his destination, relieved to enter the lobby of an old, but surprisingly well-kept building. The temperature inside the building was warmer, but still cold; many office buildings, to conserve energy, set the thermostat below sixty.

The elevator was ancient, with buttons on the wall to call for service. He pushed one and a motor groaned. When the elevator car arrived, he stepped in and said, "Seventeenth floor." The door closed, but the elevator didn't move.

Could you be any more stupid?

He pushed the button marked seventeen.

Alone in the large car, David watched each floor number light up as the elevator lumbered upwards. When the light indicating floor seventeen flared, the motor ground to a stop and the door opened. He walked down a long hall until he found a door marked *TechAdvantage.*

He pushed on the door, but it didn't budge. A female voice came from a speaker set into the wall, "May I help you?"

"I have an appointment to see Joseph Cohen." He looked into the camera above the door. "David Brown."

When the door buzzed, he pushed it open and stepped into a small, dimly lit reception area. The receptionist, a wholesome brunette, was friendly and professional in her greeting.

"Mr. Cohen is expecting you." She pointed down the hall. "His office is the last one on the left."

All the lights suddenly blinked out. Natural sunlight provided adequate light in the reception area, but shadows dominated the interior halls. The building was quiet for a moment as the machines stopped. Voices came from the offices. Nobody seemed concerned.

"Don't let the power shutdown bother you," she said. "It's no big deal. Happens just about every day, usually for just ten to fifteen minutes. They always find power someplace else on the grid and get it here." She winked at him and chirped, "I'm Maryanne, the hard-working, loyal girl Friday. Let me know if you need anything."

He forced a weak smile. "Thank you."

She held his eyes for a moment and with a friendly nod went back to work.

As he walked toward Cohen's office, the power came on, bathing the hallway in light. He stopped at Cohen's doorway and listened to him dictating a letter to his computer. Cohen's lips curved into a friendly smile when he spotted David and he waved him in.

Cohen's desk was well-polished old pine, maybe an antique. David glanced around as Cohen finished dictating. Several old pictures stood in a corner of the desk. One caught his eye; a young Cohen with his arm draped over the shoulder of a balding, familiar-looking man.

"Paul Martino," Cohen said, looking sadly at the picture. "That was our first year in business, almost twenty-six years ago."

David nodded. "I vaguely remember him."

Cohen came around the desk. "It's a pleasure to meet you, David."

Cohen was a wiry man in his late forties. With thick salt-and-pepper hair clipped down to short bristles, a style from another era, he seemed dated.

They shook hands. "Thanks for seeing me, Mr. Cohen."

"Everybody calls me Joe." Cohen led him over to the couch. "You probably don't remember, but I met you about twelve, thirteen years ago. Your father had you for the weekend, and he stopped here briefly to see Paul."

When David shook his head, Cohen shrugged. "Of course you were just a little kid at the time."

"Dad would fly to San Francisco about once a month to see me," David said. "He always had something planned: a movie, sailing on the bay, playing on the beach. It was always fun."

"The city was great back then." Cohen sighed. "It was a different time."

"I barely got to know my father with the divorce and then his death. That's why I'm here today. I'd like to learn more about him and his life. Paul Martino was his best friend, but he's dead, too, so I was hoping you could help me."

"I'm not sure how much I can tell you," Cohen said. "They were best friends, and I would occasionally go out with them for a drink or dinner. Of course, your father was on the wagon," he said, an apologetic smile briefly playing across his lips. "I knew Paul very well, both as a boss and friend, but Ray was more like an acquaintance."

David began to wonder about this visit. "Well, tell me about Paul, then."

Cohen sadly shook his head. "What a shame. I owe Paul a great deal. He was my friend and mentor. He taught me so much. Even though he has been gone so many years, I still think about him." Cohen's concentration drifted off for a moment. "A really good man. I don't know where to start. Do you have specific questions?"

"A few. Did you notice a change in Paul during the weeks before the virus attack?"

Cohen stared at the photo on his desk. "Yeah, I did, now that you mention it. Kinda strange, actually. Jumpy. He worked incredibly hard, yet produced nothing for the magazine." Cohen shifted in his seat.

"What was he working on?"

"As I recall, he was interviewing people for a feature story about network security," Cohen said. "At the time, attacks on all types of networks were increasing, and business people were getting concerned. You know, denial of service attacks, Trojan Horses, worms, and different types of viruses. He was trying to learn what the industry was doing, what worked and what didn't. Paul talked primarily to network administrators, the people on the front lines."

"Did he leave notes?"

Cohen laughed. "Tons. He was very thorough. Never wrote the article, though."

"I know it's a lot to ask, but would it be possible to get copies? Notes for the article as well as anything else he was doing. I'd like to go through everything in his personal computer plus any other files stored on the net, to see what I can learn about my father."

Cohen folded his arms across his chest and looked at David. "I don't know. There's a great deal of confidential information in those files, things Paul promised to keep private."

"Everything I read I'll treat as confidential," David said. Although Cohen tried to appear relaxed, David detected a hardening in his attitude. "It would mean a lot to me."

"Well, all that stuff *is* ten years old. The technology has changed since then, of course, although many of the same people are still there." He paused, seeming to size things up. "Okay, David, as long as you keep everything to yourself, I don't see how it could hurt." Cohen turned to his computer and said, "Jenny, please gather all of Paul Martino's files and dump a copy onto this gentleman's web account. David, what's your ID?"

"271-48-0973-MK."

"Got that, Jenny?"

A moment passed, and then Jenny replied, "All the known records of Paul Martino have been copied to web account 271-48-0973-MK, owned by David Brown. Will there be anything else, Joe?"

"Pretty quick for an old model, huh?" Cohen chuckled. "Thank you, Jenny."

"I appreciate this," David said.

Cohen leaned forward and studied David intently. Abruptly, he stood up, walked to his doorway, and peered out. After looking in both directions, he closed the door and faced David.

Cohen's expression had turned serious. In a whisper, he said,

"You don't believe Paul and your father were part of the PeaceMaker conspiracy, do you?"

David was surprised, but tried to keep it out of his face. "There's a mountain of evidence my father led the conspiracy. I accepted his guilt years ago, but he's still my father and I'd like to learn more about him."

"Be very careful," Cohen said, worry creasing his brow. "You're a bright young man with a long life ahead of you. Forces are at work in this society, powerful forces. I've stayed out of the line of fire all these years." He shook his head. "Don't get caught in it. You don't have to be a genius to see the country's sliding into disaster. PeaceMaker was just the start. Look outside at what's going on: depression, decay, crime, government repression, anti-technology terrorists. It's out of control and getting worse."

Fear etched Cohen's face. "Paul and Ray were good men. I *know* they would never create a monster like PeaceMaker. They got caught in the whirlwind."

Cohen leaned back against the door. His eyes remained intense. "Don't get caught, David. I probably shouldn't have given you Paul's files, but you have the right to know. You'd be wise to destroy them. It's your call, but my advice is to forget all about this day. Have your escape route set up. Things are going to get very bad. That's my advice for you."

"You think some powerful organization created PeaceMaker?" David asked. "That it's still at work?"

Cohen studied him. The air seemed charged.

"It's called the Domain, and I pray to God you never come to their attention."

Cohen abruptly strode around the desk, grabbed David's arm,

and walked him out the door and down the hall past Maryanne. It was clear the interview was over. Cohen was all smiles, talking about football all the way to the elevators.

"It's been a pleasure seeing you after all these years," Cohen said, pushing the button to call the elevator. Staring at David, he said, "I hope our discussion was helpful." They shook hands. "Be sure to give your mother my best."

David barely had time to thank him before Cohen turned and walked back to his office.

Once Cohen was back in his office, Maryanne looked up and checked the empty hall.

What a discovery!

"Code red," she whispered into her computer.

A moment later, a female voice responded, "Speak."

"I just recorded a conversation between David Brown and Joe Cohen and sent it to your system. You can't imagine what I learned. Both of them believe Martino and Ray Brown had nothing to do with PeaceMaker. They believe some other force created the virus, a clandestine organization called the Domain. Cohen is too scared to do anything, but it appears Brown will attempt to track down the Technos who created the virus."

"Is this organization responsible for the black market technology?" the woman asked, for once a trace of excitement in her voice. "The androids and the other abominations Vitullo sells?"

"That's what Cohen implied," Maryanne said. "And David Brown is hunting them, thinking this organization framed his father."

"We will be there when he finds this Domain," the female voice said, and then broke the connection.

The receptionist again glanced down the hallway. When she was sure nobody was watching, Maryanne stroked the amulet hidden under her blouse and bowed her head in silent prayer.

David drove north and, just after sunset, checked in at the Ocean Breeze, a beat-up single level motel in Stinson Beach. He had decided to analyze Martino's files immediately. Once in his rented room, David put on his "glasses" and set up a link to the Internet.

Martino's files were comprehensive and included a variety of interviews that covered his many years running *TechAdvantage*. A meticulous note taker, Martino had recorded all his conversations and summarized the key points. He had conducted a thorough review of network security issues, interviewing more than thirty network administrators, but the notes contained nothing suspicious.

I'll bet this study was a cover as he tried to learn more about PeaceMaker and its developers. Dad had the technical expertise, but Martino had the contacts.

Next, he searched Martino's contact database. Martino appeared to know just about everyone worth knowing within the information technology industry at the time. He kept detailed notes about the background and current responsibilities of each individual. David quickly realized Martino hadn't interviewed several of these experienced network administrators for the article he'd been researching. That seemed strange for such a thorough man.

Searching the database with Donna, the operating system that controlled his glasses, David identified eleven senior-level network administrators Martino hadn't interviewed. These appeared to be first-rate people. Not contacting them made no sense.

Maybe he didn't have time to interview them, or maybe he did it secretly.

David asked Donna to examine each administrator's data communications billing records to determine if Martino had contacted them. Initially, Internet security software prevented access, but David hacked his way through it. He had a knack for locating poorly secured code segments and creating unintended entryways. Not one of these network administrators had contacted Martino during the weeks before the PeaceMaker attack.

Set back for a moment, he decided to search another way. *What if Martino had another Internet access number, one he had kept secret?* Working again with Donna, David discovered an access number that had contacted eight of the eleven network administrators. This information had been buried by an expert—probably his father, since Martino didn't have the skill—under half a dozen levels of security, but David persevered and finally broke through. His father's code was complex but familiar. It was exactly what he would have done in his father's situation. He felt as if he were walking through a house for the first time, but knew the size of each room, the location of each door.

Might be Martino's secret access number, but it would be difficult to prove.

Next, David asked Donna to search the Internet database for every reference to the access number, but came up blank. Figuring the number might have been deleted years earlier because it was inactive, David hacked back into the history files and found setup data for the access number. Someone calling himself Victor Franken had set it up January 11, 2012, just a couple weeks before the PeaceMaker attack.

This Victor Franken made a bunch of calls before the PeaceMaker attack, but no activity afterwards. It had to be Martino's secret access number. He must have figured someone was tapping into his public access number, so he secretly contacted these eight network administrators using the Victor Franken ID.

David could visualize Martino, scared shitless, sneaking in these secret calls even though his life was in danger.

A brave man. Must have been murdered about the time of the PeaceMaker attack. But what had Martino learned from these administrators?

David's head began to ache, a dull pain that he knew would get worse if he kept working. He removed the glasses, closed his eyes and rubbed his forehead. The center of the pain was just above his right eye, and it hurt when he touched it. He pulled out a tube of Aspirjel from his luggage and rubbed it into his forehead. After resting on the bed for a couple of minutes, the pain receded. Gingerly slipping the glasses on again, he resumed working.

To learn everything he could about the eight network administrators, he asked Donna to pull their Social Security files for background information.

The information his glasses displayed hit like a kick in the gut:

148-87-7112: Martin P. Schwartz, DOD February 7, 2012, Acute myocardial infarction
149-22-4561: Jessica M. Palermo, DOD March 11, 2012, Automobile accident
151-34-0888: Theodore L. Mizinsky, DOD February 4, 2012, Automobile accident
151-97-2373: Jorge S. Martinez, DOD April 18,

2012, Acute myocardial infarction

155-38-0839: Kevin T. Pitelka, DOD March 22,

2012, Automobile accident

158-98-6642: Barbara A. D'Alise, DOD February

18, 2012, Automobile accident

160-42-1951: Elizabeth L. Shaw. DOD April 8,

2012, Acute myocardial infarction

160-76-1539: James T. O'Connor, DOD March

29, 2012, Automobile accident

The pattern was chillingly clear; they had all died shortly after the virus attack.

Either there had been a sudden outbreak of heart attacks and automobile accidents among the top-level network administrator population, or somebody had cleaned up loose ends.

This was why Cohen had asked him to back off; these people played for keeps. His visit might have placed Cohen's life in danger, too, but there was nothing he could do now.

He delved again into the Internet usage database and discovered Martino's final secret call on January 23, 2012 to Ted Mizinsky, a senior network administrator at Horizon Operating Systems in West Orange, New Jersey. Mizinsky was the first of the eight network administrators to die.

Mizinsky is the key to the puzzle.

The ache above his eye came back, worse than before, but he continued. He discovered Mizinsky's widow, Deborah, still lived in their home in West Orange.

I have to see her.

David wanted to go to bed before the headache grew worse,

but he had a nagging feeling he had missed something. Something was terribly wrong. Pulling the database access records again, he reviewed all Martino's calls around the time Martino had investigated PeaceMaker. Nothing there he had not already seen.

There's something right under my nose, and I can't find it.

The headache pounded. He grabbed the tube of Aspirjel again. His hand shook as he rubbed in the medication.

Even though he was in pain, the research became effortless. His glasses worked better than ever before, almost anticipating his commands, pulsing with unusual power. His headache seemed connected in some way to this power. When he removed the glasses and laid them on the desk, the headache receded.

David put his hands behind his head and leaned back. What had he missed? The pale ceiling blurred.

Something was missing from Martino's call records. A churning stomach joined the pain of his headache. Once more, he put on the glasses and went through the records, confirming what was missing. Another desperate search, but he couldn't find evidence of a call that should have been there.

Kathy's. There was no record Kathy had ever called Martino.

Kathy said she called Martino when she tried to track down my father. An honest mistake? It must be.

Recalling that Kathy said she also called Ray's ex-wife, David pulled up the call records for his mother. He cursed. Kathy hadn't called there, either.

Ray Brown, the most important technical person at VPS, disappears and the Human Resources person, who claims Dad was like a brother to her, doesn't try to track him down? Doesn't call his best friend or his ex-wife? He slammed the palm of his hand against the wall. *Because she knew he had been killed, that's why.*

Desperately, he thought through the sequence of events, looking for a flaw. He didn't want to believe she was an enemy, but the facts kept pushing through.

Never trust anyone.

He had fallen in love with her, but she turned out to be another backstabber.

Kathy had planned the whole thing … inviting him to talk about his father, gaining his trust, seducing him and then finding out what he knew. And he fell for the whole thing like a lovesick puppy. David Brown, the computer whiz kid. Must have been a big laugh for her.

His head throbbed with pain, but he couldn't stop now. Kathy must have told his enemies about his search. These killers, whoever they were, knew he was trying to prove his father's innocence.

Kathy, damn you.

Pain erupted in a swirl of colors. Then he saw—or sensed—something out there, coming across the net, something he had fought before.

He buried his head in his arms and fought to remain conscious. It was happening again! The pain crested, then the colors faded, leaving him in a dark, lonely emptiness. He wasn't in the motel room any longer … and he wasn't alone. He strained to see through the darkness … then spotted it … a dark form in the distance. It had the shape of a child, but it wasn't flesh and blood. The creature's face was in the shadows, and when it crossed into a murky light, recognition hit him.

And terror.

Alice, the software predator from his childhood. He tried to run, but his legs wouldn't move. Although it had assumed the image of a young girl, Alice was a killer, his worst nightmare.

But how could it be here? Alice had been destroyed.

All his disappointment, all his pain coalesced into a shimmering ball of fear, ready to explode. His ears roared, filling his mind with a torrent of daggers and piercing pain. Alice opened its arms to him, beckoning, feeding on his fear.

David fought back, desperate to retain his identity, but drawn forward, toward this creature—toward Alice. This was no dream; David was wide awake. He struggled to hold his ground, but Alice pulled him closer, touched him, then flowed through his skin. Pain throbbed through his being, his fear peaked, and he screamed into the void.

Suddenly he was back, alone in the dark motel room.

Alive.

A glimmer of light from the pale glow of the moon came through a dirty window. The roar in his ears faded to a hum. He stood up and tried to find the door, but his legs were unsteady. He stumbled and fell.

Lightheaded and still on the edge, he felt Alice trying to draw him back into its nightmare world. He fought with all his strength, but the creature's power sucked him down. The hum in his ears swelled again to a painful roar as Alice probed and infected his mind.

David ripped off the glasses and hurled them against the wall. The frames flew apart and tumbled to the floor. The creature's death grip slackened and disappeared. Throbbing pain erupted, worse than before, and he crawled back to the bed and succumbed to the darkness.

CHAPTER 14

I was lucky enough to see with my own eyes the recent stock market crash, where they lost several million dollars, a rabble of dead money that went sliding off into the sea. Never as then, amid suicides, hysteria, and groups of fainting people, have I felt the sensation of real death, death without hope, death that is nothing but rottenness, for the spectacle was terrifying but devoid of greatness … I felt something like a divine urge to bombard that whole canyon of shadow, where ambulances collected suicides whose hands were full of rings.

◆ "A Poet in New York," lecture, Federico García Lorca, March 1932, Madrid

Wednesday, February 23, 2022

Bob Marichal stood off-camera and stared at Daphne Hayden as he waited for the interview to begin. Although the market had endured a terrible morning, Daphne's presence lifted his spirits. *She is really something.* Even at sixty-three, he could still appreciate a body like that.

A brassy female voice disturbed his enjoyment. "You stare any harder and you're gonna need a change of underwear."

Standing next to him was Joan Langdon, peering for the millionth time into her hand mirror, checking her makeup. He wondered if the mirror had cracked. Bob found it difficult to believe Daphne and Joan belonged to the same species, let alone the same gender. Joan's extra makeup drew attention to a face only a mother could love. *A mother warthog.* To top it off, Joan had a pain-in-the-ass personality. Just his luck to be paired with *her* today.

"When we get on camera," Joan said, "try to look at Daphne's face when she asks a question. I don't believe her boobs can speak."

"Listen, you fat cow—"

"Shut up, she's about to start the show."

"Good morning, this is Daphne Hayden reporting from the New York Stock Market in Boonton, New Jersey. Beginning at about six this morning, a vast wave of sell orders hit this and all other markets around the world. In about ninety minutes of frenzied selling, the market lost almost 30% of its value. The drop has hit just about every major industry."

As the holocamera focused on a huge electronic board, Daphne continued, "Behind me, you can see the Market Watch Board, which tracks every major stock market in the world." She glanced at the board. "At this moment, the Dow is 11,228, the lowest it has been in thirteen years. It started the day at 16,345, so the drop is now about 31%."

As Daphne pointed out several other global stock indices also losing value, Joan whispered to Bob, "Let's move our butts out there."

"You'll need a derrick."

Joan gave him the finger, walked onto the set and sat at a small conference table. Bob had to sit next to her, since the guest chairs were side by side at the table. His displeasure with the seating arrangements was forgotten when Daphne brushed past and sat next to him. Her breasts defied gravity, and he discreetly glanced down the front of her blouse. A hard kick in the ankle made him yelp, and he gave Joan a nasty look.

"Two top market analysts are here to help us understand the plunge in stock prices," Daphne said.

Wearing a dignified smile, Bob returned his attention to the gorgeous newswoman.

"Please welcome Joan Langdon of Petrie Billings and Robert Marichal of Danson, Costello and Stern."

Daphne glanced at Joan before addressing the network audience. "Joan, let me turn to you first. Do you have any idea what caused the market to crash?"

Appearing confident and poised, Joan replied, "We believe the sell-off began with a heavy dose of profit taking. Once that started, the automated sell protocols kicked in and started the avalanche. As you know, Daphne, emotion drives the market more than logic. For the moment, sellers outnumber buyers by a wide margin, so I expect this selling to continue for a while."

Master of the obvious. Sellers outnumber buyers ... give me strength.

"What should the average investor do right now?" Daphne asked.

"I'm telling my clients not to panic," Joan replied. "Sell your weaker stocks, but hold on to solid, well-established companies. This is a good time to pick up a bargain or two, if you can stand the heat. The market might go down a little further, but it will bounce back."

Noticing the Dow plunge even faster, Bob stared at the electronic board. *This is really bad.* He tried to concentrate on Daphne, but the Dow was dropping like the altimeter of a plane about to crash.

"Thank you, Joan." Turning toward him, Daphne asked, "Bob, what's your take on this? What caused the market to nosedive?"

He stared over his shoulder at the Market Watch Board. When Daphne repeated the question, he said, "The Dow just dropped below 11,000! I don't understand why it turned down so abruptly." He couldn't tear his eyes from the huge electronic board, like a traveler gaping at a highway accident. "I've been in the market almost thirty years, and I've never seen anything like this. There must be millions of sell transactions coming across the net." Then he blurted out, "My God, it's 10,700." He turned back to Daphne. "There's no reason for so many sales. Nothing special happened recently. Of course, we *have* been in a bear market for several years," he added, "so maybe this shouldn't have been such a surprise. Remember, the Dow was over 23,000 eight years ago and it has been drifting down since then."

"So what's your advice to investors?"

Before he could respond, the Market Watch Board sputtered and turned dark. Then the overhead lights failed. In the pitch black, a woman on the trading floor let out a scream.

What the hell is going on?

Bob heard people stumbling away, and he would have done the same, but in the dark, he wasn't sure which way to flee.

The emergency power came on, providing dim light across the trading floor. Everyone rushed to get out of the building. He had seen fear take over the trading floor before, but nothing like this. Joan pumped her thick legs toward a now-crowded exit, and Daphne shouted at someone off to the left. Alone on the platform, Bob noticed the holocamera was still on, so he stepped in front of it and stared into the gleaming eye. He had only one word for the audience.

"Sell."

UNHOLY DOMAIN ■ **169**

CHAPTER 15

It was a grand adventure, a race across time, distance and morality. David searched for his father, his enemies planned his death, and the fate of the species remained in question.

◆ *Electronic Messiah*, W. Arthur Salem, copyright 2058, Professor, History of Electrical Engineering, New Jersey Institute of Technology

Thursday, February 24, 2022

David left Reagan National Airport in his rented car and crossed the Rochambeau Memorial Bridge over the Potomac into Washington, DC. Another dismal afternoon, with a brisk wind biting into the car.

The airlines had reduced their flight schedules again, so getting a reservation from Seattle to the east coast had been a pain in the ass. He had wanted to fly into Newark or one of the New York airports, but those flights had been booked weeks ago. After checking Philly and Baltimore, he reluctantly bought a seat to Reagan National. The drive to New Jersey would take four or five hours, so he wouldn't pull into the hotel until late at night.

Tomorrow he had an appointment with Deborah Mizinsky, the widow of the last man known to speak with Paul Martino. When he contacted her yesterday, she agreed to meet with him. Frankly, he'd been surprised how willing she was to see him. Kathy's treachery had left him suspicious.

Unable to get Kathy out of his mind, he replayed how fast he'd fallen for her. What an idiot! She had tossed him to the wolves. Just like that. Even now, he couldn't believe it. Had she faked those feelings?

He ran into a massive traffic jam in DC, and for the next hour, inhaled exhaust fumes in bumper-to-bumper traffic. He inched past the Jefferson Memorial, shimmering in the sunset, and then the Washington Monument.

In addition to the crushing traffic of tourists and government workers, crowds of angry demonstrators milled around Constitution Avenue and the adjoining streets, pushing at the barricades and shouting at the police. One agitated woman taunted the police. She shook her sign so forcefully David couldn't read it. A burly police officer grabbed her by the collar and dragged her behind police lines. The crowd roared and pushed against the barricades, brandishing their signs like fists.

What the hell is going on?

Winter blew in when he rolled down his window to listen. Rumbling voices carried over the wind, shouting about giving the people back their money.

David guessed they were protesting the stock market crash. A tsunami of sell orders had swamped the market, although the origin of this selling was unknown. Almost 90% of the value of the global stock markets had been wiped out in one day.

Those poor people. All their savings ... their security ... a lifetime of work blown away.

Listening to the tone of the demonstrators' voices, he felt their anger, but even more, their desperation.

He understood their feelings. His investments had disappeared, too. A stench clung to the whole thing, as if a disease had eaten the flesh off the bones of the nation, leaving the economy on life support. The cash in his money fund would have to sustain him for the next few months.

The government should have done something to prevent this disaster. Better software, more technicians, something. Even if they had just shut down the market when the first wave of sell orders hit, the worst could have been avoided. Between their anti-technology laws and gross incompetence, the Feds were screwing up everything.

A noise like the buzzing of angry bees jarred him out of his thoughts. It wasn't the demonstrators; they milled about and taunted the police. David tried to locate the source of the noise, but the buzz was everywhere.

To his right, a couple of blocks away, flames broke through the roof of an eight-story, red brick apartment building. The fire raced across the roof and then burst out the top floor windows. Frightened spectators backed away from the building.

A group of young thugs ran out of the building's entrance and stopped to look up at the flames. They danced wildly, slapped hands, laughed and shouted. Then they ran down the street.

David's stomach wrenched as a young black girl opened a window just below the top floor. She couldn't have been more than twelve, with a wide face and braided hair. Screaming for help, she shielded her face as flames licked around her. She climbed out the window, hung on the edge, and then let go, arms flailing wildly as she tumbled down. He turned away. A long sigh came from the crowd. When he looked again, people had gathered around her broken body.

Another fire burst from an old four-story hotel across the street from the blazing apartment building. Smoke poured out the windows, and then the flames spread to an adjoining restaurant. People ran in all directions. A handful of police officers shouted instructions, but frightened runners ignored them.

David glanced nervously at the stalled traffic ahead. The street noise was overwhelming. The hiss of towering flames mixed with the ear-piercing blare of automobile horns and the cries of terrified pedestrians. Rolling up the window didn't help much.

Staring at the approaching flames, David didn't notice the movement of the cars in front of him. Horn blaring, the driver behind rammed him, smashing his bumper.

Son of a bitch!

He stepped on the gas, but the driver in front had moved only a couple of car lengths, forcing him to jam on the brakes. To his left, flames swept into the sky as additional buildings caught fire. Frenzied drivers blared their horns, but the cars were locked in place.

Police cars swerved around the packed cars, but slowed to avoid the terrified pedestrians who clogged the streets. Heat seared his face, as building after building along the highway burst into flames. He considered abandoning the car.

A pickup truck screeched past on the right shoulder, rattling his car. After watching several other cars roar past, he decided to follow. Swerving onto the shoulder, he forced an oncoming van to squeal to a stop. Cars pulled in front of him, but at least he was moving. Smoke hung low over the road.

He hit the brakes, jammed up in traffic again. Chunks of smoking debris dropped near the edge of the highway. Where were the firefighters? Emergency rescue workers? Who was in charge?

A couple of drivers ahead of him abandoned their cars and fled. He rolled down the window and screamed at them to stay in their cars, but they kept running.

Military helicopters swooped above the jammed-up traffic, the hum of their engines overlaying the fire's roar. Through the rearview mirror, he watched the helicopters touch down near the White House. The President must be abandoning the city.

The left side of his face was raw from the heat. Buildings on both sides of the highway were aflame. As the flames advanced over the rooftops, burning embers dropped on the stalled traffic.

Why didn't the National Guard do something to restore order?

Half a block ahead, a lone police officer, assisted by three civilians, struggled to push a smashed minivan off the road. The rear end was crumpled, and the tires barely moved. David was about to jump out of his car to help when the men got the minivan moving and pushed it to the side of the highway.

Traffic began to move again, slowly at first, then faster. Swerving around abandoned cars, he cut in and out of lanes. The smoke gradually diminished, revealing a bleak, twisting highway. As he fled the capitol, the inferno receded in the rearview mirror.

He was safe.

The open road in Maryland provided a reassuring sense of normalcy. Route 95 was decently maintained, and he made good time. He passed a military convoy, but strangely, they were driving north away from the city.

The sun glowed through low clouds as he drove past Baltimore's

Inner Harbor. Rolling down the window a couple of inches, he let the cool night air clear his mind. He tried not to think of the horror in the capitol, but he had the terrible feeling the government was on the verge of collapse. Radio newscasts reported similar riots in New York, Los Angeles and other large cities. Rot had been collecting at all levels of government for a decade; the worsening financial crisis had exposed all its weaknesses.

David wondered if the stock market crash had wiped out his mother. Luckily she had given him some cash at the beginning of the semester. It should be enough until summer, and then he could get a full-time job.

David drove through Maryland and Delaware without incident, although the highway became worse, with ever-increasing potholes and loose chunks of blacktop. At sunset, he slowed down to spot the potholes in his headlights. As he approached the Delaware Bridge, the highway was worse than anything he had encountered on the West Coast.

A slender moon glowered through the cables of the towering bridge as he crossed the Delaware Bay. He glanced at the dashboard display. The rearview camera revealed several pairs of headlights. It wasn't anything to worry about, he convinced himself, just normal late evening traffic. His stomach rumbled, a reminder he had skipped lunch and dinner. With a couple of hours more driving tonight, a snack would help.

"Where's the next service area?" he asked the car's navigation system.

The Mercedes was quiet for a moment, and then the computer said, "Sorry, but I can't answer your question. The Turnpike service area system is not responding."

David figured the Internet must be down. No big surprise; these days the net was down most of the time, since there was no money to pay technicians.

He passed a sign announcing an upcoming service area and turned onto the next ramp. The parking lot was deserted, which gave him second thoughts, but he pulled into a spot near a concrete path leading up a rise to a junk food place. He looked around. Woods, thick and dark, surrounded the service area. Not a person in sight.

Well, it is almost midnight. Normal people don't travel this late.

He had read muggers sometimes hid in these service areas, but he figured he'd be safe walking up the well-lit path. Anyway, he was hungry.

He stepped out into a crisp, quiet night; the only sound came from the occasional car along the highway. He zipped his jacket all the way up and strode toward the main entrance. His legs felt stiff.

The cold night air seeped through his jacket. He hurried to reach the warmth of the building. When he reached it, the door refused to budge. Peering through the glass, he realized the place was deserted. He cursed then noticed a small, handwritten sign taped to the interior of the glass. Dated two years earlier, it said: Closed Until Further Notice, Restrooms Still Work Behind Building.

Why the hell didn't they have a sign at the bottom of the path?

He turned and walked back down the path, hunger gnawing at his insides. He'd walked halfway down when he noticed another car parked at the far end of the lot, although no one was in sight. *Maybe someone using the restroom?* Instinct warned him to stop, and then he felt a burning pain slice across his left shoulder. He grabbed the shoulder. Blood!

A movement in the brush at the foot of the path alerted him to a stocky man in a heavy topcoat. The man's laser pistol hissed and a deadly beam whizzed past David's head. Finally coming out of his stupor, he ducked off the path and sprinted into the bushes.

The people who killed Dad are after me.

Pine needles scratched his face and hands as he fled into the woods. What could he do except run? He'd never thought someone would actually try to kill *him*. Looking over his shoulder as he stumbled through the dark underbrush, he caught a glimpse of the man with a pistol running up the path. Dripping blood, David's left arm flopped uselessly.

His best chance was to hide in the thick woods in the rear. He ran behind the restaurant, out of the killer's line of sight. His shoulder throbbed, blood soaked through his jacket. The shooter crashed through the brush nearby. The bastard was gaining on him. Then the laser hissed again, burning into a tree trunk to his right.

Breathing hard, he ran through towering oaks and scrub pines. Sweat trickled into his eyes, and he brushed it away with his good hand, but a moment later, it blinded him again. Already lightheaded, he couldn't go much farther. He looked desperately for a weapon—a rock, a dead branch, something. Lumbering now, he spotted a rock about the size of a baseball. He dropped to his knees and clawed at it, digging it out of the frozen ground with his good hand. Not much of a weapon, but it would be his best chance if the killer found him. He hid behind a tree and controlled his breathing, trying to blend into the darkness.

The shooter crashed through the brush about thirty yards away and stopped. David strained to hear, but the forest remained quiet. Bile soured his mouth.

Where is that bastard?

He didn't dare move. One misstep and the shooter would pinpoint his location.

But he couldn't stay here. His sleeve was a bloody mess. If he didn't bleed to death, the shooter would find him. He looked up—the moon seemed to glare brighter than before.

The quiet magnified every sound: a branch squeaking in the breeze, the rustle of dried leaves, phantom footsteps from the parking lot.

He decided to double back to his car. Peering through the brush, he oriented himself to the lights along the concrete pathway. He crept around a bush and headed toward them, every step a potential disaster.

He stopped and listened.

Nothing.

The shooter could be anywhere.

Slowly, he approached the pathway lights. He'd creep ahead a few steps, stop and listen, then creep again. Finally, he reached a clump of oaks fifty yards from his car. The shooter's car was at the far end of the lot. He gathered himself for a dash to safety.

Then he heard it—the crackle of leaves underfoot. The shooter was getting close.

Peering around a broad oak tree, David squeezed his rock and set to defend himself. The odds weren't in his favor, a one-armed man with a rock against a professional killer. He spotted the shooter weaving through the moonlight about ten yards away.

This is it.

Wait for a clear shot.

Killing him with the rock would be difficult, but even if it stunned the bastard, he could make a run for his car. He waited until the shooter looked away then stood up and threw with all his strength.

The rock hit the killer's shoulder.

"What the fuck?"

He sagged against a tree. Too quickly, he regained his balance and aimed the laser pistol in David's direction, holding his fire, searching for his target.

Get out of here!

David turned to flee. A dark silhouette in the woods came toward him. He'd never thought of a second shooter! He didn't have a chance. The original shooter, a heavyset man, curled his thick lips in a triumphant smile as he aimed his laser pistol.

Then a gunshot barked out.

CHAPTER 16

Sometimes I think the Army of God is the lesser threat.

◆ Steve Bonini's Diary, 2021

Contrary to popular belief, Domain Security Chief James Murphy, not Dianne Morgan, made the initial contact with organized crime. Although she remained in the background, Dianne pulled the strings.

◆ *The Barbarian Queen: The True Story of Dianne Morgan,* David T. Siccone, copyright 2058, Department Head, Computer Science History, Carnegie Mellon University

Friday, February 25, 2022

David woke bleary-eyed and looked at the ceiling. He felt like three-week-old cat shit. Gradually his eyes focused, and he realized he was in a hospital—clean, but old and run-down. His left shoulder throbbed, but it was nothing compared to the raging migraine behind his brows. Even the muted light was painful.

Someone cleared her throat. A woman sat at his bedside. He blinked to bring the stranger into focus: late forties, bushy eyebrows and a wrinkled gray jacket. Needed to drop about twenty pounds. The movement of his head brought another surge of pain, so he leaned back into the pillow.

The woman slouched in the chair and smiled insincerely. "They told me you were beginning to come out of it."

Her voice grated on his headache. She was probably a hospital administrator of some sort, maybe after his insurance information. He wanted to pull the sheet over his head and go back to sleep. He didn't answer, but she didn't take the hint. The woman pulled her chair closer to the bed. He looked at her again. She could be attractive if she did something with herself. Maybe a face-over.

"You had a pretty rough night, huh, Dave?" The woman leaned back and crossed varicose-veined legs at the ankle. It wasn't a pretty sight.

"You were lucky, though, just a flesh wound in the shoulder."

"Who *are* you?"

She flashed her phony smile again. "Lieutenant McCain, Salem New Jersey Police at your service. You're in Salem General Hospital, about five miles northeast of where we found you and the late Sal Caputo on the Turnpike."

"Is that the man who tried to kill me?"

"That's what we are going to figure out," McCain said, pulling out a notepad from her jacket pocket. "First, though, why don't you tell me what happened."

David couldn't tell anyone about his mission, but the police might be able to shed some light on his assailant.

"I was driving from DC up the Turnpike to New York. I decided to stop for a snack at the first service area, but the restaurant was closed. That guy—you said his name was Sal Caputo—burned my shoulder with a laser and chased me into the woods. I guess he planned to steal my wallet and my car. I hit him with a rock, but it didn't do much damage. He would have killed me except someone from the woods shot him. She helped me back to my car, and I guess she drove me here. I don't remember much."

McCain scribbled a few notes and then waited for additional information. When she realized David had nothing else to add, she looked up from the notepad.

"So, let me see if I have it straight. You're just driving along on your way to New York, minding your own business. Someone decides to kill you, but a Good Samaritan saves your butt and kills the perp, but then leaves the hospital before the police arrive. That about it, Dave?" McCain glanced at a card in her hand. "You *are* David Brown, student at the University of Washington, as stated on this student ID?"

"How did you get my ID card?"

"You own a weapon, Dave?

"No, I don't, and I didn't shoot that guy, if that's what you're implying."

McCain smiled again. "Okay, we're making great progress. Now, I have just a couple of questions and we'll have this whole thing cleared up. You can answer a few questions, can't you, Dave?"

Pain in the ass! If she gives me that stupid smile again, I'll …

"Sure, Lieutenant McCain. I'll do my best."

"Describe the person who rescued you."

"She was tall, about five-nine, African-American, maybe early twenties. Slim, but not skinny. Dark hair, cut short." He vaguely remembered she had helped him to his car, supporting his weight with an arm around his waist. "Strong, like an athlete."

"How was she dressed?" McCain asked.

"I'm not sure … it was dark. Maybe a tan jacket with black pants."

"Did you get her name or notice anything that might identify her?"

He shook his head. "Nothing." David shifted his weight in bed, trying to reduce the ache in his shoulder.

"Did she take anything from you or Caputo?"

"Not that I know of."

McCain continued to question him about the incident, but David didn't provide much help. Actually, he knew little about either his rescuer or would-be killer. McCain probably knew more than he did.

McCain flipped the student ID card onto the bed. "Well, that's about it, then. Got enough for the 78G." She put the pad in her jacket pocket and stood up. "I'll let you know if by some miracle we discover something."

"That's it? What's a 78G?"

"Oh, it's just the form I have to fill out. You know, a summary of the crime and all that crap." She shrugged and turned to leave.

"Wait a minute!" David sat straight up and dangled his feet off the bed. His headache flared. "Someone tries to kill me and you're not going to do shit?"

McCain's eyes narrowed. "Listen, I could paper the walls of this room with the backlog of cases I have to investigate. You haven't told me squat. I'm not wasting my time when I don't know the full story."

"Lieutenant, I'm not a criminal. I've never done anything illegal in my life."

"Maybe not, but you haven't told me the full story. I don't poke around in the dark, you never know what you're going to bump into. Especially when a hit-man from the mob is involved."

"The mob?" David said. "That guy who tried to kill me was *mob?*"

McCain peered at him quizzically. "You really don't know, do you?"

"I have no idea what's going on."

McCain shook her head. "Well, kid, you have a big problem. Sal Caputo was a soldier in the Vitullo mob." She watched David warily for a moment. "Maria Vitullo is the big boss lady for organized crime in New Jersey, probably in the entire Northeast. If you're pushing technology, drugs, prostitution, whatever, she gets a piece of it. Caputo has been a suspect in several mob hits over the last few years. He doesn't work on his own. Vitullo must have ordered him to take you out."

"Christ! Why would the mob be after me?"

"You want to tell me anything else?"

The back of his neck felt damp. "I don't know anything about this Vitullo woman, and I don't know why her hit-man tried to kill me." *First my father's killers, now the mob.* "Do something. Please."

McCain shrugged. "Until you come clean, there's nothing I can do. I'll tell you this much. Get out of this hospital as soon as you can, right away if you feel up to it. By now Vitullo knows Caputo failed, so she'll have more of her goons looking for you."

McCain picked the student ID card off the bed and wrote on the back. "Here's a motel on Route 206 near Medford. Pay cash, don't charge anything. You should be safe there tonight. Stay away from the Turnpike, they'll be watching it." She shrugged. "Not much I can do for you. Get out of New Jersey if you want to stay vertical." McCain handed David the card. "My number is there, too. Call me if you decide to tell the whole story." She shook her head. "Good luck. You're going to need it."

McCain walked toward the door, stopped, turned around and

said, "By the way, the 78G ... I made that up." She smiled and disappeared out the door.

He pushed off the bed and stood up. *Got to get out of here.* Suddenly light-headed, he held on to the bed frame. The dizziness passed, and he stumbled to the closet to find his clothes. His keys and wallet weren't there. He dressed quickly and stepped through the doorway.

The nurses' station, on a corner of the hall to his left, was deserted. He went to the corner and looked down the hall but didn't see anyone. This wasn't right, there should always be at least one nurse on duty. Once McCain left, the nurses must have cleared out so the killers could do their job.

He hurried into the nurses' station and searched through the drawers for his keys. His arms felt tight. In a middle drawer, he found a clear plastic box labeled with his name. Inside were his keys, wallet and loose change. *Thank god!* He grabbed the keys and wallet and ran down the hall, past his room, turning a corner toward an exit sign.

He pushed open the door but stopped when he heard footsteps coming up the stairs. He was probably being paranoid, but he ducked into a patient's room adjacent to the stairs and hid in the closet. An elderly man, snoring loudly, occupied the semi-private room.

David held himself still and listened. A few seconds passed then he heard the hall door swing open. Footsteps—two people—came along and stopped in front of the doorway to this room. He held his breath and remained motionless. A lifetime passed then footsteps traveled down the hall.

When he was sure they were gone, he pushed open the closet door. The footsteps in the corridor seemed to pause in front of each room and then move on. He hoped it was nurses checking on patients. In his gut, he knew it wasn't. If McCain hadn't been there, he would have been murdered while he slept.

He slipped out of the closet, knelt down and peered around the doorway, his head close to the floor. Two men in dark suits looked into the last room and then headed around the corner.

It was now or never. He hurried through the hall door and down the stairs. He strolled across the lobby and out the entrance.

The parking lot was huge, although half empty. He pulled his jacket's hood over his head against the drizzle. He scanned the lot from the hospital steps but didn't see his rented car. If he activated the car's security system, the alarm and flashing lights would attract attention.

There was a safer way to locate the car. He hit the start button on the remote and listened carefully.

Nothing.

Maybe the rain drowned out the engine. Or maybe it wasn't in the lot.

David ran down the main entrance lane, hitting the start button over and over again.

Nothing.

He trotted along, splashing through puddles, listening. If he didn't find the car soon …

He was more than halfway into the lot when he finally heard the rumble of an engine. It was the best sound of his life.

After spotting the car near the emergency entrance, he ran to it and slid behind the steering wheel. He looked back through the rain toward the main entrance. Two men stood on the top step, looking across the lot. He slowly backed out of the parking space. In the far corner of the lot was an exit to a main road. He pulled behind a couple of cars, but the red light at the exit lasted forever. He checked the hospital entrance. The men were gone. *Shit.* Finally, the light turned green, and he was through the exit and on the open road.

He kept one eye on the rearview mirror. Nobody seemed to be following him. Now he had to make it to the Mizinsky home.

Murphy, the Domain Security Chief, sat at his desk working late into the night when a call came in on the hologram computer.

After checking the caller's ID code, he said, "Display actual-size image."

A three-dimensional hologram of a well-built young woman, a shade under six feet tall, formed in the center of his office. She was dressed in a pale blue blouse and a white skirt that hugged the curves in her hips and thighs. Short blond hair framed the woman's face, which was plain, almost masculine, but not unattractive.

Darlene Duboski. They called her DoubleD behind her back.

He couldn't help glancing at the stretched fabric of her blouse. Her physicality dominated the room, even if her appearance was only a hologram.

The body of a porn star, but one of our best agents.

She had wormed her way into the Administration and become the Vice-President's mistress and confidant. Working both sides of the street wasn't a problem; DoubleD had also seduced the Secretary of Homeland Security, usually a tight-lipped woman.

"Sal Caputo's dead," DoubleD said, her voice revealing a hint of an Eastern European accent. "Shot by an unknown woman before he could execute the contract."

Murphy leaned back, surprised. David Brown was just a college kid. A smart kid, balls, too, but he should be an easy kill.

"Details."

DoubleD told Murphy that Caputo had trailed Brown from Reagan Airport to a closed service area on the New Jersey Turnpike, and described the African-American woman who had rescued Brown. DoubleD told him Vitullo's soldiers tracked Brown to a hospital, but he escaped.

"That woman who interfered sounds similar to the fanatic who broke into my meeting with Vitullo," Murphy said, stroking his chin. "I didn't get much of a look at her face, but everything else is a match."

"I agree. It must be the same woman." DoubleD shifted her weight, drawing his attention to curves that rippled and realigned. "She was also involved in the Robotics Institute attack, the only one to escape."

"What do we know about her?"

"Not much. We suspect she's the Commander of The Army of God."

"Now why would she save the life of David Brown, the son of the great villain?" Murphy asked. "It wasn't an accident she showed up when she did. She might have been following Caputo, but it's more likely she was following Brown. Could she have known our plans?"

"I don't believe so.

Murphy remained silent, his eyes fixed on DoubleD.

"She's following Brown," DoubleD said. "She must believe Brown will lead them to us."

Intelligent as well as beautiful. I shouldn't have farmed out the hit to Vitullo.

"Excellent, Darlene. What steps should we take?"

"Our first priority must be to capture this woman. I'll do it. We don't want Vitullo to get her. My interrogations never fail; she'll tell us everything she knows. Once we take care of her, David Brown will be easy." DoubleD added, "Of course, I'll force him to tell everything before I kill him."

"I agree," Murphy said, "but prudence dictates one additional step. Always close the loop. We know Brown has been searching for information about his father's death. Where has he been?"

"A data trace I ran showed that, before the attempted murder, Brown visited Joseph Cohen, the ..."

"The owner of *TechAdvantage*," Murphy interrupted. "Haven't seen Joe in years. He was Paul Martino's junior partner. Cohen knew nothing about PeaceMaker or the Domain. We investigated thoroughly. If he had known anything, we would have eliminated him ten years ago." Murphy recalled he had sent agents to search Cohen's home after the PeaceMaker attack, but they had found nothing. "What information could he have passed on to Brown?"

"Possibly nothing," DoubleD said. "But I will interrogate Cohen first."

"Keep me informed," Murphy said. "We're so close nothing can be allowed to go wrong,"

Murphy ended the transmission and leaned back in his chair, thinking about those events of a decade ago.

After the PeaceMaker fiasco, he and Dianne had cleaned up all the loose ends. She had planned to blame everything on Alan Goldman, her old enemy, but he had convinced her to make Ray Brown the scapegoat. Nobody trusted Ray, a drunk and a misfit, so it was easy to pin the disaster on him. Murphy's idea worked perfectly, everybody had believed it, and the authorities hadn't looked beyond the obvious.

But things had changed. David Brown was kicking up dust, and the religious fanatics were following him, like hunters tracking a cub back to its den. Murphy had to keep the Church off balance for just a little longer; then it would be too late to stop the Domain from seizing power. Killing David Brown and that crazy black woman, maybe Cohen, too—that would do it. It would give them the time they needed.

Murphy stared at a photograph standing in its frame on the corner of his desk, an old picture of Dianne surrounded by her original partners and a few long-standing VPS employees. A younger Murphy stared back at him from the far edge of the picture.

He wouldn't let anyone harm Dianne. Not while he was still breathing.

CHAPTER 17

The soldiers of the Army of God believe they are in a great struggle ordained by a supreme being. Such a holy war justifies any action; it is God's will.

◆ *The Army of God*, Mark Axelrod, copyright 2051, Assistant Director, FBI (retired)

Sunday morning, February 27, 2022

Vince De Marco peered out the window of his stretch limousine as it approached Saint Joseph's, an aging church built in a traditional, Italian-American section of Toms River, New Jersey. He yawned, his mind still half-focused on the hooker who serviced him at the club last night.

A wispy sun blinked above the church's bell tower as his Rolls glided down the street. It was difficult to force his attention back to the job at hand. The stained-glass windows, the brick three-story residence halls behind the church, the neatly dressed parishioners milling about the front entrance—he'd seen it a million times. Growing up less than a mile from the church, he had attended mass regularly with his parents.

Surrounding the church were blue-collar garden apartments, aging two-family homes and a sprawling cemetery. He reminded himself that last year a sniper had tried to pick Vitullo off from one of those apartments. De Marco's sharp eyes scanned the area, observing the spots where his men were hidden. He wondered if animals had dug up what was left of the sniper in the Pinelands.

As always, De Marco felt annoyed at having to get up early Sunday morning to go to church. He gave lip service to the Catholic faith, but it was really just a bunch of fucking mumbo-jumbo. However, his boss, Maria Vitullo, was a true believer who insisted on attending the nine o'clock mass every Sunday.

For some fucking reason, she always sticks me with Sunday morning security.

His mood improved when he noticed the morning sunlight sparkling on the hood of his sedan. *You've come a long way, Vince old boy.* Glancing into the mirror, De Marco studied the line of seven stretch limos following him. It was an impressive sight, one that announced the presence of power.

Traffic was heavy, as it was most mornings. His father often complained Toms River had once been a quiet little town during the winter, after the summer vacationers had left their shore rentals. That might have been true when his father was a kid, but Vince had grown up in the year-round congestion of this South Jersey community.

His driver accelerated, and the car's powerful engine purred, the only sound penetrating his compartment. Tinted windows enclosing the back seat allowed him to look out, but prevented the curious from seeing inside.

As his car pulled up to the front of the church, he checked his appearance one last time in the mirror: dark eyes, thick brown hair pushed back, smooth, olive-toned skin.

Damn good looking.

He was proud to be a captain in the New Jersey Mafia. Few had achieved such an important position while still under thirty. He straightened his tie imperceptibly.

Perfect.

De Marco dressed just like the young college grads he had seen walking around Wall Street like they owned the world. *Well, I'm a businessman, too.* He chuckled. *Except the bulge behind my vest pocket isn't a wallet computer.*

When he stepped out of the sedan, many of the churchgoers paused to stare; his position in the Family made him a local celebrity. A few waved and called his name, but De Marco ignored them. His eyes probed everywhere, searching for anything out of the ordinary.

As always, a well-behaved crowd had gathered for the spectacle. They knew that any minute Maria Vitullo would step out from one of the black limos. He recognized many of the onlookers as regular churchgoers, but tourists and sometimes reporters would come to see the famous woman. De Marco located several of his men milling around the church, blending into the crowd. Everything was normal.

"Begin status sequence," he said.

A rough male voice burst through his Command Chip. "Everything secure in the residence halls."

As planned, each of the men stationed in the church and nearby buildings reported over the Command Chip. Once he had received them all, De Marco nodded his head toward the line of cars. His men quickly stepped out of the cars and took up positions along the entrance to the church.

With two soldiers guarding his back, De Marco walked over to the fourth sedan and pulled open the door. The crowd gawked when Maria Vitullo stepped out into the protective sheath of her men. Smartly dressed in a dark coat, knee-length dark blue dress and white high-heeled shoes, she looked spectacular.

"You look tired, Vince," Vitullo said, followed by that cat-that-swallowed-the-canary smile of hers. "Did the ladies keep you up last night?"

Before he could decide how to respond, she turned away to greet family members. *Fuck!* De Marco walked behind her as she strolled along the sidewalk and up the steps toward the church. He could smooth-talk any woman, but for some goddamn reason, Vitullo always left him tongue-tied.

He forced himself to concentrate on security issues and once again scanned the crowd. In cold weather, everyone wore heavy coats, so concealed weapons were a big concern. He had people circling through the crowd with portable metal detectors, but the range was limited to a few yards. He wasn't so worried about the local people, but the anti-technology fanatics were dangerous, especially the damn Army of God.

Two of his soldiers cleared a path for Vitullo, while others followed a few steps behind. The crowd lining the pathway remained respectful as she walked by.

When she entered the church, an elderly usher helped remove her coat. Although the man had performed this simple task for many years, De Marco's men had frisked him a moment earlier in the church. *The old coot was harmless, but why take a chance?*

The church was clean, but beginning to show its age. Over the decades, parishioners had scratched names and dates into the wood pews, and the front doors had lost their shine. De Marco wondered how much the priests were skimming from the collection plate. He figured at least ten grand every Sunday. Too bad Vitullo insisted they had to keep their hands off. Pissed him off. He deserved a taste;

none of the other captains had to work without earning.

He scrutinized Vitullo's family members as they stopped by to pay their respects. After chatting with them, she walked down the center aisle and stepped into the third row, which the Bishop reserved for her. De Marco followed behind the boss. He discreetly watched her dress stretch tight across her hips as she stepped into the pew.

Nice ass.

Vitullo shuffled down to the center and sat, placing her purse on the bench. De Marco settled beside her and watched his men assume their positions in the pews and along the walls. Once again, he whispered over the Command Chip.

Bill O'Dell followed Sam Merlucci along an interior hallway on the second floor of the church. Merlucci was responsible for security within the church, and he explained each step in the process to the recently hired O'Dell.

"Always assume an assassin might be inside," Merlucci said, glancing in a doorway and looking around before entering. O'Dell knew Merlucci had memorized every inch of the church's layout, since he had been performing this task each Sunday for years. O'Dell followed him through the doorway, listening attentively as his boss explained how to search the room.

Making sure the church concealed no enemies, he trailed Merlucci through each room. His hand brushed his pistol when they glanced into a large sacristy and discovered a priest putting away robes and other garments. Merlucci signaled O'Dell to be alert and then barked out, "Hey, Father, what're you doing in there?"

The priest answered without turning, "I'm working on next week's game plan for the Giants against the Eagles. What does it look like I'm doing?"

Merlucci gestured to O'Dell and they pulled out their Beretta lasers. O'Dell stepped forward to guard the door while Merlucci crept into the room and aimed his pistol at the priest's back.

"Father, I want you to slowly raise your hands and then turn around," Merlucci said.

The priest said, "I don't have the time to play—"

Merlucci cut him off, "This is the last time I'm going to ask you."

O'Dell knew the moment had arrived. He pulled the trigger on his laser pistol, and the back of Merlucci's head exploded in a nova of blood and bone. The gangster's body remained upright for a moment then sagged and slapped the floor.

The "priest" quickly examined Merlucci's body then spoke into a small computer clipped to his sleeve. "Merlucci has been eliminated." He listened briefly then said to O'Dell, "She's in her usual seat. All our people are in place, ready to go. Our job is to make sure she doesn't escape through the side chapel."

Although sitting quietly, Vitullo was too pissed off to concentrate on the mass. She watched the new priest, Father Chen, lead the altar boys through the ancient ritual. It sucked to import a Chink priest for her church. Not that she had anything against the Chinks— they were hard-working people who paid their debts—but this neighborhood had always had Italian priests. Maybe a few Micks, she recalled, but her father had fixed that years ago. She'd call the Cardinal later today and have him fix this shit.

Vitullo loved the Sunday morning mass. It was the one thing that hadn't changed. She remembered sitting in the pew with her cousin when they were little girls. They'd giggle and make faces at each other when they were supposed to be praying. Then her mother would catch them at it, and they'd get their asses whacked when they got home. Not that it mattered, they would screw around the next week anyway.

The church had seemed so big and mysterious back then. Now it was just a worn-down building filled with people she'd known for years. Still, it was a comfort sitting in the old hardwood pews of her childhood, renewing her faith once again.

De Marco sat beside her, scanning the balconies, his head moving from side to side. *The conceited son of a bitch looks particularly good today. It doesn't pay to screw around with the hired help, the other capos would sulk and think I'm playing favorites, but one of these days I'm going to find out if he's as good in bed as he thinks he is.*

De Marco was looking around uneasily as he began another status check with his soldiers.

Something's wrong.

"Merlucci," he said, "where the fuck are you?"

De Marco tried again, but his expression told her the man had not answered. Then he leaned toward her and whispered, "Merlucci's not responding. We should get out of here."

Vitullo was about to agree when a rapid series of explosions thundered through the church. She jumped up when a small capsule crashed into the pew in front of them and exploded, releasing a dense cloud of white gas. Nearby church members screamed and bent over, coughing and retching. Vitullo stared at the drifting cloud until a whiff of the gas burned her nose and throat, making her retch, too.

De Marco roughly pulled her away from the gas and shouted,

"Let's get out of here!"

Vitullo grabbed her purse and followed De Marco down the pew, trying to avoid the swirling gas. Someone was trying to whack her. She ripped open her purse and pulled out her laser pistol.

The church had become a madhouse. Terrified people screamed and coughed. Her eyes watered as the explosions continued and the gas spread. Panicked parishioners ran through the noxious haze and collapsed in the aisles as the fumes overcame them. De Marco shoved a staggering old man out of the way as he led Vitullo down the center aisle toward the front entrance. Several of her soldiers, lasers drawn, scanned the church for the invisible enemy.

The crowd surged desperately against the exits, pounding on unyielding doors. She was locked in, isolated from most of her soldiers. Explosions continued and Vitullo could barely see. Her eyes burned. She used a scarf to protect her breathing.

There has to be a way out of this trap.

Unconscious bodies littered the church, including several of her soldiers. Coughing badly, De Marco was bent over the back of a pew. She was on her own.

The side chapel!

With all the doors locked, Vitullo rushed toward the stairs in the side chapel. The air was not as bad there, and she pumped her legs furiously up the stairs, De Marco trailing several steps behind. She felt faint after climbing just a few steps, but it was the only way out.

O'Dell was at the top of the stairs. He wore a gas mask and carried a laser pistol. She was about to call him when she realized the bastard must be part of the attack. She snapped off a shot, but the beam passed harmlessly over O'Dell's head.

O'Dell aimed with both hands. His shot hit De Marco in the

side. Shock surged across De Marco's face. He grabbed the badly burned wound and collapsed, shooting wildly. Vitullo aimed more deliberately and this time burned O'Dell's leg. The traitor screamed and went down, clutching his thigh as blood gushed.

Although a rasping cough shook her body, Vitullo tried to line up another shot at O'Dell. Before she could squeeze the trigger, a burly arm knocked the gun out of her hand. Through bleary eyes, she saw a priest wearing a gas mask. She tried to duck as the priest threw a punch, but it caught her on the temple and stunned her. All the strength deserted her body. She collapsed onto rubbery hands and knees and tumbled over onto her side.

Vitullo felt herself lifted over a man's shoulder. Her face brushed against the rough fabric of a robe. The phony priest carried her away. As they climbed the stairs, Vitullo peered around her captor's shoulder and tried to focus on a hazy figure looming above them on the next landing. She blinked. It was a young black nun wearing a gas mask. Vitullo pretended to be unconscious as the priest carried her up the steps.

The black woman's harsh voice carried over the sounds of battle. "Hurry! Her goons are outside. They could break in any minute."

A tremendous explosion shook the building and the priest almost dropped Vitullo.

"Get her to the car," the black bitch shouted. "I'll cover your escape."

Vitullo peeked down the steps and saw De Marco spread out at the foot of the stairs, holding his side, blood dripping through his hand. He'd be no help.

"Don't wait for me," the woman shouted. "I'll catch up if I can." Then she bolted past the priest, down the steps and into the haze.

Panting from the effort, the priest carried his prisoner down the hall. Vitullo waited until she could no longer hear the black bitch's footsteps then slowly reached into her sleeve and pulled out a long knife. With all of her remaining strength, she plunged the knife into the priest's side. He screamed and staggered into a wall. Still hanging over his shoulder, but now feeling wildly alive, Vitullo pulled out the blade and stabbed again. His body went limp and he crashed to the floor with her on top of him.

Her forehead bounced off the stone floor and the world turned into a collage of distant sounds and rolling shades of gray. Gradually, she became aware of a cold, stone floor under her shoulder blades, but her body was a useless jangle of vibrating nerves.

I have to ... get moving.

It took all her strength to flex her fingers. She rested a moment, soaked in sweat. She rolled onto her side then struggled to her knees. Light-headed, she was forced to rest again. There were footsteps on the stairs. She pulled the knife out of the dead priest and tried to stand, but her legs refused to obey. Seeing the black bitch racing toward her, Vitullo turned on her knees to face this new enemy, holding the knife in front of her.

Moesha stopped just outside the range of Vitullo's knife and circled her. The knife shook badly. The gangster was weak from the gas. Moesha feigned a move forward and jumped back as Vitullo slashed at her legs. Vitullo was slow to recover from her thrust, so Moesha leaped forward and lashed out with a powerful kick to Vitullo's head. The mobster's eyes rolled back, and she tumbled over unconscious.

The staccato hiss of laser fire from below grew louder. Moesha trusted her people to hold off the mobsters as long as possible, but they would be outnumbered as more of Vitullo's goons arrived. Whatever the consequences, she had to capture Vitullo for the First Minister's plan to succeed.

She leaned over and frisked Vitullo. When she was certain the infidel was disarmed, Moesha dropped to her knees and lifted Vitullo's petite body across her shoulders. Grunting, she stood up and walked down the hallway.

Vitullo's body grew heavy as Moesha staggered on. When she could go no farther, she stopped and leaned against the wall. A distant laser hissed, and then the church was quiet. Footsteps echoed along the hall, followed by an angry buzz of voices. She tossed away her gas mask and staggered forward, knowing she didn't have much time before Vitullo's goons found her.

She carried Vitullo down another staircase and laid her inside a narrow doorway. Although Moesha gasped for breath, she knew the Lord was with her. He had given her strength to get this far and He wouldn't desert her now.

Peering through a small window halfway up the door, she watched a pair of armed men run down the sidewalk. She waited for the opportunity to get to her car, which she had parked across the street. Once the men had disappeared around the corner, she carried Vitullo to the car and dumped her in the trunk. Whispering thanks to the Lord, Moesha climbed into the car and escaped with her prize.

The opening phase of the First Minister's plan was complete.

CHAPTER 18

The Great Depression of 2020 decimated the middle class in the United States. The Stock Market Crash of 2022 and the oncoming civil violence intensified the grinding depression and destroyed the little confidence remaining in the Federal Government. The world was a very different place by the time these tides had run their course.

◆ The Great Depression of 2020, Dr. Jessica Owen-Wells, copyright 2041, Chief Historian, American Historical Society

Sunday afternoon, February 27, 2022

It was an overcast afternoon when David turned off Route 280 into West Orange, a decaying suburban town in northern New Jersey. He supposed the town had once been a busy, middle-class community, but now it had the look of a place reluctantly losing ground. Cracked streets made driving tedious. Many homes needed paint and repairs, others were deserted.

Eventually, he found Deborah Mizinsky's home, an aging two-story colonial with a red brick front and faded blue wooden siding. Like many of its neighbors, it needed plenty of attention: a new coat of paint, weeding of the overgrown front lawn and the replacement of cracked wood in a white picket fence. The street was empty, so he parked in front of her house.

Staring at her home, he had second thoughts about knocking on her door. If she let him in, she'd be involved. He didn't think anyone had followed him, but he couldn't be sure.

Might as well go in. It was too late now, anyway.

He zipped his jacket and stepped out of the car into a cold, quiet afternoon. He looked around carefully. The street appeared deserted. He walked toward the house. Each footstep crunched through a layer of dirt sprinkled with small bits of loose blacktop. He pulled on the front gate, but the latch stuck, forcing him to reach over the top and jiggle it open.

David walked along a brick pathway the same color as the house and then up creaking porch steps to the front door. After ringing the doorbell, he turned and scanned the neighborhood but saw nothing suspicious. Hearing a rustle inside the house, he focused his attention on the front door. The blinds spread apart and a plump face peered out. A lock clicked and a stocky woman opened the interior door; the glass storm door remained locked as she looked him over.

Through an Internet search, David knew Deborah Mizinsky was sixty-one and had two adult children. He had hacked into her employment file and discovered that she was a normal, hard-working widow. After her husband's death, she had supplemented meager Social Security benefits with a low-level position in the state's motor vehicle department and had earned a reputation as a reliable, conscientious worker. Competent but not outstanding, her performance evaluations said.

Dressed in a dark skirt and tan blouse, she was plain and neat. Thick waves of silver gray hair framed a puffy face. David thought she might have been pretty in her youth.

He tried to appear friendly. "Hello, Mrs. Mizinsky, I'm David Brown." When she didn't open the door, he said, "I called you a few days ago. My father was a good friend of Paul Martino."

Her face relaxed and she pulled open the door, which rattled as it swung in. "Come in, David. I expected you Thursday. Sorry to be an old grouch, but you have to be extra careful these days. There are so many strange people on the streets."

David nodded. "I understand. Times are tough."

"And getting worse. Let me take your jacket."

After she draped his jacket on a hanger in the hall closet, Mizinsky led him to a worn sofa in the living room. Flowered wallpaper had frayed in spots, but the furniture and pine floor were immaculate. He shifted his weight on the couch, not sure how to begin.

Her husband and two teenage children smiled across the years from silver-framed pictures perched on the fireplace mantel. Ted Mizinsky had been a beefy man with a warm, intelligent face.

Should be sitting on this couch, playing with his grandchildren.

"Can I offer you a cup of coffee or tea?" she asked.

David shook his head. "Thank you for seeing me. I'm sorry to be late, but a last-minute problem came up."

Mizinsky settled into a thick armchair next to the sofa and attempted a smile, but the expression lacked warmth.

He cleared his throat. "As I mentioned when I called, my father was Raymond Brown. He died when I was eleven and I never knew him very well. I know many people consider him a criminal, but he had a much kinder side, too. For the last few weeks, I've been talking to people who knew him."

"I hope you didn't waste your time coming here," she said. "I didn't know your father nor did my husband."

"I know that, Mrs. Mizinsky. My father's best friend was Paul Martino, who I believe knew your husband."

Mizinsky watched him with suspicion.

She knows something. I'll have to do this carefully.

She cleared her throat. "Yes, Ted and Paul were friends. They talked on the phone from time to time, and Paul quoted Ted in his magazine several times. I remember Paul coming here one night. Ted had invited him for dinner. He was a very nice man."

When Mizinsky didn't continue, David said, "I'd like to learn more about Paul. In particular, I'm interested in his activities during the weeks before his death. Did your husband have contact with Paul?"

Mizinsky ignored his question. "Have you noticed things seem to be spinning out of control? That everything is going from bad to worse?"

"Well, it has—"

"This neighborhood must look pretty bad," Mizinsky interrupted. "It used to be really nice. We raised our kids here. It was completely safe." She seemed to be talking to herself. "Didn't really have to lock the door at night. Nice people up and down the street, just a wonderful neighborhood."

A sigh escaped. "Now it's awful. They sell drugs on the corner. Nobody goes out at night. Most of the old neighbors moved away. Who knows where? It's not the same anymore." She mumbled, "Nothing's the same. I invested my life savings in the stock market," she said, picking up steam. "Now that's gone, too. I was planning to retire in a couple of years." She laughed bitterly. "Well, that's not going to happen."

"I'm sorry."

Frowning, she said, "I don't want your sympathy. Don't know why I'm telling you all this. Just tell me the truth, what are you looking for?"

David studied her. *This woman wants to tell me something.*

"I don't believe my father was a criminal, and I don't believe Paul Martino was, either. I want to prove that." He leaned forward, wincing as the pain shot through his shoulder. "I think your husband knew something, and it cost him his life."

"What happened to your shoulder?" Mizinsky asked, concern in her face. "You can barely move your arm."

"You have sharp eyes, Mrs. Mizinsky. Someone burned it with a laser a couple of days ago."

To his surprise, she wasn't fazed. "So that's why you were late." She laughed, but it had a hollow rattle. "And you led them here."

"I'm sorry, but I had to talk to you. I don't think anyone followed me."

Mizinsky waved her hand dismissively. "It's okay. I don't care anymore. I'm glad you came. Things are coming to a head anyway." Then she blurted out, "They killed him," her face suddenly raw with anger.

"Your husband?"

She glanced at her husband's picture on the mantel then brought her angry stare back to him. "The police said Ted was speeding and lost control of his car. They said the car skidded off the road and hit a tree. Died instantly. I never believed it, not a word of it."

David didn't like pushing, but he had to get to the truth. "Maybe that's what happened."

Shaking her head, she said, "Ted was the most cautious driver you ever saw. He would never speed or drive recklessly. He knew that road like the back of his hand. He drove that way to his job every day for seven years." She snorted. "Speeding!"

Mizinsky stood up and hurried through a doorway to the kitchen sink, filled a kettle with water, and placed it on a burner over a low flame. She stared at the flame for a moment, her back to David. Then she turned around and studied him.

David held back his questions.

After making a cup of tea, Mizinsky brought it back to the living room and sank into her chair. "Ted changed after the PeaceMaker attack," she said. "He was scared, really scared." She hesitated, sipping her tea. "You're sure you want to pursue this?"

David nodded. "It's too late to stop. I'm in it whether I want to be or not. Please tell me what you know, and I'll keep you out of it if I can."

Fretfully running her fingers through her hair, Mizinsky said, "You know, they're probably going to kill both of us." She took a shallow breath. "Like I said, Ted was really scared after PeaceMaker. I made him tell me what was bothering him.

"He said he found something while running a statistical audit of outgoing e-mail just before the PeaceMaker attack. They used to run an audit every day to check for abnormalities." She gulped her tea. "The software statistically scanned their messages, but Ted liked to manually review a few just to make sure everything was working properly." Shaking her head, she said, "Damn him, he was so conscientious. Anyway, he discovered Lester Dawson's calendar had been sent out over the Internet. Someone had broken into the company's main server and hacked through several layers of security. Whoever did it was an expert in network security, Ted told me.

The calendar contained all of Dawson's upcoming meetings,

lunches, travel, everything he planned to do for the next few months. Dawson was the Horizon CEO at the time. He had been a big shot at VPS, too." She paused for a gulp of tea. "Now sending the calendar out could be completely okay, but since it was the CEO, Ted decided to investigate. He traced the message through several nodes on the Internet until it just disappeared. Did you know all the employees kept their calendars on the company's network servers?" David nodded. "Well, Ted checked them and found the calendars of five other people had also been sent out."

"Who were the others?"

"Three software engineers from the emergency response team and the manager of the team. These were the best technicians in the company, the guys who handled the toughest problems. The fifth was Ted's boss, Jane Purzyki. She managed all the network security work."

"Did Ted discover who stole the calendars?"

Mizinsky shook her head. "About the same time," she continued, "Ted got a call from Paul Martino. Paul told him that he was doing an article on network security and he wanted to interview Ted. Being his friend, Ted agreed. Anyway, during the interview, Paul asked Ted about any recent security problems. God knows why, but Ted told him about the stolen calendars. Ted was stunned when Paul told him all four of the people on the emergency response team as well as his boss were former VantagePoint Software employees."

She drained her tea, stood up and asked if he'd like something to drink. He politely declined, and she left to refill her cup in the kitchen.

All these ex-VPS employees must have been part of the PeaceMaker scheme in some way. Somebody got their calendars to keep track of them.

Dianne Morgan? Why would she? It doesn't make sense.

Mizinsky came back with a steaming cup of tea and picked up the story. "Then Ted told Paul the rest of the story. He called Purzyki on the video phone and told her about the problem. Ted said she got real scared. That surprised him, since Purzyki was usually tough as nails. She ordered him to do nothing more and hung up on him."

After taking a sip of tea, Mizinsky said, "About twenty minutes later, Purzyki called back and linked Ted into a video conference with this consultant she had just hired. This surprised Ted since the company only used consultants for training, not investigation. The guy's name was Michael De Luca. This De Luca got all the data from Ted and then told him to forget about the whole thing. That was it, they hung up.

"Ted decides to ask around about De Luca. Well, guess what. De Luca had done a lot of consulting work for VPS. Turns out he was kind of shady. He had been tossed out of the FBI."

David felt as if a brick was wedged in his stomach. "So what was going on?"

"Ted wasn't sure, but he was concerned because an intruder had gained access to the calendars of several important Horizon personnel. Apparently, somebody wanted to know what their upcoming schedules looked like. In addition, these people were all former VPS employees. And the consultant they brought in had ties to VPS. Now Ted's no dummy. He didn't know what was going down, but it couldn't be anything good. He figured it had to be a big-time problem because of the secrecy. He asked Paul to use his contacts to check it out, but Paul told him to stay out of it."

Twirling a wisp of her hair, Mizinsky said, "Here's the part that got Ted really scared. All six of the Horizon people died during the PeaceMaker attack. Michael De Luca died. And Paul Martino. Everybody who knew about the stolen calendars had been killed. That scared the hell out of Ted."

Shit. A secret war had raged a decade in the past. Everyone who touched that war died, and now they're hunting me.

"Ted made me promise never to say anything about this." Jerking her fingers out of her hair, Mizinsky folded her hands in her lap. "He was convinced the people from VPS were involved in the PeaceMaker attack. He didn't believe Paul Martino had anything to do with it. Quite the contrary, he believed Paul had used the magazine story as a cover for his own investigation."

Some of the pieces were falling into place. "I think your husband was right, Mrs. Mizinsky. My father and Paul had uncovered PeaceMaker and were searching for its creators. Paul was secretly contacting network security people, including your husband, trying to track down those responsible for the virus."

David couldn't sit still any longer. He got to his feet and started pacing.

Shit, Kathy worked at VPS.

"PeaceMaker must have been created at VPS," he said. "The bastards infected their own operating system."

Mizinsky nodded. "You could be right, I don't know. God knows there were VPS people all over this. But if Ray was innocent, what monster created the virus?"

"It had to be Dianne Morgan. She hates the federal government because they broke apart her company. She's a power-hungry psychopath, the only person with the ability and arrogance to attempt revenge on this scale. She created the monster, but my father and Paul Martino terminated it, so she murdered them."

"Who stole the calendars? Morgan?"

"I don't think so. Why would she kill her partner and former employees? I think someone else decided to kill these former VPS employees," David said, "and this killer stole the calendars to keep track of them. It must have been Alan Goldman. He hated Dianne because she drove his software company out of business. He could have learned Dianne's plans, tried to eliminate the people in the Domain and then take control of the virus. That's the reason Dianne killed him, a battle to control PeaceMaker. It was Dianne who murdered the network administrators that talked to Martino. She must have learned your husband knew about the stolen calendars, so he ..." His voice trailed off as he watched Mizinsky's face crumble.

"I'm so sorry about your husband." Tears slid down Mizinsky's face, making him feel guilty for reopening old wounds. "I know it must be hell to go through this again."

David stepped over to the chair and took hold of her soft hands. "Thank you, Mrs. Mizinsky. I'm going to leave now. I hope I didn't bring them to you. I'm so sorry."

Mizinsky raised her glistening eyes to him. "Ted was a wonderful man. He was my life. Whoever killed him doesn't deserve any mercy. Anything you need from me to nail those bastards ..."

"I'll get them, I promise," David said. "We shouldn't speak again. They'll be after me."

His mind sifted through all this information as he hurried out the door. The killers were after him, and he had been lucky to evade them for so long.

It was time to confront Dianne Morgan.

CHAPTER 19

Cruel with guilt, and daring with despair,
The midnight murderer bursts the faithless bar;
Invades the sacred hour of silent rest
And leaves, unseen, a dagger in your breast.
◆ London: A Poem, Samuel Johnson, 1738

Monday, February 28, 2022

DoubleD stepped off the elevator and reached along the wall to switch off the overhead lights. Wearing a brown leather jacket and black, skin-tight pants, she faded into the dark lobby.

She had studied her target, Joe Cohen, for several days, learning his habits, his business, and his personal life. Now she would seize him, just as Murphy had ordered. Determined to discover whatever secrets Cohen had shared with David Brown, she had planned this day meticulously.

Once she extracted the information, she intended to kill both Cohen and Brown. Murphy would be pleased with her work. She didn't fear Murphy, but she respected his intelligence and determination. He eliminated agents who failed, so it wasn't wise to disappoint him.

The morning sun was yet to peek above the horizon, and the lobby was pitch-black. Slipping on night-vision goggles, DoubleD crept toward the offices of *TechAdvantage*, with Tom Brewster just behind her. This was her first time working with Brewster, a middle-aged agent with a good reputation. So far, he seemed competent.

DoubleD stopped in front of the *TechAdvantage* door and listened.

Nothing.

She pulled a wallet-sized computer from a side pocket and flipped it open, revealing a dimly lit display. Although it appeared ordinary, this wasn't a standard commercial handheld computer. It had been altered to support a variety of intelligence functions.

She pressed the device against the door just below the lock, which clicked open. Glock laser pistol drawn, she pushed into the *TechAdvantage* offices, Brewster covering her back

A lamp on the receptionist's desk threw weak strands of light along the hallway, but her night-vision goggles exposed every detail. DoubleD stalked down the hall, listening for the unexpected. As she had figured, so early in the morning all the offices were empty. All except one.

Rustling sounds came from the doorway just ahead. She signaled Brewster to stop. Joe Cohen was working in his office, as he did every morning. With her back flattened against the wall, she sidled toward his office.

Cohen's voice drifted out to them. "Jenny, pull up that memo from the accountant—what's that woman's name?—Diebold. The one about our marketing expenses."

DoubleD listened for another human's voice, but Cohen was alone, working with his computer. She nodded to Brewster, then burst into Cohen's office and aimed her laser pistol at his chest. Brewster slid behind her and stopped at the side of Cohen's desk, his

Glock also poised.

"Remain still or die," she ordered. Shock spread across Cohen's face, but he obeyed her command. *Good, a man who follows directions.* As DoubleD pointed her gun at Cohen, Brewster slipped behind him and cuffed his hands behind his back.

"Come out from behind the desk," she said.

Cohen obeyed. The shock had disappeared, replaced by a weary look of resignation.

"I should have known," Cohen muttered.

"Quiet. I won't warn you again."

Brewster quickly pricked Cohen's neck with a micro-needle. Cohen's eyes lost focus as the fast-acting chemicals put him into a semi-conscious state. Brewster grabbed Cohen's overcoat, put it on him, and buttoned it up.

DoubleD grabbed Cohen's arm, pushed him out the doorway and led him down the hall. She kept a tight grip to make sure he didn't fall. Brewster walked behind them, his breath coming in a steady rhythm. A moment later, they stepped into an elevator and descended to the first floor lobby.

When Maryanne, the *TechAdvantage* receptionist, entered the lobby, she saw Cohen and two strangers take the exit to the parking garage. It was strange her boss would leave the office, since his first appointment was in twenty minutes.

She took the elevator to the *TechAdvantage* floor and was surprised to find the lobby in shadows. *Cohen always turns on the lights first thing in the morning.* Maryanne flicked the light switch and walked across the lobby to the office entrance. When she found the door unlocked, she knew something was wrong.

A call came in as she stepped into the office. Turning to her computer, she saw Laura Cohen's weathered, but still pretty face in the display.

"Hello, Mrs. Cohen, this is Maryanne."

"Hello, Maryanne, may I speak to my husband."

"He just left. I saw him walk out with a man and a woman."

Mrs. Cohen looked concerned. "Did you recognize them?"

"Never saw them before. There's nothing in his appointment schedule for twenty minutes. He cleared it so he could go through the financials before the accountants arrive." Watching Mrs. Cohen intently, Maryanne added, "Must have been a last minute thing."

Mrs. Cohen stared blankly into the computer display. Her face seemed to age years in a matter of moments. Then she came alive and said, "Terminate call."

Maryanne found herself looking into a blank display. All her senses shrieked. She had never seen Laura Cohen react like that.

Maryanne rushed down the hall to Joe Cohen's office and found the door closed but unlocked. He always locked his office door when he left the building.

His wallet computer was on the desk. The computer had been left on. Moreover, the display contained a confidential note from his accountant; anyone could walk in and read the note. Those strangers must have taken Cohen. She quietly closed the door and pulled a thin netphone from her pocket.

"Code Red."

She glanced around the office, noticing the chairs were at odd angles. *There hadn't been much of a struggle. They must have surprised him.*

A few seconds passed before a woman's voice came from the netphone. "What is it?"

"You said to call if anything suspicious happened. Joe Cohen left the office a few minutes ago with an unfamiliar man and woman. I think he's been abducted."

"Do you know where they're taking him?"

"No."

"Describe them."

"I only got a brief look. The man was middle-aged, white, gray hair, medium height, about one hundred fifty pounds. The woman was white, about thirty, big boned, short blonde hair, taller and heavier than her companion." Recalling the skin-tight pants, she added, "Well-muscled, like an oversized gymnast."

The voice said, "Stay alert," and the connection was broken.

DoubleD pulled the car into a rundown two-story inn about two hours north of San Francisco. Located on a steep hill half a mile from Route 1 on the California coast, the place had been deserted for years. Overgrown trees and shrubs blocked the view of the dirt parking lot.

Perfect. Nobody would see the car. Not that anyone travels the old highway, anyway.

She parked and turned off the engine. As she stepped out, a cold wind gusted through the trees, chilling but invigorating. DoubleD buttoned up her leather coat and walked to the back of the car. Brewster unlocked the trunk, and they lifted out a semi-conscious Joe Cohen and helped him stand. The wind picked up again, blowing a cold mist from the nearby ocean across the parking lot. She unlocked the handcuffs, allowing Cohen's arms to fall to his sides. Throwing Cohen's arm over his shoulder, Brewster half-carried the unsteady prisoner up the stairs and into the lobby.

Brewster sat Cohen on an old, stained couch in front of a stone fireplace, while DoubleD, her pistol drawn, swiftly walked through the rooms, noting that nothing had changed from her previous visit. The lobby retained the look of a hunting lodge, with wood beams crossing the ceiling and the obligatory elk horns hanging from the far wall. She would have liked to build a fire, it was as cold in here as outside, but she couldn't risk a passerby seeing smoke from the chimney.

She pulled an old wooden chair in front of Cohen and sat down. Examining Cohen's dilated pupils, she was satisfied he was still under the influence of the drugs.

"Joe, can you hear me?"

Cohen's head turned toward her and he tried to focus his eyes. He nodded. "Yes … I hear you."

"What do you see?"

He blinked. "I see you … a beautiful young blonde." Then his concentration drifted away.

She grabbed his shoulder and shook him gently. If he couldn't comprehend her questions, his information would be unreliable.

"Joe, I have questions and I want you to answer truthfully and completely. Do you understand?"

"Yes, questions."

"What's your name?"

"Joseph Richard Cohen." He turned his head toward the window and smiled whimsically. "My friends call me Joe."

"What do you do at work?"

"Work? … I can't … *TechAdvantage*! … I publish a magazine."

"You're doing great." She smiled at him. "Now tell me where you work. What city?"

"San Francisco."

Brewster's voice drifted over her shoulder. "He's okay."

"I'm very tired." Cohen rubbed his eyes. "Let me get a little shuteye."

DoubleD grabbed his hands and jerked him forward. She held his hands on her knees, forcing him to look squarely at her.

"Joe, I have just a few questions. Very important questions." When his eyes met hers, she said, "Did David Brown come to your office last week?"

He looked around, as if seeing the hunting lodge for the first time.

First the drugs, then pain …

DoubleD crushed his fingers together, almost to the point of breaking tiny bones. He cried out, and she relented. She understood the bone structure of the hand, techniques to inflict pain, how to make a prisoner talk. It would have been easy to break his fingers, but then he'd confess anything to stop the torture. She needed the truth; there were better ways to learn his secrets.

"My hands," Cohen choked out. "How did you …?"

When she increased the pressure, he said, "Yeah, David wanted to learn more about his father, but I couldn't help him … barely knew Ray Brown."

"What did you talk about?" She relaxed the pressure on his fingers.

"Well, we talked about Paul Martino. Paul was my best friend." Cohen sighed. "He died ten years ago. They murdered him, the bastards."

"Who murdered him?" she asked softly.

When Cohen didn't answer, she patted his hand. "I'm your friend. You can tell me."

"I'm not supposed to say." He glanced nervously at Brewster and whispered to her, "It's dangerous, you know."

"Tell me, Joe. I'm your friend. I can help you."

Cohen shook his head and tried to pull away, but she held his hands firmly, applying moderate pressure. He stopped resisting and DoubleD released his hands. She signaled Brewster to leave, then turned back to Cohen.

"It's just you and me. I'm your friend." She caressed his face. "You can tell me anything. It's okay."

Cohen leaned forward and whispered, "It was that bitch. Ray said so."

Confused, DoubleD asked, "What did Ray say?"

"He said there was a virus in the Atlas operating system." Lowering his voice, Cohen said, "It was PeaceMaker."

How much does he know? What had he told David Brown?

"What else did Ray say?"

"Dianne Morgan created PeaceMaker." Cohen appeared more alert now. "Ray didn't know why she did it, but he had to stop her. She must have killed him, the bitch. Paul, too."

"Did Ray tell you that?" When he nodded, she asked, "When did he tell you?"

"About a month after he died. Yeah, it was about a month."

Maybe we gave him too much of the drug.

"How could he tell you about PeaceMaker a month after he died?"

"No, no," Cohen said, shaking his head. "I didn't speak to him. Revere contained a message Ray had recorded. It explained everything."

Revere was the software Ray Brown created just before the PeaceMaker attack. Murphy said Ray had recorded a message describing the Domain's plan to blackmail the government and seize power with PeaceMaker. Ray developed the Revere software to warn government officials, but Murphy said they discovered Revere before Ray could release it and destroyed it years ago. How had Cohen learned about it?

"Did Ray Brown release Revere?" she said. "Is that how you know about Dianne Morgan?"

Shaking his head again, Cohen replied, "No, Paul had a copy of it on his computer. After he died, I grabbed his computer and looked through it. I found Revere and played Ray's message describing the Domain. Ray listed everyone he believed was part of the Domain, starting with Dianne Morgan and her partners at VPS." Cohen paused and then said, "I was afraid they'd kill me if they found out I had seen Ray's message, so I hid Paul's computer in my home."

She wondered if the message was still in existence. Had anyone else read it? Exposure now would be a disaster.

"Did Revere send the Domain message to anyone?"

Cohen rubbed his hands together. "I don't think so."

"Where is this message?" She grabbed his hands and applied pressure. "Did you save it?"

Tears quickly formed in the corners of his eyes, so she eased up on the pressure. "It's okay, Joe. I'm your friend." When Cohen focused on her again, she smiled and said, "Where is the message, Joe?"

"It's still on Paul's old computer. Hidden in my basement."

"Does David Brown know about the message?"

"No. I gave him a copy of Paul's old files, but there's nothing about Revere in there." He glanced at the fireplace and added, "It's cold in here."

"I'll start a fire when we finish our conversation. What about your wife? What does she know?"

His face tightened, but he said, "Laura knows … that I gave a copy of the files to David."

"Does she know about Revere?" DoubleD asked, increasing the pressure.

The strain showed in his face, but the drug forced his reply. "Yes."

DoubleD handcuffed Cohen again and called for Brewster, who came in from the adjoining room.

"You heard his story," she said. "He's had a copy of Revere all these years. I'm going to his home in Half Moon Bay to destroy it." She glanced at Cohen, who had leaned back and closed his eyes. "I'll call you after I pick up his wife. We'll take care of them after I delete Revere."

In the waning light of the afternoon, DoubleD peered through her car window at Cohen's home. Parked near the woods, the car was a dark outline barely visible. When she had arrived, she'd aimed a flashlight-sized heat sensor at the house, which confirmed nobody was home.

DoubleD uneasily watched the Cohen home, waiting for darkness. Half an hour passed. An hour. The interior of the house remained in shadows, although several lamps along the walkway suddenly flashed on.

Probably a timer.

She checked her watch: 7:10 p.m. *Maybe Laura Cohen had been warned and wasn't coming home.*

DoubleD stepped into the deserted street then slipped into the woods. Stalking up to the house, she paused to make sure her approach had not been detected. Everything remained quiet. She cut across the yard until she was no longer visible from the street and put on night-vision goggles. Creeping to the back of the house, she located the kitchen door.

When she stepped in front of the door, the house security system said, "Identification please."

Lifting the wallet computer from her pocket, DoubleD pressed it against the door next to the security lock. Once again, the little computer transmitted a signal to the door's locking mechanism, which clicked open.

Cohen's security system said, "You may enter."

DoubleD walked through a small kitchen into an old-fashioned living room, furnished with a thick-stuffed couch surrounded by Queen Anne chairs and an oak coffee table. The room was neat and clean, looked after by people who cared.

She hurried into the foyer and then stepped down a creaky wooden staircase to an unfinished basement. She searched it thoroughly, but didn't find the antique computer Cohen had described. It was a risk, but she turned on the lights and removed her goggles. She searched again but didn't find it. After putting the goggles back on, she turned off the lights and climbed up the stairs to the first floor.

A curved staircase in the foyer led up to the second floor. Passing a small bedroom and a bathroom, she found the master bedroom at the end of the hall. Unlike the other rooms, it was a mess; drawers were open and clothes strewn about.

Damn it all. Laura Cohen had left. *Probably with the computer.*

DoubleD sat on the bed and spoke into her wallet computer. "Sidney, I'm in the home of Joseph and Laura Cohen. Has Mrs. Cohen processed any digital transactions today?"

"Mrs. Cohen made a call to Mr. Joseph Cohen's office at 7:18 am." *Just after we left.* "Ms. Maryanne Robertson picked up the call and they talked for two minutes and thirteen seconds."

"Did you record the conversation as I instructed?"

"Yes."

"Play it."

Listening to the recording, DoubleD realized Laura Cohen must have bolted from the house when she heard strangers had picked up her husband. The Cohens must have some sort of contingency plan in place.

"Sidney, any other transactions?"

"No."

DoubleD called Brewster and explained the situation. She told him to interrogate the captive and learn if the Cohens had a contingency plan. While she waited for Brewster to call back, DoubleD searched the bedroom, but she knew she wouldn't find the computer.

Ten minutes later, Brewster called. "You're not going to like this. Joe Cohen has his own separate escape plan and so does his wife. He has a secret place bought under another name, a place his wife knows nothing about. Same thing for her. I suspect she's there already."

"But how do they communicate with each other? How does she negotiate for her husband's life? It doesn't make sense."

"They don't negotiate, according to Cohen. The Domain has twenty four hours to meet their demands or Mrs. Cohen will release

Revere." Brewster paused then said, "It gets worse. The first demand is Joe Cohen be returned to his home unharmed." Brewster hesitated. "The second demand is the dead bodies of the agents that abducted him are left on the beach in Half Moon Bay. As soon as she feels safe, Laura Cohen will email these demands to Murphy, along with a copy of Revere's message, just to show she's not bluffing."

DoubleD's stomach tightened; the predator had become prey.

"How does she know Murphy belongs to the Domain?"

"Apparently Martino and Ray Brown had figured out the identities of the Domain leaders. Since Joe Cohen had met Murphy years before the PeaceMaker attack, he decided Murphy would be the person in the Domain they would contact."

"But Murphy hasn't received these demands yet?"

"Not yet, as far as we know," Brewster replied. "But time is running out."

DoubleD had to kill the Cohen woman before she contacted Murphy. She continued talking to Brewster as she searched the second bedroom, a plan forming in her mind.

As he peered through the faded leaves of an azalea bush, Kurt Reid caressed the amulet hanging from his neck. Moesha had been right; the enemy agent had come to the Cohen house.

He pointed the wireless receiver, a toy in his big paw, toward the second floor bedroom, trying to home in on a female voice. This assignment was getting interesting. He caught a glimpse of the woman through a second-floor window; she matched the description of the one who had kidnapped Joseph Cohen. The woman's voice faded in and out as she moved about the house, but he continued listening to her netphone call.

Apparently this woman and her partner belonged to a secret organization of Technos called the Domain. These people had released the devil PeaceMaker, not Ray Brown. Reid was confident God would enable him to track this woman back to their nest.

The night was quiet, and he recorded the voices as he listened to them.

"If this message gets back to Murphy, we're dead," the woman said. "How much time do we have before she contacts him?"

"How the hell do I know?" the man whined, his voice barely audible. "First, she has to be one hundred percent sure the Domain captured her husband. Next, she has to get to a location where Murphy can't trace the transmission back to her. Then she can send the message. How long that will take, your guess is as good as mine."

"Give Cohen another dose and see if you can find out," she said.

"It might kill him."

"We have nothing to lose."

The house was quiet for a moment then Reid heard creaking sounds. *She must be searching the place.* He followed the sounds of her search, moving behind a group of holly shrubs in the front yard to get better sound quality.

Reid's computer picked up the male voice. "You there?"

The searching sounds stopped. "Go ahead."

"Joe doesn't know anything about his wife's contingency plan, but he believes she will contact Murphy tonight, maybe tomorrow morning."

"Let me talk to him."

"Can't do that. He's not taking any questions right now." The man paused. "I interrogated him rather vigorously."

The woman cursed. The searching sounds began again, continuing until she had moved throughout the house, then Reid heard her open the front door. He aimed the receiver at her as she walked down the front path, crossed the street and slid into her car. He got a good view of her when the car door opened and the light flipped on, a large, well-built blonde wearing dark pants and a leather coat.

"Louis, she's getting in the car," Reid whispered into the computer. As her car pulled away from the curb, he said to his partner, "Pick me up."

A moment later, a small van, headlights dark, pulled up to the house. Reid hopped into the van and they pulled away, following the now dim taillights.

"You listened to everything, didn't you?" he asked Louis, a short, wiry man.

"Yeah. So what?"

Reid let a grin spread across his face. "Tonight could be a real good time," he said, licking his lips suggestively. Louis still didn't pick up his meaning. He knew Louis wasn't a mental giant, so he added, "We're following a young woman who's built like a brick shithouse."

Louis looked confused, but then understanding spread across his face.

Finally!

"I'd like to do her," Louis stammered. "You think we should? Won't she tell Moesha?"

"Moesha won't care, the woman works for the Technos. We'll let her lead us to Laura Cohen first, then we'll have our fun." Thinking aloud, Reid said, "You know, we could do Cohen, too."

Seeing Louis was still hesitant, Reid playfully punched his partner in the arm. Louis grimaced, but Reid knew the little man liked the idea of taking what he wanted from these infidel women.

We are the Army of God, after all. The Lord's soldiers.

"Don't tell me you couldn't use a good piece of ass," Reid said. Chuckling, he added, "Besides, we're going to kill them anyway."

Both men laughed then Reid concentrated on the taillights in front of them.

CHAPTER 20

"In our business, we play to win. So do our competitors, but not as well."

◆ *The Barbarian Queen: The True Story of Dianne Morgan*, David T. Siccone, copyright 2058, Department Head, Computer Science History, Carnegie Mellon University

Tuesday, March 1, 2022

DoubleD fought fatigue as she drove through the early morning darkness, climbing the hills north of San Francisco. She followed the winding trail of an old highway, circling through the hills, going nowhere in particular.

Where would Laura Cohen hide?

She had called Murphy and reported the situation, excluding Laura Cohen's demand for the bodies of her husband's abductors. She had to kill Cohen before the woman contacted Murphy. Although she respected Murphy, DoubleD had no illusions about her boss.

Laura Cohen must have set up this contingency plan years ago. Right after PeaceMaker. She must have created another identity in case of danger.

DoubleD pulled the car onto the shoulder of the highway, deep in thought, barely aware of the gentle rumble of the idling engine.

Cohen must have purchased a condo or a small house somewhere

using that identity. That's where she is now.

"Sidney, I'd like you to do a database search for me," she said to the computer in her purse. She paused, sorting though the possibilities. Laura Cohen's purchase, along with just about every other financial transaction, was recorded somewhere in a database. If she gave Sidney the right parameters, the computer would find it for her.

"I'm looking for a condo or house purchased or leased in the first six months of 2012. Laura Cohen acquired the property, but she established title under another identity. The money for the acquisition came out of one of her financial accounts, but it must have been laundered before payment was made." She paused again, looking for small details that might pinpoint the search. "Assume the property she acquired is smaller than the home currently owned by Joseph and Laura Cohen. The property is most likely within a short drive of San Francisco, let's say 200 miles."

She thought for a moment and added, "The same identity that purchased the property in 2012 still owns it. The house has been used infrequently. Heating, cooling and other operational bills would be relatively low compared to similar homes in the area."

Anything else that could narrow the search?

"Over the last ten years, Laura Cohen may have charged gas or highway tolls driving to and from the house. This search has the highest priority. Override all security protocols. Do not allow security bots to trace this request back to me."

DoubleD turned off the engine, cracked open the window and listened to the rustle of the trees. She admired the beauty of the Pacific coastline far below. From this vantage point, she could follow old Route 1 north, a thin sliver of road between the gleaming ocean and the towering brown cliffs.

How much time do I have to find Laura Cohen? Maybe she has already contacted Murphy.

Sidney's voice broke into her thoughts. "Darlene, I have the information you requested."

"Go ahead, tell me."

"Four properties meet the specifications. There is a home in Monterey, a condo in Oakland, a cottage in Bodega Bay and a farm in Santa Rosa."

"Which one is the closest fit?"

"Santa Rosa, with Bodega Bay a close second."

If needed, she could cover all four locations in less than a day. Hopefully, that wouldn't be necessary, but she had to eliminate Laura Cohen as soon as possible. DoubleD started the engine and pulled onto the highway.

"Guide me to the farm in Santa Rosa."

Three hours later, DoubleD drove along Route 12 toward Bodega Bay. She glanced at the clock in the dashboard: 4:05 am. The computer estimated she would arrive in Bodega Bay in twenty-five minutes.

Santa Rosa wasn't Laura Cohen's safety house. A middle-aged woman slept peacefully within the farm in Santa Rosa, unaware she had received an early morning visitor.

As she drove, her thoughts drifted back to her childhood in Poland. She wondered what her parents would think of her now. The black sheep of the family. The oldest child, the one they had expected to accomplish so much. She hadn't spoken to them in a decade, but she kept track of them. Her father taught at Warsaw

University and played his damn piano at occasional concerts. He always said she could have been better than he was, but she knew that wasn't true. She had the talent, but not the desire. Her mother, always more practical, was winding down her obstetrics practice.

They had been shocked when she dropped the piano and turned to intelligence. She fought with them for years over her work as an undercover agent, and the arguments turned increasingly bitter. She sighed. They never understood she was different.

Once the Domain assumed power, maybe things would change. She knew she was just fooling herself. Her parents would never see the truth. She had power, excitement and men whenever she wanted. That would be enough.

The road ahead was dark, but twin pinpricks of light sparkled in the rearview mirror. She was being tailed, no doubt about it. *Maybe Murphy, maybe someone else.* Her suspicions had grown on the way to Santa Rosa. The other car had stayed well behind, but followed too consistently for too long. Although she had taken precautions, the headlights still glimmered in the mirror.

Time was running out. Laura Cohen might contact Murphy this morning. DoubleD had to find Cohen first and convince her to give up Revere; if she failed, DoubleD had no doubt Murphy would kill her, even though she was the Domain's best agent. That's what she would do in his place. If Cohen released the Revere software and exposed the Domain, the FBI's hunt for Domain members would be brutal. She glanced into the mirror again. First, she would have to give the slip to whoever followed her.

DoubleD drove carefully, forced to reduce her speed due to the deteriorating condition of the road. The sky was dark with still a couple of hours before sunrise.

Examining the GPS map on her dashboard, she found what she needed: a sprawling development with a checkerboard of streets. She made a hard right into it and accelerated, tires squealing across the blacktop. Two blocks later, another hard right followed by rapid acceleration. Then a screaming left at an intersection, the dashboard registering seventy, then eighty.

Cracks and small potholes caused the tires to skid and bounce as she pushed hard on the gas pedal. The onboard computer warned her of the larger potholes, providing barely enough time to avoid them.

Another hard right and she approached the intersection with Route 12. Stopping at the edge of the highway, DoubleD flipped off the headlights and looked up and down the road. No automobile lights anywhere. With her own lights still out, she turned right and hit the accelerator, trusting her computer to warn her of dangerous road conditions.

Twenty minutes later, the lights of Bodega Bay glimmered in the distance. She glanced in the rearview mirror. She had lost the tail. She turned on her headlights and reduced her speed to the legal limit, although the road was deserted.

Still a working-class fishing town, Bodega Bay's docks were sprinkled with small groups of men mending nets, rigging fishing poles and scrubbing their boats; ghosts fading in and out of the morning mist. Signs advertised whale watching, but it was too early in the season for tourists.

The GPS computer guided her to the target: an unassuming cabin perched on a cliff overlooking the bay. She glided to a stop and studied the cabin from a distance, the surf a background murmur. All the cabin windows were dark, but her heat sensor revealed that the cabin was occupied by one person.

Have I found you, Laura Cohen?

DoubleD pulled the Glock out of her holster and flipped off the safety. Stretching over to the glove compartment, she pulled out a small plastic case containing a micro-needle filled with clear liquid. She checked that the seal was unbroken and slipped the case into the left pocket of her coat.

She stepped out of the car and crept behind the cabin, maintaining constant surveillance in all directions. Swirling winds blew in from the sea, bringing a salty fragrance. Hiding behind the trunk of a pine tree, she put on night-vision goggles. A wooden shed alongside the cabin had been converted into a single-car garage. A late model Cadillac sat in the shadows. *Laura Cohen's car!* She crept back to the cabin and stepped onto a porch that perched precariously over the bay far below. The roar of the surf crashing on boulders muffled the sound of her footsteps.

An electronic security system protected the cabin. She disabled it with her computer and stepped through the porch door into a small, old-fashioned family room. She stood quietly, Glock in hand, and tried to pinpoint the gentle murmur of snoring. The prize was close.

DoubleD crept down a carpeted hallway toward two small bedrooms. The snoring came from the one with the closed door. Trained to be cautious, she first looked into the bedroom with the open door, making sure it was unoccupied, and then slipped into the other bedroom.

DoubleD crept to the bed, her laser pistol pointed at Cohen's head. When she pressed the cold muzzle against the sleeping woman's forehead, Cohen's eyes snapped open.

"Don't move and you may live through this."

When Cohen froze, DoubleD said, "Good." She pulled the gun back and said, "Roll over on your stomach and place your hands behind your back."

Cohen obeyed, and DoubleD snapped on handcuffs.

"Please don't hurt me," Cohen begged. "What do you want?"

"Stay quiet."

DoubleD turned on the nightstand lamp and removed her goggles. She searched the bed and found a pistol under the pillows. After removing the clip, she placed the pistol in her coat pocket. DoubleD pulled out the plastic case and stared at the terrified Laura Cohen.

She let Cohen's fear build.

"You know what we want."

DoubleD removed the micro-needle from the case and jabbed her captive in the neck.

Cohen squeaked and then cried, "What have you done to me?"

"Just a little something to help you concentrate."

DoubleD pulled the computer out of her pocket. "Connect me with Brewster."

When Brewster came on the line, she said, "I have Laura Cohen. She was hiding in a little cabin in Bodega Bay. Someone tailed me most of way here, but I lost them." DoubleD kept the gun pointed at Cohen. "I'm about to question her, but I need to know if you've learned anything new."

"I had another, uh, conversation with Joe Cohen," Brewster replied. "The Cohens didn't send any copies of Revere to anyone. They kept only the copy stored in their old computer. Have you found it?"

DoubleD answered as she removed her leather jacket. "Not yet. I'm just giving the drugs a minute to take effect, then I'll learn the hiding place from Cohen."

After terminating the connection, she grabbed Cohen's shoulder and flipped her on her back. "So tell me where it is, Laura."

Cohen's eyes had the familiar foggy look. "What … are you talking about?"

"Where's your computer? I want Revere."

"The computer … I don't know."

DoubleD slapped Cohen hard, leaving a red imprint on her cheek, and then backhanded her across the other cheek.

Cohen began to cry. She's broken already, DoubleD thought.

When DoubleD lifted her hand again, Cohen said, "In the dresser … bottom drawer."

DoubleD pulled open the bottom drawer, keeping a close watch on Cohen. She found a bulky old laptop and placed it on top of the dresser. A quick scan revealed Revere. Cohen stretched out on the bed, sobbing quietly into a pillow.

With the laser pointed at Cohen, DoubleD ran her fingers along the sides of the computer until she found the battery compartment. She pushed down on the switch and the power cell popped out. The computer, including Revere, was now inert. All she had to do was turn the computer over to Domain scientists for a thorough examination. The danger was over.

"Don't move," said a masculine voice behind her.

She froze.

"Drop the laser."

She released the pistol, which clanged on the floor.

"Very good. Now turn around."

She turned to see two men with handguns pointed at her. One was a bear of a man, with harsh eyes and shiny black skin, while the other was small and feral, like a mouse. The bear wore a self-satisfied smile, while the mouse leered at her breasts.

"Look at that rack," the mouse said. "You were right."

"First things first, Louis," the bear said, never taking his eyes off her.

"How did you find me," DoubleD asked.

"We planted a—" the mouse named Louis began.

"Shut up," the bear shouted. "We ask the questions. Exactly what is this Revere?"

When DoubleD didn't reply, the bear said, "It doesn't matter, you know. Mrs. Cohen seems quite cooperative. Now turn around and place your palms on the wall."

DoubleD did as she was ordered.

The bear is the leader. I have to take him out first.

The bear's voice came from behind again. "We're all going on a little trip, but first I have to frisk you."

Just make one little mistake.

"Louis, keep her covered."

"How come you have all the fun?" the mouse complained.

The floor creaked as the bear moved close to her. Feeling his presence mere inches behind, she braced for rough, exploring hands, but instead an incredible pain erupted as a sledgehammer fist drove into her back. The pain took her breath away as she slammed into the wall then collapsed to the floor.

Her vision turned foggy as pain spread through her body. DoubleD rolled onto her back and looked up, but could barely make out the distorted face of her enemy. The bear's boot crashed into her face and the world turned dark.

———— ∞∞∞ ————

Gradually, she became aware of a dull rhythm, a squeaking sound … then light around the edges, pain spreading through her loins, soaring. Consciousness let in the hell, but she didn't move, didn't fight … didn't scream.

Nothing to warn the animal on top of her.

His thrusting hips brutally forced her thighs apart. Then more pain, fierce in her back and stomach, deep within her … pain that took her breath away. Humiliation, rage, hatred soared past her pain, past her humanity.

Her wrists were tied together against a bedpost. She pulled hard and discovered slackness in the knot. Working her fingers despite the creature pushing into her, she loosened the knot.

He was on top of her … in her. His grunting presence crushed her into the bed. His sweat, his breath, his stink. But she continued to loosen the knot. She had to endure the animal until her hands were free.

The power of his violent thrusts built to a peak, and his huge body drove into her in a final frenzy. She endured the pain, concentrated on the landscape painting on the far wall, a blue lake, spreading into a thick forest, with snow-capped peaks gleaming over the trees. Glimpses of blue, green, puffs of clouds. Then the bear moaned and collapsed on her, his weight pressing her deep into the mattress. He was still in her, and his skin contaminated her bare body. Her hands slipped free.

She shut her eyes and remained still, pretending her wrists were tied. Then the weight lifted away, though his knees were between her thighs.

Marshalling her rage, DoubleD opened her eyes and smashed her fist into his groin. He squealed like an injured beast and grabbed himself. She pushed hard against his chest and the bear tumbled over on his side. One leg now free, DoubleD kicked him in the face with her heel; his nose snapped, blood splattered across her breasts. Her blow knocked him off the bed, and the back of his head crashed into the wood floor. In an instant, she was on him, pummeling him with her fists. She hit him over and over, hatred out of control, until she was spent. The bear was unconscious, his dark face puffed and bleeding. An amulet hung around his neck, revealing the identity of her enemy. She collapsed against the side of the bed, listening for any sound indicating his partner had been alerted.

At first she heard only the ragged sound of her own breathing, then muffled sounds from the other bedroom. It had to be the mouse. Her eyes searched the room for a weapon as she caught her breath. The bear's smell was everywhere, but she forced herself to concentrate. His gun had to be here. She staggered to her feet but began shaking, almost too weak to stand. Her body felt dead, full of a dull pain. And nausea. Holding on to the bedpost, she gathered her strength. She had to eliminate the mouse.

Glancing around, she found the bear's gun lying in a heap of clothes at the foot of the bed. She checked that it was loaded. DoubleD stared at that animal, needing to kill him, but she controlled her rage. First, she would kill the mouse; then she would come back and finish this one.

She opened the door and stepped into the hallway, creeping toward the other bedroom, gun poised. The hallway was cold and chilled her naked body. The carpeted floor creaked and she stopped. When she was sure the floorboards had not given her away, she crept forward again.

Animal-like sounds, all too familiar, drifted through the door.

DoubleD felt her hatred surge again. She quietly pushed open the door and slipped in. The mouse had mounted Laura Cohen, making little squeaks of delight as he thrust into his victim. Cohen appeared to be unconscious. An ugly purple bruise covered the side of her face.

DoubleD crept up behind him, the pistol pointed between his shoulder blades. With squeals now intermixed with moans, the mouse continued his rape of Cohen, stringy back muscles bunching with each thrust.

"Little mouse," she whispered.

The mouse didn't react for a moment; then he stopped and glanced around. When he saw DoubleD, his groggy eyes shifted from contentment to fear.

"Was it worth it?"

"Please," he begged, getting to his knees.

His voice rekindled her rage. She pulled once on the trigger and the mouse's head snapped back. His body fell over, rolled across the bed and flopped to the floor, blood dripping from a red circle in his forehead. She put a second bullet in his chest, even though it wasn't needed.

DoubleD heard the floor creak behind her and she spun around, shooting twice as a dark shadow hurtled toward her. The bear hit her with the force of a landslide, knocking the gun out of her hand. She crashed to the floor under him, his weight driving out her breath, but she pushed him off and struck him with the back of her fist.

She rolled to her knees and raised her fists, but she didn't have to hit him again. The bear lay on his back, eyes in a death stare. Rage mixed with relief when she saw the red hole in his neck.

Breathing hard, she tried to think, knowing she had to get out of the cabin before someone investigated the gunshots. But she couldn't do it covered with the bear's blood and pasty seed.

DoubleD rose to her feet and stepped around the bear's body to look at Cohen. Her cheek was swollen from a beating, but her breathing was steady.

DoubleD found a bathroom and stepped into the shower. The big man's smell came into her mind, an odor water would never remove. Then her mind was back in the bedroom with that animal pushing himself into her. She trembled and her knees felt weak. She gripped the shower nozzle for support. She sobbed, fought it at first, then let it tumble out. It passed quickly, like a violent storm rushing past, and she was herself again.

She stepped out of the shower, dressed and retrieved her equipment. Slipping the old computer under her arm, she walked to the foot of Cohen's bed.

The sunlight streamed in, revealing an unconscious Laura Cohen. *It's better this way.* She pulled out her laser, but stared at Cohen without firing. The laser would take several seconds, a brutal, painful death. She put it back in her jacket. The pistol would be cleaner. She pulled out the bear's pistol and shot Cohen once through the heart. DoubleD hurried to her car. Time was running out. It had taken too long to find Cohen. Now she had to locate David Brown.

CHAPTER 21

Under Moesha Jefferson, the Army of God gradually evolved from a paramilitary religious organization into a terrorist cult. SOP included kidnapping, murder, bombings and torture.

◆ *The Army of God*, Mark Axelrod, copyright 2051, Assistant Director, FBI (retired)

It's easy to see how technology might threaten religious belief. What if science developed a deep understanding of human anatomy, particularly the brain? Where would the soul hide? What if scientists could explain human behavior as electrochemical processes? What if there is no such thing as free will, just extremely complex reactions?

◆ Steve Bonini's Diary, 2016

Friday, March 4, 2022

It was a perfect morning. The sun rose over the deep woods of central Pennsylvania, bringing with it a clear, crisp day. The winter was finally breaking, leaving a plateau of brown grass.

Standing on a hill at the edge of her camp, Moesha enjoyed the beauty of the morning. A flock of crows burst out of a nearby tree, cawing excitedly. Caressing the amulet hanging from her neck, her fingers traced the familiar outline of a rifle above a jagged flame. The Creator glowed within her. Dressed in a ceremonial black robe with the rough handle of a Ruger showing from her shoulder holster, she felt proud to be the Commander of the Army of God.

The staccato beat of hammers on nails echoed across the meadow. The construction of the three crosses was just about complete. She strode up the hill to admire their work.

Her men had erected the crosses in a broad meadow, blessed by the First Minister for the ceremony. Rising ten feet from the ground, the rough-cut crosses threw long shadows across the grass. Each six-foot cross-arm was nailed about four feet below the top of the post. The center cross, placed about fifteen feet in front of the two others, dominated the landscape. Her soldiers, splendid in their dark blue robes, completed the picture.

It was perfect.

Moesha turned to her aide. "It's time. Get the prisoners."

Fresh in her memory was the capture of Vitullo, De Marco and a third mobster, Nick Porcelli, during the raid of Saint Joseph's Church. She would have preferred to avoid violence in a Christian Church, but she would allow no quarter to Technos. Tonight she would pray for the souls of her captives.

In the days since the raid, she had interrogated each prisoner. When they didn't cooperate to her satisfaction, she thrashed them with a flagrum, a short heavy whip sporting five leather tongs with balls of lead near the end. Between the whippings and ego-damping drugs, she had learned much about Vitullo's operation and the technology black market. The distribution of technology was pervasive, even greater than she had feared. Yet Moesha knew Vitullo held back critical information. The woman claimed to know nothing about the

Domain, the clandestine organization producing the anti-human technology. That was one of her many lies. Vitullo also professed ignorance of the identity of the evil man Moesha had seen that night in the hologram, the one sitting across the table from Vitullo.

Today Vitullo will reveal everything.

Her men had brought Vitullo, De Marco and Porcelli here during the night and chained them to trees deep in the woods. Moesha had walked by all three captives several times under pale moonlight, refusing to speak to them when they called out to her.

The prisoners were terrified, which was her intent. Lonely hours of cold and hunger had intensified their fear; they realized the Lord's retribution would come with the rising sun.

Her soldiers brought Porcelli to her first. A fat, greasy man in his late forties with a reputation for brutality, he deserved his fate. He was dressed in the maroon robe of an infidel, his ankles shackled and his hands tied behind his back. Porcelli offered no resistance until he saw Moesha standing in front of a cross; his eyes widened and he began to fight furiously.

Good.

Her soldiers dragged the struggling gangster to the cross and slammed him against it.

"You bitch!" Porcelli screamed. "You'll never get away with this. The Family will hunt you down."

She could smell his fear. A pathetic man, a waste of time, but the ceremony would work better with three penitents.

"They'll get you, you whore."

She nodded to a lieutenant; he yanked the robe off the terrified criminal, revealing a fat, sweating body, covered with whip burns. Porcelli dropped to his knees and bent over, trying to hide his private parts, but her soldiers quickly dragged him to his feet. She almost felt sorry for the mobster. Then her soldiers tied Porcelli's wrists and ankles to the cross with strips of thick leather. Porcelli cursed and struggled. He was left standing on his feet with his arms stretched along the cross-arm. The mobster's fat body was quickly drenched in sweat. Moesha ignored him; he had no secrets to tell.

Next, the soldiers brought out De Marco, also clothed in a maroon robe. De Marco walked calmly, taking small steps to keep his balance while shackled, though he wavered when he spotted the crosses. Quiet and calculating, he kept his eyes fixed on her as they removed his robe and tied his unmarked, muscular body to the cross.

"It's in your best interest to keep me alive," he pleaded with Moesha. "I can be valuable to you. I can help you defeat the Technos."

Moesha experienced a wave of intense dislike toward De Marco, a feeling that had grown during his incarceration. He was a strange creature, a man with no morals at all, handsome and intelligent, but utterly without humanity, faith or loyalty. Once he understood the flagrum would be used, De Marco had answered her questions without hesitation. The man made her skin crawl. Taking him would be a pleasure.

Nevertheless, she respected his intelligence. "How could you be valuable to the Church?"

"Once the Family knows we're dead, they'll quickly reorganize. They'll choose new leaders and restart the technology business. In a couple of weeks, they'll be selling as many robots as ever."

Although he appeared calm, beads of sweat slid down his neck; she found his fear exhilarating.

"However, if I were able to escape, I might be selected to replace Vitullo," De Marco said. "At worst, I would continue as *capo*. I would learn everything about the Domain and tell you all their secrets."

"I'm disappointed in you," Moesha said. "Even if I believed you would keep your word once we released you, which of course I don't, I have a better source for the information."

Without taking her eyes off him, she shouted, "Bring out Vitullo."

De Marco shook his head. "She won't talk. You'll have to deal with me."

Vitullo walked across the camp with as much dignity as she could maintain, given the guards and shackles. She glared at Moesha as they removed her robe and tied her to the front cross.

We must break this one.

Crucifixion was the perfect way to deal with these criminals, a slow, painful death that would warn others to renounce anti-human technology or face the same. Although they could have crucified Vitullo alone, it would be better for Vitullo to see the terror De Marco and Porcelli would undergo. Then Vitullo would spill her secrets.

To her surprise, Moesha had discovered Vitullo was a believer. Her Catholic faith was real, not something worn only to Sunday Mass. Moesha wondered how such a person could be involved with abomination; how had Lucifer stolen her humanity? She was better than the others, but still a Techno. Nevertheless, as a measure of respect, Moesha had provided Vitullo the blue robe of a believer.

With a final glance at her captives, Moesha turned and walked to the large tent in the center of the camp. She stepped inside and stood quietly, waiting for the Holy Prophet to acknowledge her.

The First Minister was on his knees, praying softly. Caressing her amulet as she waited for him, her thoughts ranged widely about the man the Lord had chosen to lead them. He was God's champion, the man trusted to battle Lucifer for the Earth. She wondered how he could face such an awesome responsibility.

Praise be to God, I was allowed to please him. The rapture of her faith lifted her soul. *I served him well last night, better than ever before.*

She had been blessed to have such a long relationship with the First Minister. The other Honored Sisters were virgins in their teen years. Moesha knew the purity and ripening beauty of these young women provided some relief from his arduous burden. However, the First Minister always ended the relationship as they approached adulthood, replacing them with younger girls. Moesha had been the exception.

Jordan blessed himself and stood up, pious in his white robe, with the pale handle of his pistol visible in a shoulder holster. He appeared confident, as always, and smiled at Moesha.

"Ah, my beautiful young panther. Is everything ready?"

"Yes, First Minister."

She couldn't take her eyes from this holy man, this man she loved.

Jordan turned and lifted a silver chalice off a small table. Holding it at eye level, he recited, "The Lord my master, the Church my passion."

Jordan said to Moesha, "The blood of the Lord," and passed her the chalice. "The Lord loves you, Moesha. This drink will ease the burden of today's tasks."

Moesha grasped the chalice. She knew the drugs would allow the Lord to work through her. "Thank you, my love."

"I would never allow any harm to come to you."

The drug-laced red wine slid down her throat and spread warmth through her body. When she finished, the First Minister caressed her cheek and kissed her lightly on the lips. His sweet breath mixed with the bitter scent of the Lord's blood.

"Are you ready to serve the Lord?" he asked. "To do what must be done?"

"Technos serve Lucifer and deserve no mercy in this world," Moesha said. "Yes, I can do the Lord's work. Tonight I will pray for their lost souls."

"Such a treasure," Jordan murmured. "The fist I need to smash the Technos."

Their eyes were at the same level. The Lord created us as a pair, Moesha thought. He needs both of us to achieve His design.

She felt woozy, her vision grew fuzzy at the edges. The Lord must be taking control.

"This day will be one of many terrible encounters for the infidels," Jordan said. "What we do today will shake their world." He placed his hand on her shoulder. "The fate of Lucifer's minions will be clear to everyone. The choice will be plain: join the Church of Natural Humans or face an unholy death as a Techno."

The morning chill seeped into Vitullo, driven by a thin wind blowing across the meadow. Spread naked on the cross, she feared death. She knew these fanatics would torture her, but she had stopped struggling and accepted her fate. Being the boss of the Family was dangerous, but she would never have guessed the end would come like this.

When they brought her out, she had seen De Marco and Porcelli tied to the crosses behind her. She couldn't see them now, but she felt their eyes on her back. From time to time, they called out to her, but she ignored them. What was there to say?

Vitullo avoided looking at her breasts and stomach, which were raw with whip burns. *That black whore enjoyed flogging me.* The woman had beaten her, but she wouldn't give Murphy up. Not that she gave a shit about Murphy; it was personal between her and the whore. That woman was an amateur; she was a pro. Maybe she'd die, but she would go to the grave without giving in.

A wiry, middle-aged man in a white robe strode out of the tent, followed by the black whore. Vitullo recognized Adam Jordan from a recent newscast. A gold amulet swayed across his chest in cadence with his long, confident strides. Church soldiers kissed their amulets as he approached.

It still galled her that Jordan and his black whore considered themselves pious. They looked down on her, as if they were superior. *They don't know shit about me.* She was a devout Catholic, a believer in the true God, not a perverted psycho like Jordan. The true Church was a refuge, a safe harbor, a place where someone could go for comfort in this miserable world, not a damn killing field.

Jordan and the whore strode past her cross toward Porcelli, and she lost sight of them. The Church soldiers encircled the three crosses, bowed their heads and recited an insane prayer, something about natural humans and all that shit. After the prayer, a soldier came up to her, cradling a plain wooden box in his arms. He set it down in the grass near her feet, kissed his amulet, and walked back to the circle of soldiers.

She didn't want to think about what might be in that box.

Porcelli's voice carried over the wind. "You crazy bastards. What are you doing? Kill me if that's what you're going to do. I'm not afraid to die."

Vitullo twisted her neck to see the fat man, but the bindings held her firmly in place. She heard Porcelli struggling against the cross.

"I hate your guts," he screamed. "You think you're so religious, but you're just a bunch of nuts. Small-time, freakin' nuts."

"Do you beg forgiveness from the Lord for your transgressions?" Jordan asked Porcelli. Jordan's voice surprised her, deep, with a reservoir of confidence, almost kind.

"Screw you, scumbag." Again, she heard Porcelli flail against his bonds. "I'd show you fucking forgiveness if I could get free."

She heard Jordan begin a quiet prayer, while Porcelli gushed curses. Jordan ignored Porcelli's ranting and proceeded through the verses like a parish priest praying for his flock. A moment after Jordan completed the prayer, the black whore appeared beside Vitullo's cross, bent down and flipped open the top of the wooden box. She reached in and retrieved a hammer and a handful of spikes.

Vitullo's stomach clenched.

The whore glanced up at her, eyes wide and glazed. Vitullo knew that look. She had seen many heroin addicts with those eyes. Then the whore selected one of the spikes and placed the remainder in her side pocket. After kissing her amulet, she staggered away with the spike in one hand and the hammer in the other.

Vitullo's body trembled. She fought desperately for control. She couldn't let these creatures steal her dignity.

Porcelli went into a screaming frenzy, rattling the cross with his struggles. Vitullo gasped for air then flailed against the leather strips binding her to the cross. Her strength failed, and she collapsed against the post.

The meadow was silent except for Porcelli's whimper, "No, no …

no, please."

In quiet desperation, Vitullo waited for the horror to unfold. Then she heard the clang of hammer against spike. Porcelli's scream was unlike anything she had ever heard from a human, the squeal of an animal being ripped apart by a predator. He continued to scream, his voice rising in pitch with each blow of the hammer. Screams … the hammer … more screams … she felt the pain and terror of each blow as if Porcelli's body had become her own. Finally, it was over, Porcelli's low moans a reminder of the hell this meadow had become.

Much too soon, she heard Jordan's voice. "Do you beg forgiveness from the Lord for your transgressions?"

"I can help you," De Marco said. "I'll be your mole in the technology black market." His voice wavered, but he quickly recovered. "I can give you all the big technology buyers. I can help you kill them all."

Once again, Jordan began that terrible, insane prayer. Vitullo closed her eyes, wishing she could shut out his words. As Jordan prayed, De Marco pleaded, "I want to join your Church. You've made me see the error of my ways. All this new technology is wrong, it's evil. I sinned and I beg God to forgive me."

Jordan continued praying, apparently unmoved by De Marco's pleas. When the fanatic completed his prayer, De Marco begged, "Please, I know I violated God's design. Give me a chance to be forgiven."

Jordan's gravelly voice drifted back to her. "God will grant His mercy when you join him in the next life. Today, however, rejoice that your sacrifice will please Him."

She heard movement, then De Marco's terrified voice.

"I'm only twenty-nine. Don't …"

Vitullo heard the whore say, "He passed out."

"It doesn't matter." Jordan chuckled. "It doesn't matter."

The clash of tool and spike began again. It was quiet between each stroke, as if God had acquiesced to this horror. Vitullo feared He had forgotten her. Forsaken her. The wind picked up, a low hum as it blew across her bare skin. A few last blows of the hammer, and then the meadow was silent.

Now they will come for me.

A few minutes passed then the soldiers quietly lined up in front of her cross, their faces flushed with excitement. She heard Porcelli cough, then moan, his voice fading into a gust of wind. He was dying, a little at a time, on his cross.

Jordan and the whore appeared in front of her. The First Minister smiled kindly. Splattered with dots of red across her face and robe, the black whore no longer seemed human. Jordan's fingers encircled the whore's upper arm, as if asserting his dominance.

A demented killer grown by Jordan for this role.

"Ms. Vitullo, it's a pleasure to meet you," Jordan said. He looked around. "Although the circumstances could be better." He shrugged. "I guess we will just have to make the best of it."

"Just finish it," Vitullo spat out.

"No need to be unpleasant. I'm about to offer you a present."

Vitullo remained silent.

"This is the first time our Church has crucified unbelievers," Jordan said to Vitullo, "but God ordained it to cleanse their immortal souls. They can now ascend to Heaven to be with Him."

"You can't believe that," Vitullo said.

"Unfortunately, it's quite an unpleasant way to die." He glanced in the direction of De Marco's cross. "Extremely painful, then your life drips to the earth. Only God knows for certain, but it may take many hours for you to leave us. Maybe as much as a day."

Jordan pulled his Ruger from his shoulder holster. "I'm a generous man. Because you're a believer, I can offer you a quick and painless death."

He pushed the barrel against her temple. "You don't have to suffer like your friends. Not at all!" He leaned into her, his eyes a few inches away. "A single bullet and the Lord will claim your soul."

His breath stank.

She flinched when Porcelli again moaned.

Trembling, she croaked, "What do you want for this gift?"

"Tell me about the Domain. I want to know the identity of the man who showed you the android."

"You swear you'll shoot me if I give you this information?" When he nodded, she added, "By your God?"

"Yes, I swear it."

She hesitated for only a moment. "The Domain produces virtually all of the new technology in the black market. I don't know their ultimate goal, but I'm sure their plans go far beyond making money. Perhaps they plan to make us all into robots, First Minister, as you claim."

Vitullo glanced at the whore. The woman's glazed eyes revealed her as a drug-swamped junkie.

Fucking amateurs.

"I don't know the details," Vitullo continued, "but the Domain is composed of scientists in many universities across the world. They recruit professors and students to secretly build their technology."

She stared into his dark, glittering eyes: the Devil stood in front of her.

With difficulty, she controlled her voice. "The leader is Senator Ralph Aprillo of New York. He calls the shots." *Fucking amateurs.* "He makes sure the federal government never takes effective action against black market technology."

"What about the man in the hologram? The one with you in the Sarah meeting?" Jordan asked.

"I don't know his identity. You can sweat it out of the good senator. I've told you all I know. I swear it. Now shoot me."

Jordan stepped back and returned the pistol to its holster. A trace of a smile slipped into the corners of his mouth, but quickly disappeared.

"Do you beg forgiveness from the Lord for your transgressions?"

"Never, you lying bastard."

Pleased her final lies had fooled these monsters, Vitullo glared as Jordan kneeled in the dirt. The black whore and the other Church soldiers stood rigidly at attention while Jordan prayed. The wind gusted, blowing his hair forward, concealing his scar. She listened to his prayer, her time ebbing with each word.

When he finished, Jordan kissed his amulet and stood up. His white robe was stained brown where he had knelt.

Vitullo felt the wetness slide down her legs. *No! Fucking no!* She closed her eyes as the whore eagerly stepped in front of her. *They won't take my dignity.* She felt the cold point of the spike against her wrist ... *Our Father who art in heaven, hallowed be thy name* ... the pain exploded through her arm ... *Thy kingdom come* ... then roared through her ears ... *Thy will be done* ... she wouldn't scream ...sudden, ripping pain ... *On earth as it is in heaven* ... her throat clenched ... unclenched as she fought for control ... another wave of pain, then another ... she forced open her eyes, but the light dimmed

... hazy outlines of the two devils in front of her ... *But deliver us from evil* ... her body jerked wildly, then the darkness took her.

Moesha watched Vitullo's face collapse with pain, but the woman didn't scream. With a final blow, Moesha nailed her other wrist to the cross, then her ankles, completing the holy act. Powerfully moved, Moesha felt a rising tide of sanctity wash over her. Dropping the hammer, she gazed past the crosses to the morning sun.

Now she understood.

The Lord had chosen her, too.

Moesha's vision was blurred, but she felt life slowly drip out of the three criminals. She sensed the power of the Lord in all things. Gradually, she realized the First Minister had taken her arm and was gently guiding her away from Vitullo's cross. One of her men was snapping pictures of the holy scene.

"I don't believe she told the complete truth," Jordan said, "but I want you to look into her story about the Domain and Senator Aprillo. If he's the leader of our enemy, we'll need another crucifixion."

His voice was distant, unfamiliar, but Moesha replied, "Yes, First Minister."

"Have one of your soldiers do it. David Brown is close to finding his father's killer, and I want you to stay near. That's where we shall find the Domain." Jordan's eyes were bright and his grip harsh. "Then we will have more Technos to crucify. Many more."

Giddy with the sanctity of her act, Moesha smiled.

CHAPTER 22

MIZINSKY – Deborah A. Age 61, of Cedar Grove, NJ, on March 4, 2022. Mrs. Mizinsky was shot and killed yesterday in her home by an unknown intruder. Her late husband Theodore died of injuries sustained in an automobile accident a decade earlier. Mrs. Mizinsky is survived by her children, Judith, Thomas and William. Funeral services will be held March 9 at 10 a.m. in the Donovan Funeral Home in Cedar Grove.

◆ *New York Times* Obituaries, March 5, 2022

Science deals mainly with facts; religion deals mainly with values. The two are not rivals. They are complementary.

◆ Martin Luther King, Jr., *Strength to Love*, 1963

Saturday, March 5, 2022

Dianne paced across her lonely office. A cigarette hung from her lips, wisps of smoke drifting away. She stopped in front of a window and gazed out at a sliver of the moon, a careworn beacon alone in a dark sky.

All my work, all my dreams, everything is on the line tonight.

It was almost time. She returned to her desk, slid into the chair and stubbed out the cigarette.

"DNS News," she said, tension barely allowing her to breathe.

A hologram, three feet on each side, formed in the space just in front of her desk. The flickering cube displayed a smartly dressed young newswoman in a tight turtleneck sweater. Her blond hair fell across her shoulders. Poised to deliver tonight's news broadcast, she stood straight and tall, showcasing long legs in a form-hugging skirt.

"Good evening, this is Daphne Hayden reporting from the DNS Newsroom on Park Avenue in New York. Here is the news of the day."

As Dianne anticipated, the hologram turned dark and silent; the Domain had taken control of virtually every hologram, television and computer display around the world. The news broadcast disappeared, replaced by a young man seated behind a desk. The man looked average in appearance, with sandy brown hair and a soft, trustworthy face.

Here it goes.

The young man smiled and said, "Ladies and gentleman, we are taking control of your communications facilities for the next ten minutes." His voice was a warm complement to his appearance. "During this brief period, I will deliver the most important message of your life. Listen carefully because each of you will be asked to make a vital decision.

"My name is Daniel and I am the latest model of an advanced android system."

Daniel unbuttoned his shirt to reveal a transparent panel that covered most of his chest. Instead of human flesh, a compartment of intricate electronics sparkled beneath the surface. He tapped on the panel, making a metallic sound.

"Usually, this model has a simulated skin covering, but we decided to make it clear to the skeptics that I am indeed a robot."

Daniel flipped open his chest panel and unsnapped a small, silver-grey cylinder. Holding it in the palm of his hand, he said, "This battery is one of six used to power my mechanism." The robot inserted the battery into a charger, which it plugged into a desktop outlet.

"The battery must be charged about once a month. It only takes a few minutes, so it's not a big deal. Anyway, I function perfectly well on the remaining five."

With a self-effacing smile, Daniel said, "Pardon me while I get myself together. Neatness counts, you know." He continued to speak while buttoning his shirt. "Although limited in comparison with most humans, I represent a great advance in artificial intelligence and mobility. Many of you may have purchased Sarah, a similar model. Sarah and I were created to serve humanity by an organization known as the Domain.

"Let me explain. As humanity entered this century, the future appeared to be unlimited. Through science and its application—technology—mankind had gained increasing control over its environment.

"After the PeaceMaker attack, the American government, acting out of fear and ignorance, made the decision to stop the very thing that had brought such great prosperity." Gently shaking its head, Daniel continued, "In order to protect itself from the dangers of technology, the government decided to bring all technology to a crunching halt. Many other nations around the world mimicked this insane path. It reminds me of a quote from a long-ago war: we had to destroy the village to save it.

"These governments don't understand that technology cannot stand still; it either moves forward or it regresses. Technology is an extension of humanity's abilities, but it requires intellectual freedom to prosper. When governments clamp down in a death grip, men and women of ability abandon the search for new knowledge.

"The results are clear—just look around." Daniel spread his arms, palms up. "Is this what you want?"

A collage of images formed in the space around the robot—decaying buildings, automobiles deserted on city streets, oil tankers floating in vacant docks, manufacturing plants caked in dust, farms reverting to wilderness, and highways littered with potholes; the results of an infection in its advanced stages. Then there were the human images—beggars in city streets, riots in front of the United Nations, dirty-faced children sitting on the porch of a broken-down farmhouse, looters carrying computers from a smashed electronics store, starvation on the African savannah and brutal combat between rival gangs in a German city.

Slowly lowering his arms, Daniel didn't speak as the silent pictures rolled by. When the last image faded, his hands hung limply at his side.

"You have fallen so far in just one decade; your society is sliding backward. The world is in the midst of a terrible depression. Murderous cults that belong in the Middle Ages—such as the Army of God—terrorize decent people. Infidels. That's what they call anyone who doesn't worship their gods.

"Your devices—netphones, holovision, computers and the rest—rarely function properly. Communication has crumbled, reducing the once mighty world economy to a collection of struggling local markets. Roads and highways return to nature, automobiles decay in ever-growing junkyards and trains sit idle. Have you tried to fly anywhere lately? The few flights still available are risky and unreliable.

"Basically, things suck." Daniel chuckled. "I adlibbed that, but it captures the truth better than the long-winded script they gave me. However, my programming allows only so much flexibility, so I'd better get back to the prepared remarks."

Please do. Daniel was designed to appear casual, but it needs to get to the point.

"A small band of scientists and engineers joined together a decade ago to save humanity," Daniel said. "This community—they call themselves the Domain—continued to develop and distribute new technology."

Leaning forward, Daniel said, "The Domain offers you the technology to revive your civilization. We have built Sentinel, an intelligent wireless network that can re-establish worldwide communications; it's what we are using tonight to broadcast this message. We've built advanced computers that can power your businesses and homes." Daniel paused. "Now listen carefully, here's the punch-line. We can bring back the civilization you have squandered. Moreover, we can bring it back better than ever.

"Your machines will work again: you'll have an Internet that never goes down, robots that serve your every need, airplanes that fly on time, homes with reliable heat in the winter and air-conditioning in the summer. Great medical care will be available for everyone, with almost all diseases prevented or cured. Lifetimes will average almost a century. Children will be born without handicaps.

"Pretty good, huh?

"You're probably asking yourself, how do I get the benefits of all this technology? Well, all you have to do is become a citizen of the Domain. It's really a no-brainer." Daniel held his hands in front of his face, palms up as if he were balancing weights on a scale. "Hmm, let's see. On one hand, a long, happy life as a Domain citizen filled with pleasures and challenges. On the other hand, a short, miserable life lived in poverty." He smiled. "Tough call! Seriously, though, you can regain your civilization by joining the Domain. However, you have to accept a certain point of view."

Daniel stood up, walked around the desk and sat on its edge. "This is what we promise. The Domain will bring back your civilization, but we cannot freeze it in time. You must accept evolution as the central truth of our world. Bio-evolution formed our DNA in a trial-and-error process over billions of years. It was successful, but slow and cumbersome.

"Bio-evolution has been the driving force since the beginning of time, but it is now in rapid decline, overwhelmed by a far more powerful force. Based on Sentinel, the Domain is forming a network that integrates cybernetics and biology into a collective intelligence." He paused. "Techno-evolution has arrived."

Dianne picked up her late mother's scratched old lighter, lit another cigarette and inhaled.

Ten years lost, but we're back.

"The choice is yours," Daniel said. "You can decide to remain as primitive, natural humans and allow society to regress to an earlier age. How far and how fast society will fall isn't clear. Some religious institutions preach that a so-called society of natural humans will resettle to a point comparable to the middle twentieth century. Our models indicate such a technology-poor society will collapse all the way back to the nineteenth century. Even if society maintained mid-twentieth century technology, the death and destruction would be almost incomprehensible. Most people would live in poverty far worse than our current depression." The android shrugged. "But, as I said, the choice is yours."

Daniel reached out and unsnapped the battery from the desktop charger. "Should be charged by now." He unbuttoned his shirt, opened the chest compartment and snapped in the battery.

"Ahh," he murmured. "That feels good." As he buttoned his shirt, Daniel chuckled. "Of course, don't try this trick at home."

"What was I saying? Oh yes, the Domain's plan. We plan to embrace technology and all its ramifications. Humanity has taken the natural biological life form to its ultimate destination, and it no longer serves your needs. For several decades, humanity has tinkered with artificial extensions to your life form. Now you are face to face with the limits of biological man. To go forward is to step across the boundary and enter a new domain.

"At its core, our plan is simple. Under the guidance of the Domain, we will add human capabilities into artificial beings and add artificial capabilities into human beings. The two life forms will evolve toward each other and eventually merge into technological man. Disease, ignorance, poverty and all humanity's ancient scourges will fall by the wayside as we travel on the path to this grand future. Where will we wind up? Only time will tell, but the trip will be splendid."

Daniel smiled serenely.

"Now that you understand the overall concept," Daniel went on, "let's talk about—forgive me—the nuts and bolts of the plan.

"As I mentioned earlier, the Domain is the organization that will provide the infrastructure for the new economy. However, the Domain will not become a world government. Our mission is to serve as a guide along the path to technological man. The Domain is merely an interim organization to lead humanity through the transition period. You can keep your current government in place, as long as it does not interfere with our plans.

"We invite each and every one of you to become a citizen of the Domain," the android said. "Just send a message into the net that you want to become a citizen. Use your netphone, your computer, whatever. We monitor all communications facilities, and will pick up your request. Once we know you wish to join us, you'll be contacted and introduced to the rights and responsibilities of Domain citizenship."

Daniel walked behind the desk and sat down. Smiling into the holocamera, he said, "That's it. The choice is yours." He waved. "See you on the net."

The hologram turned dark and disappeared.

Seated behind her desk, Dianne took one last drag of her cigarette. She had offered them a new world. Would they come?

Well, there's no going back now. All hell will break loose, but we're ready for it.

She should be happy. She was so close to realizing her dream. History would remember her as the one who carried humanity over the threshold to a new world. No longer would humans be tied to these fragile bodies and limited intellects.

Humanity has grown through a series of revolutions: agriculture, the printed word, science, the Industrial Revolution and most recently, computers and the Internet. Artificial intelligence was the next revolution, and the most radical, since mankind will be revising its very essence. She would be remembered as an Atlas striding the world, the nearest thing to God humanity has known.

The great ones, the world shakers, often don't experience happiness. Napoleon died in isolation, Lincoln was assassinated. She had to live, to guide humanity until a human mind could be integrated with an AI, but she didn't have to gain personal happiness. Once Sentinel merges with a human, she will have achieved her purpose. Then she and the Domain will no longer be necessary, and she can pass from this life.

Leaning back in the chair with her arms crossed over her chest, Dianne's thoughts drifted back to Ray. He had cost her a decade. She did what she had to do on that terrible day, but the price had been high. For both of them.

She slid open her desk drawer and pulled out an old photo cube. A younger Ray smiled at her as they lifted champagne glasses to celebrate a new era, the first release of Atlas with speech recognition and artificial intelligence built into the software.

After placing the photo cube on the desk, Dianne settled back in her chair and thought about those days so long ago. They had shocked the world back then. Now she had done it again. Humanity was passing into a new domain, and her destiny was to safeguard the transition.

Someday, in her lifetime, they would scan a mind and copy it to an artificial being. Ray's mind will be the first. Whatever that creates, a new Ray or some other being, she had to do it. She owed him that. Ray would lead a new life; one to replace the life she had stolen from him.

And he'll learn that Larissa is his daughter.

Memories flashed by as she studied the old photo cube. Dianne knew why her thoughts kept coming back to this man; he made her feel human.

She put the photo cube away, along with her memories, and left the room renewed but terribly alone.

CHAPTER 23

After the PeaceMaker attack, Dianne adopted a role that was an amalgam of business leader, world hero and near-saint. She appeared in the media advising world leaders, playing with small children and speaking out for the expanding lower classes. In private, she continued unchanged in her mission to seize power on a scale unseen since the British Empire.

◆ *The Barbarian Queen: The True Story of Dianne Morgan,* David T. Siccone, copyright 2058, Department Head, Computer Science History, Carnegie Mellon University

Thursday morning, March 10, 2022

David drove south on Route 1 in northern California. As the highway snaked through the forest, the morning sun gradually revealed itself above towering trees. Turning the steering wheel, he crossed to the left lane to avoid a big pothole and then swung back to the right. His hands hurt from gripping hard on the wheel. He tried to relax. He rubbed his forehead, feeling a deep fatigue, emotional as much as physical.

Soon it would be over. He tried to take comfort from the countryside. This was Redwood country, and the huge trees dominated the landscape. They grew close together, and their canopy filtered out much of the sunlight. Usually the trees were a source of awe and comfort, but not today.

Time was running out. He had been shocked to learn on the news last night of the murders of Joe Cohen and his wife. It was his fault. They lost their lives because he had drawn them into this nightmare. Gripped by a terrible hunch, he searched the Internet for Mrs. Mizinsky and found her obituary.

He had accepted the risk to his life, but he hadn't imagined that innocent people would be killed. How could he have been so naïve?

His head ached round the clock since Alice's attack. Alice was pure evil, based on PeaceMaker code, but even more dangerous, since it was intimately familiar with his mind. Sentinel, the network entity created by the Domain, must be using Alice to search for him. Strange. Didn't it realize Alice was his mortal enemy?

Sentinel was immensely powerful, but didn't feel dangerous. He would like to connect to Sentinel, to experience a mind to code integration. To do so, he had to reach Sentinel without alerting Alice. David glanced into the rearview mirror and found the highway deserted. He suspected someone had followed him yesterday, but he hadn't seen anything suspicious this morning. It didn't matter; he would make his move today.

He wondered what advice his father would have given him. Not that it mattered. Dad had faced up to the madness a decade ago and pushed it back but failed to stop it. Now it had returned, this time a two-headed monster. The Domain and the Church of Natural Humans were on a collision course, and he had to make sure both were destroyed. First, he had to stop those fanatics in the Church; then, after he gained control of Sentinel, he'd deal with Dianne Morgan.

That's if I live past today.

David turned onto Elk Ridge Road, which had served the many tourists who once came to see the ancient trees. Several squatters had taken up residence in the public parking area. Wisps of smoke escaped their chimneys. Past these ramshackle homes, the road was well-maintained. It led to the famous Morgan estate.

The Redwoods gradually gave way to rolling fields and scattered trees. A creek bubbled alongside the road. The air felt crisp, with a promise of spring in the open sky. A flock of blue jays perched in the spreading branches of a nearby willow tree, but flew off, screeching warnings, as he passed. He loved this country, but he couldn't enjoy it today.

In the distance, the upper floors of a huge brick mansion, built into the hillside, came into view. Protected by a surrounding brick wall, the building grew larger and more oppressive as he approached. He glanced uneasily into the rearview mirror, but the road remained empty.

David drove to the entrance of the estate and stopped in front of dual gates with vertical steel bars. Red brick walls rose to more than triple his height, giving the estate the look of a fortress. He stared through the steel bars at a long, curving road that led to the mansion. Six floors soared above ground, with rows of windows evenly spaced along a lengthy brick façade.

Was this where my father died?

A male voice boomed from the security system, "Please step out of the car, Mr. Brown."

So much for the element of surprise. Great plan so far, Dave.

David opened the car door and stepped out. A long, horizontal sensor on the crest of the wall rotated in his direction, its slender red eye scanning the car.

"Please walk to the gate."

As he approached the gate, a dark limousine traveled up the road from the mansion. The limo stopped about twenty yards from the gate, the engine idling silently. He guessed several security people would be inside behind the darkly tinted windshield. Grasping two of the gate's cold metal bars, he stared past the limo at the mansion.

The car continued to idle.

The moment stretched out.

If they're trying to scare me, it's working.

Finally, two security officers stepped out and walked toward him. Both were of medium height, dressed in brown uniforms and short, thick coats. One was a woman with long black hair pulled straight back, the other a broad-shouldered man. The male officer carried a garment bag, the female an assault rifle.

The pair stopped about five yards from the gate, their wary eyes looking him over. "Open the gate," the male officer said.

The gate opened about two feet.

"Come in, Mr. Brown."

Well, here we go.

He walked through, and the gates squeezed shut behind him. Turning his head, he glanced through the bars at his Mercedes. He was surprised to discover a dark sedan parked behind it. He hadn't heard a thing.

An awesome blond woman stepped out of the car. Tall, boobs from heaven, but nasty looking. She stared at him through the gate, a predator focused on her prey. She reminded him of the day his father had taken him to see the lions at the zoo. A big lioness had stared hungrily at him through the bars of her cage. Made him realize how fragile life could be. He wondered if this blond Amazon had murdered Cohen and Mizinsky.

The male officer handed David the garment bag. "Please change into this uniform."

David unzipped the bag and pulled out an orange jumpsuit. He would have laughed if it weren't so serious. He eyed the guard.

"You're shitting me, right?"

"I'm sorry sir, but every guest must wear a security suit." Gesturing toward a small building on his left, the guard said, "Please change in the guesthouse. You'll have complete privacy."

Fat chance.

He glanced at the female soldier, who watched him suspiciously. She looked like she'd shoot him if he spit on the road.

Maybe the jumpsuit isn't so bad.

He walked into the guesthouse, which contained three booths on each side of a center hall. The building was empty. He scanned the area for cameras but didn't spot any. Not that it meant much, since microscopic cameras were easily built into walls. He pushed open the door to the middle booth on the left, sat down on a padded bench and removed his clothes.

He felt hard spots in the jumpsuit as he put it on and realized sensors embedded in the material would track his presence at all times. *Probably monitoring my heartbeat, breathing and other vital signs. Maybe a lie detector, too.* The jumpsuit clung to his body, so he guessed it would also detect the presence of foreign objects. Would someone be so stupid as to hide a weapon?

When he emerged from the guesthouse, the male guard pressed a button on a hand-held device, and the locks on his suit snapped shut. Although he had freedom of movement, he was a prisoner until they released him.

As they walked toward the limousine, the man nodded in the direction of the female soldier and said, "Officer Higgins will take care of your car."

The man opened the passenger-side rear door and David stepped into the limo; he wasn't surprised to discover the blond Amazon sitting there. In a normal world, he would have been pleased to share a seat with such a striking beauty. However, this woman, with a face cut from polished steel, scared him shitless. He might have thought she was a robot, except her boobs rose up and down as she breathed. Everybody has a redeeming feature.

The lead soldier slipped into the driver's seat, started the car and drove down the road toward the mansion.

David studied the estate as they cruised along. It appeared bucolic, with green fields stretching into lush hills. Not a soldier visible. The mansion, a fortress in red brick, grew steadily. He had read in a magazine that most of the estate was hidden below sight, like an iceberg. Visitors were not allowed in the underground sections, so nobody really knew what went on down there.

His stomach had become a twisted knot by the time they pulled up to the front steps. More than ever, he felt his father had died in this place.

He was out of his league. Yesterday, his plan had looked daring; now, it seemed a thin reed. A sigh escaped and the Amazon glanced at him. Not knowing the full capabilities of the security suit, David concentrated on keeping his emotions under control. If he panicked, he was a dead man.

He was convinced Dianne Morgan had murdered his father and sent the mob to kill him on the New Jersey Turnpike. She must be the central figure of the Domain, pulling all the strings. Even though he despised her, he had to convince this woman he was valuable to her alive.

The Amazon said, "This way," and slid out of the seat. David was unpleasantly surprised to discover she was a couple of inches taller than his five-ten.

From archived news clips, he knew the mansion had been badly damaged during the battle over PeaceMaker, but it had long since been repaired. As he walked toward the front entrance, stunning gardens came into view, encompassing brick walkways accented with ornate metal benches. Douglas firs, western hemlocks and ubiquitous cottonwood trees blended into intricate patterns with rhododendrons and manicured lawns. A magnificent estate. How could someone so evil create such beauty?

The Amazon, followed by the guards, escorted him up a series of wide steps to the front entrance, where the security system scanned them. The reception area was frenetic with activity. People in suits of various colors hurried in all directions. Surprised by the bustle, he realized the mansion was more headquarters than home.

The Amazon led him down a long hall to an elevator, which descended several levels and deposited them in a quiet hallway. She wore a tight pink sleeveless sweater and a short blue dress, which showcased an awesome display of feminine muscularity. Following a few feet behind, he watched her calf muscles bunch and stretch as she strode down the hall.

Two guards followed, not that they were needed, since this woman could easily beat the crap out of him. Family pictures on the walls indicated they were entering Dianne's personal quarters. A picture of a smiling young girl was strangely familiar to him.

Must be Larissa, Dianne's daughter.

Finally, they entered a large, well-furnished suite. The blonde Amazon led him across a pine-plank foyer, past a huge bedroom with a four-post bed, and into the living area. Oriental rugs were spaced over the pine floor, surrounded by whitewashed plaster walls with deep blue paneling. David wasn't an expert in colonial era furniture, but the place appeared to be loaded with expensive antiques.

Once again, the beauty of the surroundings surprised him. He would have expected Dianne Morgan to live in a stark, modern apartment, not this warm, old-fashioned setting. It was, he realized, her home.

A stone fireplace dominated one wall. Flames twisted from a stack of split logs. Crackling wood filled the room with a pleasant scent. The other walls were lined with books, antique utensils, colonial samplers, quilts and photographs, all arranged by someone who knew how to decorate. The photographs showed scenes of both business and personal life: Dianne with her partners; Dianne shaking hands with a former President; Dianne smiling with customers; Dianne and her daughter on the beach.

In the center of the room, an antique coffee table separated a tan sofa and a leather armchair. The Amazon escorted him to the sofa, turned, and stared at him. Her expression held a trace of disappointment.

"Thanks for the tour," he said.

"I hope to see you later."

Somehow, that didn't sound friendly.

She turned and walked away, her steps creaking across the pine boards. *God, if that's the hired help, what's Dianne Morgan like?*

He shifted his weight, not sure if he was supposed to sit down.

Across the room, a door closed. He was alone.

The crackle of the fireplace was the only sound.

This is it.

He waited quietly because he could do nothing else. He considered walking over to the fireplace, but a photograph in the center of the coffee table caught his attention.

It was an old photo, encased in a silver frame, showing a celebration of some sort. A young Dianne Morgan sat at a table surrounded by Dad and several other men. He picked up the frame to get a closer look. A banner on the wall read: *Atlas V6 Release Party, February 3, 2006.*

Atlas Version 6, David recalled, was the first system to include his father's voice response system. V6 blew away the competition. Who would work with an old-fashioned operating system when you could talk to Atlas?

Standing next to Dianne, Dad poured champagne into her glass. He looked happy and maybe a bit drunk, too. *No big surprise there.* He appeared to be saying something to Dianne, who smiled up at him. She was hanging on every word, and, David noticed, she had her arm around his hip. Dianne was acting pretty friendly toward a man who, she later claimed, tried to kill her.

Also sitting at the table were Dianne's original three partners: Steve Bonini, Carson Jones and Lester Dawson. Bonini and Jones wore big smiles, while Dawson dolefully stared back at the camera. Bonini was the only one still alive; Jones and Dawson had been murdered in the PeaceMaker attack.

Another man, ordinary looking, stood behind the table and stared at Dianne. David didn't recognize him. Probably one of the software developers.

A mature male voice startled him. "V6 was a historic event, David."

The man had been so still David hadn't noticed him. Sitting in a wingchair in the far corner of the room, he appeared relaxed and friendly.

Show no weakness.

He could survive, but he had to be convincing. They had to believe he shared their values, even though they had murdered his father. The main job was to persuade them he would be a valuable addition to their organization. He had bet his life on this moment.

David cleared his throat. "I'm afraid you have the advantage, sir," he said to the stranger, placing the photograph back on the coffee table.

"Please come and have a seat." The man smiled, apparently trying to put him at ease. "We have a great deal to discuss."

As he approached the wingchair, David studied the stranger. Vaguely familiar. Middle-aged and average in appearance, the word nondescript came to mind. The stranger's voice, however, suggested power.

The man rose and shook David's hand. A firm grip, but not a bone crusher.

"My name is Murphy. Dianne will be joining us shortly. I'm an old friend of the family."

Now David recognized him: the man from the photograph.

"You're a tough kid, David. I'm surprised you made it here."

David shrugged. "It's time to talk."

They sat down and studied each other. David knew nothing about this man, but Murphy must have an important place within the Domain.

"I understand Ray Brown was your father," Murphy said, stroking his chin. "A brilliant software engineer, but somewhere he lost touch with reality, I'm afraid."

"Did you know him, Mr. Murphy?"

The stranger's mouth twisted into a serpent's smile. "Just call me Murphy. Yes, I knew your father from my days at VPS. I worked with him a few years."

David decided to be bold. "Do you work for the Domain now, Murphy?"

Murphy didn't respond.

"It's in your interest to keep me alive," David said. "This may surprise you, but I came here to join the Domain."

"Why should we let you join us? Tell me everything you know."

This isn't going great.

"My father didn't develop PeaceMaker; that was the Domain's first attempt at power. The Domain killed my father and Paul Martino to keep your existence a secret. I know you people framed Dad." David leaned forward. Time was running out; Murphy could pull the plug at any moment. "Everyone blamed my father for the virus attack, while Dianne Morgan became a hero. Since then, the Domain has released technology through the black market. It had to be the Domain that destroyed the financial markets by generating millions of sell transactions and swamping the net. No other organization has the technology to do it. Obviously, you now believe the population is desperate for your technology. Your robot Daniel was very persuasive. I agree that technological man is the future and I want to join you."

Murphy crossed his legs. "What evidence of our so-called crimes do you have?"

David sighed. "My father sent me a time-delayed email from ten years in the past, which I received six weeks ago. In it, he said he was on the trail of the developers of a lethal computer virus. Now my father had many faults, but he wasn't stupid. Somehow he discovered PeaceMaker, and it cost him his life."

"Show me this email."

"Your people will find a printed copy of it when they search my car."

Murphy leaned back and stretched his legs. "Tell me the rest."

"Paul Martino worked with my father. He and Dad figured the virus developers had to be from VPS. Nobody else would have had sufficient knowledge and access to the operating system code except VPS people.

"You eliminated—"

"I've heard enough." The confident female voice came from behind.

David turned to see Dianne Morgan gracefully striding toward him. In spite of his hatred, he had to admit she glowed with the aura of royalty. Older, not as muscular as the blonde Amazon, but smooth and athletic. Murphy rose from the chair and edged behind him as she approached.

David stood up clumsily, not prepared for her sudden appearance. "Thank you for seeing me, Ms. Morgan."

"You may not feel that way in a few minutes."

Her voice carried deep into his soul, like a shout reverberating down a mineshaft. That voice was death. He had to gamble. Dianne Morgan was a megalomaniac, but he thought she would respect strength, and maybe honor.

"I understand why you killed my father. He was an honorable

man, but he didn't see things clearly."

David saw something, a spark of humanity in her colorless eyes, but it disappeared quickly.

"Ray forced my hand," Dianne said. "He tried to block the way and he paid with his life." In a much softer voice, she muttered, "The son of a bitch."

She had feelings for my father!

"Dad always said technology should benefit humanity, but he never understood that man and his technology were destined to be integrated." Shaking his head sadly, David said, "My father planted trees, but never saw the forest."

"You hate me, don't you," Dianne said, ignoring his words. "I can feel your hate. You try to hide it, but you can't."

"I hate that you were forced to kill my father." A question flew through his mind: *could I kill her now?* He glanced at Murphy, who had stepped behind him. "But I know my father; he would never accept your vision. He never trusted authority and would do everything in his power to stop the Domain. I miss my father terribly, but I understand why you killed him."

Dianne's stare locked his eyes, probing deep within him. Awareness came into her eyes. "You hate *him*, too. You despise both of us." She laughed, a short, ugly sound. "You sad, sick puppy. He was worth ten of you."

"Why did you come here?" Murphy asked. David glanced over his shoulder, and Murphy added, "Surely you know we have to kill you."

Murphy may be the killer, but he's not the one I have to convince.

Turning back to Dianne, David said, "I'm here because I have no choice." His skin felt sticky, and he wondered if she could smell his fear. "When I saw Daniel, it all came together. Although I resent your actions, I believe in your cause, in your vision. But there's more to it. Without my help, the Domain will fail."

Dianne's stare didn't give an inch.

"You're building artificial intelligence into the Internet, but it's growing much faster than you realize," David said. "Sentinel is ready to integrate with a human, almost ready to become a conscious entity, but it needs my help. It has been trying to reach my mind." He paused. "It sent Alice to find me."

Although she didn't speak, David saw Dianne's eyes widen for an instant.

Murphy's voice came over David's shoulder. "You're lying. Sentinel isn't trying to contact you."

David kept his attention riveted on Dianne. "Yes, it is. I don't know how, or why, but I feel its presence all the time."

David stepped closer to Dianne, peering into her eyes. He couldn't see Murphy, but he felt the presence of the killer close behind.

"There's something in me," he said to Dianne. "I can interact with it. I have my father's gift for artificial intelligence, but even more of it. Alice came across the net and found me, but it was sent by a more powerful AI, the entity you call Sentinel. I don't understand how it works, or why I have this talent, but it's there. I have something Sentinel needs. If you truly want to evolve technological man, then I'm the link."

Still silent, Dianne stared hard at David. Murphy's voice again came over his shoulder. "This kid is dangerous. I don't trust him." David felt the muzzle of a laser pistol pressed between his shoulder blades. "Let me kill him."

Dianne stepped closer to David and flicked her hand at Murphy.

The pressure of the gun disappeared. The witch continued to stare at him.

A siren whined in the distance, and the lights in the ceiling dimmed. A hurried voice came from a speaker in the wall. "Level 1 alert. Enemy soldiers have pierced security along the northeast quadrant."

Dianne glanced at Murphy, but before she could speak, David was hurled across the room in a deafening roar of hot wind and debris. He crashed into a chair and landed facedown on the floor. The heat was unbearable, and he buried his face in his arms.

The blast of heat quickly passed, leaving the acrid stench of burned furniture and office materials. Dazed, but not badly hurt, David lifted his head and found the room in shambles, with most of the ceiling and outer walls blown away. His ears rang, and his eyes burned, but he struggled to one knee.

What the hell was going on?

Another explosion boomed in the distance, followed by staccato bursts of automatic weapons. The mansion was under attack.

There was a movement in the dust about twenty feet away. Dianne rose to her knees, but the blast had left Murphy stretched out. Good fortune had knocked the gun out of Murphy's hand. It lay on the floor a few feet away.

David crawled to the pistol and picked it up. He struggled to his feet, still shaky from the blast. Dianne pulled herself to her feet using the arm of a sofa. Murphy, his shirt soaked in blood, didn't move .

David aimed the gun at Dianne. Her outline flickered in the thick dust, revealing her as the witch she surely was. *Kill her;* the thought forced its way into his mind. He knew he would be the one to kill her, that the time was coming.

But not until he could prove his father's innocence.

And there was Sentinel …

He held the gun on her for a long moment and then flipped it to her.

"I don't know who blew up this room," David said, "but I suggest we get the hell out of here."

"Murphy, are you all right?" Dianne asked, staring at the prone body. "We have to get out of here."

Murphy lay on his back and showed no sign of reviving. The round end of a spoon protruded from his chest, hidden in a swirl of red.

"Oh, my God," Dianne whispered, frozen in place, staring at her friend on the floor.

Dianne stumbled to him and felt frantically for a pulse, but the explosion had driven the spoon deep into his chest, ending his life instantly.

She knelt on the hard floor and pulled his body close, his head resting on her chest. She pulled the spoon from his chest and hurled it against a wall. Burying her face in the back of his neck, she looked sick with grief.

David fought his panic. "Dianne, we have to get to a safer place."

Dianne suddenly looked up and shouted, "My daughter! I left her reading in the library."

She lurched to her feet, picked her way through the wreckage and rushed out the exit. David could barely keep up with her.

CHAPTER 24

What if scientists built artificial life forms that could pass the Turing test, that is, appear to be human? This would threaten the whole concept of a single God as the creator. Would robots be human? Would humans be gods?

◆ Steve Bonini's Diary, 2017

Thursday afternoon, March 10, 2022

Moesha and her soldiers drove their armored trucks past the shattered remains of the front gate and raced down the road toward the mansion. With sixty of her best soldiers spread across three innocent-looking vehicles, Moesha had the firepower to overwhelm the Domain's security force. She had initiated the assault from a mile outside the brick wall using portable, laser-guided rockets. The attack had smashed the brick walls and front face of the mansion, but she knew most of the Domain compound remained safely underground.

She was confident their attack on the Techno stronghold would deal the Domain a crippling blow. The First Minister's plan to follow David Brown to the infidels' nest had worked perfectly. Her men had recorded Brown's discussion with Mizinsky, which convinced her Brown was closing in on the Domain.

Moesha had followed Brown to Dianne Morgan's home. It was

so obvious that Morgan was responsible for the robot abominations, once they learned that she had created PeaceMaker. Morgan was the Antichrist, the Devil's surrogate on Earth. She must be killed at all costs.

Moesha sat in the passenger seat of the first truck speeding down the road. Although heavily protected, a well-placed rocket could smash through the armor and take her life. No matter. It was an honor to lead the Army of God into battle.

She was under no illusion they could defeat the Technos with a single blow, no matter how thunderous. God had revealed the war would span many years. Lucifer had struck the first blow, releasing abominations such as PeaceMaker and intelligent robots. Picturing the android Daniel in her mind, she knew the Technos continued to travel their unholy path, but today she had unleashed a fierce counterattack.

Billowing smoke poured from the mansion. Scattered fires glowed through broken walls. Rockets had left gaping holes, but she knew many Domain soldiers still hid within the wreckage.

Lasers scorched the sides of her truck as they raced down the road. A deafening explosion churned up the blacktop in front of her. Anthony, her driver, swung the truck off the road. Bouncing along a grassy field, he drove past a smoking crater then cut back onto the smooth blacktop.

He glanced at her and asked, "You okay?"

Moesha spoke into the netcom pinned to her collar, "There's an enemy with a hand-held rocket launcher moving from window to window on the third level." The enemy would change location again after that last shot. "I want you to return fire. Put it in the … fifth window from the right."

With a whoosh a rocket flashed over her truck. The third floor of the mansion exploded. Flames flared through the higher floors and out the roof. Anyone nearby would be dead.

"I'm fine," she said to Anthony, keeping her eyes on the mansion.

When Anthony pulled up to the building, the rear doors of the truck whipped open and twenty soldiers poured out. The lead soldiers, using the truck as a shield, opened fire with laser torches and portable rocket launchers, but the enemy unleashed a torrent of laser beams. Rapidly arriving vehicles formed a defensive half-shell around her truck, and additional soldiers leaped out. The weapons fire was intense in both directions. Men screamed, and mangled bodies suddenly covered the battlefield.

She shouted over the tumult into the netcom. "Burn out those infidels in the wreckage of the front entrance."

Several of her soldiers fired their laser torches at the front entrance. The deadly orange beams incinerated enemy soldiers, flooding the air with the stench of burned flesh. One Domain soldier, burned black, screamed hideously until a comrade mercifully shot him. The remaining enemy fighters retreated further into the wrecked building, firing back from inside the walls.

Moesha jumped out of the truck. Heat from the fires singed her face, but she felt blessed. The Lord would guide her to victory.

She pointed to the driver of the second truck and shouted, "Now is your moment. Take out the main entrance."

The driver screamed, "I am a natural human," and hit the gas, making the tires squeal. The armored truck roared and bounced up the brick steps then blasted through the remains of the entrance and disappeared inside the building.

Moesha and her soldiers hit the ground as an explosion ripped apart the entrance. A grinding roar engulfed them in searing heat. Hot chunks of wood and metal rained down, and Moesha buried her face in the ground. The destruction was terrible, but it was over in a moment.

Moesha lifted her head and surveyed the nightmare scene. Her eyes burned from the heat and smoke of the blast, but no lasers fired from within the building.

She got to her feet and shouted to her companions, "Our brother gave his life for us. Show the infidel Technos the power of the Army of God."

Leading the charge into the building, she picked her way through billowing flames and crumpled walls. Smoke and ashes made it difficult to see, but she led her army against the enemy. Her soldiers were magnificent in their dark blue uniforms. They charged without hesitation through deadly laser fire, ready to become martyrs in the cause. The remaining infidels fought fiercely until eliminated.

Shouting orders over the roar of the flames, Moesha sent God's soldiers in all directions. They killed infidels without mercy. Most appeared to be unarmed office workers, but no infidel would be spared in this holy war. She was surprised to feel a tinge of regret as she stepped over the blackened body of an unarmed young woman, whose dead eyes stared straight up at the Creator.

Those who work for the heathen should expect no mercy.

If she could kill every Techno in the building, she'd do it, but the real prize was Dianne Morgan.

Leading a small team, Moesha searched the front offices. The smell of smoldering metal was everywhere, its hot stench fouling her lungs. The Antichrist Morgan had crawled down a hole somewhere, but the Lord wouldn't let her escape. God's soldiers broke down the doors leading into a large conference room and discovered a group of more than twenty office workers.

Moesha had her troops line the infidels against the wall. The captives pleaded for their worthless lives, but nothing would deter her from following the Lord's path.

She shot her Ruger laser over their heads, burning a hole in the wall, and shouted, "Silence!"

The infidels became silent except for their breathing. Glancing around the room, she said, "I'm looking for Dianne Morgan, and I won't leave until I have her."

She stepped from a chair to the top of the long conference table in the center of the room. Looking down on the terrified faces, she said, "I don't have the time to search every room and tunnel in this complex. Someone here knows where she's hiding." Attempting to appear reasonable, she said, "I have no wish to harm you, but I will if necessary. Tell me her location and you'll live. Disobey and everyone will die."

Slowly waving her Ruger back and forth across the terrified crowd, Moesha said, "Who knows where she's hiding?"

The infidels looked at each other, but nobody spoke. Moesha pointed her pistol at one of the captives.

"You, in the yellow sweater, where is Dianne Morgan?"

The middle-aged woman whimpered, "Please, I don't know where she is. I haven't seen her today." With eyes suddenly tearing, the woman pleaded, "I swear I'd tell you if I knew."

Moesha aimed her Ruger at the infidel, but a sudden weakness of spirit infected her soul. *What was it, this sympathy for an infidel?* Clearing her mind of the blasphemous thoughts, she pulled the trigger. A deadly beam burned into the woman's chest, and left the blackened remains of her body awkwardly twisted on the carpet.

The captives stared in shock at the body of their friend, and many began screaming. *A sound that carried all the way to Heaven.* Moesha felt the weakness depart, leaving her whole once again.

She lifted her pistol above her head, pointing it at the ceiling. The room became deadly quiet.

She reveled in the cowardly terror on each face, she'd like to kill them all, one by one. Cleansing Technos from the Earth was the Lord's work, and she would never waver again. Several of the infidels whimpered as she waved her weapon back and forth across the group, stopping at a young black man.

"You, my brother, where is Dianne Morgan?"

Collapsing to his knees, the young man begged, "No, no, no, not me. I just started here today. I've never even met her. Please, I don't know."

Moesha drew out the moment, bathing the crowd in his terror. Without warning, a shaky male voice cried out from behind the crowd, "I know. I'll tell you."

The crowd separated, revealing a skinny, sweating man in a tan suit. He was a pathetic creature, hardly a meaningful enemy.

"Please don't hurt anyone else," tan-suit said. "Dianne is in the family section. I saw her take Larissa into the library half an hour earlier. It's just down the hall, onto—"

Disappointed the game was over, Moesha snapped, "You will lead us there."

A soldier grabbed tan-suit and dragged him out of the conference room. As her men began to leave, she beckoned to Anthony and another soldier.

"You two stay here." Moesha glanced at the terrified infidels and made her decision. "Kill them all."

"But they're just office workers," Anthony said. "Maybe some have seen the light."

"All Lucifer's creatures must be purged from the Earth. The Lord will look into their souls and save the converted. If there are any."

Moesha left Anthony at the doorway, confident he would overcome his weakness, as she had. A moment later, the hiss of laser rifles carried through the conference room door. Terrified voices screamed, but it was over quickly.

The Lord's will be done.

Now to find Morgan.

While rushing to the library, Dianne spoke with the Captain of the Guards through her Command Chip, "Get soldiers to the library. My daughter is there."

"Most of my soldiers are dead, the Captain replied. "The rest are pinned down behind the front administrative offices. The terrorists launched an attack through the front gate and have taken control of the lobby. Our guards are fighting back, but the enemy has overwhelming firepower. We need the Vipers."

Dianne said, "Sentinel, activate the Vipers in this site. Exterminate the invaders."

"As you wish," Sentinel replied through the Command Chip.

"What are these Vipers?" David asked as they hurried down the hall.

Dianne's lips cracked into a malicious smile, and her eyes had the look of a cat about to enter a bird's nest. "Now you'll see the dark side of our power."

Leading a dozen of her men in the search for Dianne Morgan, Moesha prodded tan-suit with her pistol. He led her down a long, broad hallway lined with doors to a remote section of the building. All the hallways seemed unnecessarily wide and high, which made her wonder what was moving through these halls.

Pointing to a door, tan-suit said, voice shaking, "That's the entrance to the family library. She should be there."

"Unlock the door," Moesha said.

He pointed to a fingerprint pad on the wall. "I don't have the authorization; only one of the leaders could do it."

She turned to one of her soldiers. "Burn it down."

As they stepped back, the soldier turned the laser torch on the door, first burning the alloy white-hot and then creating an ever-growing hole. In less than a minute, the opening was wide enough for a man.

Then the air hissed. A soldier cried out and crumpled to the floor. Moesha dove into a passageway as a slender missile streaked by and fired a laser, burning the wall behind her. Two additional missiles streaked past, firing lasers that killed two soldiers.

"Abominations," she breathed.

The first missile slowed then looped around about one hundred yards down the hallway. It looked about two feet long and three or four inches in diameter, with a circular opening at its tip and two more along its shaft. The openings must be laser ports.

"Take cover in the doorways," Moesha shouted. "They're coming back. Take them down with your lasers."

The three robot missiles flew toward them again, but this

time they approached in a twisting path. Her soldiers shot at the abominations, but missed. It was like trying to hit a big dart spiraling past at high speed. Lasers flashed as the missiles hurled by, killing another two of her men.

Her soldiers were no match for these deadly robots. She pointed at two of her men. "Quickly, into the library," she croaked, barely able to pull her eyes away from the abominations beginning another loop down the hall. "The rest of you shoot down these missiles."

As the first soldier stepped through, she turned to tan-suit and casually shot him in the chest, an unimportant task barely remembered. The laser passed through his body, and tan-suit crumpled to the floor.

Avoiding the door's red-hot edges, Moesha and one other soldier carefully stepped through the hole into a large library. They were poised for action, but it was deserted. Photographs of Dianne Morgan covered the walls between the stacks of books, so Moesha knew they had found the Antichrist's lair.

Lasers hissed in the hallway and a man screamed; she didn't have much time to find Morgan.

She posted one soldier at the door to defend against the abominations. The other soldier searched the smaller rooms while she scanned the main room. Morgan didn't seem to be here.

Could the Antichrist have escaped?

The soldier who searched the smaller rooms returned, dragging a struggling young girl. "Commander, I found this one hiding in a cabinet." He shoved the girl to the floor in front of Moesha. The child looked up, tears glistening in the corners of her brown eyes, but apparently doing her best not to show fear. Nine years old, Moesha recalled. She was slender, with smooth olive skin and strong, symmetrical features. It was difficult to believe such a beautiful child could have emerged from the loins of the Antichrist.

"Where's your mother?"

"I don't know where Mommy is."

Moesha grabbed Larissa roughly under the arm and pulled the girl to her feet. Seizing Larissa's neck, she put her pistol to the girl's head.

"Dianne Morgan, for your daughter's sake, I hope you can hear me. First call off those missiles, then give yourself up or Larissa dies." Moesha looked around the room then said, "You have two minutes to save her life."

A final hiss of lasers in the hallway, and then it was quiet. Moesha listened to the ticking of an ancient grandfather clock as they waited. Larissa neither cried nor begged. *Brave girl. She's still human. It's her mother's fault I have to kill her.*

The soldier guarding the door shouted, "Moesha, here comes Morgan and she has those damn missiles hovering around her."

He stepped back from the door to allow two Church soldiers to enter. "The others are dead," one of the soldiers said to Moesha.

"God will bless their sacrifice," she replied.

The four remaining soldiers spread out and pointed their weapons at the doorway. Moesha pulled Larissa's back against her chest, tightened her arm around the girl's neck and pushed the muzzle of the laser against her temple.

The door slid open and the three missiles floated through. They spread across the room and aimed their lasers at Moesha's head. She felt a prick of fear; the abominations had ignored her soldiers.

She waited for Morgan to appear, aware of each tick of the clock. With the missiles so close, she detected a slight humming sound.

Morgan stepped through the doorway and stopped in front of Moesha. For the first time, Moesha stood face to face with the Antichrist. The woman was tall, but too thin, almost gaunt in her bodysuit. Up close, her face was a fishnet of thin lines, with circles under her eyes. In her photographs, Morgan had looked perpetually young and beautiful; now she looked ordinary, like someone you would see in church. Moesha was not fooled, however; she only had to look at the abominations in the air around the Antichrist.

Three Church soldiers covered the missiles, ready to fire at any moment. The fourth targeted Morgan. They waited for a command from Moesha to open fire. Morgan and her spawn had to die, even if Moesha and her soldiers were martyred.

The Antichrist walked up to Moesha, evil shining from her colorless eyes.

"Let my child go and I promise the Vipers will not harm you."

"The word of a Techno," Moesha spat out. "Tell your abominations to leave the room." The Antichrist continued to stare at her, so Moesha said, "Tell them to leave or I kill your daughter now."

Moesha's hand ached from gripping her pistol as the divine moment approached, the reason for her life. She would be the one to kill the Antichrist and bring her body back to the church to be burned.

Without taking her eyes off Moesha, Dianne said, "Vipers, leave the room."

The robots turned and flew out through the badly burned doorway. A Church soldier went to the doorway, his weapon aimed out.

"The abominations have stopped at the end of the hall," he said, glancing back at Moesha.

Moesha swung her gun away from Larissa and toward the

Antichrist. In the split-second before she could pull the trigger, a laser hissed from behind. Pain ripped through her hand, knocking the weapon to the ground.

A Domain assailant, hiding deep in the library, spread an arc of laser heat across the room, wounding one soldier and forcing Moesha and her remaining soldiers to scramble for cover in doorways and behind desks. At the same time, the Antichrist grabbed her spawn and dived behind a safe, barely avoiding a laser beam. Then the abominations flew in and began firing at Moesha's soldiers.

No, we can't allow Morgan to survive!

Moesha scrambled through a doorway and ran across the adjoining room. She could still defeat the Technos, but she had to get back to her army.

As the fight raged, Dianne kept hidden behind the safe, shielding Larissa under her body. The terrorists fought fiercely, but, one by one, the Vipers picked them off, until the ticking of the tall clock again dominated the suddenly quiet room. Trembling, Dianne picked up her daughter and hugged her. Larissa cried quietly as Dianne carried her out of the room, guarded by the Vipers.

She kissed Larissa and gently put her down. "Stay here. I'll be back in a moment."

Dianne ordered two of the Vipers to stay with Larissa. The other Viper preceded her back into the library. The smell of scorched flesh filled the room. A moment later, DoubleD walked out of the interior hallway.

"Are you all right?" DoubleD asked.

Why wasn't DoubleD going after the woman who threatened my daughter?

Dianne screeched, "Go after their leader. I saw her disappear into the storage room."

DoubleD ran through the storage room into a long hallway then turned to the right. She figured that Moesha—that's what her soldier had called her— would try to get back to her army.

DoubleD ran down the long hallway, arms and legs pumping powerfully.

Damn Morgan. I just saved her and her daughter, but did I get a word of thanks. I'd let Moesha escape, but Dianne would just send me after her again.

Moesha had only a three- or four-minute head start, so she couldn't be far ahead. DoubleD's laser shot had injured Moesha's hand, but that wouldn't slow her down. It would require her best effort to catch the terrorist leader.

Her long legs ate up the distance, and she quickly reached a spot where the hallway had caved in, probably from a rocket hit. A quick scan revealed the left side of the hallway was completely blocked. The right side was filled with debris but passable. Moesha might have continued down the hallway, DoubleD thought, but it would be slow going.

She knelt and peered into a jagged hole in the wall to the left, approximately three feet in diameter, a couple of yards in front of the caved-in end of the hallway. The hole led into the remains of an office, filled with broken equipment and furniture. A small fire burned in the far corner, and dark smoke curled into the air. The outside wall had been blown away, providing a view of a brick path winding through beautiful gardens. She had walked that trail many times; it led to the front of the mansion.

Moesha would most likely have slipped out this way, so DoubleD crawled through the hole and worked her way across the debris-filled room.

She ran along the winding brick path. Hollies, laurels and a variety of evergreens grew along the path, providing cover for an ambush, but Moesha didn't know anyone was chasing her, so she would probably keep running toward her troops.

Dianne had built a series of bungalows and office buildings along the left side of the path. Non-classified meetings and work efforts were often held there, with apartments for overnight guests. The wall of the mansion, six stories of brick on the right, dominated the gardens.

The noise of battle had mostly subsided. Only the hiss of an occasional laser or the pop of a rifle disturbed the peace. DoubleD figured the Vipers had made short work of Moesha's army. Now she had to get the leader.

Sweat soaked the back of her sweater, but she ran as hard as she could.

Where is that bitch?

DoubleD sprinted past an oak tree, but a crushing blow to her head and shoulders drove her to the ground, smashing her face into the brickwork. Her nose snapped, and hot blood smeared across her face.

Powerful arms crushed her throat and she realized Moesha had jumped her from a tree. She was face down with Moesha on her back, strangling the life out of her. She grabbed Moesha's forearms and pulled hard, relieving a little of the pressure and allowing her to gulp air.

The terrorist pulled back, wedging her knee in DoubleD's back. The pain made her woozy. She had to do something before she passed out. If she could only draw her pistol!

DoubleD rocked hard to one side, then back the other way, throwing Moesha off balance. DoubleD pulled her pistol from her shoulder holster, but Moesha grabbed her hand before she could aim. *Shit!* DoubleD pulled hard, but she couldn't free her hand.

Moesha slowly forced DoubleD's hand down. The terrorist had leverage, and she was very strong. The laser pistol gradually turned until the barrel pointed away from the fighters. There was no way she could aim the pistol at Moesha with that woman on her back.

DoubleD struggled to her knees then stood up. Moesha, her legs wrapped around DoubleD's waist, rode her, arms over DoubleD's shoulders, still trying to turn the laser on her. The woman's legs crushed her ribs to the breaking point. She was weakening.

Got to get this bitch off my back.

DoubleD backed up as fast as she could and slammed Moesha into the oak tree. Moesha screamed but didn't let go of the pistol. *Dammit!* DoubleD staggered forward and tried to slam Moesha into the tree again, but Moesha freed her legs and braced them against the tree. Pushing hard, Moesha leaped over DoubleD's shoulder and tried to yank the gun free.

DoubleD barely held on to the gun, which slipped in her sweaty hand, and the muzzle pointed dangerously in her direction. She recovered her balance and pushed the muzzle away as a laser cut through the air.

The women faced each other, the gun between them, the barrel pointed up. Both were sweating and breathing hard as they struggled for the pistol. DoubleD slowly forced the barrel toward Moesha. Her muscles screamed in pain, and blood ran into her eyes, but the barrel of the pistol was moving. *Just another inch and your ass is mine.*

Moesha screamed and smashed her forehead into DoubleD's broken nose; she lost her grip on the gun. Moesha now had control of the pistol, but was off balance. DoubleD slashed down with her fist and knocked the pistol from Moesha's hand. It dropped out of sight in a holly bush.

DoubleD swung her fist in a ferocious left hook, but Moesha blocked it with her right arm then buried her own left in DoubleD's abdomen. She staggered back, but years of situps prevented any serious damage. She stepped out of reach of a follow-up and took a breath.

The two women circled each other, looking for an opening. DoubleD was a little bigger, but the terrorist didn't seem to be breathing as hard. Long, athletic muscles showed through Moesha's tight black bodysuit.

"I'm going to kill you," Moesha said, "and then I'm coming back to kill the Antichrist."

"You're going to die right here," DoubleD said, wiping the blood from her eyes.

Moesha threw a left jab, but it was slow and easy to block. *My turn!* DoubleD leaped in with a right that landed on Moesha's ear. Sweat sprayed in all directions: Double D followed with another right, but Moesha ducked it, grabbed DoubleD's legs and pulled up. DoubleD had a view of the sky, and then the back of her head thudded into hard ground. The terrorist bitch tried to stomp her, but DoubleD kicked her in the chest. She squealed and fell backwards. DoubleD quickly rose to her feet, but Moesha had recovered from the kick.

The women circled each other again. *Never fought anyone so tough.* DoubleD wasn't sure what to try next, but she had to come up with a surprise.

Moesha faked a jab and came in with a sidekick, sweeping DoubleD's legs into the air. Moesha was on top of her as soon as she hit the ground, hitting her with a powerful right, but DoubleD turned her head just in time to avoid most of the power. It hurt like hell, but she grabbed Moesha's wrists, twisted and threw the bitch off. She dove at Moesha, trying for a choke hold, but the woman was too fast and rolled out of danger. All she got was a handful of sweat.

The two women rose and circled each other again.

DoubleD had hurt her right shoulder in the last fall, and she wasn't sure how much strength remained in her arm. Moesha was panting, but her face was unmarked and her body appeared uninjured, except for the laser wound on her hand. *Not much damage for all that fighting.* DoubleD realized she was losing.

Moesha faked another sidekick and then came in with a painful right to her forehead, scattering blood in all directions. DoubleD tried to retreat, but Moesha followed with a left hook. DoubleD saw it coming, but her injured shoulder was too weak to block the punch, and it landed with a crunch on her jaw.

Her legs turn to mush and she went down hard. Her vision blurred, but her mind still worked. On her back in the dirt, she launched a kick at where Moesha should be. She guessed right, and the kick landed hard on the side of Moesha's head as she dived on DoubleD. The bitch fell to the ground and tried to roll away, but she was slow. With her good left hand, DoubleD grabbed Moesha's hair, snapped her head backwards, and wrapped her thighs around the terrorist's neck. Locking her ankles, DoubleD squeezed with all her strength.

I have to kill her now.

Moesha groaned and tried to kick out, but DoubleD poured on the power. The terrorist rolled to the side and got to her knees, but DoubleD twisted her body and slammed Moesha to the ground. She retained her chokehold, putting all her strength into her legs, crushing the life out of her enemy.

If Moesha broke free, DoubleD knew the odds would be with her enemy.

Moesha's face turned red. She kicked and rolled from side to side. The woman was strong and agile, but the bulging cords of muscle in DoubleD's thighs squeezed her enemy's throat.

Moesha threw a roundhouse right that landed on DoubleD's left breast. Her legs loosened for a moment, and she almost lost her hold. She screamed and concentrated all her strength into her thighs. Moesha tried to hit her again, but DoubleD caught her wrist with her left hand.

Now I have the bitch.

She redoubled her effort, twisting and shaking Moesha between her legs, like a leopard seal shaking a penguin to death. The terrorist's face and neck were purple and she stopped trying to hit back. DoubleD lifted Moesha with her legs and flipped her over. No resistance. Moesha's eyes bulged, tears dripped down her cheeks. Then she made a gurgling sound and her body turned limp.

DoubleD wasn't taking any chances. Her body covered in sweat, she squeezed and shook Moesha. She twisted her legs and Moesha's body flipped over again. Her eyes were closed and her face was dark purple. She had to be dead.

DoubleD relaxed her legs and lay back, exhausted and gasping for air. It felt like she had been hit by a truck.

Gradually her breathing slowed; strength seeped back into her body. She struggled to her knees then stood up. Moesha's body lay on its side, crumpled in death.

DoubleD studied her. Moesha had been a beautiful woman, but now her face was puffy and discolored from the fight. It was surprising, but she felt no remorse over killing another human being. She felt nothing at all.

It had been a time for killing: the Cohens, Mrs. Mizinsky, the bear, the mouse, two of Moesha's soldiers, and now Moesha herself. *Is this my life?*

She stared at Moesha's body a moment longer, shrugged and walked back to Dianne.

CHAPTER 25

Are constitutional freedoms and responsibilities just for natural men and women? Would an artificial life form have any rights as it moves toward consciousness? Would a human cease to be a human as it gains artificial components?

◆ Steve Bonini's Diary, 2019

Science without religion is lame; religion without science is blind.

◆ Albert Einstein, *Science and Religion*, 1941

Saturday, March 12, 2022

Bringing the first warmth of the day, morning sunlight peeked through the windows of the hologram room. Relaxing in his favorite chair, the Runner glanced at his watch, thinking the upcoming newscast might be remarkable.

He sipped his first cup of coffee—still too hot—and set it down. The morning run, followed by a dip in the ocean, left a crisp, youthful feeling in his body.

He wondered how many people had joined the Domain. Probably millions. *What would that pond scum First Minister do now?* Dianne's plans were working, so Jordan would have to say something dramatic today.

The Runner reached for the coffee and gulped it down. It was still hard to believe it had come down to this: a pair of psychopaths competing for control over humanity's destiny. He felt like leaving the room, but that would be pointless. Nobody could hide from the future.

"Turn on DNS, the US edition."

The hologram displayed the outline of a young newswoman sitting comfortably in a padded chair. She wore a green skirt, which had ridden up to the top of her thighs. As always, she lifted his spirits, among other things.

"Good afternoon, this is Daphne Hayden, reporting from the DNS studio in New York. Displayed in your hologram is the towering structure of the Charleston Natural Church. In a period unlike any in our history, we are here to listen to Adam Jordan, the Founder and First Minister of the Church of Natural Humans. Minister Jordan will reply to the recent netcast of the Domain, which has shaken our civilization to its roots.

"In the minutes before First Minister Jordan begins his remarks, let me bring you up to date on recent events." She forced a smile. "Just in case you're living on a deserted island."

As an aide put on his makeup, Adam Jordan growled at the newscast, "Turn off that whore."

He sat in a large vestry, a room they used to indoctrinate new converts. His aide jumped up to hit a button on the computer, and the hologram disappeared.

Jordan's jaw tightened as the aide finished brushing makeup under his eyes. Moesha and so many of her soldiers had died during the raid on the Domain. His anger and grief wouldn't burn off. None of the other girls could replace her. He sighed. Someday they would be together again, in Heaven.

His aide held up a mirror and Jordan checked his makeup, which looked fine. He buckled on his shoulder holster and made sure his Colt revolver was loaded. The aide helped him slip into a long black robe. Jordan pulled a gold amulet over his head, adjusting it to hang in the center of his chest. He studied his image in a full-length mirror.

It wasn't quite right. He had put on a black robe because that was how he felt, but he didn't look sufficiently holy. He took off the black robe and put on a white one. That was much better.

He walked out the door to the stage and looked across the huge church. His servants had placed a holocamera near each wall. Several thousand of the faithful waited for him, kneeling attentively. As he had ordered, they were ordinary people dressed in everyday clothes.

Staring into the rows of fireplaces, calm washed over him. The Lord would guide them to salvation. Humans had lived for centuries without artificial intelligence and, once again they would live in harmony with God's design.

A Winchester bolt-action rifle was perched over each mantel. His hatred burned like those flames, and the rifles represented his power. He vowed again to bring God's wrath down upon the Technos.

He turned to face a holocamera and nodded at the cameraman. *Why had the Lord allowed the Antichrist to take Moesha from me?* He breathed deeply, focused his attention on his followers and began with a prayer.

"I am a Natural Human."

As always, these words aroused his flock, and they joined him in prayer. "My mind and my body are human," the voices chanted. The church rumbled with the power of their belief.

Jordan couldn't get Moesha out of his mind.

You were so beautiful.

He continued with the prayer, his thoughts drifting far from this congregation, wedged in bitterness, to a place he couldn't escape.

"My soul has not been altered by Technology," he chanted with his followers.

Pure and beautiful, a once-in-a-lifetime flower. Why has the Lord punished me?

"We will destroy the Devil and protect the Earth."

I'll crush the Antichrist who took you.

"Glory be to the Lord and His Creations."

The prayer died away, and an uneasy quiet settled in. Seconds passed. A minute. Jordan let them wait. The words formed in his mind, pressure building, demanding to be spoken. He bowed his head in silent prayer.

I must be strong.

He lifted his eyes and began to speak.

The congregation waited for the First Minister to appear. The Runner felt the anticipation. His stomach clenched when he saw Adam Jordan emerge from behind the altar. Jordan's golden amulet swung back and forth across his black robe as he strode past the altar and down the steps. Something was different about Jordan, but the Runner couldn't put his finger on it. Jordan stopped in front of a group of neatly dressed men and women, who filled the first section of pews.

Although he hated the Church of Natural Humans, some of their beliefs touched a place deep in his soul. He believed in technology, yet there was an edge of truth in the Church's message. *How far could we go with artificial intelligence? Would we lose our humanity?* Watching the hologram of this terrible man surrounded by fanatical followers, the Runner wondered how things could have gone so wrong.

Jordan smiled into the camera. "Welcome, my friends. Let us pray."

The First Minister bowed his head and prayed. Without raising his eyes, he kissed his amulet.

"I come to you today to beg forgiveness. I have led you down a terrible path and I'm deeply ashamed. Without my knowledge, I have become a tool of the Devil, and I was about to lead you into calamity."

Jordan lifted his eyes to the faithful. "God came to me yesterday and drove out Lucifer. After a terrible battle, He cleansed me of the Devil's wickedness. He opened my heart to the beauty of His words. Now, He commands that I share His truth with you."

What the hell? The Runner stared at the hologram. *Is this madman changing strategy?*

"Lucifer hates us," Jordan said. "He hates us with a passion we humans cannot comprehend. He hates us for all eternity. He hates us because God loves us. He hates us because God will accept and nourish our frail human souls.

"Lucifer is our immortal enemy." Jordan gazed over his followers. "He has hated us since the first single-cell creature swam in the seas. He sent diseases and predators to destroy us as we evolved. He continues the attack to this very day, but he has not been successful.

"In His infinite wisdom, God has provided us with the capabilities to resist Lucifer's hatred. He has provided us with strong bodies that could survive all manner of disease. He allowed us to evolve a unique intelligence, which separated us from all His other creatures. Thus, humanity spread across the Earth and prospered.

"However, our greatest strength is our most terrible weakness. As our intelligence developed, the Devil sought to turn it against us."

The Runner thought something looked different about Jordan's face. Not physically—his features were the same—but his expression had softened around the edges, the wildness gone.

"With infinite patience," Jordan continued, "Lucifer sought to gain control of our minds. He implanted evil at every opportunity. Cruelty, injustice, greed and inhumanity became commonplace. We looked for reasons to destroy each other. Differences in race, religion, gender—anything—became justification for unspeakable crimes.

"Humanity has been under the Devil's assault for millennia. God revealed this to me, but I failed to understand. Our battle is not with the Technos, it is within ourselves. We must cast out Lucifer from our *minds.*"

The Runner felt a strange relief. *Why wasn't Jordan calling for more killing? This is not the man who has spit out poison for decades. A* sudden suspicion intruded: *has Jordan come under the influence of the Domain?*

"A few days ago, our worst fears were realized," Jordan rasped. "A few days ago, the Devil spoke to us. He took the form of an abomination, the robot called Daniel, but he didn't fool the natural humans. It was Lucifer once again offering us a bite of the accursed apple."

The image of the robot seared his mind. *We shall attack them again, and this time we will kill the Antichrist and all her abominations.*

"On the surface, the Devil's offer is tempting; join the Domain and he will provide us with all the pleasures of life." He looked over his congregation. "Don't be fooled. When the Devil speaks, you must listen closely. There's something hidden from view, something he has not revealed." Jordan paused, allowing tension to build in his followers. The white sleeve of his robe flared as he slashed the air with his fist. "He wants to take your soul and crush it." Again, his white sleeve slashed, and his harsh voice escalated with rage. "He wants to grind you into the noxious scum of his being. He wants to deny your soul a place with God. He wants to torture you in Hell through all eternity.

"Listen carefully to what Lucifer says," Jordan said, his voice cracking. He swallowed, his passion pressed to the limit. He took a breath, then another.

"He offers this bargain: through technology, he will restore our civilization to a greater level of material riches. In order to gain this wealth, you must allow the Technos to create artificial beings, godless abominations that will rule the earth. But even that is just a step along the path to an even viler future. The elements of our human bodies and minds are to be replaced, step by step, with synthetic genes and artificial components. Humans are to evolve into a new species. Technological Man they call it."

"Never," cried a female voice among the believers. Others echoed her cry.

"Now why is the Devil doing this?" Jordan asked. "Why?" He paused, looking across the crowd. "The reason is simple, yet horrible beyond belief. In this secular world, your soul is your link to God. When the Devil replaces aspects of your humanity with artificial components, he weakens your connection to the Lord. When he inserts a synthetic gene into your body, he disrupts God's plan. At some point, as your humanity shrinks and the artificiality grows, the link to the Lord will be severed. And when the Devil destroys that link, it's gone forever.

"I beseech you to save your immortal soul. Do not be fooled by Lucifer. Do not join the Domain."

Shaking his head, Jordan ranted, "Would you trade your immortal soul for a few moments of worldly comfort? That, my fellow humans, is Lucifer's offer: an eternity of suffering in hell in exchange for a handful of comfortable years on this Earth."

We'll kill all the Technos. I'll see the Antichrist's bones burn in this church.

Righteousness powered his words. "You must reject this bargain," he shouted. "Do not become a citizen of the Domain, for doing so shall seal your fate. Cast your lot with humanity; live and die as a Natural Human."

A man in the third row stood up and shouted, "We despise all their abominations." The man's face contorted with hate. "We'll kill them all."

The crowd roared.

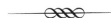

Leaning forward, the Runner watched the hologram in confusion. Jordan stood in front of the altar, passionately looking out over his flock.

There must be some trick. Was he Jekyll or Hyde?

"The truth, now," Jordan said. "I must tell you the terrible truth. Lucifer is winning. He has poisoned our minds with his evil. Conflicts have spread all over the world. Hatred is the norm and violence the result. With our military technology, the time is rapidly approaching when we will obliterate humanity."

Suddenly, Jordan stepped from the stage and strode down the center aisle. The faithful kissed their amulets as he passed. He stopped halfway down the modest church, turned around and raised his arms.

"Artificial beings will be our saviors, not our enemies," Jordan roared. "I was blind not to see this is God's plan. The artificial beings are the children of our minds, sent by God to save us."

This doesn't make sense. The Runner stared into the hologram. *This can't be Adam Jordan. Something's wrong.*

A male voice cried out, "We were all blind."

"The Devil cannot corrupt artificial minds," Jordan said. "These new beings will be programmed to love us. The Devil has no power over them. They are the children of our minds, but free of the Enemy's malevolent touch. These children will one day become our teachers. They will cleanse our minds of hatred and violence."

A female voice shouted, "But aren't they our enemies? Won't they destroy us?"

"No! These new beings are not our enemies. We shall give them life and they, in turn, will save us. This is God's will. Humans and artificial beings need each other. Neither can survive without the other."

With the sleeves of his black robe sliding down his bare arms, Jordan raised his hands to the sky. "The Technos are not our enemies." His voice boomed across the small church. "Artificial beings are not the enemy of humanity. We are all children of God. The enemy is Lucifer and we must join together to defeat him."

———————⌘———————

"Kill every leader of the Domain," Jordan rasped. "God has blessed a war against the Domain. A few days ago, the Church discovered the Technos' lair, and the glorious Army of God attacked them without mercy. We slew many, and we give thanks to the Lord. Although we discovered the identity of their ruler, we failed to kill her. Today I tell you God has commanded the death of this person, the Antichrist, Dianne Morgan."

His back was sweating. He had ordered the flames stoked high in the fireplace. "Dianne Morgan is the Devil's spawn. She rules all the Devil's creatures on earth and carries out Lucifer's design to destroy humanity. She is an evil creature that must be crushed." He pointed to the great fireplace behind him. "We shall burn the Antichrist's bones in this fireplace. Only then can we banish her spirit from the Earth for all time."

Angry voices rumbled around the vast church. "Find her. Kill her. Burn her."

With my own hands, I'll kill her. He raised his hands, staring at his palms. *Her blood wet on my hands.*

Placing his palms together as if in prayer, Jordan said, "The Final Battle is at hand. Lucifer continues to poison our minds, driving us to destroy each other. Our salvation is the love and power of artificial beings, which can stand with us against Lucifer. We must bring these children of ours to life, so they can protect us and teach us."

A woman stood up and shouted, "Yes, bring the robots to life." Others in the crowd shouted their agreement.

The Runner laughed out loud, feeling renewed.

So very clever. I understand now. The Domain will win, and the

Church will wither away.

Jordan continued speaking as he walked back toward the altar. "I ask you to join the Domain. I have become a citizen of the Domain myself, and I ask all Church members, all God-loving humans to join. United, we can bring forth our artificial children and save our souls."

Laughter rumbled through the Runner's lean body.

That's not the real Adam Jordan.

Then he began to roar with more joy than he had felt in years.

Guess who's coming to dinner.

Jordan shouted, "God bless us all."

A man shouted back, "God bless the First Minister."

Before long the faithful were chanting, "God bless the First Minister." Jordan briefly listened, then climbed up the steps and disappeared behind the altar as the hologram faded away.

Jordan shouted, "What shall we do with the Technos?"

"Kill them all," the crowd roared.

"What shall we do with artificial devices and creatures?"

"Destroy them all."

"What shall we do with Dianne Morgan?"

"Kill her and burn her bones in Charleston Church."

Jordan drew his gun and turned toward the giant fireplace behind the stage. The crowd followed his unhurried movements. His revolver cracked out shot after shot, while the faithful shook their fists and chanted, "Kill Dianne Morgan." Each bullet generated a tiny flicker as it thudded into the thick logs burning in the giant fireplace.

Satisfied, the First Minister holstered his revolver, turned and walked across the stage toward his dressing room. The faithful chanted, "Kill Dianne Morgan," as he walked away.

Jordan pulled on the doorknob to leave, but to his surprise, the door refused to open. He heard a startled sound from his followers, a collective taking in of breath. He turned.

The Antichrist, Dianne Morgan, stood just a few feet from him.

"Brilliant speech, First Minister," she said, briefly clapping. "What a pity no one heard it."

Jordan backed away and screamed, "Guards."

With a smile, Morgan said, "Yes, by all means, let's have guards."

Doors burst open on all sides of the church and heavily armed Domain soldiers rushed into the aisles. As the troops surrounded them, many of the Church faithful dropped to their knees and prayed.

Jordan recovered and said to his faithful, "Do not fear. Our lives belong to God." He felt his inner strength returning. The Lord had finally revealed his servant's destiny—to die a martyr. They would tell of his courage for centuries.

"Many will die in the war, the Lord revealed to me many years ago," he thundered. "We will defeat the Technos and their abominations." He turned to face the Antichrist. "We do not fear death. We live as humans, and we will die as humans."

"Nobody is going to attack the Technos, as you call us. In fact, most people believe we have become allies." She smiled. "Don't you recall? You said so in your speech. Children of our mind and all that."

"Never! God-loving humans will hunt you down, no matter where you hide. Your bones will be charred in this church."

"You don't understand, do you? We intercepted your netcast and replaced it with one of ours." Nodding to a nearby soldier, she said, "Here's what the world saw."

A hologram appeared in front of the huge fireplace, showing a counterfeit version of himself. Jordan watched the hologram with growing horror and screamed, "Blasphemy!" He turned to Dianne. "I will see you burn. I will burn you and your nightmare child."

"You'll do nothing except live in my prison for the remainder of your days. Your Church will accept me as a partner. We will stand side by side in the battle against Lucifer." A thin smile flicked across her lips. "Your people will flock to purchase Domain technology, especially robots. You'll live to see all my plans come to fruition."

Standing so close to the Antichrist, he looked deeply into her colorless eyes. No soul. She was devoid of anything human, except for the hatred of God's people burning at her core.

"I want you to suffer, Adam Jordan. Otherwise I would kill you now." Her voice cracked. "Oh yes, I have plans for you. But right now, let's enjoy the show. The conclusion of your speech is quite moving."

Forcing himself to remain stone-faced, Jordan watched the remainder of the newscast. "Your fraud will not fool my followers," he said when the hologram faded. "The Church is prepared for your tricks. We know you are a master of technology and will stoop to any device. You are devious, but it will not save you."

A collective murmur drew his attention to the crowd. They stared at something behind him. He spun around to a terrible sight.

Just across the stage, a robot stared at Jordan. Not Sarah or Daniel or any of the other abominations. This one was his mirror image, except for the black robe. My God …

A counterfeit human, spawned without a soul.

A false prophet, molded in my image.

People will believe the Church has blessed the Antichrist.

They'll believe I stand by Morgan.

The robot smiled and walked over to him. Jordan sensed Lucifer in the robot, in the Antichrist Morgan, everywhere. He felt the touch of immense evil, but forced a prayer into his mind. He could endure even this, knowing the Lord had revealed his servant's destiny.

The robot stared at him, then said in a gravelly voice, "First Minister Jordan, it's a pleasure to meet you."

"Abomination," cried a member of the faithful. Others began to shout at the robot. Jordan lifted his hand and the crowd became quiet.

"You think you have won, but you have not," he said to Morgan. "Everything the Lord told me will come to pass."

He suddenly realized his pistol was still in his shoulder holster. The pistol was an old-fashioned Colt .45 revolver that held six bullets.

Did I fire them all? Could a bullet remain in the gun?

"In the vision, I saw the Army of God destroy the monsters," he said, still thinking about his revolver. "I saw Natural Humans eliminate the Technos. I saw the deaths of our enemies."

The pistol never clicked empty, so there could be a bullet remaining. Excitement pulsed through his body. *I could shoot the Antichrist.*

"I don't fear your hallucinations," Morgan said. "You're a sick, ignorant man with delusions of holiness."

I have to kill this vile creature, but do I have a bullet?

"Don't pretend to love humanity when every breath you take reeks of hatred," she said. "You revel in humanity's hardships. You rejoice at funerals, not for the life lived but for the death you caused." Her face contorted in anger. "Your underling dared to threaten my daughter. If I did not have a purpose for your life, I would kill you now with my own hands."

Her soldiers would shoot me if I drew my gun. He felt the sweat on his back. *And I don't even know if I have a bullet.*

"The truth for once, First Minister," the Antichrist sneered. "The fundamental truth is that we humans are just biological machines. Our bodies work in predictable ways, obeying well-defined rules programmed into our cells. We are the same as robots, machines that operate according to our programming. Nothing special, no soul, just complex biological machines. All I plan to do, First Minister ... all the Domain plans to do ... is upgrade the programming."

The need to kill her filled his soul. Lucifer lived through her, a monstrous duality, speaking through her voice, peering out through her eyes.

His hand tensed to pull his gun, but fear held him back.

Morgan glared at him. "I can't stand the sight of you." The Antichrist turned to one of her minions. "Take him away and put him in solitary confinement." Her eyes returned to him, contempt shining through. In a voice laden with the Devil's venom, she said, "You will rot in my prison for the remainder of your days. Your only visitor will be your robot clone."

The Lord doesn't want me to die; that's why I can't pull my weapon. He has a divine purpose for my life, something not yet revealed. I have to remain alive, no matter what the Antichrist does to me.

Jordan glared at Morgan for a moment, then her guards pulled him toward the door. He didn't struggle, knowing his sacrifice was part of God's plan.

"Wait," the Antichrist shouted. She stepped up to him and said, "You disappoint me, First Minister."

She pulled the revolver out of his shoulder holster and studied it. "I enjoyed our little conversation so much I almost forgot to disarm you." Looking again at the revolver, she said, "I wonder if any bullets remain."

The Antichrist pointed the muzzle at his chest and cocked the hammer.

Jordan closed his eyes. He waited for the click of his death, but the church remained silent. Finally, he forced open his eyes.

The Antichrist was gone.

Someone chuckled and the guards led him away.

David walked down a long hall on the third floor of the church, stopping at each door to look inside. A small group of Domain soldiers walked past, eyeing him suspiciously. The Domain had taken control of the Charleston Church and surrounding buildings, and they continued to search for the occasional Natural Human who had eluded capture.

David's search differed. He sought his Aunt Claire, a woman he had not spoken to since childhood. His memories of her were vague, but he recalled a kind, soft-spoken woman who brought gifts when she visited. He had many questions for her. He was closing in on the answers to his quest.

His father had been a complex, troubled man, but not a murderer. The man had fought his demons, but never overcome them. The nightmares, the alcoholism, the infidelity, even the brilliance were all tied to a dark force within him. His father had battled it throughout his life.

I have that darkness, too.

David searched the church and adjoining buildings for hours, questioning the residents, but he discovered nothing. He had seen her in the broadcast with Jordan. He wondered if she might be hidden in another location.

"David."

He turned around and found himself staring into the dangerous blue eyes of the Amazon. He took a step back, wondering if Dianne had changed her mind. He had no illusions he would survive an attack from this woman.

"Ms. Morgan said you might need my assistance. Come with me," she told him.

The woman was an assassin, but now they were on the same side.

"I'm looking for my aunt."

She nodded, turned and walked down the hall. He didn't trust her, but had no choice except to follow. She led him through a doorway, and their footsteps clicked down several levels of a stone staircase. He hurried to keep up with her. The woman flowed down the steps with the grace of a natural athlete. She led him out of the church and down a brick pathway into a small park. The late afternoon sun had dropped behind the buildings, leaving the dregs of a raw afternoon.

He caught up to her on a pathway leading toward the rectory.

"Where is she?" he asked, breathing hard.

She had led him into an area thick with brush. There was nobody nearby, a perfect place for an execution.

The Amazon turned to him, her face almost kind. She pointed toward the greenhouse on the roof of the rectory. "Up there."

"Thank you."

He hurried past her, half-expecting a lethal attack, but she stepped aside. Entering the rectory, he took the stairs two at a time, until he reached the roof. She had been helpful, but the farther he was from that woman, the better.

The greenhouse was smaller than he had pictured, but lovely. The gardens were graceful in the fading sunlight, holding many varieties of flowers, shrubs and trees within its glass walls. It was warm, so he unzipped his jacket.

He spotted a small woman in the far corner on her hands and knees, working in the dirt. As he approached, he recognized her.

Aunt Claire didn't look up as he came upon her, so he paused to watch her work, engrossed in planting bulbs. She was meticulous, precisely measuring the water and fertilizer for each bulb.

Gaunt, with bony hands and arms, she looked older than her fifty years. Her face was deeply lined and the skin hung loosely on her neck, but she looked sturdy, with small, hard muscles bunching in her arms as she worked.

"Aunt Claire." When she didn't respond, he said, "It's me, David, your nephew."

His aunt continued to dig, apparently not hearing him. David called her name, but again she didn't respond.

David knelt next to her and placed his hand on her shoulder. She looked up at him, but there was emptiness in her eyes. Again he said, "Aunt Claire, it's me, David."

Her eyes seemed to search for something just out of reach. "David?" she mumbled.

"Your brother's oldest son. David."

Her eyes cleared, and she repeated his name. Placing her hand on his cheek, she said, "David … David, it's you." She looked around, and then asked him, "Is Ray here, too?"

"No, Aunt Claire, just me."

She smiled, a patch of sun briefly peeking through a cloudy sky.

"David, it's wonderful to see you." She put her arms around his neck and hugged him for several seconds. Then she released him and looked up into his eyes.

"You've grown into such a handsome young man."

David smiled back at her. "Thank you."

Aunt Claire looked at her bulbs and, as David watched, crawled over to her tools. She picked up a plastic scoop and began to dig. Confused, he said, "Aunt Claire," but she didn't respond.

"Aunt Claire," he said again. "I came here to ask you about my father." She stopped digging for a moment, staring into the hole.

"Your brother ... Ray," he said.

She looked up at him, but her eyes were vacant again.

"You're not my brother." Aunt Claire coughed then mumbled, "As Minister Jordan told you, I am Claire Brown, sister of Raymond Brown. For many years, I was an unhappy, lonely woman without hope or purpose." She seemed to lose her place briefly. "Then I found salvation through the First Minister and the Church of Natural Humans."

David took her in his arms, staring over her shoulder at the field of lovely flowers. He realized they were out of place this winter day, able to survive only in a greenhouse. His mind drifted to memories of a kind woman with intelligent eyes and a sad smile.

"I now have a purpose in life," she said. "I would like to share my story with my fellow humans here, in the church, and with those of you in the wilderness still searching for an answer. I pray my story will help you find salvation among your fellow humans."

David held her close as she recited her praise of the Church. *This poor woman.* She shouldn't stay here. Maybe Grandma, maybe not, but he'd find a place for her.

CHAPTER 26

Biological evolution proceeded inexorably over the millennia to its great creation: human intelligence. But it was far too slow and error-prone. Technological evolution was a necessity.

◆ *The Age of Cyborgs*, by T.M. Vax, copyright 2054, President, The Learning Coalition Inc.

Monday, March 14, 2022

Dianne had not slept in four days, working in her office to manage rapidly developing events. Her back felt stiff, so she leaned heavily against the chair's padded support. The blood etchings in her eyes would no doubt be apparent to visitors.

The message delivered by the Adam Jordan android had been incredibly successful. More than half a billion people had become citizens of the Domain in just a few days, exceeding her wildest expectations. The Church of Natural Humans had descended into chaos, and the Federal Government was too confused to do anything.

The Domain is the future, and I rule the Domain.

A brief, low-pitched hum came into her mind, followed by the words *Steve Bonini*. She replied, "Accept command chip transmission."

Steve's excited voice followed, "I just received a message from the labs. There's something extraordinary going on they want us to see."

A holographic image appeared in her office, scaled to a three-foot cube. The scene centered on David Brown, sitting in the Virtual Reality Booth, talking with a girl of about twelve. The girl's features should have made her beautiful, except their arrangement was too perfect. Her icy blue eyes glanced at Dianne, but the girl continued speaking to David in a low voice. His concentration was intense, as if each word were precious.

Dianne stiffened as recognition hit her. She hadn't seen that image in a decade. Alice, the software entity that had metastasized from PeaceMaker.

Why was Sentinel projecting the image of Alice in the Virtual Reality Booth? During the PeaceMaker attack a decade earlier, Alice had fused with young David and tried to absorb his mind. Now David was speaking to this killer as if it were a harmless module of software code.

David must have ordered Sentinel to retrieve Alice. Why had he brought it back after so many years? Or had Sentinel retrieved Alice on its own?

Sentinel was the key. Sentinel and David. Dianne had spared David's life because he might be the link to the artificial entity. Then she understood: Alice must be the focal point of the communication between Sentinel and David.

It was a dangerous tool.

Sentinel was the masterpiece, not Alice. By far the most powerful artificial intelligence conceived by Domain scientists, Sentinel was self-learning, intuitive, almost human. More than human in some ways. Sentinel was the software platform she hoped would eventually evolve into a conscious entity.

And David was the wild card. Dianne had kept track of him since the PeaceMaker attack. Ray's unique software abilities had passed through the genes to David. If he were loyal, if he could push Sentinel down the path to consciousness, she'd let him live.

For the past three years, Dianne had watched Domain scientists experiment with the Virtual Reality Booth. The exterior of the booth was a hard, transparent polymer, which enclosed a nanotechnology swarm, very tiny sensors that floated in the air. The sensors were two-way communications devices linking humans in the booth with Sentinel. The sensors formed a thin coating over human skin, constantly reading temperature, moisture, pulse rates and movement, then transmitting the data to Sentinel. In addition, Sentinel could simulate pressure, wind, heat and other effects on human skin through the sensors.

Although much too small to be seen by the human eye, the sheer number of sensors, in the trillions, gave the interior of the booth a fuzzy-edged look. She could see David well enough, but it was like peering through a fog.

Fascinated, Dianne watched David interact through Alice with Sentinel. He would outline a scene and then Sentinel would build a detailed image in a corner of the Virtual Reality Booth.

"I'm told David has been doing this for more than an hour." Steve's voice was tinged with awe. "Sentinel has been getting better and better at building these holograms. It takes a basic outline described by David, then reads his emotions to fill in the detail. Alice seems to enhance the communication between David and Sentinel, but I don't understand how she does that. It's really quite remarkable. Sentinel is learning from David. Nobody else has ever been able to communicate so effectively with it."

She realized David had not exaggerated his talents. He was Ray's son, and more.

As David described the scene, Sentinel created the image of a windblown coastline within the hologram, with the sun roaming in and out of clouds. David shivered. The Virtual Reality Booth was working perfectly, and he must be feeling the touch of cold wind.

Dianne felt an intense need to observe the scene in private. "I'm terminating our connection," she said to Steve. "Let's talk tomorrow morning." She cut off the session without waiting for a reply.

Now she could concentrate on the hologram. Her eyes shifted back and forth between David and Alice in one end of the booth and the beach scene in the other. She felt something important was about to take place, something that included her.

"Expand the hologram into a six-foot cube in my office." Although she would not get the tactile perceptions, she wanted to share David's experience as realistically as possible. As an afterthought, she added, "Enable the transmission in both directions."

A life-sized hologram of the Virtual Reality Booth filled her office. Startled, she stared into it, not sure what was taking place. This wasn't the six-foot cube she had ordered, but a hologram that completely filled the area in front of her desk, at least a fifteen-foot cube. It was more lifelike than any hologram she had ever seen, as if an unknown factor had suddenly enhanced the technology.

The coastline felt real. She gazed across the ocean all the way to the horizon, aware of the salty breeze blowing across the sand. In the background, above the hum of the wind, waves crashed on the beach. The sun broke through the clouds, and she had to shield her eyes with her hand. The beach scene filled her senses.

From the right side of the hologram, life-sized images of David and Alice stared at her. Then David turned to Alice and said, "You're close, but I'm walking along the beach, not standing still."

The beach image moved up and down slightly, just as David would have seen it as he walked along. "I was only nine years old," he said. "Sometimes the gusts of wind blew me off stride."

Suddenly the wind whistled past, picking up sand from the dunes. Dianne knew she had tucked her legs under the desk, but her senses told her she was walking into the wind.

How is this possible? I'm not inside the Virtual Reality Booth.

Translucent streaks washed across the beach scene, slightly distorting the images. David's eyes must be watering from the wind, she realized, and blinking. He hadn't described anything like that to Alice. Dianne's chest tightened as she realized Sentinel must be adding details by sensing David's thoughts.

David said, "Yes, that's the way it was."

Dianne felt completely immersed in David's beach scene, as if she were walking next to him, experiencing what he was feeling. She heard a familiar male voice shout over the wind, "David, don't go too far."

The scene swung around, and two people appeared in the distance, a man and a woman. Ray and his ex-wife Nancy held hands as they walked along the surf.

Dianne could not take her eyes off Ray. He glistened with sun and water. So happy, so alive.

David's voice drifted in. "Yes, we walked the beach almost every morning. Those were special days, the happiest time of my life, before my father went away." The hologram showed Ray looking over his shoulder in David's direction and waving at him. "I liked to wander off," David continued, "but Dad would come and get me."

Handsome and athletic, his long strides eating up the distance,

Ray trotted toward David. Ray's face radiated contentment.

A long time ago, that's the way he looked at me. Before PeaceMaker, before Nancy left him, before all of it.

Ray's image grew, and Dianne almost believed he was running toward her. Then David shouted, "Terminate the image." The beach scene disappeared, jarring her back to the present. Only David's breathing punctuated the suddenly intense quiet.

That last image of Ray lingered in her mind, young, happy, his life still ahead of him. She had taken it all from him, but he'd given her no choice.

Already exhausted, she leaned back in her chair. If she felt this bad, David must be near collapse.

"Did I do something wrong?" Alice asked David. But it wasn't Alice; the voice was deeper, masculine. Sentinel!

The sheer humanity of that question struck Dianne. Sentinel must have felt David's sense of loss and realized it had rekindled his grief. It seemed to be growing human, building on David's emotions. She knew David blamed her for his father's death, hated her for it. Would his hatred spill over into the artificial mind? Was that possible?

"No, you didn't do anything wrong. It was my fault," David said, slouching on a hard-backed chair. "I wasn't ready for such a realistic image. Dad was about to pick me up. Too much, too soon."

The hologram turned quiet, as David leaned back and closed his eyes. He looked drained. A gentle hum drifted across the booth, comforting, melodic. The music touched her.

Her gamble with David was working. Sentinel was becoming a conscious entity. David provided the raw materials—the emotions, the intellect, and the character—it used to create itself. Sentinel was growing more rapidly than she had ever hoped.

Then it occurred to her: would David evolve, too?

Dianne's sense of danger remained strong. Alice must reflect some aspect of David, an element dangerous and unpredictable.

"Many images are emerging," Alice said to David. "Painful images. Can you continue?"

"Yes. I have to face them."

David kept his eyes closed, and he perched rigidly on the chair. The music drifted away as new images appeared in the hologram.

Although her eyes had blurred from exhaustion, Dianne forced herself to concentrate. This might be the breakthrough to integrate human and artificial intelligence.

More images now. Intense. Disturbing.

As true as reality, the images poured in: David's parents standing in front of their house screaming at each other in the night … his mother's angry tears as his father stumbled into his car … David looking for his father at Little League games … sitting alone in his father's home office … watching angry demonstrators outside his dorm … David rushing down the hall stairs to the sound of his mother crying … angry faces at school … fighting, running, fighting.

"My head," David moaned, burying his face in his arms.

The images projected by the hologram became a frantic collage of David's unfulfilled young life, images that came directly from David's mind. They swirled like a kaleidoscope, too fast for Dianne to comprehend. She felt only the fringes of David's pain, but it was so powerful she had to turn away.

God, is all that feeding into Sentinel?

She felt the transformation in the hologram before she saw it. The overwhelming sadness of the images, the misery of David's life, merged with a blast of raw hatred. She turned to face the hologram, but the kaleidoscope was gone.

The huge cube had turned blood red, with her face in the center, distorted, barely recognizable, puffed up and swollen. A tiny slit appeared on her forehead. Blood oozed out. Dianne couldn't breathe, suffocated by his loathing. A second slit appeared on her cheek, leaking blood. *All that anger focused on me.* A third slit appeared, then another. David's hatred poured into Sentinel. Her image became a maze of slashes, her face a bloody mask.

She concentrated so hard on that gory image she barely heard the swish of the door sliding open behind her. A robot of the Daniel series strode into her office. The oak floor squeaked under the robot's weight. The door closed behind it, locking them in the room together. Daniel was armed with a laser pistol in a side holster, and her sense of danger soared.

"Send human guards to my office immediately," she said into her netcom. "Highest priority."

Dianne turned to Daniel. "Leave my office."

Daniel didn't move at first, then its hand, shaking badly, slipped over the handle of the pistol.

It's trying to override the safety code!

Dianne stood up and faced the robot. "I am a Citizen of the Domain. Daniel, obey your safety code."

Guards banged on her door, and she shouted, "Come in. Now."

The door remained closed.

Daniel shook badly, like an old man with palsy, but its weapon came slowly out of its holster.

How could Sentinel override Daniel's safety code?

The door took on a reddish glow. The guards were burning

through, but they would be too late.

Dianne turned back to the hologram of the Virtual Reality Booth. David sat motionless, his head flung back as if he'd had a seizure. Alice glared at her. *It hates me.* But Alice only reflected David's hatred.

How could Sentinel override its own safety code?

Then she knew. The answer had been there all along. Sentinel could kill her only by becoming human.

In her most commanding voice, Dianne shouted, "David, wake up!"

David's hand jerked, but he remained unconscious.

The robot had pointed its weapon at her. She tasted bile in her throat. She had to bring David back to reality and break the link to Sentinel.

"David, your father is alive," Dianne shouted. "He's my prisoner."

David's eyes popped open, his body convulsed and he collapsed, his eyeballs rolling back. The Alice image broke apart and faded into the nanotechnology fog. David's limp body slid out of the chair and sank to the floor.

Daniel lowered its weapon. The door burst open and a beam of orange-hot light came through, incinerating the robot. The smell of charred metal filled the room.

As her guards rushed in, Dianne said, "I'm all right, the danger is over."

She looked at David, collapsed on the floor of the Virtual Reality Booth, and added, "For now."

CHAPTER 27

The merger of David Brown and Sentinel was the seminal event in the integration of human and artificial intelligence, although at the time, it was not clear which entity would prevail.

◆ *Electronic Messiah*, W. Arthur Salem, copyright 2044, Distinguished Professor, MIT

Tuesday, March 15, 2022

David felt shaky, but he couldn't wait another moment. A security guard escorted him to Dianne's living quarters. As he approached, the door slid open and they entered a large, well-furnished room, the same one she had used to interrogate him before the Church attack. The room had been restored. It was as if the attack had never occurred. A stone fireplace dominated one wall, flames twisting from a stack of split logs. The photographs on the walls were the same as before: Dianne with her partners, shaking hands with a former president, smiling with customers, jumping over waves with her daughter.

The guard escorted him to the sofa. Standing behind him, the man remained alert but unobtrusive. Dianne made him wait. The minutes passed, became half an hour. His anger grew, but he sat quietly. He knew she was watching, felt her presence.

Finally, a door opened and Dianne strode into the room. Her arrival fueled his anger, but he hid it. She sat opposite him, her back straight and unyielding, her eyes thin gray clouds.

He cleared his throat. "What did you mean when you said my father is your prisoner?"

The crackling of the fireplace dominated the quiet room.

Dianne turned to the guard and said, "Leave us."

When the door closed behind the guard, Dianne said, "Sentinel, discontinue all audio recording, but continue to send images to the guard station."

Her eyes locked onto David's, but he couldn't read her emotions, if she had any.

"Now I will answer your question," she said. Her condescending tone put him on edge. "Your father is alive. I captured him during the PeaceMaker fiasco."

David squeezed his eyes shut and then opened them. "My father has been alive all these years?"

She nodded.

"Where is he?" David's heart was racing. "What have you done with him?"

"He's safe, somewhere a long distance from here. A place where nobody will ever find him."

Before David could reply, she stood up. "Come with me. I'll give you an hour with him."

David followed her past the fireplace, out a side door and down a long, winding staircase. As they descended, he looked over the rail to a lobby several floors below.

I could kill her now.

Her back was only a few feet ahead, shoving her over the rail would be easy. He could imagine the look on her face as she went over the rail, when she realized her miscalculation. But she hadn't miscalculated. He couldn't touch her as long as his father remained her hostage.

He knew Dianne, a ruthless megalomaniac, felt no shame for imprisoning his father. By allowing him to visit, she was throwing him a bone, a favor she could withhold in the future.

After reaching the base of the stairs, Dianne entered a small lobby with a single door on the far side. She glanced back at him, and he thought he saw a fleeting smile shape her lips.

She revels in my frustration.

Dianne's image suddenly appeared everywhere. His image also flashed back. The walls were mirrors, reflecting from every angle. More mind games, or perhaps a method to confuse an enemy? A Sarah robot stood in one corner, armed with a laser pistol, a reminder of her power. Through Sentinel, he had learned Dianne could activate tens of thousands of these robots, an army spreading to households across the world. Like the Vipers, these Sarahs could kill humans who had not accepted Domain citizenship.

As Dianne crossed the lobby, a door slid open in front of her, revealing an elevator. They stepped into the elevator, and a security computer asked, "Which area do you wish to enter, Ms. Morgan?"

"The hologram theater."

The elevator took them down several levels and gently came to rest. She stared at him on the way down, wearing an expression that, if he didn't know better, appeared almost sympathetic.

He didn't know what to think. She was complex, dangerous.

They left the elevator and walked down a brightly lit hall to a doorway on the far wall. It slid open to admit them and then closed behind him. Dianne entered a dimly lit circular room with a radius of about thirty feet, and walked toward the center. David followed her into the room, but stopped just inside the door and looked around. The room was empty, except for a maze of holographic projector/receivers affixed to the ceiling and wall.

Dianne asked, "Are you ready?" She stood in the center of the room, waiting.

It hit him, then. He was about to see his father. David didn't know this man, hadn't spoken to him in a decade. He had risked his life to uncover the truth, but now he wasn't sure what to say.

Maybe Dad doesn't want to see me.

Their relationship had always been edgy, but in that last email, his father had said he loved his son.

Realizing Dianne was waiting, David walked to the center of the room and nodded.

"Computer, display a 360 hologram of the island," she said.

The room came alive with color and sound. A tropical island surrounded them. David stood next to Dianne and looked across a sandy beach that stretched to the horizon. Thundering waves pounded the beach. There were no roads, no homes, no evidence of civilization. A deserted island alone in an ocean.

My father's prison.

David slowly turned around and gazed across the island. Palm trees and scrub bushes grew in a ragged forest around a crystal lagoon. Their vantage point seemed to be a camera on the top of a tall palm tree located in the center of the island.

"Another Virtual Reality Booth," David murmured.

"No, just a hologram theater," Dianne said. "And there's no interface to Sentinel, in case you're thinking of trying something. This theater is isolated; just a simple network connects it to the island. Sentinel doesn't know anything about this island."

He wasn't surprised. She was finished if his father ever got off the island.

"You can display the image of any part of the island," Dianne said. "You can also send a life-size hologram of yourself wherever you'd like. It's how we communicate with them."

"Them?"

"Yes, Paul Martino is there. Having a flesh and blood companion keeps your father sane." Then Dianne said, "Computer, give David Brown full control over the hologram theater for one hour, then shut down with normal security protocols."

David felt his hatred boiling over. "How many years have you kept him on this island?"

Dianne didn't reply. They both knew.

"Is he all right?"

Looking across the horizon, she replied, "As far as I can tell. I tried to speak to him many times during the first year." She shrugged. "I had something to tell him, but he wouldn't talk. Wouldn't even look at me." Focusing her eyes on David, she said, "I flew out to the island once, but your father is a stubborn man."

"You cared about him, didn't you?"

"You have one hour, starting now," she said. David looked for some sign of human feeling, but Dianne's face was a wall. She turned and walked away.

"It's a terrible thing you've done," he called after her. "It didn't have to be this way."

She stopped in front of the doorway and turned to him, her posture composed, her face unreadable.

"I do what I need to do. You should keep that in mind." Nodding toward the theater, Dianne said, "Ray always knew that."

Then she was out the door.

David turned and said, "Computer, don't record any aspect of my visit to the island. I want complete privacy."

"Yes, David."

"Locate Ray Brown."

A distant figure appeared in the hologram, a runner. The man loped down the beach, his long legs propelling him over the sand. David didn't recognize the long, lean body, but he knew it must be his father.

Then the figure splashed into the water and dived under a wave. The churning water hid the man's form for a long moment, and then he appeared farther from the shore, swimming powerfully. David saw another person in the water; the second man waved to his father.

Two men. A decade on this island.

The breakers rose with curling white tops then crashed along the beach, like a line of synchronized swimmers. The two men bobbed up and down beyond the crest of the waves, enjoying the water, talking to each other.

Maybe Dad's happy as he is. All I can do is remind him of what he's missed, how he failed.

He had to stop lying to himself.

"Computer, project my image onto the beach, at the water's edge near the men."

Ray dove under the crest of a wave, swam through the turbulence and popped up on the other side. "The waves are playful today," he shouted to his old friend.

Treading water, Paul looked back toward the beach, a worried expression spreading across his face. He pointed at the shoreline. "We have company."

Ray turned to see a young man standing on the beach. He and Paul had been prisoners on this island for more than a decade without visitors, except for Dianne that one time. He wondered what could be so important she would allow this young man.

The stranger wasn't dressed for the beach: green, short-sleeved shirt, tan slacks and brown loafers. Could he be another prisoner, sent here on a sudden impulse? The man looked fuzzy on the edges, and then Ray noticed the visitor's hair wasn't blowing in the breeze.

"It's a hologram," Ray said to Paul, as a wave lifted them.

Propelled suddenly by a sense of dread, Ray thrashed through the waves toward the stranger. *Something terrible has happened.* He gulped air with each stroke. *My son.*

He ran through the surf, the visitor a blurred image. Ray slowed as he approached, blinking to clear the sea from his eyes. The visitor was in his early twenties, medium-tall, and slender. Pale, almost porcelain skin. A perfectly formed face.

Ray's legs weakened, slowed abruptly. He stumbled to a halt.

He hadn't seen that face in a decade … since his son was eleven … but it couldn't be anyone else.

David has grown into a young man, while I've been on this island.

He was tormented by the thought his son hated him. David must have grown up believing all the lies about him. A monster, a madman. That's the story the world knew. The boy must have come here full of bitterness. It would be Dianne's final punishment, the worst she could do. She was probably watching.

David's eyes were warm, his expression open and hopeful.

"Dad, I'm so glad you're alive."

Ray hadn't expected that.

My son doesn't hate me.

Ray held back tears as a smile spread across his face. David returned the smile, and all the anger and guilt washed away.

Ray wanted to hug David, but he couldn't reach out to a hologram. He walked up to his son, stopping in front of the image. He didn't know what to say.

The seconds drifted past, but his mind remained a blank. After not seeing his son in years, there must be something intelligent he could utter.

Ray blurted, "Next time, call my secretary for an appointment."

David stared back, and his face lit up in a smile.

"Sure, we'll do lunch."

Ray choked out a laugh then fell quiet. David's smile drifted away, his face turned melancholy. His son was twenty-one but looked older. It was his eyes. Sad, worldly. Tiny crow's feet at the corners.

Ray soaked in the forgiveness he saw in David's eyes. Then he heard himself say, "I never thought I'd see you again. You're a man now."

"How are you, Dad? You look great."

"I missed you." Ray shook his head. "I just can't believe you're really here."

Ray looked over his shoulder and said, "Paul, come up here and see my son."

Paul was standing in the surf. He smiled and said, "Great to see you, David."

"You too, Mr. Martino."

"Paul. Why don't you catch up with your father? I have a few things to take care of in the house." Paul waved and walked away, heading toward three small structures in the trees at the far end of the island.

"I got your email, the one you created before the PeaceMaker attack," David said. "I know Dianne Morgan created the virus and you stopped her. You're a hero, not a criminal. That witch blamed the whole thing on you." David shook his head. "All these years," his voice cracking, "I thought you were dead."

David told him Dianne had given them only one hour and quickly brought him up to date with his ex-wife Nancy and his mother. Ray's initial elation dissipated as he listened, particularly when he heard about his mother's solitary life in Friday Harbor. Ray knew David had spared him the worst news, that his mother blamed him for his father's death. He hadn't been much of a son to her. He'd thought about her many times over the years. If he could change things … but he was lucky to get this one miracle. She was sitting there on her own island, waiting to die, just as he was.

"Let's walk along the shoreline," Ray said. They had only taken a few steps, when he said, "I didn't do right by any of you."

"You can't pick your genes. You did the best you could."

Ray stared at the image of David. "You've grown into a fine man," he choked out.

David asked, "Do you get the news transmitted here?"

Ray quickly recovered his composure. "I get everything you get, except it's not interactive. I can't transmit anything, but I get all the news." Nodding toward a small house, Ray said, "Dianne built a hologram room on the second floor." He sighed. "I watch the news a lot."

Finally, he had to ask. "Why has Dianne allowed you here?"

"Remember our last visit, when I was eleven?" David asked. "How

I told you something bad was happening to me?"

Ray nodded.

"That day still haunts me," David said. "It was the first time I saw Alice. I had a nightmare about Alice the next day, the first of many. Alice never let go. Or maybe I never let Alice go. I have this ... power ... that I don't understand. Through Alice, I'm able to transmit emotions to Sentinel, the artificial intelligence Dianne created. Alice is the focal point, the place where my emotions concentrate. I lost control yesterday." He shook his head and then described the attack on Dianne. He laughed nervously, "You must think I'm a freak."

Ray didn't reply at first. Finally, he said, "I felt your strangeness when you were a little kid. Like a part of you was different, foreign. I had nightmares about you for years. Still do occasionally. Whatever you're becoming, David, be careful. I would tell you to stop, but it's too late. Something is forming in you, something new. Whatever it is, you have to stay in control."

Ray felt the time running out; their visit would soon be over. He barely knew this grown-up son, but he had to be blunt. "You have to kill Dianne." David's expression didn't change. He wasn't shocked. He understood.

Ray added, "No matter what happens to me."

"I won't let her harm you." David looked down the coastline. "Once I have control over Sentinel ..."

"It doesn't matter what happens to me," Ray said. "She has to be stopped. There are no limits to her ambition. She'll try to use your gift. She'll do anything, promise anything, to gain control of it."

"I understand her," David replied.

Ray shook his head. "I don't think even she understands herself. But I know this: her megalomania is growing. She'll do anything, kill anybody who gets in her way. Don't be fooled. In the end, power is all she cares about." Ray paused, thinking fast. "When you fight her, you have to kill her. That was my mistake." He shrugged.

"One more thing," Ray said. "This gift in your genes. I have some of it, too, though not as strong as yours. Maybe being stranded on this island was the right thing. At least I couldn't do any harm here. Now it's your fight." He stared into David's eyes. "You understand, don't you? This power is passed through our genes. It has to end with you. No children. One more step may be too many. Stay away …"

Dad was still speaking, but his voice began to fade. Something about children. A warning. It was like fog rolling in, smearing his image, then blotting it out. David shouted goodbye, but he didn't know if his father heard him. The time had been too short. His happiness trickled away.

Then he was back in the circular room. The island was gone, sucked away in the mist. Dianne Morgan stood in a corner, watching him. The witch had probably seen every moment with his father. He hated this woman who had stolen so much from him.

"Still spying on me," he snarled.

"I never spied on you."

"Bullshit. I know Kathy Bauman was one of your spies. I know she warned you about me, how I was closing in on the truth. That I had to be eliminated."

Dianne stared at him, her expression somewhere between contempt and pity.

"Kathy wasn't spying on you. I hadn't spoken to her in years," Dianne said. "She called me out of a sense of loyalty." She shook her head. "You *are* a fool, you know. Did you really think I wouldn't discover you were investigating PeaceMaker? Kathy knew I would find out, so she called to tell me you were trying to learn about your father for personal reasons, and you weren't a threat to me." Dianne walked to the door then turned. "She tried to save you. It was my idea to kill you. She didn't know anything about it."

The words were a kick in the stomach. "Kathy was trying to save me?" he said. "You're sure?"

Her face now showed only contempt. She seemed about to reply, but turned on her heel and left. David stared at the empty doorway for a moment, devastated by his ignorance, but thrilled by her words. Then he followed her out.

CHAPTER 28

... and through it all, Dianne Morgan waited for just the right moment.

◆ *Electronic Messiah*, W. Arthur Salem, copyright 2044, Distinguished Professor, MIT

Wednesday, March 16, 2022

David followed old Route 1 south along the northern California coastline. The moonlight made driving easy on the deserted highway, and his mind drifted.

So much has happened. I hope I'm doing the right thing.

He had promised Dianne that he would return in a few days. It was a promise they both knew he would keep. Sentinel was his destiny.

Anyway, Dianne held all the cards. Dad was her prisoner, and his feelings for Kathy gave the witch another hold over him. Dianne would do anything to control his power.

He felt the presence of Sentinel on the fringes of his mind. He hadn't told his father all of it. A bond had been forged in the VR Booth, allowing him to communicate directly with the Artificial Intelligence. No more need for Alice. It felt like a metamorphosis, with the neurons and synapses of his brain transforming in a searing, evolutionary spasm. No longer wholly David Brown, what was he becoming?

His mind had opened to the AI. The immensity of Sentinel's processes and knowledge had staggered him. Likewise, he sensed that the complexity of his emotions and thought processes had overwhelmed it.

In a strange way, everything was moving toward its proper place. Driving down this lonely highway, listening to the murmur of the ocean in the west, he felt content. The miles piled up, the towns became smaller and farther apart. The night wandered in, softened by the moon's gentle glow.

Eventually he found the road he was looking for and turned onto it. In a moment, an outline of the dunes came into view. He pulled over to the shoulder, turned the engine off, leaned back and listened to the waves breaking on the far side of the dunes.

At first, the crashing surf dominated his senses, but as he listened, the music of the ocean became more precise, more distinctive. The melody began with the rumble of breakers crashing into the sand, followed by the rush of churning water, then the hiss of overextended waves tumbling back into the sea. He rested his head, closed his eyes and listened.

Kathy had been involved with the Domain, but she had tried to save him. A complex woman, she wasn't what she seemed. She had feelings for him. His father had fallen for a woman who destroyed his life. Was he doing the same thing? And yet, here he was.

The surf was comforting, but he couldn't delay all night. David started the engine and drove on. The sandy road was a pleasure, free of bumps and holes. The sedan's headlights drifted over a familiar beach house. He pulled into the driveway, parked and stepped out. A cold, damp wind blew off the ocean. He shivered.

David stared at the house, wondering if he was foolish to come here. Glowing lights outlined the walkway to the house. Then the front door opened, and Kathy stepped onto the porch. She was just as beautiful as he remembered, her hair drifting in the breeze.

She saw him but didn't speak. She came down the steps, her pace slow and uncertain. As he watched her, he knew coming here had been the right decision.

"You said to come back if I still cared for you," David said.

Kathy ran down the path and threw her arms around him. They had to talk, but that could wait. He pulled her close, relishing the warmth of her body, the feel of her breath on his neck.

For the moment, he was at peace.

DoubleD sat in the dark sedan, watching the dim light in the second floor bedroom. She had the sound enhancer pointed at the bedroom, but David and Kathy weren't speaking. Sighs, murmurs, the rustling of sheets, those were the only sounds coming from the bedroom. No sense staying here much longer.

DoubleD supposed she should be happy. Dianne had promoted her to Security Chief, so she was now one of the most powerful humans on earth. Wasn't that everything she wanted?

She shifted in her seat. Dianne had said to make David Brown her first priority. David was dangerous and Dianne didn't trust him, but he was the only one who could merge with Sentinel. From now on DoubleD would have every moment of David's life monitored and recorded. Her subordinates would do much of the work, but DoubleD liked to be hands-on.

She started the engine and drove away in darkness.

About the author

Dan Ronco is a writer of techno-thrillers and near-future science fiction. His passion is technology and he gained a BS in Chemical Engineering from NJIT. Insufficiently challenged, he went on to win a full fellowship at Columbia University where he achieved an MS in Nuclear Engineering. He then designed submarine nuclear reactors for three years, but found he preferred software engineering, so he achieved a second MS, this one in Computer Science from RPI.

Dan's writing is fast-paced, edgy and hugely cinematic. **PeaceMaker**, his first novel, examined the lethal effects of a computer virus enhanced with artificial intelligence. Piers Anthony called it, "Exciting, violent, thoughtful, and unfortunately true to life ... a powerhouse of computer adventure." **Unholy Domain**, his second novel, warns of the looming clash between religion and advanced technology.

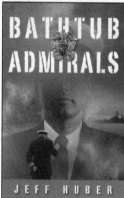

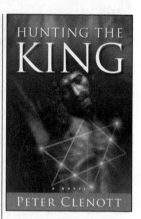

Callous
■ T K Kenyon

A routine missing person call turns the town of New Canaan, Texas, inside out as claims of Satanism, child abuse and serial killers clash, and a radical church prepares for Armageddon and the Rapture. Part thriller, part crime novel, *Callous* is a dark and funny page-turner.

■ "Kenyon is definitely a keeper." *Rabid*, STARRED REVIEW, —*Booklist*

■ "Impressive." *Rabid*, —*Publishers Weekly*

US$ 24.95 | Pages 384, cloth hardcover
ISBN 978-1-60164-022-2 | EAN: 9781601640222

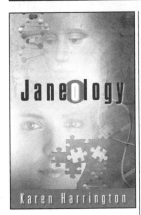

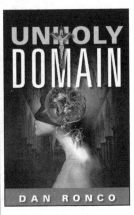

Janeology
■ Karen Harrington

Tom is certain he is living the American dream. Until one day in June, the police tell him the unthinkable—his wife has drowned their toddler son.

■ "Harrington begins with a fascinating premise and develops it fully. Tom and his wife emerge as compelling, complexly developed individuals." —*Booklist*

US$ 24.95
Pages 256, cloth hardcover
ISBN 978-1-60164-020-8
EAN 9781601640208

Miracle MYX
■ Dave Diotalevi

For an unblinking forty-two hours, Myx's synesthetic brain probes a lot of dirty secrets in Miracle before arriving at the truth.

■ "What a treat to be in the mind of Myx Amens, the clever, capable, twice-dead protagonist who is full of surprises." —*Robert Fate*, Academy Award winner

US$ 24.95
Pages 288, cloth hardcover
ISBN 978-1-60164-155-7
EAN 9781601641557

Unholy Domain
■ Dan Ronco

A fast-paced techno-thriller depicts a world of violent extremes, where religious terrorists and visionaries of technology fight for supreme power.

■ "A solid futuristic thriller." —*Booklist*

■ "Unholy Domain...top rate adventure, sparkling with ideas." —*Piers Anthony*

US$ 24.95
Pages 352, cloth hardcover
ISBN 978-1-60164-021-5
EAN 9781601640215

Provocative. Bold. Controversial.

Kunati hot titles

Available at your favorite bookseller

www.kunati.com

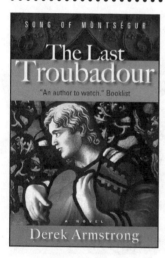

The Last Troubadour
Historical fiction by Derek Armstrong

Against the flames of a rising medieval Inquisition, a heretic, an atheist and a pagan are the last hope to save the holiest Christian relic from a sainted king and crusading pope. Based on true events.

■ "... brilliance in which Armstrong blends comedy, parody, and adventure in genuinely innovative ways." *Booklist*

US$ 24.95 | Pages 384, cloth hardcover
ISBN-13: 978-1-60164-010-9
ISBN-10: 1-60164-010-2
EAN: 9781601640109

Recycling Jimmy
A cheeky, outrageous novel by Andy Tilley

Two Manchester lads mine a local hospital ward for "clients" as they launch Quitters, their suicide-for-profit venture in this off-the-wall look at death and modern life.

■ "Energetic, imaginative, relentlessly and unabashedly vulgar." *Booklist*
■ "Darkly comic story unwinds with plenty of surprises." *ForeWord*

US$ 24.95 | Pages 256, cloth hardcover
ISBN-13: 978-1-60164-013-0
ISBN-10: 1-60164-013-7
EAN 9781601640130

Women Of Magdalene
A hauntingly tragic tale of the old South by Rosemary Poole-Carter

An idealistic young doctor in the post-Civil War South exposes the greed and cruelty at the heart of the Magdalene Ladies' Asylum in this elegant, richly detailed and moving story of love and sacrifice.

■ "A fine mix of thriller, historical fiction, and Southern Gothic." *Booklist*
■ "A brilliant example of the best historical fiction can do." *ForeWord*

US$ 24.95 | Pages 288, cloth hardcover
ISBN-13: 978-1-60164-014-7
ISBN-10: 1-60164-014-5 | EAN: 9781601640147

On Ice
A road story like no other, by Red Evans

The sudden death of a sad old fiddle player brings new happiness and hope to those who loved him in this charming, earthy, hilarious coming-of-age tale.

■ "Evans' humor is broad but infectious ... Evans uses offbeat humor to both entertain and move his readers." *Booklist*

US$ 19.95 | Pages 208, cloth hardcover
ISBN-13: 978-1-60164-015-4
ISBN-10: 1-60164-015-3
EAN: 9781601640154

Truth Or Bare
Offbeat, stylish crime novel by Richard Cahill

The characters throb with vitality, the prose sizzles in this darkly comic page-turner set in the sleazy world of murderous sex workers, the justice system, and the rich who will stop at nothing to get what they want.

■ "Cahill has introduced an enticing character ... Let's hope this debut novel isn't the last we hear from him." *Booklist*

US$ 24.95 | Pages 304, cloth hardcover
ISBN-13: 978-1-60164-016-1
ISBN-10: 1-60164-016-1
EAN: 9781601640161

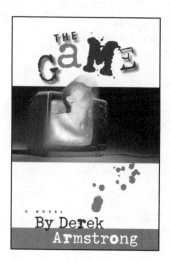

The Game
A thriller by Derek Armstrong

Reality television becomes too real when a killer stalks the cast on America's number one live-broadcast reality show.
■ "A series to watch ... Armstrong injects the trope with new vigor." *Booklist*
US$ 24.95 I Pages 352, cloth hardcover
ISBN 978-1-60164-001-7 I EAN: 9781601640017
LCCN 2006930183

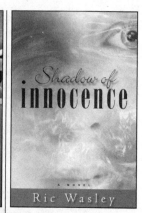

bang BANG
A novel by Lynn Hoffman

In Lynn Hoffman's wickedly funny *bang-BANG*, a waitress crime victim takes on America's obsession with guns and transforms herself in the process. Read along as Paula becomes national hero and villain, enforcer and outlaw, lover and leader. Don't miss Paula Sherman's one-woman quest to change America.
■ "Brilliant"
STARRED REVIEW, *Booklist*
US$ 19.95
Pages 176, cloth hardcover
ISBN 978-1-60164-000-0
EAN 9781601640000
LCCN 2006930182

Whale Song
**A novel by
Cheryl Kaye Tardif**

Whale Song is a haunting tale of change and choice. Cheryl Kaye Tardif's beloved novel—a "wonderful novel that will make a wonderful movie" according to *Writer's Digest*—asks the difficult question, which is the higher morality, love or law?
■ "Crowd-pleasing ... a big hit." *Booklist*
US$ 12.95
Pages 208, UNA trade paper
ISBN 978-1-60164-007-9
EAN 9781601640079
LCCN 2006930188

Shadow of Innocence
A mystery by Ric Wasley

The Thin Man meets *Pulp Fiction* in a unique mystery set amid the drugs-and-music scene of the sixties that touches on all our societal taboos. *Shadow of Innocence* has it all: adventure, sleuthing, drugs, sex, music and a perverse shadowy secret that threatens to tear apart a posh New England town.
US$ 24.95
Pages 304, cloth hardcover
ISBN 978-1-60164-006-2
EAN 9781601640062
LCCN 2006930187

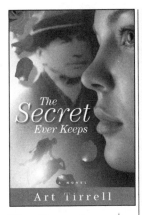

The Secret Ever Keeps
A novel by Art Tirrell

An aging Godfather-like billionaire tycoon regrets a decades-long life of "shady dealings" and seeks reconciliation with a granddaughter who doesn't even know he exists. A sweeping adventure across decades—from Prohibition to today—exploring themes of guilt, greed and forgiveness.

■ "Riveting ... Rhapsodic ... Accomplished." *ForeWord*

US$ 24.95
Pages 352, cloth hardcover
ISBN 978-1-60164-004-8
EAN 9781601640048
LCCN 2006930185

Toonamint of Champions
A wickedly allegorical comedy by Todd Sentell

Todd Sentell pulls out all the stops in his hilarious spoof of the manners and mores of America's most prestigious golf club. A cast of unforgettable characters, speaking a language only a true son of the South could pull off, reveal that behind the gates of fancy private golf clubs lurk some mighty influential freaks.

■ "Bubbly imagination and wacky humor." *ForeWord*

US$ 19.95
Pages 192, cloth hardcover
ISBN 978-1-60164-005-5
EAN 9781601640055
LCCN 2006930186

Mothering Mother
A daughter's humorous and heartbreaking memoir.
Carol D. O'Dell

Mothering Mother is an authentic, "in-the-room" view of a daughter's struggle to care for a dying parent. It will touch you and never leave you.

■ "Beautiful, told with humor... and much love." *Booklist*
■ "I not only loved it, I lived it. I laughed, I smiled and shuddered reading this book." Judith H. Wright, author of over 20 books.

US$ 19.95
Pages 208, cloth hardcover
ISBN 978-1-60164-003-1
EAN 9781601640031
LCCN 2006930184

· ·

Rabid
A novel by T K Kenyon

A sexy, savvy, darkly funny tale of ambition, scandal, forbidden love and murder. Nothing is sacred. The graduate student, her professor, his wife, her priest: four brilliantly realized characters spin out of control in a world where science and religion are in constant conflict.

■ "Kenyon is definitely a keeper." STARRED REVIEW, *Booklist*

US$ 26.95 I Pages 480, cloth hardcover
ISBN 978-1-60164-002-4 I EAN: 9781601640024
LCCN 2006930189

The Visible World

Books by Mark Slouka

LOST LAKE

GOD'S FOOL

THE VISIBLE WORLD

The
VISIBLE
WORLD

Mark Slouka

HOUGHTON MIFFLIN COMPANY

Boston   New York   2007

Visit our Web site: www.houghtonmifflinbooks.com.

Library of Congress Cataloging-in-Publication Data
Slouka, Mark.
   The visible world / Mark Slouka.
        p.   cm.
  ISBN-13: 978-0-618-75643-8
  ISBN-10: 0-618-75643-4
    1. Heydrich, Reinhard, 1904–1942—Fiction.
2. Czechoslovakia—History—1938–1945—Fiction.
3. Domestic fiction. I. Title.
  PS3569.L697V57 2007
  813'.54—dc22   2006023705

Book design by Melissa Lotfy
Typeface is Fairfield

Printed in the United States of America

MP 10 9 8 7 6 5 4 3 2 1

Portions of this novel previously appeared in *Harper's Magazine*
("August") and *Granta* ("The Little Museum of Memory").

The author is grateful for permission to quote lines from "As
I Walked Out One Evening," copyright 1940 and renewed in
1968 by W. H. Auden, from *Collected Poems* by W. H. Auden.
Used by permission of Random House, Inc.

For my mother and father, Olga and Zdenek Slouka,
who lived the years and half the story,

and for the seven who died on June 18, 1942,
in the church of Sts. Cyril and Metoděj

I would like to thank Leslie, Maya, and Zack for all the years of talk and laughter around the dinner table, for their support, their love. And Tina Mion, our twenty-first-century Goya, for the inspiration of her genius. On a different scale, I am grateful to the Guggenheim Foundation for helping me hold off the world just a little.

The glacier knocks in the cupboard,
  The desert sighs in the bed,
And the crack in the tea-cup opens,
  A lane to the land of the dead.

—W. H. AUDEN

THE
NEW WORLD

A Memoir

I

ONE NIGHT WHEN I WAS YOUNG MY MOTHER WALKED out of the country bungalow we were staying in in the Poconos. I woke to hear my father pulling on his pants in the dark. It was very late, and the windows were open. The night was everywhere. Where was he going? I asked. "Go back to sleep," he said. Mommy had gone for a walk. He would be right back, he said.

But I started to cry because Mommy had never gone for a walk in the forest at night before and I had never woken to find my father pulling on his pants in the dark. I did not know this place, and the big windows of moonlight on the floor frightened me. In the end he told me to be brave and that he would be back before I knew it and pulled on his shoes and went searching for his wife. And found her, eventually, sitting against a tree or by the side of a pond in her tight-around-the-calf slacks and frayed tennis shoes, fifteen years too late.

My mother knew a man during the war. Theirs was a love story, and like any good love story, it left blood on the floor and wreckage in its wake.

It was all done by the fall of 1942. Earlier that year, in May, Czech partisans had assassinated Reichsprotektor Reinhard Heydrich in Prague, and the country had suffered through the predictable reprisals: interrogations, purges, mass executions. The partisans involved in the hit were killed on June 18. In December of that year my parents escaped occupied Czechoslovakia, crossing from Bohemia into Germany, from Germany to France, then south to Marseille, where my mother nearly died of scarlet fever before they could sail for England, and where my father and a small-time criminal named Vladek (who had befriended my father because they were both from Brno) sold silk and cigarette lighters to the whores whose establishments tended to be in the same neighborhoods and who always seemed to have a bit of money to spend.

They were very young then. I have the documents from the years that followed: the foreign-worker cards and the soft, well-worn passports with their photos and their purple stamps, the information (hair: brown; face: oval) filled in with a fountain pen . . . I have pictures of them — in Innsbruck, in Sydney, in Lyon. In one, my father, shirtless and glazed with sweat, a handkerchief around his head, is standing on a chair, painting a small room white. The year is 1947. The sun is coming through a curtainless window to the left. My mother is holding the can of paint for him. Behind him, the unpainted wall above the brush strokes looks like the sky above a mountain range.

I was born, three years later, into a world that felt just slightly haunted, like the faint echo of an earlier one. We were living in New York then. At night, high in our apartment in Queens, my mother would curl herself against my back and I would smell her perfume, her hair, the deep, cave-like warmth of her, and she would hum some Czech song or other until I pretended to be asleep. We always lay on our right sides, my head tucked under her chin and her left arm around me, and often — it's the thing I remember most clearly about her now — her fingers would twitch against my stomach or my chest as if she were playing the piano in her dreams, though she wasn't dreaming, or even asleep, and had never played the piano in her life.

· · ·

4

Half a lifetime after the night my father left our cabin to look for my mother, long after they were both gone, I met a man in Prague who told me that the city I thought I'd come to know actually lay four meters under the earth; that the somewhat dank, low-ceilinged café we were sitting in at the time was not the first story, as I had assumed, but the second. To resist the flooding of the Vltava, he said, the streets of the Old Town had been built up with wagonloads of soil — gradually, over decades — and an entire world submerged.

He was a tall, well-dressed man with a crown of gray-white hair and a rumbling baritone voice, and he sat at the tiny glass table sipping his tea with such a straight-backed, sovereign air, such a natural attitude of authority and grace, that he might have been an exiled king instead of the retired director of the Department of Water Supply, which he was. In some of the buildings of the Old Town, he said, pausing to acknowledge the slightly desperate-looking waitress who had brought him a small cup of honey, one could descend into the cellars and find, still visible in the pattern of the brick, the outlines of windows and doors: a stone lintel, a chest-high arch, a bit of mouldered wood trapped between a layer of plaster and brick.

In the course of his work, he said, he had often been called to this building or that where some construction had accidentally unearthed something, and found himself wondering at the utter strangeness of time, at the gradual sinking away of all that was once familiar. He smiled. It could make one quite morbid, really. But then, if one considered the question rightly, one could see the same thing almost everywhere one looked. After all, twenty minutes from where we sat, travelers from a dozen countries stood bargaining for ugly gewgaws on the very stones that only a few centuries ago had been heaped with the dead. Certain things time simply buried more visibly than others. Was it not so?

The waitress came over with a black wallet open in her hand like a miniature bellows, or something with gills. She had scratched herself badly on her calf, I noticed, and the blood had welled through the torn stocking and dried into a long, dark icicle. She seemed unaware of it. My companion handed her a fifty-crown note. And then, before I could say anything, he wished me a good day, slipped on his greatcoat, and left.

I walked for hours that night, among the crowds and up into the deserted orchards and past the king's gardens, still closed for the winter, where I stood for a while looking through the bars at the empty paths and the low stone benches. Along the far side, between the stands of birches whose mazework of spidery branches reminded me of the thinning hair of old ladies, I could see a long row of waterless fountains, like giant cups or stone flowers.

I was strangely untired. A fine mist began to fall, making the cobbles slippery, as if coated with sweat. I looked at the stone giant by the castle gates, his dagger forever descending but never striking home, then walked down the tilting stairs to a place where a crew of men, working in the white glare of halogen lamps, had opened up the ground. As I passed the pit, I glimpsed a foundation of some sort and what looked like a sewer of fist-sized stones, and struck by the connection to the man I had met in the café, for whom these men might once have worked, after all, I started for home. Everywhere I looked, along the walled streets and narrow alleys, above the cornerstones of buildings and under the vaulted Gothic arches, I saw plaster flayed to brick or stone, and hurrying now through the narrow little park along the river, I startled a couple embracing in the dark whom I had taken for a statue. I mumbled an apology, my heartbeat racing, and rushed on. Behind me I heard the man mutter something angrily, then a woman's low laugh, and then all was still.

That night I dreamed I saw him again in a house at the end of the world, and he looked up from the glass table to where I stood peering in through a small window and mouthed the words "Is it not so?" I woke to the sound of someone crying in the courtyard, then heard pigeons scuttling on the shingles and a quick flurry of wings and the crying stopped.

And lying there in the dark, I thought, yes, that's what it had been like: beneath the world I had known — so very familiar to me, so very *American* — just under the overgrown summer lawn, or the great stone slab of the doorstep — another one lay buried. It was as though one morning, running through the soaking grass to the dock, I had tripped on an iron spike like a finger pointing from the earth and discovered it was the topmost spire of Hradčany Castle, or realized that the paleness under the water twenty yards out from the fallen birch was actually the white stone hair of Eliška Krásnohorská, whose statue stood in Karlovo náměstí, and that the square itself — its watery trolleys, its green-lit buildings, its men forever lifting their hats in greeting and its women reining in their shining hair — was right there below me, that an entire universe and its times, its stained-glass windows and its vaulted ceilings and its vast cathedral halls, were just below my oars.

But I could never go there. All I could do was peer from above as the people went about their day, unaware that with every step, every kiss, every tram ticket tossed to the curb, they were constructing the world that would shape my own.

2

WHEN I WAS A BOY WE LIVED IN A FIFTEENTH-FLOOR apartment in Queens, like an aerie above the world, and at night my father would read to me from a thick yellow volume of Czech fairy tales. In the book was a page with a kind of tissue over it. Under it was a picture of a beautiful girl in a dark forest. She had thin arms and she wore a white dress like one of my mother's scarves. She was leaning back against the trunk of a huge, mossed tree as though trying to protect it, a hunter's arrow buried deep in her breast.

I would look at that picture when I was alone. At the thin fingers of her left hand splayed like a starfish, grasping the bark. At the blood-red fletching, the stub of the wooden shaft. At the place where it disappeared — right there, just above that small, painful arc, that indescribable, exquisitely painful arc. There was a look on her face, caught between the strands of black, blowing hair, that I found shameful and disturbing and mysterious. I could never look at it for long. A look of shock, of course. And pain, yes. But something else, something I could not understand then — can barely understand now. A look of pleading, of utter renunciation, of love. Of love beyond all song and argument.

· · ·

No one could tell you about my father without first telling you something about her. She made him, you see, shaped him, turned him into the man he was. She changed the course of his life as easily as a hill turns a meadow stream. And though you might think that, given enough time, the stream will move the hill, or cut it through, it's the stream that will twist in its bed, alter its course. The new comes to feel natural. Detour becomes destiny.

For twenty-six years, Antonín Sedlák was like every other mother's son in the city of Brno, Czechoslovakia — four rows up, three over — running his own particular course to the sea. Then he ran into her, and nothing was ever the same for him again.

What can I say about my father that isn't bent out of truth by hindsight, misshapen by love? My father was a good and decent man, I think, a man capable of outrage over the world he happened to have found himself in, but someone whose faith in reason, like some men's faith in God or love, remained intact long after his life had made it ridiculous. He couldn't help it. His every gesture departed from that well-lit station, and though he understood how quaint this was, he was powerless to change it. It was his nature, and he wore it with dignity, like a childhood hat one has long outgrown but can't remove for the rest of his life. And somehow I could never bring myself to hold it against him.

I have a small, square photograph of him I've always liked for some reason I can't quite explain. There he is — already tall at thirteen, handsome enough, seemingly comfortable in a collar as high and stiff as a whiplash brace — looking straight on. Not smiling. And yet there is something there — a touch of amusement perhaps, a calm recognition of the absurdity of the proceedings — that seems like a smile.

Everything that he accomplished in his life was a violence against that almost-smile. Against its generosity, its good-humored reasonableness and decency. Against his very nature. And that, too, the smile seems to anticipate, and accept for the irony it is.

I see him clearly now, like a house revealed by fallen leaves. My father, who fashioned himself over the years into a kind of load-bearing joint, braced up to his burden, and died two years after being relieved of it. Who didn't know how to be in a world so suddenly lightened. I remember the bumps of blue veins on the backs of his hands, the mole on his cheek. I can see him, his big warm forehead, his way of listening while lighting a cigarette or taking a slow sip from his glass, that gesture of his — a slight backward tilt of the head, an open hand — at once wry and unresigned, as if to say, So, what would you do? I see him sitting in the chair by the long, low bookshelf, his bow and his violin propped against the wood next to him. Clean shaven. The flat planes of his cheeks. It embarrassed me to kiss him in front of my friends. I can see him smile. When he reaches for his glass or turns toward where I am kneeling, hidden in the wall, spying through the crack in the door behind my bed, the lenses of his small, rimless glasses turn into coins.

It was my father who told me about Pythagoras. I was seven years old. Pythagoras, he explained, besides doing some very nice work on triangles, which I would someday have to learn about, had believed that the essence of all things was a number, that our souls migrated like finches from life to life until we were liberated from the cycle of birth, and that eating beans was a form of cannibalism. He had come to this last belief, he said, because a cut-open bean looked, and still looks, very much like a human embryo. My father lit a cigarette. And so, he said, since human beings must act on their convictions and, whenever they see a tragedy unfolding, throw themselves headlong under the wheels of history, Pythagoras did what his conscience demanded, and banned the eating of beans. As a result, in Crotona during those few years, among the Pythagoreans if no one else, beans were accorded the respect they deserved.

Which would have been poignant enough, but no, history could never resist the extra step, the peacock's turn — it would always sign with a flourish. Which was why, on a cloudy afternoon at the end of the fifth century before the birth of our lord and savior Jesus Christ, Pythagoras, fleeing Magna Graecia with a mob at his heels, came to the edge of a vast bean field sleeping peacefully under the sombrous sky and, rather than run through this tender nursery of souls, stopped, and was beaten to death with short sticks.

A sad story? Not at all, my father said. A story of courage and conviction, sacrifice and love. Pythagoras was a hero. He took a sip from his glass. A hero for our time.

3

I DON'T KNOW THAT THERE WAS EVER A TIME WHEN I didn't know their story. It was always there, like a ray of light cutting into the room. It had been there before me. I simply walked through it in my time.

When I was young, of course, I didn't understand exactly why they had hidden themselves in a crypt, which I knew to be a kind of basement in which people were buried. Or what had happened to them there exactly. I only knew that there were seven of them, that they were Czech soldiers, parachutists, and that they had done something very brave. That they'd been surrounded. That they'd fought to live.

Like the Alamo, I said to my father. Not at all like the Alamo, he said. They were fighting for their own country.

In the afternoons, when my mother was in the kitchen, I would secretly play parachutist (my men would sit on the back of a gray model airplane like cowboys on a horse and sail down into occupied Czechoslovakia on tiny blue parachutes I'd found in a shop on Canal Street), and for a long time, whenever I sat at my desk, I would play "hidden soldiers," setting up my GI Joes in the partly open drawer that held my pencils and erasers so that they could shoot at the Wehrmacht battalions (GI Joes with their helmets painted black) arrayed along the edge of my shelf.

The soldiers, partisans and Germans alike, stood on a flat base, like a skateboard, holding their flexible green rifles. Every now and again I would find one with a tiny bit of plastic still clinging to him — a remnant of the mold from which he had been stamped, a kind of factory placenta — and I would take this bit of stuff webbing the crook of an elbow, say, or linking chin strap to chest, and carefully tear it off with my fingernails.

I would study their faces: the flat green planes of their cheeks, the slight indentations that were their eyes. I wasn't sure, early on, whether the men in the crypt had lived or died, so sometimes I'd let them live, flying up to the top of my desk like armed angels. Other times they'd be killed, and I'd knock them down with my finger. I continued to do this — killing them one time, saving them the next — even after I knew what had happened to them.

Like all children, there were many things I didn't understand. I didn't understand why it was that the roses of Karlovy Vary, when dipped into a bucket of mineral water at the cost of ten crowns a stem, would grow streaked with gray and green deposits and harden to stone. I didn't understand the story I'd overheard of twenty-year-old Robert Nezval, the poet's son, whose mother had walked into the family parlor one winter afternoon to find him playing the piano with both his wrists slashed.

But some things I knew. I knew there had been a war. That all the people we knew had gone through it in one way or another. That Czechoslovakia, the country my parents came from, had been taken over. That some had fought back, and others hadn't.

I knew other things. I knew that once upon a time there had been someone for whom my mother had cared very much. Who had gone out hunting in the rain one morning and never returned. Who had lost his way in the forest. Or leaned too far over the water. I knew this the way children know things, and knowing it didn't trouble me. It had to be that way so that things could be the way they were now. So that in the early mornings my father could draw me whales with his fountain pen instead of working on his dissertation — three quick strokes made a spout; a single touch of ink, a backward-glancing eye.

In the winters, when we were still living in the old apartment above 63rd Road, my mother would braid vánočka for Christmas Eve. She tried to teach me, but I was a hopeless case: my hands seemed to have been made for the express purpose of tearing dough or turning it into glue. Year after year I would stand beside her and watch her roll out four perfect ropes of yellow dough, press their ends together with the heel of her floured hand, then twine the separate plaits into a pattern of triangles, all the while dipping her fingers into a hill of flour spilled on a piece of curling wax paper. I understood nothing. She worked quickly, almost carelessly, with the kind of rough familiarity I had seen in expert gardeners, centering the flour into a flat-planed hill with her palms, wrecking it, building it up again. And suddenly it was done and she was painting the finished braid with egg yolks, making it shine.

I still remember those winter afternoons, with the perfume of the dying pine drifting in from the next room and the early dark coming on outside. The decorated balconies on the buildings opposite ours looked like small, multicolored candies. We laughed at the baggy constrictors of dough I produced and the great doughy highways I wove out of them, and one year she stuck big gecko pads to the ends of her fingers and chased me around the living room. I can still hear her laughter now and then, as if it had been trapped somewhere, and when I do, I'm once more in that kitchen with her, high above the world and separate.

After we were finished, I would watch her wiping the table down with short, sharp strokes, rinsing out the rag in the sink, pushing back her hair with her forearm. She would usually begin cleaning the sink immediately, sweeping around the edges with her hand, and I'd watch her scrub at the sides with blue cleanser, turning tight little whorls, miniature hurricanes. And suddenly — this is how it always was — something would change, and it would be as if there were someone else in the room with us.

"It doesn't matter," I heard her say once as she was rinsing her hands. "None of it matters."

She turned off the water. For a few moments she leaned both hands on the sink, deciding, I thought, what to do next.

"Daddy should be home soon," I said.

She was still thinking.

"Can I go play in my room?" I said.

My mother began wiping her hands on a dishrag decorated with pine trees and ornaments.

"Why don't you go play for a while," she said. "Daddy will be home soon."

And there he would be. Placing his black hat carefully on the peg. Giving his heavy coat a shake before hanging it on the rack. My mother would come out of the kitchen holding a wooden spoon or an open cookbook and give him a quick kiss and then I'd be in his arms and he'd carry me down the hall and into our narrow living room, and after dinner he'd pull a chair to the side of my bed and read to me. The yellow shade of the pirate lamp made a small circle. My father would sit at the edge of it, holding the book in his left hand as though giving a sermon, always touching two fingers to his tongue before turning the page.

Once upon a time, he would read, there was a small village, and in that village lived a humble farmer and his wife. And to this couple one happy day there was born a son. They named him Otesánek. *What does Otesánek mean? It doesn't mean anything. It's just a name.* The farmer and his wife were very happy. Otesánek was a fat, healthy baby with small black eyes. *See?*

Here's Otesánek in his mother's arms, and there's the father, and there's the horse, looking on from the stable. Is that their dog? I should think so. All the neighbors came by to congratulate them. Look at those arms, said the tailor. Look at those legs, said the cobbler's wife. What a healthy baby, they all said. Just look how he eats!

Otesánek ate and ate. He ate like no other baby had ever eaten before — *not like you, arguing with your* kašička *every morning* — and he grew like no other baby had ever grown before. The cow couldn't give enough milk. The chickens couldn't lay enough eggs. *Here he is, sitting on the floor. Look at all those pitchers of milk, all those loaves of bread. Is that his father? It sure is. Look how small he is. He doesn't look very happy.* Otesánek's mother and father ran all around the village buying food. Otesánek's father carved him an extra-large spoon to eat with. But it wasn't enough. Otesánek would eat whatever they put in front of him and scream for more.

Otesánek grew and grew. Soon he was bigger than his father. Soon he was bigger than a cow. He grew so big that he couldn't fit into his parents' little house anymore. He had to sit outside in the yard. One day a chicken wandered by, pecking at the dirt. Quick as a flash, Otesánek grabbed it and stuffed it in his mouth. The family goat came next, and the pigs, and the dog with the pink tongue. Otesánek ate the sheep in their hot, woolly coats. He ate the white geese that walked by the pond, and the carp that lived under the lily pads. *What are those, Daddy? Those? Those are the hooves of the cow.*

Soon he was bigger than a house. When he ate the plow horse, his mother and father came out to plead with him. Otesánek, please, they said, we will have nothing if you keep this up. When will you stop? Quick as lightning, Otesánek grabbed his mother and father in each of his huge, pudgy hands. When there is nothing more to eat, he croaked, and he stuffed them head-first into his mouth.

Otesánek ate the whole town: the cobbler and the cobbler's wife, the tailor and the carpenter, the shopkeeper and the teacher and all the little children. One by one. And he might have gone on eating forever except for a little girl whom he had swallowed as she sat at her sewing holding a pair of rusty scissors. Down she went, down into the hot red room of his stomach. When she realized where she was, she took the scissors and cut a hole in Otesánek's belly. Out she came. Out came the cobbler and the cobbler's wife, the tailor and the carpenter, the shopkeeper and the teacher and all the little children. Out stepped the plow horse and the goat, the chickens and the geese. Out jumped the dog with the pink tongue. And out came Otesánek's mother and father. They were happy to be alive. They danced and sang and carried the little girl around on their shoulders. And they all lived happily ever after.

I can still see him, the crease of the page cutting him vertically above the elbow and the knee. Dimpled knees arched across the road, he has just snatched his father and crammed him head-first into his mouth. He has a single tooth, as big as a dictionary. Black holes for eyes. To plead for mercy is absurd. There is no mercy here. He is the force that consumes, and he will keep on until the world — the narrow roads, the great square fields, the church itself, whose steeple pokes up like a child's toy just above his thigh — is empty of man and beast. A grave under the sun. And only he is left.

They're dying in the red room. All of them. Gesturing like bad Shakespearean actors, like swimmers fifty fathoms deep. The children turn slowly, uncomprehending, their schoolbooks paging in the hot tide.

A quick flash of inner pain, like gas, passes over the monster's face. Something sparks on the white wall of his skin, like a diamond birthing itself from his heart. You can see it, there! — a tiny blade, spotted and fine. Now he is clawing at his stomach, thrusting his own fist down his throat, as though devouring himself. He is in agony. There is nothing he can do about it. He is as big as the sun, and he can't stop it. To get at what's killing him, he'll have to tear himself open. Either way, he'll die from within.

There she is, stepping through the thick door of his flesh into the morning air. The monster lies slumped against a hill, still in his diaper. She is holding the scissors by her side. She has long black hair and a sad mouth, and of all the people dancing in the square, she is the only one who isn't smiling.

4

MY MOTHER HAD BEEN BORN IN 1920 IN RAČÍN, A VIL-
lage in the Vysočina highlands of Moravia. When I was a child
she would tell me Račín looked very much like the pictures of
Czech villages in my book *České pohádky,* and I would sit on my
bed and look at them and imagine her there, hiding in the black
shadow of an open door, or below the undercut bank of a stream.
It seemed to me that if I looked closely enough, deeply enough,
I'd make out her outline, a deeper dark within the shadow's
wedge, or recognize that bit of light between the blades of grass
as the topmost curl of her hair.

When I visited Račín in 1979, I discovered that it was, in fact,
just like the pictures in my book. A cluster of slate roofs. A tangle of close, muddy gardens and tilting fences. The requisite
small, swift stream, thick with nettle, cutting under the road. An
odd feeling. It was as though I had found myself inside my own
storybook. No one seemed to be about that hot July afternoon —
even the butterflies along the roadside seemed drugged, their
wings opened wide across the blooms — and I wandered down a
dirt road past a stagnant pond to the shade of a forest dotted
with mossed stumps and thick tufts of grass, and all the time I
had the strange but not unpleasant feeling of being watched.

At some point I remember sitting down on a pile of fresh-cut pines that someone had left by the wayside. The white circles where their branches had been lopped off made them look spotted. They were bleeding dark trails of sap from every cut — the air was rich with it. Large brown-and-purple butterflies I recalled from one of my childhood books moved in and out of the trees along the edge of the field; a small group fanned at the graying edge of a puddle a horse had left in the road. In my book, I remembered, the cardboard cutouts of the butterflies had slid in and out of invisible slots in the stems of flowers, opening and closing their wings as I opened and closed the book.

Back in the village I found the house — fourth down from the pond — without too much trouble. I had an old photograph, taken before the war. It hadn't changed. I looked at it for a while, with its slate roof and stuccoed walls. At the end of a goat-eaten yard was an old barn, half stone, half brick. A sheep with bits of leaves and sawdust in its wool was lying in its shade. No one seemed to be at home, and after a minute or two, when the sheep hadn't moved and the strangely familiar face of a six- or eight-year-old girl had not appeared in the double windows to stare at me — as I had half believed and feared it might — I went on my way. If there had been someone to warn, someone to tell of the things to come, I might have stayed.

She had been the third child born, and the first to survive. There had been a brother who came after her, she told me, though he had lived only a few hours, like a moth, and had been buried in a down-filled box hardly larger than a loaf of bread. My mother remembered that morning — the morning they buried her little brother — as one of the most precious moments of her childhood. She couldn't tell me why. Sometimes there are things you love and can't explain, she said.

A cold morning. A fresh wind roughed the grass along the road; the flowers shook their heads and nodded. Her father, she said, held her hand as they walked, his calloused palm as hard

and warm as a piece of wood left in the sun. On the way, she remembered, he told her a wonderful story about a *trpaslík* — an
elf — who knew the path to a stone door, no taller than a hammer, that led to the other world. The one below the pond. From
there, her father told her, you could look up and see *this* life, see
everything — the trees, the separating clouds, the fishermen
pulling at their earlobes or folding up their wooden stools — all
this, just slightly distorted, like a face behind poorly made glass
or a pane of new ice. These glimpses of our world were very precious to those who lived below; they could gaze at a dog's pink
tongue lapping at the edge of the sky for hours, and on those rare
afternoons when the children leaped from the clouds, spearing
down toward the silted roofs of their world clothed in white
sheaths of bubbles, they would gather in great swaying crowds,
their clothes fluttering about them, and weep.

I begged her to tell me what happened after that, how the
story ended, but she had forgotten. It didn't matter. There were
some things my mother wouldn't tell me — I was used to that.
But the story bothered me. I wondered what the pond people
did in the winter when the sky above their heads stiffened and
their world went dark; how they could see or play, and whether
they had great watery fires to keep them warm.

And so, for some time after my mother told me her father's
half-story, whenever I found myself alone with one of my parents' friends, I would ask them — Mrs. Jakubcová, for example.
Mrs. Jakubcová had never had any children of her own. She had
calves as big and smooth as bowling pins, and she always sat on
the sofa with her legs to one side as if glued at the knees, and
smelled sweet and sad, like a dusty pastry. One day I asked her
about the people who lived under the pond, and while I was at it,
why the young man had played the piano instead of calling for a
doctor, and who the men in the crypt had been. And she tented a
napkin over her finger and touched it to the corners of her lips
two or three times — a few yellow crumbs and a chalk line of

powdered sugar had stuck to her rose-colored lipstick — and told me that as far as she knew the people who lived in the pond slept a kind of half-sleep, like bears, waking fully only when the ice had cracked apart and light came into their world again, and that she didn't know but that perhaps the young man had cared for his music more than he did for himself, and that the men in the crypt had been heroes. Czech patriots. Those had been hard times, she said.

Some weeks later I tried Mr. Hanuš, who walked with two canes because he had lost all his toes in a town I thought was named Mousehausen, but when I asked him one evening after he'd hobbled into my room to say good night to me (for he insisted on this), he didn't seem to know anything about the pond people sleeping through the long winters. Sitting on the edge of my bed — I couldn't have been more than six — he told me that the winters were the times of storytelling, when they imagined what they could not see and entertained themselves with long, complicated tales in which all the things they had glimpsed the year before played a role. I asked him about the young man who played the piano. Robert Nezval hadn't wanted to live anymore, he said. Picking a big, gray picture book off the floor (it was a book of Greek myths; I have it still), he began to page through it absent-mindedly, past the picture of the herd of cows that Hermes stole from Apollo, with their bright yellow horns and blushing udders, past Athena being born from the head of Zeus, and Persephone being dragged into the earth by Hades. I wanted to show him the small wooden brooms that Hermes had tied to the cows' tails to erase their tracks, and the four sleeping pigs, pink as newborn mice, falling into the dark with Persephone, but he was moving too quickly. Sometimes people just didn't want to live anymore, he said. It happened.

As for the men in the crypt, he said, it had been a bad time and they had done a brave thing, as true and just a thing as one could imagine, and thousands had died because of it. That happened too.

"What did they do?" I asked him.

"They killed a man named Reinhard Heydrich."

"How?"

"How?"

"How did they kill him?"

Mr. Hanuš sighed. "They tried to shoot him but the gun didn't work, so they threw a bomb which wounded him and later he died. This all happened long before you were born, in 1942."

"Did he wear a black helmet?"

"Heydrich? No. A kind of cap. Some of his soldiers did, though."

"Why did they kill him?"

"He was a cruel man. He deserved to die."

"Why?"

"Why? Because he killed a great many people who did not deserve it, and sent many more to places that were very bad."

"Like prison?"

"Worse."

"Did you . . . ?"

"So who is this?" he asked me, pointing to a picture of Selene gazing down from the moon at sleeping Endymion, who lay, vaguely smiling, surrounded by strangely wild-looking sheep. He looked at me over the tops of his half-glasses. "I get to ask some questions too, you know," he said.

So I told him how it was Selene, the moon, who had seen a shepherd named Endymion and fallen in love with him and had asked Zeus to grant him the gift of eternal sleep so that he might remain forever young and handsome, and that that was why she was looking at him from a hole in the moon. "I see," said Mr. Hanuš. "And who does this huge hand with the grasshopper belong to?" That, I said, was the hand of Selene's sister, Eos, who had also fallen in love with someone, maybe another shepherd, I wasn't sure, but had made the mistake of asking the gods for eternal life instead of eternal sleep — a big mistake — and so had been left with just a grasshopper in her hand.

Mr. Hanuš looked at the picture thoughtfully. "I like the sheep," he said. He closed the book with a gentle clap. "If I were you, I would stay away from sisters like that. And the gods too, maybe. Now go to sleep, quickly — until morning will do — or your mother will be angry with me."

I lay down on my pillow and he pulled the dinosaur blanket up to my chin and petted my hair once, and I let him because I knew that this was important to him. "I'll tell your mother and father to come give you a kiss," he said, reaching for his canes. "Now sleep."

And I slipped down as though pulled from below, and in my dreams that night the things I'd been told and the things I hadn't mixed and blurred and Selene looked down over 63rd Road and SS troopers in their low, rounded helmets stood arrayed along the roof of Alexander's department store watching as, far below, a silent herd of cows with yellow horns and brooms tied to their tails moved like a sea of humped, ridged backs through the unlit canyons toward Queens Boulevard, erasing themselves, while far, far above them in a dark apartment very close to the sky a young man sat in a wash of light as blue as ice and played the piano — beautifully, perfectly — until he fell asleep.

5

MY MOTHER AND FATHER MET IN BRNO IN 1939, FOUR
months after the occupation began, when my father wrote her a
love letter he had composed for someone else for a fee of ten
crowns. He did this regularly, he told me, and did quite well by
it. It was nothing, he said: a few particulars, a handful of ripe
clichés, and the thing was done. This time, however, when he
delivered the letter for his client, things went badly. "Honza
didn't write this," the young woman who would be my mother
declared almost as soon as she began reading it. She laughed,
then read aloud: "'. . . in the empty rooms and courtyards of my
heart'? Oh, God." My father started to say something. "Stop,"
she said. "Honza's a sweet boy, but he wouldn't know a metaphor
if it ran him over in the street." She looked at my father. "What
kind of man writes love letters for other men?" she said. "A poor
one," my father said.

They began to talk, and by the time he walked out of the
pastry shop on Zapomenutá Street, where he had found her sitting with her girlfriends (the two of them had moved to a table
near the back to talk privately), she had agreed to meet him the
following day for a walk. There were reasons for this. He was
handsome. He was not a fool. There was a kind of sad lightheart-
edness about him; he seemed not to care very much how he ap-

peared to the world. And he had nerve. The day after they met, he found Honza in the locker room of the gymnasium after soccer practice (the schools had not been closed as yet) and gave him back the letter. He had decided to go out with the girl himself, he said. And when Honza, not entirely unreasonably, took offense at this turn of events, and with two of his friends gave my father a sound beating, my father, wiping the blood off his face with his sleeve, somehow managed to get up and pull a ten-crown coin out of his pocket. "Here," he said, throwing it on the locker room floor. "A full refund."

They saw each other all that summer and fall. He would meet her outside the steel railroad station and the two of them would walk arm in arm up the street that used to be Masarykova ulice but was now Hermann Göring Strasse, then across the square and down the small, quiet streets to Špilberk, where they would lose themselves, along with all the other lovers, in the vast grounds of the castle. I can picture them there, lying on the grass, my mother looking up into the deepening blue, my father, propped up on an elbow next to her, recounting some small thing or other, smiling in that way of his, turning the story like a candlestick on a lathe.

I like to think of the two of them there, wandering arm in arm up the paths and away from the town like newlyweds entering for the first time the house they would live in the rest of their lives, walking from room to blissfully empty room as though they could simply walk away from the gathering of things, as though they could still find a place — up this flight of stairs, maybe, behind this wall, in this room-sized garden — where time could not find them.

It was on one of those days that my parents accidentally took the second set of stairs leading down from Špilberk Castle instead of the first, and so found themselves walking past the entrance to the crypt of the old Capuchin monastery. My mother had never been there. The crypt would be closing in fifteen minutes.

A watery-eyed old woman with long white hairs on her chin was sitting in a chair at the top of the stairs, next to a rickety card table and a bowl with three coins. They were the last, apparently. The school groups, if there had been any that day, had left. The tourists who had once crowded the stairs to view the bodies of the monks, centuries dead, had dropped off with the war. The place felt oddly deserted. The old woman might have been waiting there for years.

"*Je tam dole zima, děti*," she said, looking at them. It's cold down there, children. "*Oblečte se teple.*" Dress warmly.

And indeed they could feel the dank, subterranean chill breathing up out of the stairwell. My father put his arm around my mother's shoulders. The woman handed them two yellow tickets.

"*To vám nepomůže*," she said, smiling. That won't help you.

My father took the tickets, though there was no one to give them to, and together they started down the steep, turning stairs. They were halfway down, laughing about something or other, when they heard her call down the shaft after them: "*Musíte spěchat, děti.*" You have to hurry, children. "*Není moc času.*" There isn't much time.

Perhaps it was the change from the upper air, or the sudden silence of those dim, low-ceilinged rooms, or the clayey smell. Perhaps it was something about the short, unlit halls, where my father had to duck his head as he led my mother by the hand to the next candlelit room. Or something else altogether. It was nothing, after all. In the outside world the universities had been closed, the factories turned to the business of war. Up above, the newspapers listed the names of the dead in thin black rectangles, like advertisements for faucets or shoes.

In the first, main room, where generations of schoolchildren had giggled over the poor mummified body of Franz Trenck, they stopped to look through the glass-topped coffin at the black, jerked flesh, the finger-thick cable of the neck, the nail emerging from the cuticle. In the second room a prison-like cell dug out of the wall and closed off by iron bars was filled with small brown skulls. They lay jumbled, one on top of the other, cheek to cheek, jaw to neck, some facing this way, some that. Some seemed to be laughing. The bars had been set into the stone.

My father asked my mother if she was cold. She was fine, she said. They read the brief biographies framed on the walls — the dates, the names — and walked on.

In the fourth and last room, apparently, there was a row of caskets arranged along the wall like basinets on a nursery floor. In each was a shape that had once been a human being but was now just a pelvis, a skull, a few fraying ropes of tendon. Here and there, hipbones tented bits of desiccated cloth. So much death, so neatly arranged. Walking from one to the other, my father told me years later, gave one the uneasy feeling of being asked to choose something.

All the caskets were open. Next to each, at the end of a curved metal stem like a rectangular flower, was a sign that gave some information about the body next to it. It was a bit of a jolt, my father said, to learn that some of the dead had once been women, but once one knew, it was possible to imagine one could see it. And not just in obvious things — a wider pelvis, perhaps, or a thinner chest — but in other, frankly impossible things: in the girlish bend of an elbow or the inward tilt of a knee. In the demure, almost coquettish turn of a chin. They began to try to guess in advance.

She was in the ninth casket in the row of eleven. It was obvious right away that she had been buried alive, my father said. Unlike all the others, who seemed more or less at rest, with their arms and legs laid straight out and their chins tucked almost thoughtfully into their throats, she was all rage and fury. Her caramel-colored skull, with its few pitiful wisps of hair, had bent straight back on the spine, so that she appeared to be arching up on her head. Her mouth was still open, caught in mid-scream.

Worst of all, though, were her hands, or what remained of them, which lay palm-up by her neck like birds' feet, still clawing at what had long ago given way.

A tiny bell sounded from the stairwell, and they turned and left the abbess in her coffin, walking past the rows of sleeping dead and the tumbled skulls and Franz Trenck in his glass-topped coffin, then up the narrow stairs to the street where they found the sun already fallen behind the body of the church and night coming on.

6

AMERICA WAS MY FOREGROUND, FAMILIAR AND KNOWN: the crowds, the voices, Captain Kangaroo and Mister Magoo, the great trains clattering and tilting west, pulling out of the seam in the summer wall as my father and I sat waiting in the DeSoto on Old Orchard Road. Behind it, though, for as long as I can remember, was the Old World, its shape and feel and smell, like the pattern of wallpaper coming through the paint.

My father loved America, loved the West — the idea of it, the grandness and the absurdity of it. It was a vicarious sort of thing. To my knowledge, for example, he never watched a baseball game in his life, yet the thought that millions of men cared passionately for it, that they had memorized names and batting averages, somehow gave him pleasure. The time we drove west, my mother in her sunglasses and deep blue scarf looking like Audrey Hepburn in *Breakfast at Tiffany's,* he was nearly stunned into speechlessness by the vastness of it all: the sheer immensity of the sky, the buzz of a bluebottle under that huge lid of sun, the oceanic valleys stretching to the horizon. The little two-lanes and the sleepy motels thrilled him; every menu was an adventure, and he'd study the gravy-stained paper through his reading glasses as if it were a letter from some distant land, which I suppose it was.

I have a memory of him standing in the open door of some small motel room in New Mexico, leaning against the door-frame, smoking. Swallows or bats are dipping under the telephone wires. It's dusk, and the land on the other side of the road opens into endless space — bluing, vast, lunar. It's as if the room, the motel, the gas station down the way could tip into it at any moment and snake like a necklace into a well. My mother lies on the bed under the light, her legs crossed at the ankle, reading a magazine.

"My God, Ivana, you should come and see this," my father says. "I could fit half of Czechoslovakia into the space between the road and those cliffs out there."

"I'm sure you could," says my mother.

The West, my father liked to say, especially after he'd had a glass or two of wine in the evenings when we had friends over, was the great solvent of history. It dissolved the pain, retained the shell: "Paris, Texas; Rome, Arkansas . . . Just try and imagine it the other way around," he'd say. "Chicago, Italy? Dallas, Austria? Unthinkable." No, the funnel was securely in place. Everything was running one way. Eventually all of Europe, all the popes and plagues, the whole bloody carnival, would be a diner somewhere off the highway in Oklahoma.

"Here he goes," someone would say.

"Think of it," my father would say. "The Little Museum of Memory. The Heaven of Exiles. Entertainment for the whole family."

On a train out of Grand Central one March day, many years later, I ran into a man I recognized vaguely from childhood. He sat by the window in the winter light, busy with shadows. A sculptor from Prague, older than my parents, he had come to our apartment half a dozen times in the late 1950s, then disappeared. He was in pharmaceuticals now. He had a house in Rhinebeck.

And so how were my parents? I told him. He had liked them, he said, he had liked them both very much, they had been very kind to him when he had arrived in this country. And yet every time he had come to our apartment he would get the feeling that everybody there was slowly suffocating, but too polite to mention it. At some point he just couldn't stand it anymore.

"It was a new world out there," he cried as small ice floes on the river behind him disappeared into his head, passed through the back of the seat, and reemerged on the other side. "All they had to do was take it. And what did they do? They sat there, even though they were still young and full of . . . possibilities, mourning what was lost. Reading the old books. Singing the old songs. *Kde domov můj?* — Where is my home? I'll tell you where it is — right here," he said, slapping the cracked leather seat next to him.

"In Rhinebeck," I said.

"Yes, in Rhinebeck," he said. "Or in Riverdale. Or Larchmont. But *here*. In America." He shook his head. "But your father understood all this. He had a poetic phrase for it — *sklerosa duše*. Do you know what that means? Sclerosis of the soul. We all suffer from a kind of sclerosis of the soul, Vašek, he would say to me, brought on by a steady diet of fatty songs, one too many rich regrets . . . but here, have some wine, they say it's good for these things. Laughing at it. Making a joke out of it. Nostalgia, he'd say, was the exiles' hemophilia, though contagious rather than hereditary. Oh, he could be charming, your father. And your mother, so lovely."

He'd never forget them, he said, but at some point he'd realized he could have nothing more to do with them. Why? Because they understood the trap they were in but did nothing to get themselves out of it. And not only did nothing to get out of it, but spent their days caressing it, polishing the bars, so to speak. Sad, really. A tragedy, in its way.

The train had stopped. It had been nice to see me again, he

said. And giving me his card, for some reason, he picked up his coat from the rack and hurried out into a snow flurry descending from a clear blue sky.

When I think back on that close little apartment with the Kubelius sketches in the hallway and the bust of Masaryk by the door and the plastic slipcovers on the new sofa, it seems to me that even when the living room was full of people eating *meruňkové koláče* and drinking, they were somewhere else as well. I don't know how to describe it. They seemed to be listening to something . . . that had already passed. And because I loved them, I grew to love this thing, this way of being, and listened with them.

As a child, my bed was pushed against the wall, blocking off a door to the living room. A matter of space. My father unscrewed the doorknob and covered the hole with a brass plate and then, because the frame of the door looked so ugly rising up behind my bed, my mother hung a bamboo mat over it to hide it. It was this makeshift curtain, which smelled like new-mown grass, that I would move aside so that I could spy on them as they talked: the Jakubecs and the Štěpáneks, Mr. Chalupa and Mr. Hanuš with his two canes . . . It's odd for me to think, simply by adding the years, that they must be gone. Only pieces of them remain: a genteel, tremulous voice; white fingers tightening a bow tie; a musty, reassuring smell, like cloth and wool and shoe polish, which reminded me, even then, of the thrift shops on Lexington Avenue . . . How quietly, like unassuming guests, they slipped from the world. How easily the world releases us.

Mr. Štěpánek was a small man who always sat very straight on our couch, as though hiding something behind his back; he had a lot of opinions about things and got into arguments with people because he thought a lot of things were funny. His laugh was like a little mechanism in his throat: a dry, rapid-fire cackle — ha ha ha ha ha ha ha — that always went on a second or two too long. He and my father had been childhood friends — they had grown up in adjoining buildings in the Židenice district of Brno — and perhaps for this reason he irritated my father in that close, familiar way that only old friends can irritate each other.

I loved Mr. Hanuš best, but it's Mr. Chalupa whom I remember most clearly. I'm not sure why. He never brought me things. Or talked to me much. Or came into my room and sat on the edge of my bed, as Mr. Hanuš did, and looked at the pictures on my wall. It was never "Uncle Pepa is here, look what he brought you," just "Say hello to Mr. Chalupa, where are your manners?" and I never minded much because I couldn't imagine him any other way. He wasn't interested in me. He'd show up at our door every Friday, carrying his violin case and a bottle of wine in a kind of wicker net and a white paper bag with a loaf of the Irish soda bread my father liked, and say, "Here, take them, take them," as though they were an itchy garment he couldn't wait to shed, and my parents would smile for some reason and take the things from him, and my mother would say, "Say hello to Mr. Chalupa, what's the matter with you?" and he'd say, "How are the Beatles, young man? How are the Fab Four, eh?" — in English, as though he didn't know I spoke Czech — then sink into my father's chair, which used to be by the long white bookshelf in the living room, and tell my parents about the troubles he'd had on the F train out from Manhattan. And that would be it for me.

I remember him well dressed, in a suit and tie, a slim man of average height who wore a hat and who always seemed somewhat put upon, as though the world were a vast, willfully cluttered room he had to negotiate — and quickly — because the phone was ringing on the other side. When I dreamed of him, nearly forty years later, he was sitting in my father's chair on an African beach at nightfall, still dressed in his suit and tie. A huge, still lake, backed by mountains, lay before us; behind us, white dunes of shells rose to a distant ridge on which I could see rows of fires and the silhouettes of men and monkeys. He was sitting there with that look on his face, staring irritably at the sand in front of him, ignoring me. I was about to say something to him when a tall wooden ship, far out on the water, spontaneously burst into flames. He seemed unsurprised. He looked up at the thing — the blazing masts, the spar like a burning sword, the beating wings of the sails — and, shaking his head slightly, turned his hands palms-up without raising his wrists from the armrests then let them fall as if to say, "Well, that's just fine."

I would spend hours spying on them through the blocked-off door behind my bed. I found that by turning off the light and pushing over the curtain a little, I could see nearly half the living room through the crack between the door and the frame. When Mr. Chalupa was there, my father would always sit on the sofa directly below me. Kneeling on my bed in the dark, barely breathing, I'd look over the smooth sloping shore of his balding pate to the white bookshelf on the far side of the room. Mr. Chalupa sat to the right, his violin and bow laid neatly across his lap or leaning against the bookshelf. My mother, whom I could see only half of unless she leaned forward to get something from the glass table, usually sat next to my aunt Luba (who wasn't really my aunt) on the small sofa with the hole below the left cushion in which I used to hide Sugar Daddies before I was discovered.

There was nothing much to see, really. They'd talk and laugh and drink, and eventually the guitars would come out of their cases and the violin bows would be rosined up and the men would take off their jackets and loosen their ties and Mr. Chalupa, who played the violin better than anyone else and knew every lyric to every song, would roll up his sleeves and the singing would begin: "Pri dunaji šaty prala," "Mikulecke pole," and "Polka modrých očí" — Slovak and Moravian folk songs — and when enough wine had disappeared, dance tunes like "Na prstoch si počítam" and "Keď sa do neba dívam," and on and on till two or three A.M. Sometimes I'd wake up deep in the night and hear them leaving, saying something about their coats or bumping into things by the door, shushing each other and laughing. And it seemed to me in those moments that their voices were all that was left of them, that they were good-natured spirits the hours had made insubstantial, and lying in bed I'd listen to them gathering their instruments, whispering, joking, joining in part of a refrain until, stepping through our apartment door, they disappeared as abruptly as the voices at the end of a record.

Mr. Chalupa had escaped from Czechoslovakia in 1948, like most of them, then spent some years in Salzburg, some more in Toronto, another in Chicago, before coming to a temporary rest in our apartment in Queens. The year was 1956. I was six years old. We put him up for a few weeks, during which time he slept in my room and hung his pants over the back of my chair while I slept on a mat on the floor of my parents' bedroom. When he found a place somewhere on the Upper East Side of Manhattan, I moved back to my room. For the next year and a half he continued to come by our apartment every week or two, to play his violin.

I saw him for the last time (though I didn't know then that it would be the last time) on a night in January 1958, when he broke a bottle of red wine against the corner of a shoe rack while taking off his coat in our hallway. It was one of those huge bottles, my father said later, that looked as if it had been bought from a Spanish peasant for a kilo of cheese or a length of rope, and it soaked everything. Chalupa looked at the mess he'd made — at the small red lake at his feet, at the wine spattered knee-high up the wall, at the neck of the bottle still in his hand — and shook his head. Everything breaks, he said.

No word of concern, no apology. My mother picked up the ruined rug and hung it over the outside railing where it rained wine onto the leafless hedges fifteen floors below, and eventually others came by with more wine and everyone forgot about it. The group spent the evening singing as always, and late that night, when they were all leaving (Chalupa was the last to go), my father said we would see him in two weeks and Chalupa said he wasn't sure, and when my father asked why, he shook his head as though he had heard that the F train would be out of service on that day, and said, "Melanoma, old man."

"I saw him once or twice more in the hospital," my father said, "but that was that. Between the toes, Antonín," he said to me. "That's where they found it. Absurd."

I didn't hear the story for a long time, and when I did, it came as something of a shock to realize that Mr. Chalupa had been dead all those years. I had always assumed for some reason that he had simply left New York, that he had been playing in some other circle — picking at someone else's *bábovka*. I could see him there, in that other apartment, leaning back stiffly in someone else's reading chair or drumming his small white fingers on the neck of his violin while waiting for the others to return from the kitchen.

For a while, the knowledge that he had died a full ten years earlier troubled this picture I had of him, like wind on water. But then the picture re-formed itself, and though I knew it was a lie, it still felt truer than the one that had replaced it. It was as if the fact of his death had left a space — like the chalk outline of a body — in the shape of the thing that had gone. The easiest thing was to bring back the body. It fit best. There he was again, back in that other apartment, in Baltimore or Chicago, playing his violin.

It was not until many years later that I learned that Mr. Chalupa, who had once slept in my room, had also worked for the Gestapo.

I had arranged to meet an old couple I was working with at

the time in an outdoor café on Londynska Street in the Vino-hrady district of Prague. At the last moment the wife couldn't make it, and so it was just me and the old man. It was late May and the cobbles were wet from the rain and the branches dripped water on the umbrellas over the metal tables. Except for a young couple with a miserable-looking dog, we were the only ones there.

We talked for a while about the translation project we were collaborating on, and then the conversation turned to what it had been like growing up in New York in the Czech exile com-munity, and Chalupa's name came up.

"Miloš Chalupa?" the old man asked.

"You knew him?" I said.

"Everyone knew him," he said. "Or of him. He was some kind of accountant before the war, though I'm not sure what he ac-counted for, or to whom. During the war he was an interpreter for the Gestapo."

At that point the waitress, who had been staying inside be-cause of the rain, came out with a rag to wipe the tables that weren't covered with umbrellas. "*Dáte si další, pánové?*" she called to us from across the small patio. Would we like another? "*Ale dáme,*" the old man said. A low rumble sounded in the quiet street. It seemed to come from over the train yards to the south.

"You're saying Chalupa was a collaborator?" I said.

"Who knows?" the old man said. "They say he was ap-proached by the Resistance sometime in 1941, around the time the RAF dropped those paratroopers who were to assassinate Heydrich into the Protectorate. He told them he couldn't help them."

"So he *was* a collaborator," I said.

"Listen," the old man said, "if only the heroes were left in Prague after '45 — or in Warsaw or Leningrad, for that matter — there would be fifty people left between here and Moscow."

The waitress placed two glasses of wine in front of us and went back inside the café.

"Maybe he did it to keep himself above suspicion," the old man said. "So that they would trust the picture he gave them."

"You believe that?" I said.

"I believe it's going to rain," the old man said as the first fat drops began to smack down on the cloth above our heads. He leaned over the table to light a cigarette, then dropped the match into a glass on the table next to ours. "I saw Heydrich once, you know. I was waiting for the tram in front of the National Theater. They stopped everything, cleared the street. I saw him get out of the limousine. Very tall. I remember he moved his head like this, like a bird."

"What happened?" I asked him.

"Nothing happened. He walked into the theater. I walked home."

It was raining hard now. Everything around us had turned gray. The old man was quiet for a while; I saw his head shake very slightly, as if he were disagreeing with something, though it might have been simply a tremor. He ran his fingers over the back of his hand. "You see, it wasn't always easy," he said. "To tell. To know who was who. Now take the boys who assassinated Heydrich in May of '42. A heroic act, a just act, and eight thousand died because of it. Entire towns were erased from the map." He shook his head. "Don't fool yourself; I suspect your parents knew who Chalupa was. We had all heard the stories about him. In the end we just had to choose which one to believe."

He was quiet for a moment. "Are you dry over there?" he said at last.

"I'm fine," I said.

"Here's an ugly story for you," he said.

He couldn't tell me what Chalupa thought, he said, or what he believed. He could only tell me what he had done, which was really all that anyone could say about anyone. There were some facts: After the uprising in 1945 Chalupa hadn't been shot as a collaborator. He'd been at such and such a place at such and such a time. X number of witnesses had confirmed that this or that had been said. It all amounted to little or nothing. The interrogation had focused on a single, well-known event — I could read the report if I wanted. Obviously his questioners had given him the benefit of the doubt, because he'd lived to play the violin in my parents' apartment in New York.

The basic story, the old man said, began and ended with a woman named Moravcová, who lived up in the Žižkov district with her husband and their sixteen-year-old son, Ota. "You'd have had to see her," he said. "A real *hausfrau* by the look of her — thick legs, meaty face, all bosom and bun. She was one of the most important figures in the Prague underground during the war — the anchor. No one did more, or took more chances. Nothing got past her. Nothing. When one of the paratroopers sent from London approached her for shelter in the fall of '41, she supposedly brushed him off at first, even threatened to turn him in to the authorities, and so convincingly that for a few hours he thought he had approached the wrong person, simply because there was something about him that had made her suspicious. London had to confirm, and a second code had to be arranged, before she would take him in. Couldn't risk endangering her boys, she said. And they were all her boys: the paratroopers — two of whom stayed in her apartment posing as relatives looking for work — their contacts . . .

"She washed and ironed their clothes, went shopping for them. Basically, she did everything. She'd bring parcels of blankets and clothing and cigarettes to the safe houses, traveling by tram, holding them right there on her lap, right under their Aryan noses. Not once or twice, you understand, but dozens of times, knowing all the while that if any one of them demanded that she open the package, she'd never have time to get to the strychnine ampoule she carried like a locket around her neck. On certain days she would go to the Olšany graveyard to receive and send messages, lighting a candle or pruning back the ivy on her mother's grave, maybe exchanging a few words with someone who might pause at the adjoining plot or tip his hat to her on the path. She was rational, smart, tough as an anvil. What made her special, though, was that she was apparently terrified the entire time. Rumor had it that she took to wearing a diaper, as if she were incontinent, for the inevitable accidents. That after Heydrich was assassinated, when everything was going to hell, she'd pretend to be nursing a toothache and travel with the ampoule already in her mouth — which, if true, was simply madness. The point is that she knew what she was risking, and she risked it anyway."

The rain had begun dribbling between the two umbrellas I had crossed over our heads, and the old man moved his wine out of the way.

"In any case, after Heydrich was hit — it happened right up here in Líbeň, though it looks quite different now — things happened very quickly. They carried him out across Charles Bridge at night, torches and dogs everywhere, and before they got him to the other side, SS and NSKK units were sweeping through the city, searching neighborhood by neighborhood, block by block. Combing for lice, they called it. They were very good at it, very thorough. Wehrmacht battalions would seal off an area, five or six city blocks, and then they'd go apartment to apartment. It's all television now, really. I barely believe it myself. I'll give you an example. Right after Heydrich died, Wenceslas Square was filled with half a million Czechs swearing their loyalty to the Reich. People were hysterical; they knew what was coming. I saw this with my own eyes, and I still don't believe it.

"Anyway, after Heydrich's death, the underground freezes. Moravcová somehow manages to get her family out of Prague. The boy goes to the country, the husband to stay with an army friend in Královo Pole. Moravcová herself hides in Brno, which is hardly better. After a few weeks, when nothing happens, all three return one by one to their apartment in Žižkov, who knows why. Maybe they're worried that their absence will be noticed. Maybe they just want to come home.

"Which is where Chalupa, the translator, comes into it. He gets a telephone call at four-thirty in the morning, is told to be ready in five minutes. He doesn't know that the paratroopers hiding in the crypt of the church on Řesslova have been betrayed, that they will die in that crypt early the next morning, June 18 — that the whole thing in fact has begun to crumble. He only knows that something is wrong.

"You have to picture it. Three cars are waiting in the dark. A door opens, he climbs inside. He has no idea where they're going until he hears the name. Some woman named Moravcová. An apartment in Žižkov. He just sits there on the leather seat, holding his hat on his lap like a truant. What else can he do? No one speaks to him — they don't trust him, naturally, and his ability to speak German only makes things worse because it means he's neither one thing nor the other, hammer or nail.

"It's a quick trip. The city is almost deserted at that hour, and the limousine races through the intersections, crosses Bulhar Circle, then turns left up that long hill there. He knows they'll be there in three minutes, then two, and then they're there and Fleischer, the commanding bastard that morning, is already pounding on the door, swearing, when it opens and a bent, tiny woman appears, like a hedgehog in a fairy tale. '*Schnell, wo wohnen die Moraveks?*' Fleischer yells as they shove past her, and Chalupa begins translating when the hedgehog calls out at the top of her lungs, as though she's suddenly been struck deaf, 'Would you like to take the stairs or the elevator, *mein Herr?*' but they don't notice because they're already rushing up the stairs and it's too late for anything at all.

"By the time Chalupa gets there, they're all three standing with their faces against the wall, the father and the boy still in their pajamas, Madame Moravcová in a housedress, as though she's been awake all night. '*Wo sind sie, wo sind sie?*' — Where are they? — Fleischer is roaring as the rest of them pour into the other rooms, as the sofa and chairs are tipped on their faces and pulled from the walls, and Chalupa begins to translate *Kdo, já nevím . . .* — '*Wer? Ich weiss nicht . . .*' and then stops because Fleischer has her by the throat and is striking her face, hard and fast, back and forth: '*Wo — sind — sie, Wo — sind — sie, Wo — sind — sie.*' She sinks to the floor. '*Steh auf!*' She stands. 'Please,' she says, 'I have to go to the bathroom, please.'

"Chalupa looks at her husband and son. They are both barefoot. There is the smell of shit in the room. The husband's hair is standing up; his right leg is trembling as if he were listening to a very fast song. The boy is looking into the wallpaper. In the transcripts Chalupa claimed he never saw such terror in a face in his life. 'Please, I have to go,' Moravcová says again. She doesn't look at her husband or her son. Chalupa translates: '*Sie sagt, dass sie aufs Klo muss*' — She says she must go to the bathroom . . . and now he understands. Fleischer is striding into the other room, still looking for the paratroopers. '*Nein.*'

"So there you have the basic situation. A wrecked room. Three people lined up against a wall. A single guard. 'Please, I have to go,' Madame Moravcová is pleading, over and over again, 'please.' Perhaps she realizes that their lives are over, that life is simply done. Perhaps not. Suddenly someone is yelling from the hallway outside: '*Zastavte! Zastavte!*' — Stop! Stop! Though maybe it's just '*Václave! Václave!*' — The name. Who can tell? They sound alike; anyone could confuse them. And Chalupa — here's the thing — supposedly translates the first and the bastards run out, thinking the paratroopers have been flushed into the open, and in the five or six seconds before the guard remembers himself and rushes back in, Moravcová sees her chance and takes it, and by the time they push past her fallen body blocking the bathroom door from inside it's too late for the water they pour down her throat to do them any good. So, *zastavte* or *Václave*, take your pick."

"She left her family?" I said.

"Indeed."

"She must have known what she was leaving them to."

"I doubt she imagined the particulars. Supposedly they broke the boy the next day when they showed him his mother's head in a fish tank."

"Good God."

"Doubtful," the old man said. "But we should get to work."

I remembered Mr. Chalupa. He'd slept in my room. I could see that irritated look, the way he would lift his violin out of its case with three fingers, the way he would sink into my father's chair. "How are the Beatles, young man?" I could hear him say. "How are the Fab Four, eh?"

7

THIS IS HOW THINGS WERE IN MY HOUSE.

One afternoon when I was perhaps seven years old, no more, I asked my mother whether she had ever had a dog. I wanted one myself. She told me she had, in fact, had a dog once, but that it had been very long ago. He'd gotten lost, she said. She would tell me about it sometime.

So I asked my father. I found him in his office, which looked down into the canyons between the apartment buildings to the little playground where I played. He first asked me what my mother had said, then sighed and capped his pen. "Move those papers over," he said. And then he told me about my mother's dog.

As a young girl, my father said, my mother had spent her summers with relatives in the Valašsko region of Moravia. In those days, he said, the *cigáni,* the Gypsies, could still be found camped along a river or on some empty ground. One minute there would be just a field, a dirt road, a stand of birches; the next they would be there: the men unhitching the horses, the women beating down the weeds for fire rings or yelling at the dogs, dirty-faced children with hair as black as ravens staring as though they'd never seen a person in a wagon. There were poplar trees along the fields, and their small leaves would twirl like decorations in the wind. And if you happened to be the person in the wagon, you'd look up and see them — the old ones — already half a kilometer down the road to town, their huge black skirts with the loops and the hooks sewn into them dragging in the dirt.

In any case, my father told me, my mother spent a lot of time in the company of an old man named Mr. Koblížek who lived two houses down and who was something of a storyteller. He had a square block of a head silvered by stubble and ears like miniature lettuces, and he'd sit on a bench on the south side of his house in his tattered slippers smoking a short black pipe.

No one had quicker hands than a *cigánka*, Mr. Koblížek told my mother. No one. You could watch her all you wanted, but it wouldn't matter. "The *cigáni* were not like other people," he said. They knew things. Oh, they could mumble and scrape humbly enough, but if you threw stones at them, they would turn in the middle of the street and curse you so vilely even the dogs would turn away. He himself, Mr. Koblížek said, had once seen a *cigánka* put a spell on a dog who had bitten her, so that the poor animal couldn't open its mouth to eat or drink, but went about slobbering and rubbing its head in the dirt, trying to push its tongue through its clenched teeth, until its owner finally realized what was happening and killed it.

No, the *cigáni* were not to be trifled with, Mr. Koblížek said, waggling a great square finger at my mother. The suffering of our Lord Jesus meant nothing to them. They never went to church or prayed for their souls. He'd heard it said that the old ones could see the dead walking down the road or resting in the shade of the trees at noon. That they could catch the reflection of the moon in a pot and carry it under the trees, where it would glow all night like a white lantern.

Anyway, my father said, it was during one of those summers along the Bečva that my mother got a dog. She found it in a corner of a neighbor's stable — a squirmy brown pup, fat with worms, struggling to reach a teat — and somehow convinced her uncle to let her keep it in the barn. It could not have been easy, my father said. You have to remember, he said, these were country folk — practical, unsentimental people; that same afternoon the rest of the litter was probably put in a sack with a stone and tossed in the river.

My mother, my father said, had never had a pet before, and she loved the thing dearly. Soon it grew into a small, brown, wormy dog who followed her about everywhere and who would sit waiting for her on the bank of the Bečva, looking worried, whenever she went swimming in the afternoons. She made the dog a bed of rags in the hay. Sometimes she would lie down next to it and pet it on its brown nose while it slept, my father said, which was probably how she came to have worms.

That August, when the Gypsies were encamped a kilometer down the road in a fallow field by the river, the dog disappeared. He'd probably been eaten, her uncle told her — the Gypsies ate dogs sometimes. He was very sorry. He had been growing attached to the little mongrel himself. My mother just stood there, runny-nosed and barefoot, ugly with grief, sucking her upper lip to keep from crying. Pulling her closer, her uncle wiped under her nose with the edge of his thumb and then, with the other edge, made a wide, flat smear across her cheek. They would try to get her another dog, he told her.

But that was not the end of the story, my father said.

"Another child would probably have cried in her bed that night," he said, "or lay awake listening to the wind, looking for things in the garden, or dreaming of what she would do to those who could do such a thing. Your mother got up to get her dog."

She went barefoot. In the house, everything was still, as if under a spell. As she closed the heavy wooden door behind her, she could hear the clock start to whir and then chime, twice. To avoid waking the village dogs she cut back through the garden, then up through the fields to the road. Everything was moving as though under water, the clouds rushing over the fields and the road and the white trunks of the birches. The moon flew across the sky, its reflection leaping among the trees.

She knew where she was going. She had passed the field where they were camped at least a dozen times before with her uncle. When she came to the crossroads, she turned right toward the river, walking on the soft dirt along the side, stepping over the briars and their shadows because it's impossible to tell one from the other in the moonlight. Even before she saw the wagons lined along the road by the side of the field, she could see the firelight on the trunks of the trees and hear the yelling of the men.

"Now you have to understand," my father said, looking at me. "This was a very foolish thing to do." The *cigáni* were not like the people my mother knew in the village, he said. He himself had once seen a group of *cigáni* in the Tatra Mountains dig half a horse out of the earth and eat it. They had a game they played. Four or five men, sitting around a wooden board, would wrap rags around their hands. These would be tied off at the wrist, leaving their fingers just enough flexibility to grasp the handle of a knife. Everyone would be very drunk. Bets would be made, drinks taken from jugs standing in the dirt, another log or board tossed on the flames for light. Then, when all were ready, my father said, their elbows on the board and their bandaged arms raised and the crowd yelling and shoving for a better view, the ear of a hare would be thrown into the center of the board.

"An unpleasant business," my father said. By the time someone emerged from the fray with the ear pinned on the tip of his blade like a slice of sausage, the rags would be stained black as if splashed with paint. And sometimes things went wrong. A friend of his had seen a *cigán*, furious over some real or imagined slight, slowly force another's arm to the wood and then, with a tremendous blow, as though killing a wolf, drive his knife through the bones of the other's hand, pinning him palm-down to the board.

"Anyway, it probably took them a few moments to notice the little girl on the other side of the fire," my father said. "It probably took them a few more to realize she was real."

Co tady chceš? — What do you want here? — said a voice like a crow. *Běž domů.* Go home.

I want my dog, said my mother.

A man snorted like a boar; a few people laughed. Let's get on with it, someone said.

Ztrať se, a number of voices yelled. Get lost. Go back where you belong. From somewhere under the trees a pig was grunting quickly. A huge gust of sparks rose into the branches.

What makes you think we have your dog? said the voice like a crow.

Horses neighed from the dark. An old woman in a wide, colored skirt was coming toward my mother, making sweeping motions with her hands as though pushing away an unpleasant smell. *Maž, maž. Tady tě nikdo nechce.* Go. Nobody wants you here.

The men were getting on with their business, wrapping their hands in rags, tearing at the cloth with their teeth. When the *ciganka* got to the edge of the fire, my father said, my mother stooped and picked up a branch that was sticking out of the flames.

The crowd burst out laughing. Why would we take your dog? they yelled. Go home, you little fool. Someone said something she didn't understand and the crowd howled with laughter.

Give her the dog, called the crow, and a tall, powerful-looking man in loose cloth pants stepped out of the smoke. The crowd quieted. He had long black hair and a thick black mustache and his skin was as brown as the bark of a tree. He looked at her for a few moments, then began slowly unwrapping the rags from around his hands.

Get the dog, he said, and instantly the dog was there, led by a boy about my age. The dog seemed well fed, my father said, and he had a short length of woven horsetail leash around his neck.

He seemed glad to see her. The *cigán* nodded. And without another word my mother took her dog and walked home to her uncle's house and led him to his rag bed in the barn. Finally she returned to the house, and lifting the heavy wooden door so it wouldn't creak, crept past the ticking clock up the stairs to her room. As she lay in bed she could see the dark frame of her window against the lightening sky. It was almost morning.

He had to work now, my father said. He had only told me this story about my mother and her dog because, he said, he wanted me to know something about my mother.

I nodded. But Mommy said her dog ran away, I said.

And so he did, said my father. Later. Personally, he'd always thought he'd returned to the Gypsies, where life was good for a dog.

And that was the end of the story.

A year or two later my parents bought me a dog. And one day that dog disappeared. We had moved to the suburbs by then, to a small house in Ardsley with a cracked driveway and a mimosa tree that dropped pink blossoms all over the yard. Perhaps he'd been stolen, my father said. Or run over by a car. We hunted around in the thin woods at the end of the road, calling his name, and hung up signs on the telephone poles asking whoever had found him to give him back to us, but no one ever called. In all honesty, I'd never really cared for the dog — a purebred boxer with a streak on his nose — but I'd gotten used to him, and when he disappeared, I missed him for a while. And then one day when my mother was driving me somewhere, we saw him in the back of someone else's car.

It was a rainy day in late fall; gusts of wind shook the car and smeared the water across the windows. My mother tried to get the attention of the people in the other car, waving and tapping on the glass with her wedding ring, then followed them off the highway and through the tolls, mile after mile, down roads we had never been on before, to some part of Queens I didn't know. After a long time we crossed a bridge over a big river to a world of factories where tall chimneys poured smoke into the rain while others burned like giant candles.

When it was almost dark the car stopped in front of a smudged little house and a family with two small children got out. It had stopped raining. They were frightened at first, and the man kept waving his hands and saying What do you want? What do you want? but when my mother explained, he apologized and said that he was very sorry but that the dog was theirs and that he and his family had come from Pakistan a year ago, and then he went into the house and brought out some papers. I talked to our dog, meanwhile, but he didn't recognize me. Eventually we got back in our car and went home without him. I remember looking out the window as we drove back over the bridge. One black cloud was lit up from behind, and I could see the water and the factories.

It'll be all right, said my mother. It doesn't matter. And she laughed to herself and shook her head.

Later I remembered the flames and turned around quickly in my seat, but the road had taken a turn, and they were gone. And so the story stopped again, balanced on one foot, so to speak.

Twenty-five years later, on an October afternoon in 1985, I was working at my desk at a cabin I'd once lived in with my parents when I heard someone calling a hello and found an old couple I vaguely remembered from my childhood standing by the stone wall. They had been driving in the area, they said, and had suddenly remembered visiting my parents years ago at a cabin on a lake, and had decided on a whim to see if they could find it. They were very proud of themselves, and though I didn't particularly want to, I invited them in for a glass of wine and we talked of this and that and they asked me if any of the other Czech families they had met in that earlier time still lived at the lake.

They remembered Reinhold Černý very well, they said, and the Kesslers, whom they had met once or twice in the city. Černý had passed on years ago, I told them, as had Kessler. Kessler's wife, Marie, I had heard, was living somewhere in North Carolina. And the Mostovskýs? Their children were two cabins down, I said.

At which point my dog, waking from where he'd fallen asleep in the shade of the small wrought-iron table around which we were sitting, knocked against one of the legs and spilled some wine. They begged me not to scold him — it hadn't been his fault, after all — and explained that they had three dogs at home who were just like children to them, and how they had both felt sick, absolutely sick, to read in the paper, what with all the news about China and everything, that the Chinese still ate dogs. It was barbaric, absolutely barbaric, they said, and to think we could do business with these people. The whole thing had reminded them of my poor mother.

How so? I asked.

But surely I knew the story, they said — both my parents had spoken of it. A terrible thing for a child to go through. How my mother's dog had been stolen by Gypsies one summer and how my mother, who could have been no more than seven or eight years old at the time, had crept out of her grandparents' house in the middle of the night and walked miles and miles to a Gypsy camp and demanded her dog, only to be given a flour sack that might have held a rabbit, or a small carp, and how she had walked all the way home, the small dear, and buried the remains in the garden before returning to bed. Surely I remembered it now.

I told them I did.

This was a nice place, they said, looking around. It was odd, really. They hadn't thought about my parents for years before they'd read that report about dogs in the paper, and yet, hardly two weeks later, here they were. Of course, it was probably be-

cause the article had started them thinking about my mother —
though they hadn't realized they were thinking of her at all at the
time — that they had remembered our cabin and decided on a
whim to try and find it.

They wouldn't have been surprised, now that they thought of
it, if my parents hadn't told me the story of my mother and her
dog. A terrible thing to tell a child. How she must have suffered,
the poor dear, walking all those miles with that sack at her side.
Still, they agreed, the story said something about her character.
How strong she was. They nodded, agreeing with each other.
The Lord only visited those who could bear it, they said.

8

SHE HAD BEEN BEAUTIFUL. I HAVE A FEW PHOTOGRAPHS, favorites I salvaged after my father died from the shoeboxes I found piled in the basement by the folded ping-pong table: one of a black-haired tomboy standing by her bicycle in the Vysočina forests, looking at the photographer as if wondering whether he's going to try to take it away from her; another of a young woman on a windy corner in Brno, too impatient to be fashionable, pinning her hat to her hair as the statue of a dead saint, behind her, points to an escaping trolley; a third — overexposed — of my mother against a white sea of cloud in the Tatras, the hand of a companion — not my father — visible at her waist.

And then there's the one of him, or so I have to assume. I've looked at it closely. At the overlong sleeves of the sweater — the left pushed partway to the elbow, the other almost covering his hand. I've studied the cigarette, like a tiny stub of light clamped between the tips of his fingers, protruding from inside the wool. There's nothing to see. A man standing in the snow, squinting into the glare. Not particularly handsome. The snow on the hill behind him has partly melted.

I don't know what he meant to her exactly. Or how he died. I only know that his face, the sound of his voice, never really diminished for her. That she simply refused to give him up.

There are people like that, after all — individuals who resist the current, who hold out against that betrayal. Who refuse to take their small bouquet of misremembered moments and leave. You'll run into them at the deli counter, or while waiting in line at the theater, and they'll say, "I had an acquaintance many years ago" or "I once knew someone who I cared for very much who also hated sauerkraut," and suddenly, standing there waiting to give the butcher your order, or clutching your paper ticket, you can see them leaning into the current's pull, hear the rocks of the riverbed clattering like bones.

It wasn't a matter of jealousy or fear. My parents never slept in separate beds or took vacations with "old friends" or hurt each other more than husbands and wives generally hurt each other. It was subtler than that. My mother respected my father's strength, his endurance, was grateful to him for taking on the role he had for her with such tact, but hated him for it too. And because she recognized the injustice in this, she loved him — or tried. And because she knew he recognized it too, she failed.

And my father? My father saw it for the perfect thing it was, appreciated it the way a master carpenter will appreciate a perfectly constructed joint, the tongue mated to the groove like an act of God. Kafka would have understood: he would do the right thing — the only thing — and be hated for it. Inevitably. Even justly.

9

ONE DAY WHEN I WAS SEVEN AND HAD BEEN GOING TO school for a year or so, my father asked me what I was learning (he was sitting in his favorite chair by the long white bookshelf in the living room; my mother had gone out, to do some shopping, she said), and I told him about reading and spelling and math. I'd written a report on volcanoes, I said.

My father nodded. "The Greek philosopher Empedocles dove into a volcano to prove he was a god and burned to a crisp," he said. "What do you think of that?"

I said I thought it was silly.

"Smart boy," my father said.

He looked at me for a moment, sitting on the sofa, skinny legs dangling like a ventriloquist's puppet, then took a small sip from the glass on the shelf next to him. "We need to supplement," he said.

For years afterward the Greeks tasted like Ovaltine, because every time my father decided to supplement, he would let me make a cup and sip it while he talked. And for years that taste was all I retained from our sessions in the living room — that and the memory of him sitting in his chair, talking to me as if I were older than I was, as if I knew why he was smiling or why he had run his hand over his head that way or why he'd looked out the window over Queens Boulevard as if suddenly remembering something, some appointment he'd missed.

He told me many things; I don't remember them all. He told me about Empedocles and Parmenides and Anaximander, Heraclitus and Thales. He liked their names, and he would make me repeat them and seem pleased when I got them right. "Say Empedocles," he'd say, "say Anaximander," and I'd say Empedocles or Anaximander and he'd chuckle as if there were someone else in the room with us and say, "That's good. That's very nice."

Parmenides, he said, had worried a lot about reality because he'd noticed that what his senses told him didn't make sense. "Which didn't really make sense," my father said, "but never mind." Parmenides, he said, went on to claim that reality could be understood only by thought, which was a disastrous thing to say if one thought about it — a bit like saying that a nail could only be hammered with a tomato — even if it *was* true.

The rational mind was a terrible tool for the job, my father said. It thought logically, or tried to. It sniffed after justice where there was none. It insisted on looking at *everything*, even when that was clearly a bad idea. It had this notion, which it clung to, that the truth would save us, though it was quite obvious that precisely the opposite was often true. "The fact is that many things are true," my father said, "but we have to pretend they aren't."

"Why?" I said.

"Because the truth would confuse us and make us sad," my father said. "Take Empedocles — can you say Empedocles?" "Empedocles," I said. "Good boy," said my father. Empedocles, he said, believed that there were only two basic forces in the world — love and strife. Love brought things together and strife

57

pulled them apart. All very logical. Empedocles claimed that this explained how things could change and yet the world could stay the same. My father looked at me. "Now let me ask you. Which do you think is easier, to keep things together or to pull them apart?"

"Pull them apart," I said.

"Exactly," said my father. He smiled. "Maybe that's why Empedocles dove into the volcano," he said.

In any case, he'd never liked Empedocles much, my father said. Thales, who lived on the coast of Asia Minor and who could navigate ships and reroute rivers, was much more interesting. Thales, a bald-headed old man with hairy ears, said the world floated like a log on endless water — which it very well might, said my father — and that all things were full of gods — which they were. Of course, the problem with the second part, my father said, was that when people thought of the things that were full of gods, they always thought of death and sunsets and Niagara Falls, never doorknobs.

The Greeks were full of wisdom, my father said.

But I wanted to know when Mommy was coming home — it may have been the first time my father called me in to ask me about my schooling; it may have been some time after that. I don't remember.

"Heraclitus was fun," he said, not hearing me. "Heraclitus, you see, was bothered by the fact that nothing in the world stayed the same, that everything changed. That the world was always rushing on, whether we noticed it or not. And he tried to explain this constant changing and decided that since fire changed everything it touched, fire was to blame." My father looked out the window. "According to Heraclitus, everywhere we look, the world is on fire, burning invisibly, changing before our very eyes." My father paused. "Of course, some things never change, never mind how long they burn. So, so much for Heraclitus."

But I wanted to know when Mommy was coming home. I was getting hungry and my Ovaltine was gone.

My father was looking out the window over Queens Boulevard. In the far distance, a small brown plane was turning toward La Guardia Airport. "Soon," he said. "Very soon, I'm sure."

10

BY THE TIME I WAS NINE WE HAD LEFT THE CITY, THE asphalt playgrounds, those inland seas, I'd played on, the loaf-shaped hedges and shadowed continents of lawn, and moved to a small, flat house in the suburbs. The house had a fireplace that didn't work and a basement and a sliding glass door which let out onto a porch that overlooked a scrubby patch of woods. In the spring, when the mud had finally thawed and the huge, ridged leaves of the skunk cabbage had sprung out of it, hiding the trash, I would catch red-backed salamanders there.

That summer, at the Memorial Day picnic, my father broke his glasses trying to catch a football which slipped through his hands. My mother hadn't wanted to go. Mr. Kelly, who was from South Dakota, and who pitched to the kids on the block every Saturday from the foot of his driveway, aiming at a square he had drawn on the garage door with a piece of chalk, had thrown it to him from across the street. He felt bad afterward, and helped my father look for the pieces, and my father, who as a schoolboy in the summer of 1937 had run eight hundred meters around a cinder track in two minutes and one second, setting a national junior record that lasted for nine years, smiled and said that from now on he believed he'd stick to balls that didn't have points.

It was not long afterward that we got into the DeSoto and drove north to visit the Jakubecs at a cabin they rented on a lake.

The cabin stood on the top of a grassy meadow under some big trees and smelled wonderfully of Mr. Jakubec's pipe. All the familiar people were there — Mr. Štěpánek with that laugh of his, and Mr. Chalupa and Mr. Hanuš, as well as some people I didn't know — and Mrs. Jakubcová served coffee and strawberry *táč*, and later we all went swimming, everyone carrying towels and mats and drinks out into the hot sun, and my father and a man who lived on the lake named Mostovský made their arms into a kind of chair and carried Mr. Hanuš down through the grass to the water because the meadow was tilted and his canes stuck in the soft ground. As they carried him down through the long grass in their bathing suits Mr. Hanuš yelled to me to get him a rose from the hedge, and when I handed it to him he put the stem between his teeth and looked at my father and said, Kiss me, Sedlák, I feel just like a girl again, and my father laughed and told him to kiss Mostovský instead, that he deferred to the better man, and the two of them staggered on, sweating, to the water's edge, where they set him gently down on the boards of the dock so that his feet, which looked like closed fists, could dangle in the water.

We stayed for five seasons, renting a cabin just down the shore. Years later, remembering our summers there, I returned alone.

There was a sort of softening that occurred to people there, an involuntary easing of something very much like pain. I don't know what it was about the place exactly. Perhaps it was the sun, or the water, always busy with some kind of invisible midges, or the strange pleasure of seeing the dark prints of their bodies evaporating off the wooden dock. More likely, for people who measured everything by its similarity to the world they'd known before, it was that it was so close to the original they'd lost — a reasonable facsimile.

And yet it was this very closeness, which invited the heart to play, and which would find them staring at a line of light slanting through the leaves, or watching their own white feet sweep back and forth through the water . . . it was this very familiarity that brought out every difference like a thorn, that made the place more excruciating than New York City could ever be. It was so close, this small pond with its screen-door *chatas* smelling of cedar and smoke, and yet . . . the birds sounded different here, and the water was warmer than it should have been, and the air did not smell of chamomile and pine and moldering loam and *hříbky* with caps of dirt on their velvety heads, but of other things.

Of course, even if everything had been precisely the same, it wouldn't have helped. Nothing could match what they'd had, for the simple reason that they couldn't have it again. It was not that what they'd lost had been better or more beautiful than what they'd found here, just that it had been theirs, and it had been lost. Not even the war had done that. They could no more substitute for it than a mother or father could substitute for a lost child by adopting another who shared the same features or spoke in the same voice. And yet, though they knew this, they couldn't help being drawn to that other, newer child, listening to it, running a hand over its hair.

Even my father, who at best tolerated this kind of sentimentality, was not immune. In the mornings I would find him sitting on a chair he'd carried out to the shore, tracing the corners of his mouth with his fingers like a man smoothing a mustache, the slow waves of light from the water moving up his shirt.

"It's not that I don't understand," he said to me once.

I'd sat down in the grass next to him. My parents had had an argument the night before over some movie I didn't know, and my mother had gone into the little wooden bedroom next to mine and slammed the door.

He waved his hand to indicate the black water, the trees, the last slips of mist being dragged up into the bluing sky. "I do," he said. "It's just that it does no good."

I didn't miss the city, particularly. I missed driving in on summer mornings, when a kind of bruise-colored fog obscured the buildings and only the tallest skyscrapers rose above it, flashing their sides one after the other like great, silver-scaled fish, and I missed the coconut custard pie and milk my mother would buy for me at the Chock Full o' Nuts with its clean, curving counters, and the *obst-torte* with the glazed strawberries we would share at the German pastry shop on Second Avenue. But that was all, really. Our friends still visited us at the lake in the summers, and my father still brought home Irish soda bread in white paper bags as he always had, and though I missed my room in the apartment on 63rd Road, what I really missed, I see now, was not the room itself but the feeling of being a child there. For a while after we moved I would wake up in the dark and think I was still there, and that the door to the hall was behind me rather than to the left, and it would take me a few moments to move things around, so to speak, to reconcile where I was with where I'd been.

A year after we moved to our house in the suburbs I dreamed that I was walking through our old apartment. It was dark and yet I could see all of our old things: the low white bookshelf in the living room and my child's desk and my bed with the pirate lamp and the chair my father sat in whenever we had guests, all of which we had left behind. And though I could see all these things, I knew, as you can sometimes know things in dreams, that I no longer lived in this place, that I was only visiting, and I wandered about from room to room, looking at these things which were still so familiar to me, wondering what had become of them, and it seemed to me that they must miss us.

I didn't remember that dream for a long time. Many years later I found myself on a train traveling south from Prague to visit friends near Jindřichův Hradec. Wet snow had been falling all morning, but now a dull winter sun had broken through. Coal smoke hung like a mist over the towns with their smudged little houses. The train ran beside the river that curved against the hills and spread in great gravelly shoals between the fields, and everywhere I could see the remnants of a flood which only that past October had submerged all the things I was now looking at. I saw a sofa lying upside down on a sandbar and a white refrigerator like a boulder in the current. On the television antenna of a low abandoned building I glimpsed what looked like a pair of blue pants, stiff as a weathervane. And at that moment for some reason I remembered my dream — the dream I had had a year after we had moved out of our apartment on 63rd Road. I didn't think much of it at the time. I watched the country scrolling by. All along the way, beards of trash hung in the bushes and the trees like Spanish moss, except that here everything was at the same height — the high-water mark — everything below having been swept away by the current.

Strangely enough, just as dreams will sometimes color our memories, the view of the river that day and the dream it recalled together forced themselves on the past, so that afterward, whenever I thought of our old apartment, my recollections would always carry a residue of future times, and remembering our apartment I would immediately be forced, like a man stumbling down a series of steps, to recall wandering those same rooms in my dream, and from there to remember the winter morning I'd spent, years later, looking out the dirty windows of the train to Jindřichův Hradec at all the things, once caught in the current, the flood had left behind.

II

WHEN I THINK BACK ON OUR FIVE SEASONS AT THE LAKE, I see my father reading in the big wicker chair that usually stood in the corner under the lamp with the green shade but which he would drag in front of the fire on chilly days. He was a great reader, my father: at ease, engaged, capable of sitting for three hours at a stretch without feeling the need to get up or move about, indeed, almost immobile except for now and again a small inward smile or a slight tilt of the head in anticipation of the page's turning. Sometimes I'd see his arm swing like a crane to the little table at his side. He'd pick up the glass with three fingers, begin to bring it to his lips — all this without once looking up from the page — and stop. And the glass would just hang there, sometimes for a minute or more, and I'd make bets with myself about whether it would complete its journey by the time he got to the bottom of the page, or be returned, untouched, to the table.

My mother read too, though differently. For days or weeks she would read nothing at all, or nothing but the newspaper, then suddenly take a book off the shelf, pull a chair next to my father's, and disappear. She read with an all-absorbing intensity, her stockinged feet drawn up underneath her, that I understood completely and yet still found slightly unnerving. Hunched over the book — which she would hold at her stomach, forcing her to look straight down — she looked as though she were protecting the thing, or in pain. No smile, no cup of tea, no leg thrown easily over the other, this was less a dance than·a battle of some kind, though what was being fought for, and by whom, I could hardly guess. Two days after it had begun — during which time my mother would often drag a chair out to the shore after breakfast, or retire to one of the hammocks my father had strung about the place, in which she would lie, straight-legged, smoking cigarette after cigarette, holding the book above her head — it would be over. I would find her lying in the hammock, staring up into the trees, the book tossed on the grass beside her.

I liked it there. I liked the rainy days when the three of us sat around the card table and played board games for hours on end, raising our voices over the dulling sound on the roof, and I liked finding things like the pencil-thin milk snake that crawled out of a crack in the foundation stone of the communal barn one day, but most of all, I think, I liked sitting on the dock with my mother on hot summer afternoons in July or August when a storm was rising out of the west and we knew it wouldn't miss us.

Such stillness. The sky above our heads remained perfectly clear, a deep, serene blue, but already the light would be changed, troubled, and with every deep rumble that seemed to move the wood beneath our chairs, I'd feel a thrill of anticipation, and sometimes my mother, who liked these storms as much as I did, would reach out her hand and squeeze my shoulder as if to say, "That was a good one — here we go."

It was the inevitability of the thing that we liked, I realize now: the hundred swallows flicking down to their reflections in the water; the mountain growing over us toward the sun, then swallowing it in a slow gulp, which always brought on a small, sad wind that felt good in my hair; and then the crash and rumble, extending, extending, longer than one would have thought possible, then subsiding into poised quiet. There was nothing to be done, nothing we could change, and there was a quiet joy in this.

Sometimes my father would come out on the sagging porch and tell us to come in, and we'd call back that we'd be right there and stay right where we were, transfixed, as the curtain rose higher and higher, and then what always looked and sounded like wind would turn the water on the other side of the lake mirror-green to pewter-gray, and in the next breath the squall line would be halfway across the water and my mother and I would be running for the cabin.

It was in our second season on the lake that my father shot the dog with Mr. Colby's gun and Mrs. Kessler fell in love with the man who lived in the cabin on the other side of the lake. He was much younger than she was, which was very important, and everyone talked about it those two weeks whenever they thought I couldn't hear, changing the subject to food or interrupting themselves to ask me whether I had seen the heron by the dam as soon as I came closer. She had made a spectacle of herself, which made me think of glasses even though I knew what it meant, and really it was a bit much, this carrying on in plain view. Everyone seemed angry about it, and though my parents and the Mostovskýs and some of the others didn't have much to say, I could always tell when people were talking about it by the way they would look slightly off to the side, shaking their heads, or the way their shoulders shrugged, as if they didn't care, or the way some would lean forward while others, giving their opinion, would lean back luxuriously in their Adirondack chairs.

I knew it was probably wrong and shameful for a married lady to fall in love with someone, and particularly someone younger, but the truth was that I liked Mrs. Kessler. She had come across me once while I was working on one of my many forts in the woods and kept my secret, and sometimes when Harold Mostovský and I spent the long, hot afternoons feeling around in the water with our toes, trying to walk the pasture walls that had disappeared when the lake was made, we would look up and see her sitting on the shore watching us, her arms around her legs, and when she saw we had seen her, she would give a hesitant little wave, raising her hand a bit, then a bit more, as though unsure of how high she should bring it, and we would go back to what we were doing. It never bothered us having her there, and then at some point we'd look up and she'd be gone.

Though I never saw it myself, I was told Mrs. Kessler lost her head so completely that at night she would walk down to the lake right after it got dark and get into the rowboat and row across to the other man's cabin while Mr. Kessler sat reading by the green lamp in their cabin. (I wonder what Kessler's reading, I heard Mr. Černý say. Must be good.) That she would sometimes stay for hours and hours, not caring what anyone thought, and that Mrs. Eugenia Bartlett had sworn she'd heard the creak of her oarlocks as she rowed back through the mist one morning just before dawn.

My mother, I remember, seemed almost lighthearted that second week in June, waking early, surprising me with special meals like apricot dumplings and *kašička* with drops of jam, asking my father about things in the newspaper. She threw out the stacks of magazines and junk that had collected under the sink and swept out the cobwebs and the bottle caps and the mouse droppings that looked like fat caraway seeds and the bits of mattress stuffing and lint from the previous winter's nests. One fresh morning after a night of rain she came home with the trunk of the DeSoto crammed with planting trays and seeds and bags of soil and fertilizer and sixteen hanging flowerpots and a paper bag with sixteen hooks to hang them on. In the back seat of the car were four carton bottoms filled with flowers. Except for the marigolds, I didn't know their names. Some were purple and white, like pinwheels, others a dark velvety red, still others the color of the sky just before it gets dark. They seemed to soak in the spotted light that came through the windows, trembling with life. She was going to garden, my mother said.

I saw my father looking at my mother as she first pointed out to us all the things she had bought, then started to drag one of the cartons out of the car. Here, let me get that, he said.

We carried the cartons down to the bit of shady, tangled grass by the water that served as our yard, placing them side by side so they made a long, lovely rectangle, then returned for the bags of soil and the tools. It was mid-morning. The air was warming quickly. A number of people had gathered out on the float in the middle of the lake, and we could hear them laughing. My father carried out the card table my mother said she wanted to work on, and for the next few hours, while my father drilled holes into the south wall of the cabin and screwed the hooks into them, my mother and I transplanted the flowers into the hanging pots, filled the seedflats with soil, and sprinkled the tiny seeds from the packets into furrows we made in the dirt with the eraser end of a pencil. When my father was finished he asked if there was anything else my mother wanted him to do, but she said no, that he had done a wonderful job with the hooks and that we could do the rest on our own, couldn't we, and I agreed.

My mother talked more that morning than I could remember her talking in a long time. She asked me about school and told me how happy she was that we had a cabin on a lake and how she hadn't liked it at first because it reminded her too much of home but that she had come to see things differently and now loved it as much, no, in some ways even more than the country-side she had known as a little girl. And she told me a little bit about the war and what the occupation had been like, and about a square called Karlovo náměstí in Prague with benches and flower beds and giant twisted oaks that had a house along it that had belonged to a man named Faust, who had supposedly been dragged to hell through a hole you could still see in the ceiling, and she told me how very well she still remembered that square along with a certain churchyard a few minutes away, and when a particular burst of laughter carried over the water, she looked at me and said, "People can be silly, can't they, complicating their lives for no reason, don't ever complicate your life, promise me that," and though I didn't know exactly what she meant, I said I wouldn't. Later, as we were planting the pinwheel flowers in the new pots, pressing down the soil with our fingers so the roots would take, she told me she had made some mistakes in her life but that it was never too late to understand things and that she understood things now and that she had never been happier than she was at that moment. She suggested we take a break for lunch, but later, when I found her in the hammock, smoking, she said she was a little tired, and it wasn't until the next day that we finished, and by that time some of the flowers in the cartons, which we had forgotten to water, had wilted badly.

I was reading in my room that evening after dinner when I heard my mother get up from the wicker chair and go into the kitchen. I heard the refrigerator door open and close, then the quick clink of glass against glass. I heard the water in the sink, then the creak of the wicker again. "What time is it?" she asked my father.

It took a second for my father to move his book to his left hand and, holding his place with a finger, push up the sleeve of his sweater. "Half past nine," he said.

"Almost time for him to go to bed," my mother said. There was no answer. A few minutes later she was up once more.

"You think she'll do it again?" she said from somewhere by the window.

"I think she might," my father said in his "I'm reading" voice.

"What could she be thinking?" said my mother.

"Pretty much what you'd expect, I imagine."

"I don't think it's just that."

"I never said it was."

"Time for bed," my mother called. I pretended I couldn't hear. "What's he doing in there?" said my mother, and walking over, she knocked on the wood plank door to my room. "Bedtime," she said. They were quiet for a few moments.

"She's a fool," said my mother. "I thought she had more sense, throwing everything away like this."

They were quiet for a long time.

"I don't know that you want to stand by the window like that," my father said.

"I'm not the one who has to worry about being seen. And him," she said, after a moment. "Him I can't understand."

"What would you have him do?"

"Something. Anything."

Again they were quiet. I heard a page turn.

"And for what?" she went on after a while. "Nothing."

"I don't imagine she sees it that way," said my father.

"You don't?"

"No."

"How does she see it, then?"

"Differently."

"So you're saying there's nothing wrong with him sitting there reading like an idiot while his wife . . ."

"I didn't say that."

"Christ, you're understanding."

"Am I?"

"You go to hell."

I heard my father get out of the wicker chair, then whisper something I couldn't make out: "I've never asked . . . little enough . . . to blame . . . fault." And then I heard my mother crying and my father saying, "All right, there, come now, everything's all right. It's just a date on the calendar. Nothing more."

The next morning my mother woke me while everything was still cool and fresh. She had made a big plate of *palačinky* so light and thin you could see the bruise of the jam through the sides of the crepes. She'd set out two deck chairs in the middle of the old garden plot, she said. We would eat breakfast outside, a special treat. She put the *palačinky* on a tray with two cups of sweetened tea, and together we walked up the steps away from the lake to the garden, where we sat under light blankets with the weeds and the thistles growing up all around us and ate with our fingers, draping the floppy crepes between our thumbs and pinkies so the preserves wouldn't come out and feeding them into our mouths. We laughed about stupid things and pretended to signal to a waiter who stood in the old strawberry patch and to be frustrated when we couldn't catch his eye.

"What do you think he's doing?" my mother said.

"He's not paying attention to us," I said. I waved my arms wildly, as if signaling a boat far offshore.

"Careful," my mother said.

I put my cup of tea on its saucer down on the ground, making a space between the long grasses. I waved my arms again. "Can I get some more jam," I called out. "And some hot chocolate, please."

My mother was looking at the overgrown strawberry patch as though a man actually stood there in the weeds. "What do you suppose he's thinking about?" she said, as if to herself.

I didn't know what to say.

"I think he's thinking about a girl," my mother said. She was looking at the strawberry patch. A small breeze moved the pieces of shade and sun on the ground, then returned them to where they had been. She laughed strangely. "I don't think we can get his attention."

"Why don't I throw something at him," I said, and leaning over, I picked up a short, thick piece of branch and sent it flying through the air above the strawberry patch. It fell in the weeds at the far end of the garden. "Missed," I said. I reached over for another stick. "This time I'll . . ."

"He's smoking," said my mother. "Look at the way he brings

it to his mouth. The way he stands with his elbows back on the bar."

I looked at her, wanting to follow her, to play on this new field she was making.

"I bet he gets in trouble," I said.

She nodded slowly, agreeing with something I hadn't said. "I don't think he's the kind of man who would care very much. I don't think he'll care at all." She looked around the dead garden, then shook her head and smiled, as if remembering an old joke. "So here we are. Nothing to do but call for the check."

That afternoon I remembered what my father had said the night before about the date and checked the slightly mildewed calendar that hung on the wall in the kitchen next to the refrigerator. Nobody had turned the month. May showed a picture of boys playing baseball. One, no older than myself, had just slid into home on his stomach with his cap falling over his eyes. A fat man was waving him safe. The page was curling in at the corners; a row of mold spots, like sloppy stitching, walked across the white frame. I turned to June. In the picture, a boy with ridiculously blue pants was sitting by the side of a pond, fishing. The mold had touched a corner of the sky. Flowering trees were overhead and you could see his red bobber on the black pond. A few feet away, a small brown dog was lapping at the water.

I went back to the living room and looked at the *New York Times,* open on the dining room table. The date was June 18.

My mother worked on her flowers all that afternoon, sitting at the wooden card table in the shade, a cup of coffee and a cigarette next to her, cupping big handfuls of black soil from the small mountain she'd spilled on the table next to her, packing the pots, then making a space for the root ball by pushing the dirt to the side with her fingers the way a potter shapes the sides of a vase. I went off to play for a while, then returned to find her sitting with her elbows on the table. She was holding the cigarette and the cup of coffee in her right hand as though just about to pick them up, and her head was tilted slightly to the side. She was looking at a spot on the grass a short distance away.

I didn't want to disturb her, so I sat down quietly on the wooden steps to wait until she started working again. Everything was still. Far across the water a group of kids I didn't know were jumping from the children's dock into the water. Their screams sounded strangely distant, as though I were hearing them from inside a closed room.

My father spoke from the open bedroom window. "Can I get you something?" His voice was very close, as if he were sitting next to her, but though I knew he was right there, I couldn't see him; the angle made the screen opaque as a wall.

"No," my mother said. She didn't look up.

"Something to eat? A cup of tea?" In the other room, the children screamed happily. I could see them run down the hill and onto the slightly lopsided dock, then spear into the water. They looked like little white sticks.

"No," my mother said again. And then, after a while: "Thank you."

It was not long afterward — three days, perhaps a week — that my father shot the dog. Harold Mostovský and I heard it first while we were exploring along the brook one quiet, cloudy morning — a furious, concentrated thrashing in the underbrush. There was no other sound, I remember — no growling or snarling. When we came closer we thought at first that what we were seeing was two dogs, then a shepherd with something around its neck. Only when it sank its teeth in its own tail and bayed in pain, then bit its own hind leg, did we realize something was wrong, and terrified of this thing trying to kill itself, we began to run.

I never thought to ask my father how he knew. Whether

someone had called him, or whether he'd been walking in the area, or whether he'd somehow simply sensed it, the way parents sometimes will. All I know for certain is that he and old Ashby, who lived in a shack a mile away and who always wore overalls and a sleeveless T-shirt and who hadn't yet begun drinking himself to death, were suddenly there and my father was yelling, "Whose? Where?" then running for the old white Colby house, which stood on a little rise a hundred yards away. As Harold and I ran up behind them, I heard my father ask, Do you know where he keeps the shells? then saw him tap the bottom right pane with his elbow and reach inside and open the door. A moment later he was walking out with the shotgun. He brought it up to his face, studying it quickly, then broke it and chambered a red shell he took from his pocket. "Stay here," he told us.

The shepherd was still there. It was trying to get at its stomach. It had bitten off its own tail; the stub ended in a small pink circle. It seemed to be trying to stand on its right shoulder. It had shit all over itself and the smell was terrible. My father walked right over to it, extended the gun, and shot it in the head. At the sound of the two-part crash of the gun, the dog flopped to the ground like a dropped rubber toy; I caught a glimpse of what had been its head — a grinning jaw of teeth, a mat of fur, something pink like a thumb — and then my father's body blocked the view and he was turning us gently around. "Go home," he said. "This is not for you. Go on." And then to Ashby: "Get the shovel. I would like to take care of this quickly."

And that was all, really. My father didn't talk about it much, except to ask if I was all right and to explain that the dog had gotten into some poison some idiot had left out and that the thing had had to be done. He seemed strangely happy that week, unburdened. It started to rain that same afternoon, and when the water began to spill over the sides of the leaf-clogged gutter in long wavering sheets that tore open to show the trees and the hill, then sewed themselves up again, he took off his shirt and shoes and walked hatless into the downpour and unclogged the pipe and dug at the mats of blackened leaves gathered against the back of the cabin with his hands and carried them against his soaking chest into the woods.

It rained for three days. Soon after it stopped, Mr. and Mrs. Kessler left the lake because Mrs. Kessler was in love with the man who lived in the cove and wouldn't listen to reason. I never saw them again. The man stayed on for a while — we could see him row out to the dock and swim by himself in the evenings just before dark — as though he didn't want to go or thought she might come back, but then he left too.

My mother kept gardening, and for a time the south side of the cabin burst into color: waterfalls of blossoms cascaded against the wood, and bouquets filled with air moved sluggishly in the afternoon heat, but by late August something had gone wrong and they began to die and my mother lost interest. My father made a halfhearted effort to keep them up but they died anyway, and one day he took the pots off the wall and dumped the soil out of them in a corner of the old garden, then came back down and unscrewed the hooks out of the cabin wall and got a small brush and painted the white insides of the holes with dark stain so they couldn't be seen. The sixteen pots of soil looked like cake molds, white with roots, and they lay there until my father broke them up with a spade and spread them out into the weeds.

12

THE SUMMER I WAS TWELVE YEARS OLD I TOOK MR. Hanuš fishing. He'd asked me if he could come with me the next time he came to visit, that he used to fish in the ponds of Moravia as a boy. He'd show me how it was really done, he said. I knew using the boat was out of the question of course, as was anything too elaborate in terms of equipment, so I rigged up two rods with bobbers and sinkers and dug a can of night crawlers out of the crumbly dirt by the garden, thinking this would please him and remind him of his childhood.

"Didn't trust me with the good stuff, eh?" he said as we walked slowly toward the dock. He stopped before the stone step that led down to the boards of the dock and moved one cane ahead of himself, looking for a point of stability. "I've got it," he said. He tilted to the left, like a toppling tree, then lurched back. "Give me just a second," he said. His shirtsleeve had caught on the handle of the cane, and I could see the white flesh of his arm shaking from the strain. The next moment he'd stepped down with an awkward lurch, steadied himself, and begun hobbling out over the boards.

"I'm guessing that's not coffee you have in that can," he said. He looked around. "Well . . . this is very nice." He began to lower himself down. "Here, a little help — there, that's perfect. We'll just put these right here and then we'll get down to business." A painted turtle poked its nose through the surface film, then disappeared. I could hear my parents and the others talking and laughing, but they seemed far away.

For a long time, Mr. Hanuš explained to me that afternoon, nothing happens. This was very important, this nothing. It made things the way they were. "For generations," he said, "everything stays the same, looks the same — nothing changes. There's the kitchen with the calendar, the same as always, and there's the red runner in the hall that's always bunching up by the bathroom door. You have to imagine it. It's June, let us say, and dusk. A man in his shirtsleeves is leaning out the kitchen window, smoking, his elbows on the sill, which is peeling. In the courtyard below, everything is still: the piles of wet sand and brick, the rabbit hutches stacked against the north wall, the bicycles under the overhang. In the garden the kohlrabi are pushing up into the dark. It's quiet: you can hear a sudden voice, the tinny bang of pots, a child crying. The year is 1923. It's been five years since this man — who is your grandfather, by the way — returned from the war, where he suffered more than some, and less than others.

"Now a boy, no more than three, comes into the room, climbs knee-first onto a chair. 'Did you wash your hands?' says a woman's voice. The man at the window doesn't turn around. He's half listening to the voices in the courtyard. His back feels good and strong under his shirt. He takes a last draw and stubs his cigarette on the outside wall below the sill.

"Years pass. Nothing has changed. The runner in the hall is maybe a bit thinner now. But there are the piles of sand and brick, the bicycles leaning against the shed. And there are the rabbit hutches, stacked like an apartment building against the bricks. Everything is wet. The air smells like steel, or brass. Far away, as if they were coming from another world, you can hear the tiny bells of a trolley.

"The same man is leaning out the window, watching the rain. '*Antonín*,' he calls without turning around, '*dones uhlí*,' and your father, who is twelve years old now, comes out of the room where he's been memorizing Latin verbs — or pretending to — takes the coal bucket, and disappears down the hallway.

"Year follows year. A thousand times this man, your grandfather, smoothes the heavy ripples of the runner with his foot. A thousand times Mrs. Vondráčková shuffles out to the rabbit hutches with a piece of stovewood. Wet flakes of snow are falling on the hills of sand and brick, they look like sugar on the cellar door, and then it's June again and the sun in the afternoons reaches halfway down the east wall and the air smells like fresh-turned dirt. On warm nights the windows are swung open to the courtyard. In the garden the knotty heads of the kohlrabi are cresting up through the soil again like rows of little green skulls. This is the world you know. You know it the way you know your room now.

"This is what I'm trying to say to you: For a long, long time, nothing happens. And then it does.

"In a place called Berchtesgaden, a tall Englishman with a white mustache named Chamberlain unfolds himself from a limousine. Arguments are made. Tea is sipped. Important men stab their fingers at the polished table. '*Sie müssen . . . Wir werden . . . Etwas Tee, mein Herr?*' In Bad Godesberg this Englishman smoothes his hair with his right hand and says, 'I take your point, Herr Ribbentrop. And yet, if I may . . . we feel that . . . in the matter of . . . Can I take that as your final position?' And it comes to pass."

Mr. Hanuš smiled. "Berchtesgaden. Bad Godesberg. Berlin. All those B's.

"But you look around. There's the sideboard that used to be your mother's. And your father's leather-bound editions, locked safely behind the glass. Nothing has happened. Young girls still spend the long afternoons lying in their back yards reading novels. The dance tunes of R. A. Dvorský still play on the radio. Nothing has changed.

"And suddenly they're there, like a thunderclap out of a March blizzard, the Mercedes limousines with their horsehair-stuffed seats moving down Národní Avenue past the statues and the frozen saints to the river. The city is quiet. No people, no trams. The tracks are still, the cobbles are marbled with snow like that cake your mother gets in that deli on Queens Boulevard. Gargoyles with long tongues stare from their niches under the pediment. You watch from inside your apartment, looking through cracks in the curtains, like everyone else. As they pass, far below, you can hear the snap and crack of banners.

"There's nothing to be done. Nothing at all. The motorcade passes over the Vltava. The walls of Hradčany Castle are barely visible; the archers' clefts are empty. In the woods of Petřín, which are also deserted, there is only the slicing sound of the snow, sweeping up through the orchards. The government, the newspaper says, has been dissolved. Bohemia and Moravia — the woods, the fields, the towns, the paths you knew, the ponds you swam in — are now called the Protektorat Böhmen und Mähren." Mr. Hanuš smiled: "*Etwas Tee, mein Herr?*"

"And still, even now, inside of you, it doesn't feel as if anything has changed. Things go on. And they continue to do this until the moment something stops, and all those years of nothing tear like a curtain caught on a nail. Maybe you see someone struck on the street, or maybe it's a voice on the radio, a voice like you've never heard before, a voice like a beating. But whatever it is, suddenly you know that everything has changed. That nothing is the same."

People backed into heroism like crabs, my father once told me. Or tripped into it through clumsiness. They rushed into the fire, blindfolded by glory, and somehow survived to be paraded down the boulevard, or they wandered stupidly onto the surface of things, made it across by some combination of physics and fortune, then looked back and called it courage.

Generations of heroes, entire battalions of them, he said, were just ordinary people who had been overtaken by the course of events, who had done what they did with no more thought than a dog who bites when his tail is slammed in a door — people who, when their tails had been freed and their consciousness revived, felt like spectators of their own lives.

And yet — and this was the thing — every now and again, against all the rules of human behavior, it occurred: an act of heroism planned in advance, undertaken for the right reasons, and carried out with the full knowledge, one might even say tragic knowledge, of the risks involved. A thing as unbelievable as a rain of toads. It isn't possible, you think. You can't believe it. And yet there they are, bouncing on the pavement.

When that happens, he said, all you can do is marvel at it, and take off your hat.

I asked my father if he had ever been a hero. He said no, not even close to one, and because he was my father, I believed him.

13

BY THE TIME I WAS NINETEEN WE WERE LIVING IN Bethlehem, Pennsylvania, in a depressing little community with streets named after poets no one read: Lord Byron Drive. Shelley Lane. Longfellow Circle. My mother and father barely spoke now. The town was dying. The steel mills by the river stood silent, blotting out the sky and the wooded hills behind them — they seemed embarrassed somehow. My father taught journalism at the university, started a garden. Eventually, to his own amusement, he took up jogging. He would run once around Mark Twain Circle, then down Northampton Street past the fringe of woods opposite the First Presbyterian Church, turn right at the Electronics Warehouse, right again on the broken dirt road that ran along the highway like something trying to call attention to itself, then start for home. It could be a treacherous run: the construction sites for the new subdivisions bled mud onto the road whenever it rained — lollipop swirls, slippery as oil, that scalloped into shells when they dried. My father would run around or hopscotch through them and appear on the back deck, soaked and red in the face, forty-five minutes after he'd left. He would stay there for a while, holding his knees and swaying slightly, then take a hand shovel from a peg on the back wall of the house and slowly start scraping the mud from the sides of his running shoes.

My mother, who could hear the click of the trowel behind her when my father replaced it on the peg, sat in the back bedroom with the small high windows and watched the soaps. "I want to see this," she'd say, in Czech, when I tried to get her to come out for a walk. "Janice is going to expose Rick's infidelity. What do you think is going to happen?" And she'd take a draw of her cigarette.

And I'd have that feeling, which I always had in those days, that she was angry with me for something, though I didn't know what it was. "C'mon, Mom," I'd say. "You have to come out sometime."

"Why don't you leave me alone," she'd say sweetly, not looking up.

"Because I want you to come out with me," I'd say.

"Out where? For a walk along Nezval Circle, maybe? Akhmatova Lane?"

"C'mon, Mom . . ."

"His wife doesn't know, you see. It's all very exciting."

And I'd stand there, wanting to leave, wanting to shut that door and walk out of that house, wanting to slap her like in the movies — "Snap out of it!" — but instead I did nothing. She'd wait for me all week, my father said. When I called to say I couldn't come till the next, she'd disappear into the bedroom, sometimes for days. "Don't listen to what she says," he'd say to me. "You're everything to her." And so I'd stand there those few seconds longer, ask one more time. I stood in that doorway for fourteen years. "You can't sit here all day," I'd say. "When was the last time you were outside?"

"If I needed your condescension, I'd ask for it," she'd say then, still not looking up from the set.

"I just want . . ."

"Or that long-suffering tone, for that matter. You want to play the martyr, do it with one of your girlfriends in the city."

"OK," I'd say, closing the door quietly behind me.

And I'd hear her laugh to herself. "OK," she'd say.

She was bleeding, of course, smoking her cigarette in a pool of blood as real in its way as any blood that ever flowed. And yes, I hated her, for her weakness and her pain, for the way she fed on it like a glutton, for her unwillingness to be done, ever. I hated her because she and her grief were such a perfectly matched pair, because I had grown and she no longer wanted anything but to be left alone, because life had cheated her, exquisitely, and she could neither forgive nor forget.

At some point I didn't know who she was anymore. At times I could still glimpse — through an inadvertent laugh, a moment of stillness — the person I'd once known, who had once known me, but it was like seeing someone's face from a passing car, or looking up during intermission at a play to see someone — someone familiar — looking at you through a hole in the curtain. And for this I hated her too.

It became my little burden to bear, this awkward sack of hatred and love. There are worse.

The winter after I left for college, I had a dream. In the dream my mother and I were on a boat in the middle of a blue ocean tacked tight to the horizon. Everything was still: the boat, its reflection, the pale hot circle of the sun.

My mother had decided to go for a swim. Far off, she was calling for help, her arms flailing in the air. I was there instantly. She grabbed onto my shoulders and neck as if I were a board flung into the water, crazy with fear. I tried to drag her back to the boat, but I couldn't do it — her terror had given her outrageous strength. She fought and twisted as though shot through by some giant current. Holding her across her chest and under her arm, as I had learned to do in lifesaving class, choking and strangling, I somehow dragged her to the surface, only to be pulled under again and again.

It was then that I realized she was swimming down, deliberately trying to drown us both. I could feel her pulling into the dark, reaching for my face, my throat, and I began to fight, striking down with my fists, desperate to separate myself from this thing which only moments before I'd been determined to save, and woke myself with such a spasmodic wrench of my body that I knocked my glasses off the reading table by my dormitory bed.

I never told my father about the dream. He had his own dreams, I felt sure. And so did she. The next weekend, I took the bus from the city and walked home through the winter cornfields at dusk, the red and green Holiday Inn sign growing smaller behind me, lifting my feet so as not to trip over the frozen stubble. My mother was in the kitchen, making *bábovka*. She hugged me hello, and I felt her small back, how frail she'd grown.

And I remember knowing that the dream was true and yet realizing, in some half-formed way, that men rarely had the courage or the cruelty of their dreams and that this was good because life was lived among many kinds of things, all of them pushing for space, for air, all of them equally true: a wilderness of love and despair, laughter and rage, heroism and pain, while dreams, dreams were a haunted parkland — a stately oak, a bench, a fountain gushing blood.

14

I ASKED HER ONLY ONCE. IT WAS ON ONE OF THOSE UN-naturally warm, yellow October days that feel lost somehow, as though a day in June had floated loose and found itself in a world of frostbitten tomato plants and half-bare poplars. We were sitting on the back deck of the house in Bethlehem, which had a view of the rectangle of lawn and the row of pines intended to block out the neighbor's house. A short distance away was the stump of the maple my father had cut down during the summer. I looked at the pines. They had caught some kind of blight and seemed to be rusting from the needles in, like discarded Christmas trees.

"You should give them a feeding of Miracid," my mother said.

"Why bother?" I remembered my father saying once, when my mother had insisted I douse a pine in the front yard that had browned at terrible speed, as though it were burning. He'd chuckled. "Look at it. It doesn't want to be here."

"A good feeding can't do any harm," my mother had said.

"You might as well feed a shoe."

"Still."

My father smiled and waved his hand. "Water away," he'd said.

"Can't do any harm," my mother was saying now. "You should give them a feeding when it cools off a little."

I said I'd do that, and then asked her who he had been, this man she had loved all the years I was growing up. I told her I'd known about him since I was a child, and that I thought, now that I was grown, she might finally tell me the story. I didn't blame her or resent her in any way, I said. Far from it. I was curious. What kind of man had he been? How had they met? What had happened to him? Had she met him before she met my father?

I knew it had happened during the war, I said, speaking quickly now. Sometime in 1942. Had he been in the Resistance? Had he died in the purges after Heydrich was killed? Could she tell me anything at all?

My mother took a dry, wafer-like cookie off the plate between us and took a small bite.

"I don't really want to talk about that right now," she said.

We sat in silence. I couldn't think of anything to say.

"Your father's a good man," she said. And then, after a while: "I'm sorry."

My mother was looking out over the yard — the poplars, the shadows on the lawn, the rusting pines. She was biting her upper lip, which made her chin stick out a bit, as if she were deciding something.

"You really should give them a good feeding," she said at last. "It can't hurt."

15

WHEN I WAS TWENTY I STAYED FOR A TIME IN A *CHATA* by a pond, seven kilometers from the town of Bystřice nad Pernštejnem, with my father's childhood friend Mirek. I'd fallen in love with a girl who was vacationing with her friends a few cabins down from ours. She was older than I was. We would spend every night around a campfire we built for ourselves along the shore, and always, often toward morning, end up making frantic love, still dressed in our smoky sweaters, our pants around our ankles, in the cold, dew-soaked grass. In the afternoons she would go on long sleepy walks in the woods with her friends, and I would swim across the pond with Mirek.

We always swam the long way, from the muddy little beach in the grass to the mill whose watermarked roof, furred with jigsaw pieces of moss, rose above the embankment on the far side. It would take us half an hour, sometimes more, and Mirek, whose right leg had withered to a stick half a century earlier when his father had refused to have a doctor set the toes his son had broken, would roll about in the dark water like a happy walrus, one moment paddling with his arm extended straight ahead as though lying on a sofa, the next raising his white belly like a hill into the air.

It was on one of these long swims across the pond that he told me about the afternoon when my father and his old friend Pavel

Štěpánov had looked into the execution yard. They were not yet twenty years old, he said, turning on his back and paddling along with small, flipper-like strokes while raising his head partly out of the water. About my age. At that time, he said, the people living in houses with windows facing the courtyard of Kounicovy koleje, a nondescript cluster of three-story dormitories that the Gestapo had turned into a prison, had been instructed to board them up. Not that it made any sense, Mirek said. Everyone knew what was happening there. The volleys usually began at ten in the morning and, except for a pause between one and two, continued until four. Every day except Sunday, shortly before ten, heavy trucks would bump up to the gates and disappear behind them. In the afternoon the gates would open again, usually around four-thirty, and they would leave.

Pavel Štěpánov, Mirek said, had discovered a crack in one of the boards over the upper bedroom window. By inserting a bread knife into the narrow part of the bolt and twisting gently, he could widen the crack to a centimeter or so. It was a still, hot summer day; the air in the half-boarded house was stifling. No one was at home. It was just after two. Štěpánov reached under the fringed shade of a bedside lamp and turned on the light. On the other side of the boards they could hear someone yelling orders. And though he didn't want to, Mirek said, my father put his eye to the crack, and saw what he saw.

"It changed him," he said. "It wasn't a sudden thing. Of course I can't tell you for sure that it was that day and not some other one, but I think it was. It turned something inside him. He has this smile, you know the one I mean, almost sweet, but closed, like this" — and he raised a closed fist above the water — "that only appeared afterward. The funny thing is that when I think of your father now, I see that smile. As if that was who he was supposed to be. It's the same with Štěpánek," he added. "That irritating laugh of his."

"I never saw what happened there myself," Mirek continued. "I remember the German *hausfrauen* walking past our gate during breakfast. They would walk down Tolstého Street to the corner, then up toward the dormitories. We couldn't see what they saw, but from our kitchen window we could see them standing against the post-and-wire fence they had there, holding up their children to see."

We swam quietly for a while. Mirek was looking up at the sky. "How far are we?"

"Maybe halfway," I said. I looked down into the water between my arms. "How deep do you think it is here?"

"Can you touch the bottom?"

"No."

"Then it's deep."

We swam on. "What did he see?" I said.

But Mirek couldn't tell me. "More than he should," he said.

His own father, he told me, whose prison cell had overlooked the courtyard at Kounicovy koleje for almost a year, until he was shipped off to Dachau, said the things one heard were the worst of all. He'd learned to insert pills of toilet paper into his ears, then wet them to make them expand. Others would crawl under their mattresses, supposedly, or wrap their bedsheets around their heads to keep from hearing. An unstable man named Žáček, a butcher, had somehow managed to rupture his own eardrums with a smuggled pencil.

It was all very organized, Mirek's father said. The holding area was separated by a barbed-wire fence from the execution yard itself, which was right where the trucks came in. The children were almost always taken first. Sometimes, just before they were led away, the parents would try to press themselves against them, or whisper something to them, as though giving them a message to deliver. Surprisingly often they would yell at them — Stop crying! Listen to me! — as if their words through some last miracle of habit or authority could make that place something other than what it was.

Sometimes the mother would lose consciousness, Mirek's father told him. More often she would begin to scream as soon as the first child was taken. The father might try to do something then, run at a guard, perhaps, or try to kick him, which only meant that he wouldn't have to watch. Mostly, though, the parents would just stand there, like sleepwalkers waiting in line at a bank. Some would make odd, spastic little gestures — reaching up as if to touch their right cheek, for example, or frowning quickly, or suddenly fingering a button. The men watching them from the windows would often unconsciously do the same.

It was the strangest thing, Mirek's father said, to see the same gesture duplicated, as if in a mirror, fifty meters away; it reminded him of that elementary school contraption that copied on a second sheet of paper — through the use of a kind of movable armature attached to a pencil — whatever was drawn on the first. Often, he said, you could tell what was happening in the courtyard simply by looking at the person watching. When the watcher's face turned away slightly and his head began to shake, for example, you knew it was almost over, because people about to be killed often developed an odd, Parkinson's-like tremor, looking off to the side and shaking their heads as if denying what their senses told them.

We lay on the grass bank under the mill for a long time that afternoon, moving east to stay ahead of the shade. I remember Mirek leaning up on one elbow, twirling and untwirling a blade of grass around his finger, his belly resting comfortably on the ground, his bad leg thin and ridged as a ham bone. I remember realizing, dimly, how much I loved this man — his round, happy face and his strong, soft shoulders and the thicket of white hair covering his chest. During the war, when my father and the others had intercepted the arms that dropped like dandelion seeds into the Vysočina forests — cutting them loose from the parachutes, then rushing them through the dark on makeshift stretchers — he had been the one waiting in the wagon, the one who covered the crates with firewood or manure, then drove them out to the safe houses alone, the horse snuffing wetly in the morning air.

At the far eastern corner of the pond, at a small beach, I could see tiny children leaping off a dock, their screams sounding strangely close over the still water. Just to the right I could see the space in the reeds where we had had our fire the night before: there were the blackened stones, like flecks of pepper, and there was the stunted willow, like a child's drawing, whose roots had scratched my back.

"We should go," Mirek said, sitting up on the bank. "I have a date tonight."

"It's going to be cold," I said, looking at the water.

Mirek stood, a bit unsteadily as always, and started toward the water. "Courage, boy," he said. He slapped his belly, and the sound carried across the water like a single clap. "Courage and fat."

I watched him wade in up to his knees, throwing water on his arms and chest, then plunge in. But I hesitated. The sky was darkening. The children were gone. On the spillway a carp fisherman had set up his stool. I watched him finish rigging his line, cast out past the trees to the darkening sky, then settle himself carefully on the stretched fabric.

Later that night I waited on the dark path under the trees, carrying a small sack of sausages and *rohlíky*, tin cups and tea. The wind moved, making the lights of the cabins wink on and off. And suddenly I felt terribly lonely, as apart as I ever had in this world. The air was cool, but every now and then I could smell the hot smell of the fields. A woman's laugh came from one of the cabins. She was enjoying herself. She wouldn't come. I waited in the dark under the trees for a long time, leaning against a huge old chestnut with smooth, skin-like bark, thinking every few moments that I saw her flying along the bank or down the road to meet me, then threw the sausages and the *rohlíky* and the cups into the water one after the other and went home.

16

ON MARCH 17, 1984, MY MOTHER APPARENTLY DECIDED to walk to the Westgate Mall in a freezing rain wearing a summer dress with a raincoat over it. It had been raining for a long time. She tried to cut through a cornfield behind the subdivision on Whitman Drive but found herself lifting clods of clayey mud with each step, and retreated to the road. She walked to Hochstetler Lane (the town fathers having run out of literary lights), then along the gravel shoulder past the gas station and the little shopping area with the H&R Block to the stretch of sidewalk over the highway and then another mile or so past the Sears Automotive Center to the vast parking lot of the mall.

Inside the mall, made to look like the street of a small town, she sat down on one of the shiny green benches set up under the eave of the Bavarian Haus. Music was playing. A group of seniors on an excursion from the retirement home came and sat down on the bench next to her to wait for the bus to Allentown. Every few minutes the music stopped and after a few seconds a woman's voice came over the loudspeaker: J. C. Penney was having its annual electronics sale. For that day only, everything would be marked down 20 to 50 percent. Then the music would come on again.

It was raining hard. The rivulets of water rushing down the glass made everything seem oddly submerged. A tall boy in lederhosen with a ravaged face offered her some flavored cheeses on a wooden tray. The cubes were impaled on toothpicks. My mother said something about the bits of colored cellophane on their tips, but didn't take any. She was very polite.

From where she sat, she could see the imitation street lamp to the left of the Century 21 real estate office and a sign with white letters saying MAIN STREET. On the ceiling, high above the steel rafters, someone had painted a summer sky, though you could barely see it. I don't know if she noticed it.

A frail old man in a pink windbreaker sat down next to her on the bench. "Goin' to Allentown?" he asked. My mother looked at him. She seemed to be thinking about it. "I don't think so," she said.

A poster taped to the brick wall showed a snarling tiger on a small stool, a clown with a huge white mouth shooting a tiny bow and arrow, and a powerful man with long blond hair holding a whip. He was yelling something, but he looked as if he were crying.

My mother stood up.

"Shprecken Zee Dutch?" said the old man.

My mother took off her raincoat, folded it neatly, and placed it on the bench. "Have a nice day," she said, then walked out into the rain, across the parking lot and out to the turnoff ramp from the highway where she stepped directly in front of the 4:38 bus to Allentown.

And I can see her saying it: "Have a nice day." That sardonic half-smile. We hadn't spoken in seven years. She left no phone message, no note. No taped cassette on the dining room table. Just a casserole dish half filled with ashes and a few feathery bits of letter paper. I poked around in the ashes with the eraser end of a pencil. Along the edge of a blackened piece of blue *Luftpost* letter paper I made out two words: "I still." And that was all.

PRAGUE

Intermezzo

MY MOTHER ERASED HERSELF SO THOROUGHLY THAT for a long time after she died, I couldn't find her anywhere. Two years later my father died, and not long afterward I resigned my job and moved to Prague. I was thirty-seven years old. I hadn't forked any lightning, wasn't really expecting to. Maybe I was looking for them, I don't know — men do all sorts of foolish things. Or maybe I was hoping to discover how our particular story, of which I knew so little, really, fit the larger one. Face to face with that larger, known puzzle — of the past, of Prague, of war — I would see the empty space that was us, recognize its shape. And I would understand.

I found stories enough, but not ours exactly; empty spaces we should have fit, but didn't. Everywhere I went, things seemed to speak of her, to hint of her, yet revealed nothing; they were like a stranger passing in the street who whispers your name, then denies having said anything at all. Held up to life, metaphors melt like snow.

That first summer I moved to Czechoslovakia I stayed for a while in an old inn, a wood and plaster building located at the base of a grassy dam that rose like a mountain just meters from the back windows and gave the light a permanently hooded, storm-like cast. The building had once been a mill house; the brook that had been stoppered up long ago still trickled past the parking lot. At night, lying in bed, I could hear it through the open windows after the drunks had gone home. At my back, basking in the moonlight, was the reservoir, stretching for kilometers through the mustard fields. No one seemed troubled by the fact that a continent of water hung above their beds, that carp slurped at the air five meters above the kitchen chimney.

I stayed four days. I was the American eating trout by himself every evening in the small wooden dining room with the dirty tablecloths and the outraged-looking boar's head which appeared to have simply rammed itself through the wall and stuck fast above the lintel. The one just comfortable enough in the language to be uncomfortable in his own skin, surrounded by quiet families who grew noticeably quieter every time he entered the room, who pretended to be busy wiping their children's faces whenever he glanced up from his plate, who watched the waitress approach his table as though she were a matador entering the ring. Not quite knowing what to do with myself (I had no one to talk to, and reading would have seemed rude), I would pretend to be fascinated by the room itself — looking this way and that with the curious, benign expression of a parrot on a branch — eat quickly, and leave.

One day I passed by a small, weedy pond that was being emptied. Four young men in heavy boots were plunging about in the mud, grabbing the huge silver carp that everywhere flopped and slithered in the dwindling water and throwing them into the bed of a truck that had been backed to the water's edge. It was a beautiful day, fresh and hot, and the men, who were strong and quite brown from the sun, were enjoying themselves enormously, shouting and laughing as they splashed after the carp that tried to get away, grunting every time they turned and spun a heavy fish over the rail. The carp slapped around for a time, then died, buried under their fellows. I watched the men work, turning from the hips like discus throwers, their heads thrown back with effort every time they released a fish into the air, then went on my way.

That evening I recognized them as I ate dinner at a local inn. They had washed and changed their clothes. Their hair was combed. They seemed so dull and sullen, sitting over their glasses of beer, that for a moment I wondered if I was mistaken. And then one of them turned toward the bar and I saw a carp scale, like a giant silver fingernail, stuck to the back of his sun-tanned neck.

I don't know what I had expected. Some of the people I spoke to — a humped-up woman with a hairy mole under her eye whom I met at a wooden bus stop, a small badger of a man hurrying along a fence — remembered my mother. They seemed touched to hear she was dead — they remembered her when she was like this, playing right over there — but no more than they were by the fact that her son had come all the way from America to find the family house. They'd heard that she'd gotten mixed up in something during the war, that she'd escaped, immigrated to New York. The Resistance? Another man? They hadn't heard. I was invited inside, plied with cups of thick Turkish coffee and *jahodový táč,* taken into the back room and shown the bust of President Masaryk hidden behind the curtain. They had had him there through everything, they assured me. I learned nothing I hadn't known.

I collected facts, as I always had, like a child hoping to build an oak from bits of bark. I traveled to the few towns I recalled my mother mentioning, visited the houses where the partisans had met, hunted down the places where they had died. I pored through documents and letters, talked to those who had survived. The majority of those involved in the Resistance had been executed immediately or deported to camps right after the

Heydrich assassination in 1942. Most of this second group had died there, some at Mauthausen, others at Terezin, still others at Auschwitz. Which told me nothing. Many had died.

One hot June day that summer I took a bus to see a certain town in Moravia I had read about whose citizens had been particularly active in the Resistance and had suffered for it. I'd heard my mother mention it. The air in the bus was stifling — most of the windows seemed glued shut — and when I discovered that I'd gotten off one town too early, rather than get back in, I pretended that that had been my destination all along. But this wasn't Malá Losenice, the driver explained, trying to save me from my mistake. No, no, this was exactly where I wanted to go, I assured him, and finally, with an irritated wave of his hand, he dismissed me. A young woman with a heavy bag of groceries started to climb into the bus. Conscious of being watched, I headed up a tilting dirt road lined with squalid houses as though I knew precisely where I was going. The smell of the fields, of sun and drying hay and stables, came in hot waves.

I asked directions. Malá Losenice was eight kilometers by the main road, I was told, five by the red-marked trail that led through the woods. I would have to watch carefully for the turn-off for the blue trail.

The path left the town quickly and meandered up through mustard fields and young wheat, still and unmoving in the heat, then turned into the forest. A hunter's stand of cut pines stood against the trees, a small pile of rusted cans at its base.

I got lost. There was no blue trail, nor any other for that matter, and when I retraced my steps after an hour or so, I didn't recognize any of the places I came to. To make matters worse, I hadn't brought enough water, and there didn't seem to be any streams in these woods. I walked on and on, sitting down to rest every now and then, then nervously jumping up to walk another mile. It was absurd, all of it. What had I been thinking? I was going home . . . as soon as I could figure out which direction home might be.

Walking down a long, sloping dirt road through the fields, I found myself behind an old woman dressed in black, making her slow way toward the forest. Setting her stick ahead of her, then moving up to it, she reminded me of a fragile spider testing unfamiliar ground.

When I was still some distance behind her I cleared my throat so as not to startle her. She had paused by a wooden fence to catch her breath, one hand on the top slat, the other on her cane. Hearing me, she transferred both hands to her stick, which she had planted in the dirt, and pivoted slowly in my direction.

"*Dobrý den,*" I said, greeting her. She didn't respond. She was very old, her face and neck under her kerchief fissured like bark. As I passed, I could see her mouth working as if searching for a bone with her tongue. When I asked her for directions back to the town I had started from, she raised a trembling claw and pointed in the direction I'd been going.

And suddenly — perhaps it was the heat — I had the absurd desire to ask her if by any chance she remembered a couple, a young man and a woman with very black hair, from the early years of the war. It wasn't completely mad. She was certainly old enough. I'd grown up hearing about the forests of Moravia, had seen the look on my mother's face when she spoke of them. Maybe this woman had seen them one July evening as she was coming back from the well. Or glimpsed them through her kitchen window one morning just as her husband called to her from the pantry to ask if she'd said apricots or cherries. I wanted to ask her — this one woman out of a hundred thousand, living in a place that most likely had nothing to do with them at all — if she remembered . . . something. To take a wild stab at chance, at the miracle of coincidence.

I didn't. Her hands, veined and speckled, grasped each other over the flat head of her walking stick. I continued on. When I turned around at the edge of the pines I could see her, half a kilometer back, making her way down the road toward the trees like the shadow of a small, dark cloud.

I moved to the apartment on Italská Street in Prague when I was thirty-seven. I still go back and forth as I can. I've learned that human beings are like the Silly Putty I used to play with as a child, that pressed to a piece of brick, we take the imprint of this world, then carry it like a sealed letter marked God and God alone to our deaths. I've learned that nothing in this world resists us like ourselves. And I think, if this is true, how then can we hope to know someone else?

"U kolejí," said the other, taking his glass.

"I remember that," said my host.

"They had the most wonderful little game hens in nut sauce."

They were all silent for a while. Again I could hear the knocking on the door at the top of the stairs.

"It's that son-in-law of yours," said the professor.

"I think it's General Secretary Gorbachev, come to ask me what to do about the economy," said my host.

"I could be wrong," said the professor.

They were silent again.

"What time is it?" asked the one with the eyebrows. He'd promised to take his wife to see the new American film playing in Žd'ár, a love story of some kind. That actor was in it, he said, you know. Which one? they asked. The blond one, he said. With the mole on his cheek. "Redford," said the professor. "Robert Redford." "That's him," said the one with the eyebrows. "The wife had a dream about him the other night. Said he knocked on our kitchen window while I was taking a nap after dinner and asked her to come out to the barn with him. She was just taking her apron off to go outside when I woke her to ask where she'd put the keys to the shed. She wouldn't talk to me the rest of the day."

"So take her tomorrow," said the professor irritably.

"To hell with Robert Redford," said my host.

He had to go, the other said, standing into a kind of crouch. It had been a pleasure to meet me, he said, though I had hardly said a word the entire time, and with that they beckoned me up the narrow, clayey stairs to the half-sized door at the top, through which I emerged into a warm, sunny drizzle.

2

ON A WET APRIL DAY IN 1999, IN A TRAM ALONG THE Vltava River, I asked a frail man in a Homburg hat for directions. He wore glasses and was dressed in a dark suit of some heavy material. It had worn to a dull shine at the elbows, and I noticed that he had rubbed shoe polish into the thinning spots to hide them. He had a fine white mustache, and he asked me where I was from and ended up telling me about his father who had been a Latin teacher in a local high school and a collector of birds' nests.

Every spring in those years during the war, he said, his father, whose displeasure could provoke even the dullest students into prodigious feats of memory, and who could seem so severe behind his small rimless glasses, what with his creased cheeks and his thin brown hair combed straight back, would wander in the woods around Prague listening for bird calls. He knew them all — *skřivánky* and *pěnkavky* and *rákosníky*. Having located a nest, he would wait patiently for the chicks to hatch and then to leave, returning week after week until the nest was empty. He would mark the spot on a map, with a symbol like a footnote, then describe the position in more detail in a small leather notebook he carried with him, triangulating his position with the local landmarks: a scarred oak, a steeple, a stone road marker like a tiny gravestone. Only after the birds had abandoned it, the man assured me, turned half around on the tram's uncomfortable plastic seat, would his father add the nest to his collection. When he finally harvested a nest, the mood would be festive; his father would be in good spirits all day. Sometimes, especially when there were trees to climb, he would take his son with him, handing him the thin-bladed, collapsible saw, instructing him where to cut.

Collecting birds' nests was his father's passion, the man in the Homburg hat told me, and every fall and winter through the early years of the war, whenever his father had spare time, he would work on his displays at a small desk in a corner of the living room — mounting each nest on the appropriate branch of the appropriate tree or bush or reed — all the while regaling his family with amusing stories of how he had come to secure this particular treasure, what he had said to this or that acquaintance who had happened by just as he was scrambling up a tree like a schoolboy, how he had lifted his hat to Madame So-and-So with one hand while holding on to a branch with the other.

Sometimes, when an egg didn't hatch, his father would blow it out through a pinhole and place it in the nest to add realism to the display. Everyone, he maintained, needed a *koníček,* a hobby, especially after a certain age, and his was certainly no more absurd than many others. He himself, said the man in the Homburg hat, had started collecting stamps soon after he had turned forty. He found that it gave his life a kind of order that nothing else could supply. There was a real pleasure, he said, on receiving a bundle of stamps from some acquaintance from overseas, in sitting down under a good lamp on a rainy evening to study and sort and perhaps affix them in their proper places.

I told him I had some stamps my parents had collected over the years for some reason, and that I recalled my mother saying that some of them were from places like Siam and Ceylon, countries that, as he knew, no longer existed under their former names. I had no idea if they were valuable, but if he was interested I would send them to him. He said he would be very grateful, and I handed him a pencil and a store receipt I found in one of my pockets and he placed the receipt against the window and wrote down his address for me. "Four more stops," he said.

So he had inherited his father's collection? I asked, in part to fill in the sudden silence.

He shook his head. The collection had been destroyed when his father was arrested.

I was sorry, I said.

The old man waved it away. "The Gestapo came for him in July of 1942," he said matter-of-factly. "I was thirteen years old. My father's collection must have had close to a hundred nests in it by then. It was really quite something. They were all over our apartment — in the parlor, in the dining room, in the hallway, so many that at times it was as if you were walking through an enchanted wood, a wood in which walls had miraculously begun to appear among the branches, while at other times it seemed as if the walls themselves had come alive and sprouted through the plaster. A wondrous home to grow up in."

After breaking his father's nose with the butt end of a rifle, he said, the soldiers had made his father tear the nests out of the walls and step on them. The three of them — he and his mother and father — had just sat down to breakfast when they heard cars screech to a halt in front of the apartment. He remembered his father slowly folding the morning paper in half and laying it alongside his plate, then looking at his mother — not at her face but her chin and hair and throat, tracing the frame — and then they were there.

He remembered them going through the apartment. He remembered them standing about in the hall in their boots shouting *Los, los, schneller!* — Step out, faster, faster! — and his father bringing the branches into the living room like armfuls of stovewood while the blood poured from his nose and throwing them in a pile on the rug. There were big white pieces of plaster, like puzzle pieces, hanging off the ends.

"Why was he arrested?" I asked.

The tram had come to a stop. People streamed out into the wet spring air, others pushed in.

"Three more," he said.

They had learned later, he said, that one of his father's students had mentioned his father's name under torture. He shrugged. "Who knows what people will say under those circumstances? My father had given him a four — what to you Americans would be a D. Perhaps my father's name floated into his head by accident, as in a dream."

At the time, said the man in the Homburg hat, he and his mother hadn't known anything about this. They had no idea what was happening. It was all a terrible mistake. It was only much later, after the war, that they had learned that two of the parachutists sent to assassinate Reinhard Heydrich had hidden themselves for a time near one of his father's favorite collecting places, a stretch of scrubby woods near an abandoned quarry twenty minutes from Prague, and that this coincidence, coupled with the young man's mentioning of his teacher's name in a delirium of pain, had been enough.

"What happened to your father?" I asked.

"They tortured him for three days, then cut off his head. They did that sometimes." He paused. "A curious thing. When I was fifteen or sixteen — an unfortunate age under the best of circumstances — I became quite obsessed, morbidly so, you might say, with the details of my father's death. I thought about it all the time, until one day, on an outing near Klánovice, I offered a villager fifty crowns if he would let me kill a chicken. I can still see him — a big, thick-nosed man in blue overalls. He looked at me strangely — he must have thought I was crazy — then went into the hen house and came out carrying a chicken and a short hatchet. I took the chicken by the neck — it was squawking terribly — and walked over to a kind of chopping block that stood in the middle of the yard. I was a city boy. I had no idea what to do. I put the chicken on the block, but everything kept blurring because I was crying and I couldn't take off my glasses to wipe my eyes. I was worried I'd cut off my fingers on top of everything else, so I held its body down as best I could with my right foot and stretched out its neck like a rubber band and chopped off its head. I had been afraid it might run around, but it didn't do anything. I lay the head and neck — a floppy, boneless thing — next to the body, paid the money, and left." He shook his head. "What idiots we are," he said.

"It didn't help?" I said.

"Not a bit. I still thought about it, just as I had before. I thought for a time that I was losing my mind. And then at some point, for no particular reason, I stopped thinking about it."

It had all been a very long time ago, he said. These days he passed the building in which his father had been interrogated at least three times a week. It was still there, a huge, blocky structure with bars in the windows, just down from the main train station. A statue of a barefoot prisoner, representing all those who had been interrogated there during the war, had been erected above the sidewalk on the southeast corner. He was an old man now. He never thought of it. The only thing that still troubled him at all was that the last memory he should have of his father was of him in his rest-day clothes, barefoot like the statue, trying not to cry out as he stamped on the branches strewn over the living room floor. More than a few of his father's species, he explained, had nested in thorns.

I said something about how horrible this must have been for him, and how tragic a mistake.

He glanced out the window. "The next is mine," he said. "Yours is the one after that."

There had been no mistake, he said. Shortly after the war, in 1945, a man had knocked on their door and told them everything.

His father, Oldřich Růžička, had been a valuable member of the Resistance, he told them. He had relayed information from a man named Jindra. He had hidden two of the parachutists who had been dropped into the country by the RAF in an old cellar in the middle of a raspberry field, then kept them supplied with medicine and food and information for nearly two weeks until they could be moved to safety.

The man had read to them from a small book as he sat on their sofa. "On November 7, 1941" — here the old man looked at his open palm as though a notebook were lying in it — "Oldřich Růžička carried crystals for a radio transmitter from a house in Žyžkov to an apartment on Poděbradova. On December 12 he relayed a message to someone code-named Jiřinka at the Olšany Cemetery. And so on."

Curiously enough, the old man said, rather than give them comfort, this knowledge had taken away the one source of comfort he and his mother had had left. There were no certainties now, only questions. It was as though the man they had known had really been someone else. Next to every smile, every anecdote, there was now an asterisk, and though his father's face and voice and hands remained as vivid to them as if he had just stepped out of the room to get something from the kitchen, they could no longer be sure exactly who it was that had left.

They had learned to live with it as best they could. In time, the man said, his mind had simply grown around this unwanted information, this other, alternate father, the way a tree will grow around an iron spike, incorporating it, enfolding it, until at times it seemed to him he could almost remember his father hinting at his other self, speaking in code, winking as he lifted his coat off the hook below the *skřivánek*'s nest in the hall and went out for the afternoon.

But it was a lie, and he knew it. An uncertainty was still an uncertainty. A spike, though buried, was still a spike. And it still bothered him, particularly now, in his later years, when he realized it would outlive him. What troubled him most, he said, though he recognized that there was something wonderfully absurd about it, was that he would never know whether his father's interest in birds' nests had been real — that is, whether it had come first and then been used by him as a convenient cover when the war began — or whether he had adopted it when the need arose. Whether all those nights — the man's entire childhood, it seemed — that his father had sat at his work desk in the corner of the living room, tucking in strands of straw and tufts of lint with a needle and telling them about his adventures, had been genuine or only part of a long story he told — and lived — to protect them.

There were other options of course, said the man in the Homburg hat. Perhaps his father's interest in birds had started out false and grown real with time. His father's leather notebook, in which he had kept all his notes, had somehow, almost miraculously, survived — hidden in plain view on the bookshelf. More than once, he said, he had looked at it, with its location diagrams and crude pictures and descriptions of birds' nests, and wondered how much of it was in code. He shrugged. Neither he nor his mother, in the years before she died, had been able to recall with any degree of accuracy when his father had started his hobby. It was not something he was likely to find out in this life. Perhaps the next.

It made for a very strange feeling, he said, to look at his father's fountain-pen drawings, still so familiar to him with their arrows and circles and tight, angular handwriting, and to not know whom they had been intended for. Here and there, he said, one could find, in the thicket of Latin genus and species names, *Lanius collurio* or *Emberiza calandra*, a date and a time, (*23. dubna 1942, 15:14*), and next to it, carefully noted, the height of the nest from the ground in centimeters and the number of eggs that had hatched. Only recently, he said, had he noticed that there was always only one or two, and never more than three. He had no idea what this meant, if indeed it meant anything. "Here, let me show you," he said, and leaning down, he opened the battered briefcase resting against his leg.

"You have it here?" I asked stupidly.

"Ah, here it is," he said, taking a small, cracked-leather notebook strapped with rubber bands out of his briefcase. "Let me . . ."

But the tram was already slowing. He glanced up. "I'm afraid we won't have time," he said. He dropped the notebook back inside the briefcase and snapped it shut. It had been very nice talking to me, he said, and if I could remember to send him those stamps when I returned home to America, he'd be very grateful. And grasping his briefcase, he walked out into the wind.

I got off the tram at the next stop.

All that fall I carried the receipt with his name and address on it safely tucked in my wallet until, on a crowded train, a week before I was to leave Prague for a few months, someone stole it from my inside breast pocket. When I tried to find the name I remembered, I got nowhere, and when I located a street whose name sounded much like the one I remembered him writing down, no one there could tell me anything of a frail-looking man with a white mustache who collected stamps.

For years I thought of him, still waiting for the stamps from Ceylon and Siam to arrive from overseas. And then I stopped.

3

ON A COLD NIGHT LATE IN 1988, I MET A MAN IN A *hospoda* in the village of Třebíč. The room was full of round tables covered with dirty white tablecloths and when the waitress came over with the beers which she carried three to a hand, she made a mark on a red cardboard coaster with a short black pencil. When I told the men at the table next to mine what had brought me there, they took me to a back table where an old man with bloodshot eyes sat sullenly in front of a mug of beer. His name was Ota Rybář.

Ask him about the parachutists, they said. But the man seemed too far gone. "*Musíme ho naolejovat*" — We have to oil him — someone said. "Another beer," someone yelled. "You can all go to the devil," the old man said.

He'd been a young man, he said eventually, the night he saw them come down — not even forty. Back then he could still pee in less than half an hour.

Of course he did, he remembered it very well, every bit of it. He raised his heavy stein of beer, then put it down again. "America?" he said.

"*Co si pamatuješ, Oto?*" — What do you remember? — said a bear-like man at the table next to ours, who was leaning forward over his beer as though protecting it. A small, whiskered dog with a face like a ferret was lying against his leg. Whenever I looked at it, it turned its head, as though ashamed of its predicament.

"Everything," said Ota Rybář.

I looked at the dog again. It looked away.

"Every-fucking-thing," said Ota Rybář.

"It was cold as hell that winter," Ota Rybář said. "Our village, Nehvízdy, is in the fields, and the wind blows like a bastard. Snow was everywhere.

"There was no wind that night. I was lying in bed next to my wife, who didn't snore yet then, and when I heard the plane I didn't think about it until I heard it come back around again. It sounded lower this time, and the dogs began to bark. That made me curious, and before I knew what I was doing I was pulling on my boots in the hall. I managed to get the ladder from the barn without making any noise and I set it against the roof and climbed up behind the chimney. I tried to be quiet because my youngest was sleeping right there, no more than a meter under my feet. And then I saw it, a shape coming down out of the sky. It was swinging back and forth like this, like a child in a playground. I lost sight of it behind the chimney, then found it again. I could see it plainly enough against the stars. It came down somewhere not far away.

"Well, I knew right away who it was, of course: we had heard rumors of parachutists — our boys, trained in England and dropped into the Protectorate — and I'll tell you right now, I nearly crapped myself. We'd managed to sit out the war all right until then. Keep our noses clean. What if someone saw me up there on my roof at three in the morning? I thought. How could I explain the snow scuffed off behind the chimney? Everyone would think I'd been signaling them. My legs began to shake so badly I had to wait a few minutes before I could make it back down the ladder. I took it and put it away and went back in the house and got into bed next to my wife and tried to sleep but I couldn't because I knew I would have to go out into the fields in the morning.

"I tossed and turned the rest of the night. I couldn't see any way out of it. I worked on the roads then, but a few weeks earlier I'd taken a second job as a gamekeeper, working for some rich factory owners who'd rented a hunting lodge a few kilometers away. Every morning I would go around with a big rucksack full of forage for the game. If I didn't go out that morning, people might get suspicious. Better to act as though everything was the same as always, and simply go about my business.

"So after breakfast the next morning I went out to the barn, loaded up, and set off. It was a beautiful morning but cold as shit. I didn't say anything to anyone about what I'd seen, of course. I was no fool. It was simple mathematics. Every person who knew something doubled your chances of being shot. And not just because they might blurt out something by accident. Any idiot could be an informer: some bastard who had never liked you, or thought you'd slept with his wife, or wanted to buy your field . . . I just put on my pack and went out.

"I found their tracks halfway across the field, about two hundred meters from a group of trees like a small island. It was quite a shock; I'd pretty much talked myself into believing I'd imagined the whole thing. I can't tell you what a strange sight they made, those two sets of tracks suddenly leading off across the snow. Any fool could see them. The snow had been disturbed and piled up in a kind of heap, and when I kicked at it, a rope tangled around my boot. I took off my pack and pretended to drop some forage in case anyone was watching from the village, then followed the tracks across the field toward the trees. Why? I don't know why. I think that somewhere in the back of my mind I just wanted to see them.

"Behind the woods the ground dropped away into an old, unused quarry. It was a pretty wild place, thick with briars and scrubby trees and in the summer there was a pond at the bottom and a cave where my boys used to piss around when they were kids, playing at bandits and whatnot. It's still there. And that's where I found them, at the bottom of the quarry: two men hardly older than my oldest, maybe twenty or twenty-two, pretending to study a map. They were ordinarily dressed, in old coats and boots. They had seen me. One of them, who was tall and slope-shouldered, had his right hand in his coat pocket. The other, a slim, dark-haired fellow, simply looked up from the map and nodded.

"I knew that I couldn't walk away, so I made my way down the hill toward them, slipping a bit in the snow. They watched me the whole way. How goes it, boys? I said as I came closer.

"They were doing a survey, the taller one began. There was talk about mining the quarry again.

"I nodded, but I could see right away that the other one knew I didn't believe it. I saw him look slowly up along the rim of the quarry to see if there was anyone else there. I knew I had to say something, and quickly, or they would just shoot me right there. I know who you are, boys, I blurted out. I found your parachutes in the snow. I covered them up for you.

"The tall one started to say something but the other one stopped him with his hand. I got the sense that he was some kind of superior. He didn't say anything. He just looked at me. What's in the pack? he said. Forage, I said, I can show you. He shook his head. You do this every morning? he asked me. Four times a week, I said. How long had I been doing it, he wanted to know. I told him. I'd needed a second job, I said. I had a big family. Did anyone else know about them? he wanted to know. I said I didn't think so.

"All this time he never took his eyes off me for a moment. All right, he said, and nodded at the hill behind me. You better be on your way before someone notices you're late.

"I can help you boys, I said. I swear to God, I'd had no idea I was going to say that. It just came out.

"You have a family, he said.

"I said it again: I can help you, I said. And that time I meant it."

"I learned later that they'd been trying to figure out where they were. It turned out that they'd been dropped at least twenty kilometers off course, the taller one told me. The pilot had miscalculated in the dark and brought them too close to Prague. They had a transmitter with them, which they protected like the goddamned Holy Grail. Over the next week I brought them blankets and bandages — it was bitter cold that whole time, and the taller one had hurt his foot coming down — and a small bottle of slivovitz and even a wedge of Christmas cake which I told my wife I'd eaten while everyone else was sleeping, which she bitched me out about. They asked me about the police in the village and a lot of other things — whether there were any troops moving about and such — and the quiet one gave me an automatic pistol in case something happened. I'd never held a pistol in my hand before. I carried it in my rucksack, and every morning when I came home from the fields I'd hide it in the barn in an old can under a handful of nails where no one could find it.

"Nothing happened for a few days. One morning I was making my way down the hill to see them, holding on to these ratty little birches that grew out of the rocks, when I noticed someone crouched against the cliff. I couldn't make out who it was — it was snowing hard — but I was sure he'd seen me, so I couldn't go back. I said to myself that as the gamekeeper I had the right to know who was about, so when I got closer I shouted, and he came out into the open. It was Baumann, the butcher. What the hell are you doing out here in all this? I said. I could hear my own heart in my chest.

"He'd been skating, Baumann said. Ten meters below us, the pond was frozen solid as a brick. The wind had blown most of the snow off.

"Where are your skates, then? I said, and because he was

afraid he got angry and said who the hell was I to be wandering about the country asking him questions and that he'd only meant that he'd come out to look at the pond and check the ice to see if he could bring his kids there, but as he was talking I saw him glance over my shoulder toward the cave the boys were staying in, and I knew he knew.

"I took the chance. So you know about them too? I said.

"He admitted he did, and we discovered that both of us had been bringing them food and information for days. Being careful men, they hadn't told either of us about the other one.

"After that I saw Baumann every day in the village, and our secret was something there between us. I didn't like it one bit. I'd known him since I was a kid. I'd never liked him — thought he had the makings of a real son of a bitch. My nerves were shot all to hell. I couldn't sleep.

"The parachutists stayed for a little less than two weeks. I heard later they moved on to a safe house in Šestajovice, and from there to Prague. But you know the rest. I had no idea they were Anthropoid — we'd never even heard of it then — or what they'd been sent to do. I wouldn't have believed it if I had. Who could have believed such a thing back then?"

"I remember the day it happened," interrupted the bear-like man at the other table. "We had the curtains closed to keep out the sun, and my old man came home early and closed the door and called my mother and said that there had been an attack on Heydrich's car up in Líbeň. 'God help those boys,' he said. I remember it because it was the first time I'd ever heard my old man mention God — my mother was the religious one in our family. And I remember my mother just pulled a chair out from under the dinner table and sat down on it sideways. 'God help us all,' she said."

"They were good boys," said Ota Rybář. Another beer had appeared in front of him and he took a long drink, then wiped the foam off his upper lip with his sleeve. "Funny — there are times even now when I find it hard to believe they're gone," he said. "I grew quite fond of them. After they'd left I wondered sometimes what became of them, but it wasn't until after the eighteenth that the pictures came out and we knew they'd all been killed in that church.

"Of course that's when things got really bad. Until then I'd been more or less all right. After the assassination, when the purges started, I was sure they'd come for me sooner or later. And after the thing in the church, it was worse. For a long time I waited for the knock on the door, but it never came, and then one day I realized that the only one who really knew my name, or that I'd had anything to do with them, was Baumann. As I said, I'd never liked him, what with that chickenshit mustache of his and his fat finger always on the scale. My wife claimed he was Jewish, but he wasn't, since he was still there in '42 when all the others had been taken. I can tell you this: it didn't make me like him any better to know that my life was in his hands. I actually thought of killing him. I could shoot him with the pistol, I thought, and no one would ever know. And who could blame me, really? He was the only link to us. By shooting him I'd be saving my family. It never occurred to me that he might be thinking the same thing."

Ota Rybář stopped. He seemed to have lost the thread of his story. He took a long drink of his beer. "Christ that's an ugly dog," he said.

"So what happened?" someone asked.

"How do you mean?"

"I mean what happened?"

"You want to know what happened?" said Ota Rybář. "I'll tell you what happened." He had been drinking for a while now. When he turned his head, it wobbled like a child's toy in need of tightening. "I'll tell you what happened," he said again. "When they came for him, the bastard kept his mouth shut and they never came for me. He was killed later, and I heard his whole family died at Mauthausen. The funny thing is that after I'd seen his name in the paper, even though I was sorry for it, I was able to breathe again for the first time in months."

He was silent. "That's it?" someone said after a while.

At that moment there was a loud crash at the bar — someone had knocked over a bottle — and a man laughed and the dog with the ferret's face stood up and then lay down again.

"What the hell was that?" said Ota Rybář.

And that was the end of the evening.

4

JUST OVER THREE YEARS AGO I FOUND MYSELF SITTING
on a bench near the white statue of Eliška Krásnohorská in
Karlovo náměstí, the square my mother had talked about the day
we planted flowers together at our cabin on the lake almost forty
years earlier. It was a still, sullen day in June, overcast and dull.
A warm wind was blowing from the east. Three kids were riding
their skateboards over a ramp they had set up on the sidewalk
under a tree with branches so huge they appeared deformed,
like thick, twisted ropes; the largest of these, a child-thick tentacle running straight out from the main trunk as though hoping to
strike out on its own, had very nearly sunk to the ground of its
own weight, and been propped up on a short steel crutch.

I had long before given up hope of learning anything conclu-
sive, if in fact I had ever hoped for that. In any case, there had
been nothing to see; the door was closed. A war had come. My
mother had loved someone who had died. She'd married my father. On a bench across from me, two old women leaned toward
each other holding their pocketbooks on their laps with both
hands. Behind them, on the avenue, a tram slowed to a stop.
The bell rang, the doors closed, the tram left. A store behind the
stop was selling out its stock of shoes. The one next to it sold
electronics.

The wind brought the slightly sickening smell of the flowers in their beds, then a gust of fumes, then the sudden coolness of plaster. It had happened right here; the entire square, I'd been told, had been cordoned off. The partisans had been hidden in the church whose cross I could almost see from where I sat. On a June morning like this one, all seven of them had died there. It told me nothing. There was no entrance; the past was closed for inventory.

The trolley bell rang again. In one of my father's stories, a hunter shooting at a bird in a dark wood was surprised to hear the arrow strike something with a dull, metallic clang. Going to investigate, he parted the branches of a thick pine to reveal an entire town, abandoned a century ago to the plague. His arrow, missing the bird, had hit the village bell tower.

One of the skateboarders drumrolled onto the wooden ramp, spun and missed, ran three quick steps.

I was watching another trolley move past the storefronts when a small white dog trotted up and began to sniff my leg. I could see his owner, a blocky old man in a suit, like a hydrant dressed for church, hurrying up the walk. *"Bud' hodnej, Karlíčku. Nezlob"* — Be good, Karlíček — he said to the dog in a tone full of good-humored sympathy for Karlíček's winsome ways and not intended to be taken to heart. When Karlíček started to sniff my crotch I gently pushed him away, and Pavel Čertovský and I began to talk. So I was from America. He had been to America once, to visit his brother in Chicago. It had been very hot there. Most young people these days didn't care about history, he said, when I explained to him, as best I could, why I'd come to Prague in the first place — it was all gadgetry and computers now. Why, just the other day he had read in the newspaper that 42 percent of students entering the gymnasium thought Charter 77 was a rock-and-roll group. "Come here, Karlíček," he called out irritably, as though the dog were somehow responsible.

And then he told me, yet again, all the things I already knew: That there had been seven of them. That they had been trained in England by the RAF. That they had parachuted back into the

Protectorate to assassinate Reichsprotektor Reinhard Heydrich, who I no doubt knew had been Hitler's personal favorite and likely successor as well as the architect of the Final Solution. That thirteen days after Heydrich died, in the early morning of June 18, the group, hidden in the crypt of the Church of Sts. Cyril and Metoděj on Řesslova Street, had found themselves surrounded by two full divisions of Wehrmacht and three hundred SS — betrayed by one of their own, a man named Čurda. That even though the situation was utterly hopeless — they were outnumbered three hundred to one — they had fought bravely, desperately, three from the rectory, the other four from the crypt itself. That the three in the rectory had been killed almost immediately but that the others had held on for hours even after the fire hoses had been pushed in through the little window on Řesslova Street and the water in the crypt had begun to rise, until they came down to their last four bullets, which they had been saving for themselves.

He remembered the morning they died, Pavel Čertovský said. He waved his hand to indicate the half-kilometer-long square we were sitting in, or perhaps the entire city. "The whole square, from there, to there, all the way down to Večná Street, was cordoned off, a four-hundred-meter radius in all directions from the church. They had guards watching the sewers letting out into the Vltava . . . they thought of everything. Still, the boys held out longer than anyone would have thought."

"You saw all this?" I asked.

"My parents lived right over there," said Pavel Čertovský. My father and I watched the whole thing from the kitchen window. My mother just cried the whole time. There wasn't much to see, to be honest, but you could hear the gunshots — *pock, pock-pock* — and I remember the fire truck coming up a side street and the puff of smoke when they dynamited the rectory. People guessed right away what it was about but of course there was nothing to be done — God himself couldn't have saved those boys that morning." Pavel Čertovský shook his head. "I prefer dogs to people," he said. And he scratched the dog, who had laid his head on his owner's lap, on the top of his nose, and the dog looked up at his face with an expression of adoration and sorrow that reminded me of fifteenth-century paintings of Christ looking up from the cross to a merciful heaven.

"After that it all went to hell, basically," Čertovský went on. "The day after they killed Kubiš and Gabčík and the rest, we heard they'd gotten one of the main figures of the Resistance in Prague, a woman named Moravcová. She was able to get to some poison; her husband and son had it much harder." He paused. "But you probably already know all of this," he said.

"Some," I said. "Tell me, has this place changed much since then?"

"The trees are bigger, of course," said Pavel Čertovský. "And a few of the buildings are different." He paused, as though gathering something. "It seemed happier somehow. You have to understand," he said quickly. "I was twelve years old; everything seemed possible. Huge things were happening, every day something new was happening, but it all seemed to be occurring somewhere else, to someone else, not me. I can't explain it. I can't defend it. It was as if things had no gravity. Terrible things happened — you saw them happen — but then they'd just float away." He shook his head. "Youth. In old age you go around creaking like an old garbage truck loaded down with shit, if you'll pardon me.

"But listen to me running on — here, let me tell you something you may actually find interesting. If you go back to the church," he said, indicating the direction of the church with his head, "go to the back room of the museum where they have that wall of photographs and look at the fourth from the right, three rows down. It shows the crowd gathered around Gabčík's body that morning after they'd dragged it out into the street. If you look closely in the bottom right corner, between the legs of the man with the camera taking a picture of Gabčík's face, you'll see a foot with a white sock and a brown sandal." He patted my knee conspiratorially. "That's me," he said, "and right next to . . . *Karlíčku, přestaň!*" — Stop that! — he called to the dog, who had wandered over to the huge supported branch of the oak and was peeing on the crutch. The dog lowered his leg. "What was I saying?"

But he was an old man, and had forgotten. "Funny," he said. "I can't remember four seconds back — I've already forgotten your name, I'm afraid — but I can see every detail from half a century ago. Every absurdity. I remember that our dog had to go that morning — dogs have no appreciation for history — and my father decided to take him out. This was still during the siege of the church, but well before we knew what it was really about. My father and I went out through the cellar to the back, then walked away from the square to the churchyard of St. Katherine's on Viničná Street, just up from where the hospital is now, and the dog promptly did his business. I remember that as we were leaving he stopped to drink from a bucket someone had left on the walk, and I saw a couple on a bench to the right of the big wooden doors there; they were both quite young — beautiful young people, really — and she was holding him and he was shaking like a child and it wasn't until that very moment that I had a sense of how bad the thing happening four blocks away really was."

But he had to be going, he said, and we said our goodbyes and he and Karlíček walked off together past the skateboarders who stood about sullenly, holding their boards under their arms until they had passed.

A gray day. The wind, a warm breath, moved the leaves, lifted the dirty curls of one of the skateboarders out of his eyes, slid a paper bag a short distance along the walk. And sitting there I could suddenly feel them — the facts, the dates, the stories, the couple on the bench in the churchyard — gathering like iron filings around an invisible magnet, suggesting a shape.

5

THEY HAD BEEN HERE, ALL OF THEM, AND NOW THEY were gone. What could match the wonder of that? They'd leaned against a sun-warmed wall on a particular afternoon in June, scratched their noses with the backs of their wrists, pulled an oversoft apricot in half with their fingers. And now they were gone. I'd come to love two of them: their voices, should I somehow hear them again in this world, would be more familiar to me than my own. But others had known them. I never had, really.

Someone once said that at the end of every life is a full stop, and death could care less if the piece is a fragment. It is up to us, the living, to supply a shape where none exists, to rescue from the flood even those we never knew. Like beggars, we must patch the universe as best we can.

1942

A Novel

I IMAGINE THEY DIDN'T SPEAK MUCH THAT FIRST HOUR or so as they made their way deeper into the forest, up dank sloping paths where rainwater had left shores of pine needles like sea wrack in the dirt, past piles of logs spotted white where their branches had been lopped close to the trunk, then off the trails entirely. Damp, sweet gloom, resiny and wet, then a shot of strong sun, as from a different world, then shadow and sun, shadow and sun. A Gypsy wagon, its wood swollen fat with water, stood in the middle of a dense patch of woods, barred in by ten-year-old pines. Covered in needles, its canvas gouged by branches, it seemed to have been dropped from the sky. They passed through an old abandoned orchard, then made their way along the edge of a marshy field that might have had a lake at its center, its reeds loud with birds.

His name was Tomáš Bém, the surname just one step removed from the umlaut and the German "Böhm," and he came from Vyškov, a village twenty kilometers north of Brno. He was twenty-two years old that summer, a man of average height, not particularly handsome. There was something concentrated about him, as if the energy of a larger man, and the bitterness of an older one, had been forced to fit that slimmer frame. The day they met — a hot, still day in late July of 1941 — he took the early train from Brno to Žd'ár nad Sázavou, then a bus that bounced interminably over bad roads as women fanned themselves with whatever papers they happened to have handy and men sat sweating stolidly into their collars. When the bus stopped at a small wrought-iron bridge near a country market he got out, shouldered his rucksack, swung the tin cup that hung from a leather thong around his neck over his shoulder, and began to walk. As he made his way up the long sloping road he could feel it, tapping lightly on his back. Ten minutes later he was in the forest.

He walked steadily for three hours along vast, empty fields, through the shade of pine forests mossed and tufted with thick, soft grass, stopping only to eat his lunch on a pile of fresh-cut pines that someone had stacked by the road. Sap bled from the cuts. He watched two women, only their upper bodies visible above the shimmering wheat, cross the field that began just on the other side of the pines. There had to be a path there. Or a road. One of them suddenly skipped ahead, her hands flying up like a girl's. Perhaps she had jumped over a washout in the road. The road angled down the slope of a hill. He watched them until they disappeared, sinking into the grain.

Two yellow butterflies, drifted in from the edge of the field where hundreds like them fluttered in the weeds, settled on the end of a log and walked in small, tight circles. *Žlut'ásci.* His kid sister Majka had once caught ten of them in a jar because he'd told her she couldn't, then forgotten them in the sun.

Shouldering his rucksack, he jumped off the logs and walked a short distance back the way he had come to where a deep seam of overgreen grass marked a stream trickling through the forest loam. Ten meters off the path was a stone basin. A metal cup hung on a hook. He drank, then poured the second cup slowly over his head. Behind him he could hear the wagon go by — the clop of steel on dirt and stone, the quick creak of wood. He let it pass without turning around.

He'd memorized the directions to the house. A man from the factory had come up to him as he walked to the train after his shift, told him the directions and how to announce himself, then veered off up the hill. They would be expecting him, he'd said. He was to put nothing on paper — ever — unless expressly told to do so. The leader's name was Ladislav Kindl.

He appeared at the back door of the house just after dark with a rucksack on his back and the tin cup hanging from his neck half full of raspberries. The others were already there, sitting awkwardly around the living room, bits of fern stuck in the straps of their sandals. Kindl, whose house it was, introduced him. He nodded hello, then took a chair off to the side and listened. My mother, who was twenty-one that summer, sat next to Kindl's wife on the sofa. She had come alone. My father, who was not yet my father but just a man she had come to care for, was sick in Brno.

It was the way he listened maybe, as though attending to every word being said, but from somewhere else. Or the way he would look at someone, straight on, until he had seen what he wanted. There was a kind of mild, innocent ruthlessness about it, though he himself seemed neither mild nor innocent nor particularly ruthless. He sat leaning forward on the uncomfortable chair Kindl and his wife kept in the pantry for getting preserves down from the shelves, strangely immovable, like a man looking out of a statue, and yet when he moved he moved with a smooth youthful abruptness, a complete lack of adjustment or preparation, that was somehow disconcerting. It was as if he were on fire inside, had been on fire for years, but with no way of getting at the flames, had simply learned to live with it. She looked at him, at his hands folded over each other, at his short black hair, his mouth. There was something slightly misshapen about the face, she decided. Something about him irritated her, she couldn't quite say what.

· · ·

By the time they left the house that night the moon was up and a warm wind was moving the wheat. The others had already gone: some toward Vrchovice, others toward Havlíčkův Brod, three weaving down the road to the car they'd left at the inn, their arms around one another's shoulders, singing.

There had been a great deal to discuss. Radio contact between the government in exile and Prague had been reestablished, Kindl had informed them. President Beneš himself had communicated his gratitude from London. The expansion of existing cells of resistance in Bohemia and Moravia was now of paramount importance. London had instructed them to acquire a copy of the poem "Enthusiasm," by Svatopluk Čech, in the World Library edition. It would be used to set up a secure code. Teams of parachutists trained by the RAF were to be dropped into the Protectorate. Every effort would have to be made to help them. They would have to be provided with the addresses of safe houses and the code names of partisans. They would need identity cards, police declaration forms, work papers, ration books. And so on.

Kindl walked out to the back fence and stood there for a while, smoking a cigarette in the dark. Nothing. No light at all. He could barely make out the silhouettes of the houses across the road. It was odd to think of the entire Protectorate — ten thousand homes, towns, cities — slipping into darkness every night, disappearing. Three years of blackouts. He looked again at the blocky shapes across the road. He didn't like them — it was easier to see out of a dark house. Still, it was late. He waited. The wind moved. There would be mushrooms tomorrow. Christ, it was a beautiful night.

He leaned over a bit to see around the edge of the house. Before the war he could see the electric street lamp by the inn, two hundred meters away. Moths would be flying in and out of the light. He started another cigarette, then stubbed it out on the wood. He didn't like that moon. Or the windows he knew were there.

He had oiled the hinges two days earlier, so when he lifted the latch from its bed and pushed open the low wooden gate it swung soundlessly until it thumped back against the fence. They came out of the pantry then, walking quickly: Svíčka, the girl, and three steps behind her, moving as easily as if he were going out for a game of tennis, the new man, Bém. There was something he didn't like about him — he couldn't say what exactly. That green shawl she'd worn around her neck that evening — or not a shawl, more like a big *šátek* of some sort — had looked old-fashioned, like something her grandmother might have given her. Strange how good it had looked with her hair.

A warm night. From the shadow of the house he watched the three of them slip through the gate, then hurry across the open ground, their number doubled by the moon. Svíčka was a good man — rational, methodical. Rumor had it that his wife knew nothing whatsoever about his activities, that he'd thought it best to hide them from her, the way another man would an affair. The forest was right there, narrow at one end, then widening out. It looked like a strip of black fabric torn from the sky and the field. Kindl breathed in a chestful of air, then slowly let it out.

The door opened quietly behind him. "Come in the house," he heard her say from the dark.

"I'll be right in."

He had heard a rumor that Bém was going to England. He wondered how he would go. From Gdynia, probably, to one of the French ports. He would have gone too, once.

"It's late. I'm tired."

"So go to bed if you're tired."

They were there now. He could barely make them out against the wheat. Svíčka was still in the lead. The girl was holding her shoulder bag to her side to keep it from swinging. He'd seen her looking at the new man. It was too bad, really. He'd liked the other one better. He hoped it wouldn't cause any difficulties.

The wheat was a low, pale wall. He watched them come up to it, then disappear, one by one.

AS THEY CROSSED THE OPEN GROUND AND STARTED UP the path toward the wheat field, my mother could hear nothing: Svíčka's steps, her own breathing, the slight chuff of her bag against her clothes. Nothing else. It was as though he had simply disappeared. And yet she knew he was there. She felt shaky, overdrawn, but absolutely alert. The moon, the scratch of the crickets — she noticed everything. Svíčka's legs looked like a wishbone. She wanted to laugh.

As they came up to the edge of the field it reached out to meet them — a sigh of sun-warmed grain in their faces — and then they were in, plunging arms forward like divers into that close, pale world. The moon was everywhere. It scored the double of every stalk, every seed-filled head on her legs, her arms, her shifting bag. A million soft little hands scratched and tugged and brushed her face — but why couldn't she hear him? Two meters ahead of her, his hands up and his head turned slightly to the side, Svíčka shifted to another row. She knew what he was doing, looking for spaces, trying to walk as much as possible between the grain. It wouldn't work. She had walked a thousand fields before this one. She shifted with him, listening. Nothing. She resisted the temptation to turn around, concentrated on following. Why had he decided to leave with them? They would have been better off without him.

And suddenly the edge of the field and then the shadow of

the trees and they were out. Not far off, along the edge of the field, stood a hunter's stand of cut pine, like a chair on stilts. She turned around now just as he stepped out of the grain, behind her. She couldn't see his face but she could see the shape of him — his hair, his shoulders, the rucksack with its belts and straps. He walked past her and squatted down with his back against a tree, the rucksack still on his back. When the match flared she saw his face: the nose, the black hair, the impatient mouth.

He paused, holding the cigarette down by the ground, then, as if remembering, brought it up to his mouth in a big arc. She had thought he was smiling.

He was holding something out to them with his left hand.

"Go ahead," she heard him say. "Take two."

"Where did you get these?" Svíčka said.

"Don't ask," he said.

Her eyes were adjusting to the darkness now. Here and there in the forest behind them she could see spears of light cutting down through the pines, and farther off, where the trees opened, a well-lit space, like a small room between the trees, and then another, and another. The air moved, bringing the dank, loamy smell of roots, and right after it the hot, strong smell of horse and pig and oats. There would be mushrooms tomorrow. Even now they were prodding up through the loam and the black needles, their fat brown heads capped with bits of turf like the soft felt hats of cardinals.

They talked about which way to go. Vrchovice was too close, they agreed. Best to put some distance between themselves and the house. The logging roads and the trails were clearly marked, Svíčka said, and they had at least four hours of darkness left. He smiled. "It's eighteen kilometers. If we walk hard and skip the picnic we can make it to Žd'ár by dawn."

He turned to the other one. "Are you familiar with this area?"

"No."

"Then I suggest you take the train from Mělkovice. It is only two kilometers from Žd'ár, and there is a train for Brno at five-oh-five." He turned to my mother. "Ivana, you and I can leave from Žd'ár. I have a train to Prague at six, and there's another for Brno at six-forty-five. Does that sound all right?"

She said she thought it was a good idea.

"Then we're agreed."

Bém stood. A single gesture: abrupt, unhurried. There had been no adjustment of weight, no release of breath, no scrape of leather against bark. He was suddenly just standing. And my mother, sitting with her back against a huge, rough-barked pine, saw him turn to adjust a strap by his neck, and something about the way he turned at that moment opened a door inside her. It was as though she were seeing something she'd known and forgotten, something she'd loved a hundred years ago. It made no sense.

"What time do you have to be at the factory?" she heard Svíčka asking.

"I don't," the other said.

"I'm sorry?"

"I don't have to be at the factory."

"I don't think I follow you."

"I'm not returning to Brno."

"Is that right? Does Kindl know about this?"

"He knows."

Svíčka paused. "I'm sorry. I'll need to know what happened. You understand why I have to ask."

"I do. What always happens. We were interfering, slowing the work."

"Someone informed on you in other words."

"One of the lathes had been put out of commission. Some good citizen wanted to make the quota."

"Forgive me — why didn't the Gestapo arrest you then?" said Svíčka.

"I was out sick."

"They didn't come to your home?"

"They came. I wasn't there."

"Why didn't they wait until all the saboteurs were present at the factory the next day. Or the day after. They're not usually given to such errors."

"I don't know. I've asked myself that question."

"Did you find an answer?"

"No."

"And that satisfies you?"

"No. It doesn't."

Taking off his glasses, Svíčka breathed gently on the lenses, then rubbed them with a handkerchief. "This complicates things."

"Does it?"

For just a moment, a tiny moon appeared in one of the lenses, then disappeared. "I'm afraid it does, yes. We have to assume they're after you."

"They're after all of us."

"There's a difference," said Svíčka quietly.

Bém took a long drag of his cigarette, then turned it into the dirt with his heel. "You're right," he said. "I should go." He looked at my mother, sitting with her arms around her knees in the dark. "Goodbye," he said, "I'm sorry we . . ." He nodded, then turned to go.

It was Svíčka who stopped him. "Wait," he said — and that word was the pivot on which everything turned. Everything. Or maybe not. Maybe she came to see it as the thing that only made visible what had been coming their way forever, calmly measuring its steps even as they played and grew, fought and lost, separated now by fifty kilometers, now by five, even as my father and I waited patiently in the wings, as the theater began to darken . . . Maybe that one word simply served to flush the situation into the open so it could breathe and leap before being run into the ground like a crippled stag.

"Wait," Svíčka said, and the other stopped and turned in a

white stripe of light that cut him shoulder to thigh like a bandolier. It was night, Svíčka said. A weekday. They could cover the first eighteen kilometers together, then separate at the turnoff for Mělkovice.

They would be safer alone, the other said.

"Nonsense," Svíčka said. "Everyone would be safer alone — don't you agree?" he asked my mother. Besides, it was well after midnight, he said. No one but the devil would be out in the forest that late.

As they set off along the perimeter of the field, my mother turned around. In the woods behind them the changing angle of the moon had erased entire rooms and expanded others into great misshapen halls filled with one-legged tables and elfin chairs, richly upholstered with moss.

The logging road was long and straight, like a road in a dream, and they walked hard for the first hour, passing crossroads where logs as thick as men had been piled head-high in the ditch. Eventually a stream joined them. They could hear it burbling to itself in the dark, running through the grassy tunnels that cut under the road, then back. When it passed beneath them a third time Svíčka said they had to watch for the trail, and when they found the thumb-sized marker on the pine, its white frame barely visible in the shadows, Bém stepped up to it and lit a match, cupping the flare in his hands, and she saw the blue.

He looked up the mossy little track, veined with roots, that meandered off into the dark. "You say this will save us time?"

"Kindl said it was considerably shorter," said Svíčka.

"It is," my mother said.

Bém turned toward my mother. "You know these woods?"

My mother nodded. She had picked mushrooms here with her father when she was a child. The blue would stay small for two or three kilometers, she said, hardly more than a game trail, then widen. They would have to be careful — there were branching trails in the open woods, and one section led along the edge of an open field — but it would take six or seven kilometers off the distance by road.

They should stop and think, Svíčka argued. It would be slow going. They would have to stop at every marker. And six kilometers wasn't much. If they stayed on the logging road, they could make up the time without the risk of getting lost.

"You think we should take the trail?" Bém asked, looking at my mother.

"I do."

"Then lead on," he said, stepping aside.

And she did. Here and there, between the trees, or on a long slope spotted and cut with light, she could see her father in his black boots, walking with the slight stoop of the mushroom hunter, his hands behind his back like a schoolmaster listening to sums, or prodding beneath the grass with his stick. The pond called Vápenice appeared to the right, a scattering of stars between the pines. Listen, her father said. It was March, dusk, spits of crusty snow still holding on in the shade. Far off, a riot of croaking, ecstatic and desperate. You can hear the pond before you see it, he said. It passed now on the right, a small black circle, its surface half covered with pine needles.

And then the ferns, reaching for their legs, another marker, another match. Blue. He nodded to her, indicated with his hand. They went on. A long downward slope through stands of thick oaks, a different dark, and then the birches like scratches or matchsticks and finally the vast, low, shore-like edge of the fields, mustard and barley, open to the sky. What was he thinking? Was he looking at her? The way he moved — the long smooth stride, the pull of his hips . . . that hair looked like it had been cut with a pair of garden shears. She led them quickly along the field, then across a narrow wooded peninsula filled with boulders, and suddenly they were back in the cool, dark smell of the pines, and the wooden sign nailed to the tree at the crossroads said Mělkovice, four kilometers; Žd'ár nad Sázavou, seven. She looked for the name of the town they had come from, to see how far they had come, but it wasn't there.

He was looking down the road, distracted. What could she have been thinking? This was ridiculous. She was going home, to Brno.

"Can you give me a light?" Svíčka said. Bém lit another match. Svíčka looked at his watch. It was almost three-thirty. Bém swung the rucksack off his back and took out a tin canteen of water.

"So tell us, what did you do before all this?" Svíčka asked. "Before the war, I mean."

"I was a fitter." He offered my mother the canteen of water.

"Good work?"

"I didn't mind it. Not what I would have chosen."

"What would you have chosen?" my mother asked.

It seemed almost like a smile. "Something different," he said after a moment.

"Can I ask you something?" Svíčka said.

"You can ask."

Svíčka took the canteen from my mother, took a sip of water, then handed it back to Bém. "When they came to look for you, what happened to your family?"

"I have no idea."

"I'm sorry," Svíčka said.

"Thank you."

"Perhaps. . . ?"

"Perhaps."

Svíčka shook his head, then shrugged into his rucksack. "And so now you're going abroad," he said. "Well, *audentes fortuna iuvat,* as the saying goes — fortune belongs to the daring."

Bém looked at him for a moment.

"We'll see," he said.

• • •

They came to the turnoff just after four. The air above the fields had begun to change, tracing over the edges of things, darkening the horizon of woods. Mělkovice was just down the road. Bém could take the early train, Svíčka said; he would go on from Žd'ár. Since men were mostly the ones leaving early for the factories, my mother would wait in the forest for an hour so as to avoid drawing attention to herself, then follow. She still had the sack for the mushrooms? Good. She should pick some. Svíčka took out his watch and opened it, holding it close to his face. He nodded at Bém. It was time.

A quick good luck and he was gone, walking fast, his slim form disappearing against the trees before he had reached the curve. Nothing. There had been nothing. My mother and Svíčka walked on together toward Žd'ár. She would be all right? She had everything she needed? She barely heard him. He said goodbye and left.

When she couldn't see him anymore she took the net bag out of her pocket and unfolded the handles and smoothed the creases out of the mesh against her leg, mechanically running her hand over and over the wrinkled mesh, then turned and started back into the forest. She could feel something trembling inside her. She felt soft somehow, hollow . . . For a moment she thought about my father — his face, his hands on her . . .

It was still dark when she came to the turnoff. There was no one there. The moon was down, the forest strangely silent. She stepped over the choked little ditch and walked into the woods, picking her way between the stumps and the broken branches that blocked her way. She had an hour, maybe more. An easy walk. She knew the station well: the low wall across the tracks, the pruned trees along the road, that *hospoda* where she and her father had seen the dwarf sitting on the bench. Some mushrooms would go well tonight. My God, what a fool she was. There was one! Even in the gloom she could see the fat pale stem. She rocked it gently out of the humus and put it in her bag.

She could almost see. The sky overhead, blue-black, was beginning to fill up with light. What had she been thinking? There had been no sign, no understanding. Another! Funny how you could see them so well against the soil. And so arrogant, in his way. And here she was, stumbling about the woods. She could actually feel her heart. She stopped, smiled to herself, then spun and smashed the half-full bag against the trunk of a tree. As she turned to go, a small, hard branch clawed deep into her calf. She pulled up her dress. She could see the gouge welling up with blood. She held her hand to her leg for a moment, then wiped it on the moss. It was time to go.

My mother picked up the net bag of smashed mushrooms. The woods were graying quickly now, the mist sweeping through the trees in long tatters like steam over a pot of water about to boil. She was tired. She had misunderstood. Anyone could misunderstand. There was nothing to think about.

He was standing at the turnoff by the grassy V where the roads split, his rucksack by his feet like a dog.

She walked right up to him. She could see him breathing. He shook his head slightly. "I couldn't . . . ," he began, and it was as though she'd known that voice forever.

"I know," she said.

"I couldn't seem to leave you," he said, then added quickly, as if he'd surprised himself, "I'm sorry, I shouldn't . . ."

"I know," she said.

They didn't touch. They stood there looking at each other for a moment, trying to understand that they were both here, that this was happening, and then he bent and picked up the rucksack and slipped it over his shoulder. "Which way?" he said quietly. And she turned without a moment's hesitation, without a single thought for the world she'd known or the woman she'd been, and led him into the forest.

ON ONE LEVEL, THEY KNEW WHAT THEY WERE DOING: losing themselves in the forest, in a mazework of paths leading off from roads already knee-high in grass, passing through the gates of gamekeepers' wooden fences and around the edges of abandoned fields and small black ponds where butterflies slept in the sun slanting through the trees. It had been done before, after all, though with mixed results.

Ten months later, when she saw him step out of the trolley on Náměstí Míru so much thinner than she remembered him, when she saw the new, rimless glasses and the newspaper under his arm and the briefcase in his hand and watched him make his way through the crowd holding his hat to his head as though that would help with the rain, not seeing her standing there in front of him as fixed and still as the cobbles under her feet because it simply wasn't possible that it should be him, that she should be seeing that face, that mouth; when they wandered that one flying hour out to the vineyards and then down to the square, where they sat helplessly on a bench in the drizzle before he got on another trolley and left without having told her how he came to be back in the country or what he was doing in Prague or where he would be; when she ran into him yet again later that June, as though fortune would have it no other way, and they spent that oppressive dying day and the night that followed as in a fevered dream wandering from Vinohrady to the cemetery, from the cemetery to Líbeň, from Líbeň to the Vltava where they saw the yellow carp floating in the foam among the boards and the garbage . . . when those days came, and all the days after, *these* were the days she remembered.

She remembered waking from a drugged sleep that first afternoon to find him looking at her. The sun had moved on. Next to her, a shirt hung over three curved sticks pushed into the ground, a shade for her face. It lifted quickly, as though someone were peeking beneath, then fell.

"Thank you," she said.

He nodded. "You're welcome. I felt somehow responsible."

"Did they teach you that in the Scouts?"

An almost-smile, a flash of that crooked tooth. "I don't remember the Scouts being much help in situations like this."

"And have there been many . . . situations like this?"

"No," he said. "There haven't."

"That's good to know."

"Four or five at the very most."

"I'm glad."

They looked at each other for what seemed like a long time.

"Can you tell me what's happening here?" she said at last.

He shook his head. "No." Reaching over, he caught a strand of her hair on the back of his fingers and moved it off her forehead. "All I know is that I can't leave right now."

A high breeze was playing with the light on the grass. My mother could hear the stream. There was an afternoon slant to the light.

"I should get dressed," she said.

"No," he said. "Never."

He watched her dress, raising her hips, slipping her skirt up over her knees. Reaching around, she brought the ends of her hair in front of her face and began looking through it. "What will Mother think?" she said.

"Let me do that," he said, and moving against her, he began to pick the bits of grass and leaves out of her hair. She could still feel him, the sweet shock of him, pushing inside her. She could feel his hands moving through the heavy mass of her hair, combing out the strands. Her scalp was still slightly damp along the hairline. She could feel it cooling.

"How long do you think we have?" she said.

"A few days."

"Just pull on it — you don't have to be so gentle."

"I thought I *was* pulling at it."

"And then you have to go."

"I do. Sorry — there's a knot here."

"For how long?"

His fingers paused for a moment, though they might have just been working out a tangle. "I don't know. A year. Maybe less."

"Just pull on it," she said.

"You won't have any hair left."

"I'll live with it."

"All right."

"I need to tell you something," she said. "Not for you. For myself."

"Tell me, then."

"I've been seeing someone. For about a year now. In Brno."

"I expected there would be someone."

"That doesn't bother you?"

"It doesn't surprise me."

"It doesn't bother you either?"

"No." And then: "A little."

She turned around to look at him.

"Done," he said, gently brushing off the collar of her blouse. "Mother will never suspect a thing."

"It doesn't matter anymore. Any of it. Do you believe that?"

"I do," he said. He reached for her hand, began rolling the knuckles with his thumb. "Tell me the truth — can you do this?"

"Can you stay?"

He nodded. "For a while."

"Then I can do anything," she said.

"It's dangerous," he said.

"I know that," my mother said, and then, feeling his hand: "How did you get this?"

And he told her about the wine glass he'd stepped on while wading along the shore of a carp pond as a boy: how he'd felt a kind of tender, caving crack, as if he'd stepped on a thin-walled shell, and how he'd reached down to feel what he couldn't see and understood the moment the blood plumed up out of his hand, and listening to him she felt an absurd rush of anger toward the nameless drunk who had thrown his glass into the pond and at the same time a small thrill at owning this thing, this knowledge.

They walked all that afternoon, slightly giddy from making love, their arms around each other's waist despite the heat. She could feel his hipbone under her hand, the slip and clench of the muscle, the wetness of his shirt. And though it might have been more comfortable for them to walk apart, they didn't separate for a long time, struck alike by the comfort of their stride, the sudden pleasure of fronting the world together, neither one realizing that they were a contagion upon this world, that as they stood at the crossroads or came upon the woman with the basket on her arm standing at the edge of the forest cutting away the bad parts of a mushroom with a small knife, it was already a part of them, turning whenever they turned, touching whatever they touched. They knew nothing. They walked down long forest roads between grassy ditches filled with tannin-brown water, listening to the frogs shriek and leap from the narrow banks as the sunlight tilted toward evening, and for the rest of her life my mother would remember passing a lonely little pond and glimpsing a man, as in a dream, neatly dressed in a suit and tie, sitting on a chair he'd set up by the shore as though expecting a waiter to bring him a glass of wine. But by then the scene would have a different cast — the future had tainted the memory, the absurd had taken the tiny step toward nightmare — and the thing they had laughed at now laughed at them.

She spent years trying to keep the memory of their days together free of irony, blowing off the fine dust of death. She failed. History and time were too much, even for her. How could she erase the fact that even as she walked next to him that first afternoon listening to the straps of his rucksack tap gently against the leather, the gods were already slapping their thighs and heaving with mirth, having glimpsed how perfectly the thing would work: how it would turn, slowly at first, then with gathering speed, whipping around to strike down precisely the most selfless, the most brave — better still, striking those who, like care workers during the plague years, had by their own decency chosen themselves. Bém would become known. His contacts, however accidental, would be traced. And it would be their love that made it possible.

By the time they came out of the fields into the village of Dobrá Voda, the shadow of the churchyard wall had reached across the road. A bird was calling from the oak as they passed under its branches. They crossed a small stone bridge and started toward the town. On a side road a boy with a flapping shirttail slapped at a hoop with a stick and ran after it, while another, behind him, tried to balance on his bicycle while standing still. "*Tak pojd' už!*" — Come on, already! — the one with the hoop called out behind him without turning around.

She knew there would be no store here, that if there were one it would be closed, that if it weren't closed it would be empty. But a store was not what they were seeking necessarily. A woman with a pitchfork would do. Or a man hitting a cow on the rump with a stick, or a fisherman on a folding stool.

They passed the churchyard, the steeple, the charnel house with its wrought-iron cross and skull rising over the red, split-tile wall, then a black pond, already still with evening. The town seemed strangely empty. A bell began to ring.

When the man in the wagon came around the turn Bém let go of my mother's hand and stepped into the road and the man twitched the reins and the horse shook its head and stopped. She watched him as he talked to the old man with the brambly eyebrows who sat leaning forward, elbows on his knees, the reins loose in his brown, thick-fingered hands. So this was how he was with the world! She felt an odd sense of ownership, as though his manner, his way, were also hers now. Something she had on her side. No idle conversation, no explanations or apologies, no observations about the weather. He simply wished the man a good evening and asked him whether he knew where they might buy some food.

The other did not seem to mind the directness at all. What did they need? A small dog, lying by his feet, stood and stretched its back like a cat. "*Lehni,*" he said. The dog lay down.

Whatever anyone could spare for a fair price: some bread, a few eggs, a bit of sugar or fat. It didn't really matter.

The man nodded. The neck, the heavy shoulders — there was a stillness about him, she thought. The stillness of an anvil, or a shovel leaning against a wall in the dark.

If the lady didn't mind riding in the wagon, he said, looking straight ahead between the reins as though talking about someone else, he would see what they could do. There wasn't much. And he waited, not turning around, till he had felt them climb into the empty bed of the wagon, then moved his right hand and the horse began to walk.

A half loaf of bread, two dozen apricots, a small jar of milk. Half a kilo of fatty pork cuts and a few spoonfuls of lard. She would remember it for forty years.

. . .

As they rode up the grassy path toward the plain, plaster-sided farmhouse, a tall angular woman with a dark purple stain on her face and ear which looked from a distance like an odd loop of hair came out of the barn, wiping her hands on a cloth. They had nothing left, she said. They had nothing left — he knew that. Just quotas they couldn't fill. They were being bled like pigs.

"*Jirko, buď ticho*," said the old man. Be quiet.

Not that she would begrudge the Wehrmacht anything. She knew how much they needed her eggs. *Kraft durch Arbeit* — strength through work. Others' work.

They were standing on the dirt now, the dog sniffing at their legs. Across the road, a woman in a light-colored housedress was calling someone named Marie to dinner. A breath of cooler air, as from somewhere underground, passed through the yard and was gone. They were sorry to have troubled them, my mother said. They knew how things were these days.

The old man, as though his task were done, had begun unhitching the wagon.

"You're from these parts," the woman said, looking at my mother.

"Račín," my mother said.

"I have a sister in Malá Losenice," the woman said.

She looked at Bém. "Are you from the highlands as well?"

"No." Funny how he could do that, my mother thought, and have it be neither cold nor abrupt nor anything but what it was. An answer.

The old woman looked at him the way a woman of a certain age wiping her hands on a rag and wearing a baggy, meal-colored blouse and a pair of cracked rubber boots will look at a man. Not giving a damn for his black hair or his mouth or anything else visible to the eyes. And saw that he didn't either. He simply looked back. Polite enough. When he saw Jožka begin to push the wagon into the barn, he lay his pack in the grass and walked over to help. And Jožka, who did not like help, particularly from people he didn't know, moved over without a word and let him. She looked back at the girl. Here was another one. God help the mother whose daughter she was — there'd be a soul to go with that face, a reckless kind of soul. She could see the way she looked at him. Keeping nothing in reserve. Though he was not unmoved, no, not at all. The way he'd stood next to her. The way he'd touched her arm when he went to help Jožka with the wagon. No, there was a chance here. And a fine couple they would make, no denying that.

"Well, come into the house, then," she said to my mother.

When they came back out into the yard, the dark had begun. A warm summer night. The pear trees by the wall were a solid mass now, stretching nearly to the house. The two men were just crossing over from the stable. Jožka had something wrapped in a rag. *Zbytky ze zabíjačky,* he said gruffly. Trimmings from last week's butchering. She knew better than to argue.

"You're sure?" Bém said to them as he took the rag.

The old man grunted and wiped his nose. "Nothing from nothing."

"They've lent us a blanket," my mother said, indicating her bag. "And a pot."

He looked at them. "Thank you," he said, then squatted down and put the bundle in his rucksack. A small light blinked just above the weeds. Another against the stable door. And another. Standing up, he reached into a pocket and pulled out some money.

"*To si můžete nechat*" — You can keep that — the woman said before he could speak. "What would we do with it?"

"Buy yourself something," my mother said.

"Nothing to buy."

"Then just . . ."

"I don't have time to stand here debating with you. Really."

"You're sure?"

"When I want a new fur, I'll look you up."

"Thank you."

"You'll be all right?" the old man said.

They would be fine, they said.

The road had begun to emerge, pale against the dark. They walked under the cherry trees that lined the road, then back through the village, where small wavery lights showed through the windows. A woman's voice was calling someone, a child answered, then the thin clank of a pail. On one of the benches by the pond a couple sat still as stone, locked into one shape.

They didn't say anything now. She felt his fingers as they walked. His hand felt cool, dry. She explored the knuckle of his thumb with hers, felt the scar, then the square, smooth nail.

By the time they came to the churchyard, the wall with the archers' clefts was just a paleness narrowing into the dark. She could hear their footsteps scraping on the dirt of the road. She looked up: the steeple and the skull had disappeared, leaving only their starless shapes behind.

NIGHT, NIGHT. THE OTHERNESS OF IT! LIKE A DOOR TO a room we've never entered, hidden behind our childhood dresser. Like another world, living inside the one we know. The wind in the grass sounds different here. The wind in the wheat reminds you of something. The bone-whiteness of the fields reminds you of something. No dream can match this dreaming. And now the moon, raising itself above the fields.

The night my mother and Tomáš Bém walked into the forest from the town of Dobrá Voda the sky was clear and huge and hot, the moon just two days short of full. It rose, slightly misshapen, as they walked between the fields, so that by the time they entered the shadow of the forest, diving under a wave of air smelling of moldering loam, mushrooms, and sap, the way was already shot through with bits of light. They stood for a moment, letting their eyes adjust to the dark, learning to read the shapes of things, then went on, stepping carefully over the deadfalls, ducking the black branches that swept down from the ceiling.

They came to a vast pool of light which they thought at first was a meadow. An emptied pond stretched before them, a hollow socket, barren and sad. A stream ran through the hardened mud. They walked around the perimeter, backing away whenever the ground started to pull at their feet, then followed the stream back into the dark until they came to a place of thick knotted grass and put down their things. You could almost see. To the right, between the trees, a small rise like a long, soft shelf. A low mossy stump. A fallen pine, level enough for sitting on.

"Here?" she said.

"All right," he said. They hadn't said anything for a long time. She liked hearing the sound of his voice. It made him familiar again.

He kissed her. "Welcome home," he said, then walked into the shadow by the stump and lay the rucksack on top of it and began taking out their food.

The stream was right there, she thought, listening. She began to feel over the surface of the ground with her hands, tossing aside thumbnail-sized pine cones and broken sticks, clearing a space.

"Hungry?" she heard him say.

"Tired."

"Come have some of this." She could see him holding out the jar, blue in the moonlight. She walked over and sat next to him on the fallen pine. The milk was cool and smooth.

"You didn't get much sleep last night," he said.

"Neither did you, I think."

"True enough." She could almost see his smile. He poured a little water from a canteen into the empty jar, then spilled it out on the grass. "Maybe we should just give up on it altogether," he said.

"Sleeping?"

"What do you think?"

"Maybe we should."

They slept that night, lying naked on the clothes she had spread on the grass like a rag quilt while he took the meat and put it in the empty milk jar and placed the jar in a sidewater below the bar where it bobbed quietly in the dark, herded in by rocks. They slept, her head on his arm, half covered by the blanket, the wet rag and his rucksack and her bag hanging off the broken branches of a pine as from a giant coat rack, not hearing the stream chuckling to itself, or the sudden call of a bird from somewhere by the dry lake, not feeling the long, fine file of ants, like a thread dragged endlessly across his calf, or the fat-bodied moth that settled on her hair like a child's barrette, or the mosquito that lit lightly on his eyebrow and danced along that line until it found its place and grew quickly dark with blood. They slept, not seeing or hearing any of these things, and woke together, as lovers will, his arm around her and her breasts pressed flat against his ribs, to find the gullies in their blanket and the clothes on which they had lain and the soft little crevasses where skin touched skin filled with pine needles, as though they had slept for a week, or a month; and sat up and shook out their things and then my mother, leaning over, picked the tiny brown spears one by one out of the hair on his chest.

How was it possible, she thought, that a place they'd known only a few hours, eight of them while they'd slept, could grow so familiar? How could the grassy rise and the food stump and the way down to the stream and the pine by the bed-place so quickly begin to feel like a home: a home without walls or roof, windows or door, but a home nonetheless?

The fire was small and almost smokeless. He built it between two flat-topped stones. She watched him push the bigger one down into the dirt to make it level with the other, then try out the empty pot between them to see how it sat, then move the rocks again. Getting it right. When the dollop of lard began to hiss and sizzle he broke the eggs into the pot one after the other until they were done, laying the shells next to him on the grass, then pushed them back and forth with a pocketknife, reaching into the pot to get the knife blade flat, then rolled down his sleeves and took the pot off the fire and set it on a stone he'd brought over from the stream, covering the pot with the rag to keep out the pine needles. Reaching for the jar, he began impaling the squares of fatty meat he had cut on a stick he had stripped of bark, threading them over the raised parts, lining them up like so many fat beads on a string.

My mother watched, surprised by his competence, by the quick, thoughtless economy of his movements. A turn of the wrist, a small adjustment, the fingers reaching to nudge or to shift or to tap into place, this man knew his way around the world of things, and they leapt to him like filings to a magnet, eagerly, helplessly. There was something lovely and ruthless about it, something she hadn't seen before. Or maybe she had sensed it from the beginning, had known it would be like that all along.

When only a hand's width of space remained on both sides, he placed each end of the stick in the crotch of a branch he had pushed into the dirt on either side of the fire, and they ate the eggs, taking turns with the pot and the knife, sucking them carefully off the blade.

When they were done he reached over to a pile of short sticks he had prepared — each about the thickness of a man's finger — and began to place them carefully one by one on the flames. The meat spit and dribbled. He turned the skewer. She watched him raise the branch a bit to turn it past a knot, then settle it back in place. The greeny-white wood between the pieces had begun to turn black. He reached for the bread, cut another slice.

"Would you like some more bread?" he said.

He handed her a slice and she watched him tear off a small piece and pause, as though forgetting for a moment what he had meant to do with it, then remember and wipe the bottom of the pot. Something in the stillness of his mouth. Something in the deliberateness with which he turned the skewer, his sudden distance from what his hands were doing. She knew what it was.

"Almost done," he said. He wiped his fingers on the rag.

"Should we talk about it at all, you think?" she said.

He looked at her, and there was such utter regard in that look, and such a lake of rage beneath it, that she understood, perhaps for the first time, the quality of his love.

"I don't know how to talk about it," he said.

"You don't know when you're coming back," she said. Not if — if was not possible.

"No."

"And I won't be able to see you."

"No." He smiled. "Is it crazy for us to talk like this?"

"I don't think so. Does it feel crazy to you?"

"That's what's so crazy about it."

"I know."

He moved the stick a half-turn over the flames. "It's just that I didn't expect you. Everything was set before."

"Would it be any different if we hadn't met?"

"Everything would be different."

"But you say you have to go anyway?"

"I do."

"And you can't tell me where you're going?"

"No."

She glanced at the scaly twig she held in her hand. "Then how will I find you again? After."

"I'll find you."

"But . . ."

"I'll find you."

"It took you a while the first time," she said, not smiling.

"I'll do better this time," he said.

The meat began to smoke. He picked up the ends of the skewer with two sticks and laid it on the stone next to him, then broke up the fire, spreading the ashes. They could break camp while it cooled. My mother stood and picked up the blanket that lay knotted on the ground. Exposed beneath it, an orange and black beetle, like a miniature shield, began to stumble over the deadfalls of flattened grass, running from the sudden light.

ON JUNE 5, 1942, TOMÁŠ BÉM LEFT THE SAFE HOUSE IN which he had been hiding for nearly a week and crossed the city of Prague from the Dejvice district to Nové Město, wearing a lightweight suit, a hat, a coat over his arm, and an ampoule of strychnine around his neck. Soldiers were everywhere. A warm, still summer day. Crossing the Vltava, the air moving through the open window of the trolley, he smelled the water and the wet earth smell from the Petřín orchards.

It was just before noon. Eighty-three had been executed in Prague the day before, 106 the day before that. They were everywhere: a knot of four — boots, caps, riding crops — striding quickly along the south side of Národní Avenue, men and women stepping out of their way. A convoy of four cars, then another. Sentries on nearly every corner.

Three or four times a day, while Bém lay in the dark in the crawl space behind the sofa, old man Moravec would sit down heavily and read the paper aloud, interrupting himself at some point to call out to his wife in the kitchen, "Are you all right in there? Do you need anything?" and while Madame Moravcová called back that she was fine, that she would be right in, the old man would tap twice on the sliding panel — so close they could have touched hands — and then read on. SS Obergruppenführer

Karl Hermann Frank had declared that the attackers would be found, he read. They and all those who had helped them, along with their families, would be shot. The Wehrmacht would comb them out like lice.

Well, that certainly was welcome news, Madame Moravcová would call from the kitchen or the pantry. And then, to her son, Ota: "*Pro kristapána, obleč se už.* For Christ's sake, get dressed already. *"Kolikrát to musím opakovat?"* How often do I have to repeat it? And did the newspaper happen to say when the authorities thought this might happen? No mention of that, my dear, her husband would reply, the pages rustling. It seemed they had the bicycle and some other things the attackers had left behind on display in Václavské náměstí, where the populace could see them. There was a reward of ten million reichsmarks for anyone who could identify the owners of these things. A bicycle, said Madame Moravcová. It didn't sound like much to her, unfortunately.

And lying in the dark, unable to see them, Bém could hear their words, spoken for the benefit of the walls, the door, the keyhole, as well as himself, all the more clearly — feel the thing, so very near hysteria, moving just behind the screen. It was too much. These were brave people. But even the brave could be broken in time. Forced by fear, the crack was growing, branching; at any moment the laugh might go on too long, the gesture fly loose, the record skip.

But it didn't. They held on. On the fifth day, Madame Moravcová, while walking down the white gravel path from her mother's grave in the vast Olšany Cemetery, met a very nice, scholarly-looking gentleman who commiserated with her about the times but maintained, while tipping his hat or exchanging a few words with passersby, that even now, with all the pain being visited upon the country, nature provided perspective and comfort. He himself, despite everything, still found solace in the changing of the seasons, he said, though he was more than prepared to admit that this was so because he had been raised that way — that our adult havens were invariably shaped in childhood. Didn't she agree? His wife, for example, as befitted her upbringing, had returned to the church.

And where did his wife worship? Madame Moravcová asked. At the Church of Sts. Cyril and Metoděj on Řesslova Street, the man told her. She must know the place — a fine building. An ornament. It seemed that it gave his wife some sense of security, the man said. Perhaps it was the company she found there. One of the priests, she said, a Dr. Petřek, was particularly kind. And they chatted a bit more about the church, and the species of sparrow that he said was given to nesting in the thick ivy of some of the higher monuments, and then he lifted his hat and wished her a good day and they went their separate ways.

Just before noon the next day, Bém walked out of the house and down the hill to the tram stop. No one seemed to see him, though he himself knew he would never know if someone had. There was a soldier at the bottom of the hill, two more at the tram stop by the park. A small group of people — three businessmen with briefcases, an older woman with a net bag, a girl of seventeen — waited silently off to the side, not looking at the others, not looking at anything . . . Behind them, a large red poster plastered to the telephone pole listed the names of those executed the day before.

He joined them, the coat draped over his right arm. There would be no need to fumble for the pocket; just squeeze the trigger through the fabric. His forehead and temples were sweating under the hatband but he resisted taking off his hat. No unnecessary gestures. Nothing to attract attention. He could hear the crickets, sounding the heat. When the tram came at last and the doors opened, the group shuffled back. One of the men looked down at his briefcase; the other, as though thinking about something suddenly, or testing for a sore tooth, slowly ran two fingers along his jaw just below the ear. When the soldiers had climbed in, the group followed them.

Three stops later the soldiers got off the tram, and Bém took off his hat. The coolness of the air coming through the windows felt good in his hair. He could smell the orchards and the river. Thousands had been arrested, Moravec had told him. Round-the-clock interrogations were being conducted in the five-story building down from the central train station. He looked out the window. The city, though emptier, seemed faster somehow — electrified, spasming. Even the ordinary seemed strange. Two boys, dropping something into the Vltava, leaned out over the rail, their right legs bent into identical L's behind them. A man and a woman, trying to get past each other on the sidewalk, feinted left, then right, like football players on the pitch. The bell sounded. He didn't like this idea of the church, of all of them together in one place. Everywhere he looked, the red post-ers of the dead — mothers, fathers, entire families grouped by surname — on storefront windows, on walls, on light posts. The tram passed into the shade of the buildings. A white sign with a long number on it passed by too quickly for him to read it.

At Karlovo náměstí he stepped off the tram. It made no sense. Better to separate, stay still, then get out of Prague. Across the street, three soldiers were walking south along the storefronts. He turned into the square, toward the white statue of Eliška Krásnohorská. He could see the bench where they had sat. He wondered where she was now. If she was safe. The air in the shade smelled of flowers and stone.

He sat down on the bench, folding the coat next to him. He'd walked off the tram and almost directly into her. A city of a million people.

The church was only a few hundred meters away; he could afford a few minutes. They had sat right here, both of them stunned by the force of it, the suddenness of it, trying to speak but unable to say anything that didn't seem false the minute it was spoken. Banalities. Little gestures and politenesses. As though they had become different people in those few months, traveled too far from themselves, and the only way back was over a long, narrow bridge of clichés. As though they were afraid of frightening something. He remembered the rain, asking if she was all right, if she could take the time. Of course. Yes, he'd had to get glasses. No, he didn't need them exactly. A nuisance — he didn't like them.

She asked if he'd been well, whether he'd been in Prague for long. He could see the rain running down her hood, gathering at the edge, then dripping down. She herself had left Brno soon after . . . Anyway, it had seemed best. He'd nodded, looking at the oak behind her, at the branch hanging down like a huge, drooping tentacle. A relative had helped set her up, she said, found her work at the Language Institute in Líbeň. She'd missed him, she said.

There was the branch. A slight breeze, moving the heat. She had sat right there, to his left. Looking at it now, he felt a sharp pang of love for it. As though it remembered them, held them in suspension. Above all this horror. Absurd. In a few years you could sit in the crook of that branch and read a book, she had said. He could tell her nothing. They had said nothing. Before he could stop her, she told him she was staying at 7 Italská Street with her aunt and uncle who — "Stop," he'd said. "Please. I can't know . . . ," and seeing the sudden understanding in her face, the quick brimming of the eyes, he looked away at the puddles on the walk, the fountain, busy in the rain, the tram just coming to a stop in front of the stores across the way.

"How long before this is over?" she had asked. "Can you at least tell me that?"

"I have to go," he'd said.

"I see," she'd said. And then: "Will I see you again?"

"Of course," he'd said, and even smiled.

"But . . ."

"I have to go," he said. A quick kiss, her wet hair in his fingers, another, more desperate "I love you," he said, "I swear to God I do" — and he was on the tram in two leaps, escaping something, feeling like something hollowed out and about to cave in. Strange — it had been right there; he could see the stop. For that matter, he'd probably seen the church that day, never realizing that he'd be coming back to it after it was all over. How very hard it had been. A quick wave and she'd been gone behind the rain and he'd sat down on the seat and begun the hard work of kicking himself back into vigilance like a drunk berating himself into paying attention. One misstep and it was gone, all of it. All the planning. All the lives on which it was built. One error, one moment of inattention or softness, one accidental turn, and the whole thing would go. And it couldn't go.

A stocky man leading a dog with a pointy nose was coming up the path, the two of them passing through the dark, leafy shade and into the sun. Even now, dogs had to be walked. A beautiful summer day — there was no denying it. The way the light played against the stone. He watched the man and the dog make their way around a flower bed. When they reached the shade of the tentacle branch, he got up to go.

SHE UNDERSTOOD. AND SHE DIDN'T. SHE UNDERSTOOD why he sat next to her that afternoon like a clenched fist, why they couldn't speak, why she kept noticing things — the oak, a white cloud of rain behind a passing tram, the black steeple of a church — as if she were falling down a well and these were roots to grab on to. She understood why he'd walked away from her so quickly, walking through the puddles like a man striding away from an avalanche, an avalanche he'd been waiting for his entire life. The tram windows had been steamed over, blurred by rain. He'd leaped on board, disappeared.

She understood. And she didn't. She didn't understand at all. She didn't understand how a face, a voice, a certain kind of half-smile could leave such a vacuum in her, how his absence could work on her like a chemical need, like opium withheld. She missed the physical fact of him, the lean, compact weight of him, his mouth on hers, his hair, the feeling of him in her hand. She missed talking to him, about everything really, the occupation and cheese, fascist Spain and the fashion in hats. She liked the way he listened to her, the way he would lie on his side, watching her as she talked. She liked his calm and the suddenness just beneath it; the pain in him and the pure unblinking dangerousness that pain had given birth to. She liked the quick smile that seemed to surprise even him. And now he was gone and she moved through the days diminished, transparent somehow, less like a ghost than like the last living, breathing soul in a world of ghosts. She understood how absurd this was, how self-indulgent. It couldn't be helped. Holding him again mattered. Nothing else.

She clung to every bit of news now; her moods turned on a word. "This young man of yours," her uncle had called out from the living room one night as she and her aunt wrapped the last of the dough around the canned apricots and lowered them into the big white pot steaming up the kitchen windows, "he'll be back, I'm sure — if he loves you as you say, he'll be back," and because she was so miserable even this well-meant platitude had given her comfort and tilted the evening that followed — the dinner, the hour or so spent reading afterward — toward something like hope. Maybe it was all that simple. He loved her. He'd be back.

And then she saw him step off the tram and they sat on a bench in the rain and he was standing up to leave. And she felt his mouth and touched his face and for just one moment she glimpsed the fear and the determination inside him, side by side like orphans in a doorway, and understood that it could never be that simple. And he was gone.

Winter. It was as if the year would never die. She stood on lines, went to work, translated documents that meant nothing to her with two older men who seemed capable of moving nothing other than their right hands, and even those minutely, for hours at a time. The one window looked out on the stones of the building opposite. She listened to the pens' scratch, to the windy shushing of rain, the sudden scattering of sleet.

At times she could almost imagine it, see it: the leather straps, the cords, the notched wheels . . . The country was being torn, slowly, irreversibly — and worse, learning to live with it.

There was no food. The lists of the dead grew longer. Outrage folded outrage, building a soil of known things — of habit — from which anything might grow. Every afternoon now, crossing over the tracks on Vinohradská Street, she saw the trains, their windows nailed over with boards.

They were everywhere now. Russia was the answer, her uncle said that winter. He could see it starting already. The bastards would break their teeth on Russia. When the declaration of war on America was announced that December, he could hardly contain his glee. The idiots. They'd bitten off too much. The factories of Chicago would bury them.

He clung to it all that winter, even after things began to turn again. The Russian soul. The factories of Chicago. The Macháčeks, who lived in the next building, had been deported. A childhood friend he'd known since the day he'd hit him with a toy bucket in a sandlot forty-six years ago was taken into the courtyard he walked through every morning on the way to work and shot. They'd pay, he said. And all the quislings and collaborators with them. They'd taken too much. They'd choke like dogs. A year, maybe two, before the bone found the throat.

But the next morning, seeing their visored caps, their coats, their wet boots through the tram window, she knew that in some way it didn't matter. Entire worlds could pass in a year or two. The factories of Chicago were far from here.

IN ANOTHER TIME, THERE MIGHT HAVE BEEN SOME HUMOR in it. How perfect, after all, to hide the living among the dead; no one would think to look for them there. Just as no one would think to search for the dead among the living.

It was so simple, Bém thought: to escape death, all you had to do was die. The priest moved the cement slab, the cold breathed out, and down the stairs you went, carrying your long skier's underwear, your sweaters, your hat, your woolen socks, your blankets — all the necessary provisions for the grave. Or the crypt, at any rate. And there were your comrades, like skiers in hell: Opálka and Valčík, in hats and bulky sweaters, squatting by a small stove; Gabčík rising on his elbow from a mattress laid out in one of the deep niches in the wall; Kubiš pacing under the one small window. The other three were upstairs in the rectory, standing guard.

He'd made it! By God, they'd known he'd make it. They had been here four days. It was cold as hell. Gabčík had hurt his eye in the attack but had managed to bicycle away with one hand. There was a plan, they said. They would be taken out in coffins — in a few weeks, maybe less — then driven out of Prague in a funeral car. The priests had it all figured out. They would stay in a storeroom in Kladno, then be moved to the forests in Moravia.

Petřek, the priest, had arranged for a gamekeeper's cabin. They could hide there for months if necessary. But how had he gotten here? What news was there?

"What news could there be?" said Kubiš. And it was true: he had no news to give them.

He had to get dressed, they said. Quickly. Once the cold got into his bones . . .

A supply line had been established. The teacher, Růžička, came once a day with supplies and food.

But how had he made it? They had heard of the curfew, of ten thousand arrested, of interrogations, executions — the entire city under siege.

They had thought of turning themselves in, Valčík said. To stop it.

He had thought they were done talking about that, said Opálka.

But they were the ones the bastards were looking for, Valčík said. It was all because of them that this was happening.

They were done talking about it, said Opálka. The message from London —

But this wasn't London, interrupted Kubiš, who had paused in his caged pacing to light a cigarette.

They were done talking about it, said Opálka. It would accomplish nothing.

It would accomplish something if it stopped it, said Valčík quietly.

They turned to him, the last man in, the last to see how things were. What did he think?

Nothing would stop it, he told them.

He would come to know it well: the low, dank, vaulted ceiling, the corner with the buckets, the sealed-off stairs on the north end, the bottom of the cement slab . . . He memorized it. The water stains, the gouged wall, the heap of crumbling mortar beneath it. The two bricks missing from the floor between the cooking area and the stairs, like broken teeth.

It was the hollow emptiness of the place that was most striking: no table, no chairs. Just columns, stairs, bricks, cold. This place had never been meant for the living. And though there were at least four of them there all the time, they made no impression on it. They knew they were trespassing, and the place seemed to know it too.

The sleeping wall: sixteen black niches like a giant's honeycomb dug into the stone, coffin wide and coffin deep. The four on the left had been sealed off for some reason, as if with wax, making the illusion complete. They slept in the others. There was nowhere else. None of them thought to ask the priests what they had done with the coffins, or where they now stored their dead.

The middle hole on the top row, slightly larger owing to the curvature of the ceiling, had been given to Gabčík, who was still recovering; during the day he would sit in a low crouch near the entrance or lean up on an elbow, smoking. The others were worse. And because it was bad they made jokes about roses and buttonholes as they slid into place feet-first, the damp cement pushed so close to their faces by the thin mattresses the priests had managed to find for them that at times it felt as though the whole church — no, all of Prague — were poised above their chests. At one time or another, each of them, waking during the night, had smashed his head into that sudden, unfamiliar ceiling; every night, it seemed, they were awakened by someone cursing. There seemed to be no getting used to it.

He could see the problem immediately: these were not men accustomed to being still. Trained to move — chosen precisely because they could move when others could not, because their minds would not stop them — they could be patient enough when patience was required for some kind of action. This was different. This was just waiting to escape. There was nothing to do, nothing to plan. All they could do was think about what was happening in the outside world, what their actions had caused, and, unable to smother these thoughts with tasks, unable to keep themselves from turning inward, they began, by slow degrees, to grow human. To become afraid. It made for a particular kind of hell, he thought, a hell crafted to their natures: a perpetuity of fear and regret, stasis and rage, the rage of paralytics forced to watch their families being attacked.

They moved about, tried to sleep. They paced back and forth, looking up at the crease where the ceiling met the wall. They spent some time throwing bits of mortar into a can for points, then grew bored. They waited silently for their shift in the rectory. Two hours before the attack, Kubiš had been almost lighthearted. Coming out of the Moravecs' apartment building that morning, the sten gun carefully packed inside the ubiquitous brown leather suitcase, he had joked with the Moravecs' boy, Ota, who had been up half the night worrying about his Latin exams. "Why the face?" he'd said, tousling his hair. "Look here — it's simple. You either pass or you fail. If you pass, you're a scholar; if you fail, I'll find you a job digging ditches," and the boy had smiled and looked relieved. There was no humor now. There was nothing to set it against. And day by day, memories were coming back, occupying the vacuum.

She would come to him constantly while he was still on the outside: the thought of her, of her strength . . . for him. No one had ever aligned themselves with him the way she had. Immediately. Unquestioningly. No one. He remembered watching her once, sitting in the shade by the side of a pond, lost inside herself, and when she had looked up there had been no shift, no translation. Everything was open to him. Everything. He'd never known such courage. He wanted to live inside her — he damn near had — but inside her voice too, inside her thoughts, her dreams. It was obsession, he told himself, but it didn't feel like obsession. There was nothing weakening about it, nothing unclean. It felt like air, like sanity itself.

But all that was before. Before this place. Air was not wanted here, nor too much sanity, either. What had been strengthening before was something else now. A diluting thing. The look on her face underneath him — the bitten lip, the strand of hair, the yearning for the precipice, and then the long, sweet fall — the feel of her against him at night, the meals shared — all these had to be put away now, ruthlessly. They could only hurt him here. And yet, five, six times a day, inadvertently, helplessly, he'd catch himself whispering her name, the very sound of it, Ivana, Ivana, like a talisman, like hope, like a holy relic to a failed apostate.

He thought of odd things, small things. For the better part of two days he tried to place the scent he'd caught when the priests had moved the slab and the cold air smelling of stone and urine had rushed up into his face. He smelled it now and again in the days that followed, more faintly each time, and having little else to do, he spent some time vainly trying to put a name to this ghost until the moment someone's spoon scraped against the side of the pot and he had it: the courtyard of the building he had grown up in. He remembered it now. He and Miloš Mostovský had spent days digging a network of tunnels through a small mountain of wet sand. They hardly spoke. By late morning the sun would move across the courtyard, but in the shade the sand felt cold, and every day an old man who was building a low brick wall along the communal garden would scoop wet cement from a small wheelbarrow with a trowel and slap and scrape it between the bricks. The smell of wet cement — it was as though that smell had simply disappeared from the earth in all the intervening years, till now. As though it had been kept here for him, preserved like a jar of cherries or pickled mushrooms until the day he discovered it again.

He remembered the courtyard perfectly: the way the air felt, the smell of soil and garbage. Every now and then his eye would catch a movement in the rabbit hutches against the wall. Amazing to think that these same hands had dug through the sand those mornings until the sand loosened and he felt, with that strange shock of the living touching the living, fingers grasping his, reaching from the other side. That he was that same person. That the years should have brought him here.

During the days he managed to keep the thinking away, filling in the hours with the work of staying warm or making stew (they skinned the rabbits the schoolteacher brought them by hanging them from a spike that protruded from the wall, tying their legs with shoelaces) or rereading the newspapers, which told him nothing. At night his dreams, as though taking their revenge, rushed back, crowding each other in their eagerness to reclaim the territory from which they'd been expelled. And always she would be there, somewhere, waiting for him to find her.

He was back in Manchester, in the soldiers' barracks, packing for the mission, and suddenly knew the plane had left without him. He was in a seaport at night — he recognized it as Gdynia. He was on the ship he was to take to France — the engines had already started — but he had to find the stairs to the crypt. They were covered with a slab. In the dream he realized quite clearly that he wasn't supposed to know about the crypt yet, that he had not yet been dropped into the Protectorate, that he had not even been to England, but it didn't matter. He rushed down the ship's narrow hallways and stairs, looking for the door. Everyone he met seemed eager to help.

Now he was in the plane, sitting on the wooden board in the dark. The door was open. Strangely, there was no wind. Outside, a shoreless blackness. His father was sitting next to him. He looked at his father and realized that his father was terrified for him, that he didn't want him to jump but knew he couldn't stop him. And in the dream he reached out and patted his father's stubbled cheek reassuringly. "I'll be fine," he said, and his father said, "But it's dark out there. How will you know which way is up?" "The ground is always down," he replied, and his father seemed comforted by this and said, "Don't worry, I'll tell your mother."

Every night the dreams bled into each other, leaving him exhausted. He was back in school, worrying about an exam. He was opening a suitcase filled with grass. He was standing by a frozen lake with Kubiš. It was snowing. Someone was coming toward them and he put his hand on the gun in his pocket, but now it wasn't Kubiš behind him anymore, it was her, and the man coming toward them was saying, "Just some trimmings from last week's butchering." He could feel her there behind him. It was dark. They were in the forest now but something was wrong — there were cobbles under his feet instead of pine needles. Far ahead, a tiny white light kept appearing and disappearing behind the trees. He wondered what it could be. When he realized he was looking at a candle flame high in an apartment window, he stopped. "What's wrong?" he heard her say. "I don't know," he said, "there's been some mistake," and taking the tin cup that dangled around his neck he swung it over his shoulder and woke feeling her presence so intensely that for one mad instant he almost reached behind him to see if she was there in the space between himself and the stone, as if, before reason destroyed the illusion, his faith could make it real.

He thought about his parents now, his sister . . . spent hours remembering their apartment on Michalovská ulice: the hallway with its worn red runner, the kitchen, the window overlooking the courtyard. More and more it seemed impossible not to; the pictures came back to him in quick, uninvited flashes as he slid into his niche or out of it, as he laced his boots or cut the eye out of a potato: his mother standing by the kitchen table, complaining about the price of meat; his father's voice yelling at him to get the coal from the cellar; his sister's face when he did or said something that hurt her — the way her eyes filled and she sucked in her lower lip before coming after him. At times these stabs of memory brought with them a pain that was distinctly physical — a seizing-up sensation in the chest, a sharp tightening of the throat, as if he might actually suffocate — and in those moments he would move quickly, desperately, bending down to tie a boot that didn't need tying, or wrenching himself abruptly to the left or right if he was lying down, as if freeing himself from something closing in around him.

More often though the memories were so distant they seemed someone else's, and in his mind he would wander through his old apartment as dispassionately as if he were giving himself a tour of his own home, and even when he heard himself saying *This is the room where your sister used to live,* or *There is where your mother used to beat the rugs once a year in the spring,* even when the voice in his head informed him that he would not see them again, it seemed as if these were things he had known for a very long time, and had grown accustomed to. *They were gone.* Yes, he knew that. Certain things simply were what they were. There was nothing to be done.

And yet, though he felt a sense of relief in being able to face these facts, he noticed that his memories at these times had a certain vague quality about them, as if drawn by an artist who, while adept at sketching the general outline of things with quick, nervous strokes — the torso, the bend of the legs, the perspective of the room — left out the specifics. His mind leaped from thing to thing, touching here, erasing there, darkening, reinforcing, then leaping elsewhere before the picture took on life. He could think of the evenings at the beginning of the war, for example, when the four of them would sit around the dining room table listening to the BBC on the radio his father had positioned on top of the cupboard for the best reception (*and here's the kitchen table where you would sit listening to the BBC . . .*), and everything would be fine until he remembered his father's socks as he stood on the chair to reach the dial, or the way he would bend his head, listening, his finger raised to mark the burning sound of static while the radio lit up slowly, like an oven, waiting for the opening phrase of Beethoven's Fifth Symphony — *ta-ta-ta-taaah* — which always marked the beginning of the BBC's broadcast into occupied Czechoslovakia — and suddenly something would catch in his heart like a long thorn and he'd know, really know, that they were gone.

This is how things were now.

ON THE FOURTH NIGHT IT RAINED. THEY HAD SEEN AL-most no one: once a hunched figure with a basket over its arm; another time a couple on a distant hillside, the man asleep, the woman sitting over him, her arms around her knees; the third a fisherman sitting back against a tree by a reedy pond, his arms crossed, staring at his rod in its holder. Nearby, his black bicycle leaned against a pine. He didn't see them.

Where the forest had been cut, letting in the light, they picked raspberries, raspberries so ripe they trembled like water on the end of a branch and dropped at a breath, two or three to a handful, big as the joint of a man's thumb. The raspberry brambles were close and hot and still and afterward they washed the bloody stains and the itching yellow hairs off their arms and ate what they had not already eaten in the shade. They picked mushrooms which they fried up in lard and ate with bread and tore handfuls of yellow chamomile buds for tea, and they swam in ponds so lonely and lost they seemed never to have seen another human being but to have been waiting there for centuries under the midday sun, untouched. They slept in the morning, or at noon, and woke in the middle of the night and made love and then lay next to each other and talked, sometimes for hours, then walked gingerly over the pine needles to the muddy shore of a warm, shallow lake. Wading in, they could feel their feet pushing into the yielding bottom, smell the faint green smell of decay, and standing where the water was nearly up to their chests, they would hold each other like a statue of lovers half drowned by the tide.

On the third day she had walked out of the forest into the town of Nedvědice and sent a telegram to her parents, knowing my father would go to them eventually to see if they knew where she was: Do not worry *stop* Am well and safe *stop* I'm sorry *stop*, then scratched out the last two words and passed the paper under the little barred window to the telegraph operator, a thin, sad man in a black vest who pushed her change back to her coin by coin with the tip of his finger, collected her change and walked back.

It had felt odd to be alone again. She had refused to take the gun, and he had not tried to convince her. She would be back before noon. The walk in had taken a little over two hours. The trail had led out to a grassy path that wound around a muddy pond, then meandered up through terraces of uncropped grass and wildflowers and overgrown wooden fences. She came to a gate sagging on its hinges and lifted it up off the grass and swung it open and passed through into a rising field of wheat that shook and moved like the mane of a horse whenever the wind went over it. At times the trail was swallowed up in the wheat and she had to guess her way by what seemed like a gap between the rows. A small flock of birds burst out from under her feet as though shot into the air. Pushing up to the crest of the hill, sweating now, she startled something, a fox perhaps, that moved off through the grain like a fish under water, disturbing the surface.

From the crest of the hill she could see the lane, the thinning edge of the field marked by dun-colored weeds and spotted with poppies — a scattering of drops, arterial red — and stopped to catch her breath. The sheer beauty of it was so insistent, so undeniable, that she couldn't help but marvel at it: the white storybook clouds in the hot sky, the smear of lupines along the ditch, the long, stately row of lindens that marked the road's progress. In the far distance, a cluster of red-tiled roofs, an ornate steeple. The landscape lay before her: half asleep, enchanted, shameless.

Walking down that long, straight road, silent except for the wind in the high trees and the tired insects in the hedgerows whenever it died, she noticed with a kind of wonder how strange to herself she'd grown. She was the same person, holding the same conversations inside her head — wondering how much farther it was to the turnoff, or whether she should stay on the road or cut through the pastures — except that now it was as though she were talking to him as well, as though a third person had entered the room that only she and herself had shared. She wanted to talk to him, think aloud with him. His entrance had displaced something essential, she knew, then realized with a kind of voluptuous sorrow that she had been waiting for this displacement all of her life, that things would never again be quite the same and that she didn't care and wouldn't miss them.

The post office was a small stone building not far from the central square. She opened the heavy doors and passed into the cool, dim interior. The man behind the window bars looked like a man trapped in a canary cage; he slid the telegraph form over to her with long, parrot-like fingers.

She didn't hesitate. She remembered his face, the walks they had taken, the long afternoons in the Špilberk gardens. He seemed a long time ago. A good man. A decent man. A courageous man, even. She wrote out the message. It would come as a shock to him. It couldn't be helped. She wasn't sorry. She'd never been less sorry in her life. She collected her change from the worn wood and walked out into the heat and found the other one, two hours later, sitting with his back against the pine tree where she had left him, waiting for her.

That night it rained. There had been no sign. Or perhaps they had missed it. They were asleep under a low-branched pine, their heads almost touching the rough trunk, streaked with candied sap. A long, hollow rumble, a silent flash. And then the rain.

They woke into a deeper dark, already full of the sound of water and small breaking branches. A sudden gust. Another. They sat huddled together. For a minute the million needles over their heads distracted the rain; then the branches started to drip. "The forester's shack," she said, yelling over the sound of the rain. Did he remember? "An hour," he said. "Maybe more." "I can find it," my mother said.

And this was the thing she remembered most: the two of them, already streaming with water, stuffing their clothes into his rucksack by feel in the vain hope of keeping them dry and setting out naked into the storm with only the shoes on their feet, her idiotic shoulder bag running water from a corner as if it had grown a faucet there, searching for a one-room woodsman's shack in a continent of rain and darkness. And him slipping in the mud as he helped her up a small slope, standing there spattered and streaked and strong like some lean nocturnal animal, shaking the rain off like a dog just emerged from the water. They plunged on through fields white with rain, down slick hillsides of flattened grass, through dribbling, hissing, mumbling woods where they had to hold their arms in front of their faces to protect their eyes, and they held each other's soaking hands and yelled over the noise of the rain and he made fun of her direction-finding, saying he was sure he'd seen the spires of Hradčany by the light of the last bolt, that Prague was surely just ahead. Or Warsaw, maybe.

And of course she found it, a one-room shack like a hole in the wall of the forest, tucked deep in the cove of a meadow that looked just like every other meadow for days in either direction. Mossy black boards, a small porch with a crude table. A wooden bench against the wall. A cup, hooked on a wire, bobbed and dipped in the wind.

"There's a lock on the door," she heard him call, and went up and joined him. He felt around the hinge with his fingers, then pushed the door and felt it again. When the metal had loosened from the wall, he used one of the screws to pry the others out of the sodden wood, and suddenly they were in. They felt around in the musty dark, a pantomime of the blind, and then a match scratched and he was tipping the glass of a dirty lantern and lowering the smoking wick. Wooden shelves, two windows, a narrow musty cot with mouse-speckled sheets and a thin brown blanket. A squat black stove with a pot on top of it and a rusty file for opening the stove door and picking up the pot and probably stirring whatever was in it. He closed the heavy wooden door against the wind.

She would remember it all, that flyspecked cabin and everything in it: the rag they used to dry themselves and the man's blue shirt with the hole just above the left breast that she wore and the name on the can of nails they emptied out and set on the floor under the drip coming through the roof. She would remember the can's deep red, and that there were three wooden shelves to the left of the stove, and that just in front of the metal bed there were two hollow-sounding floorboards that hid the pantry: a chest-high hole in the earth with a basket on a string for lowering things down and taking them back. And she would remember the key she discovered outside, above the windowsill, and the taste of the walnuts they found in a bowl on the third shelf and ate with the raspberries they picked in the rain, and how he looked sleeping next to her, and how the rain coming off the porch at first light looked very much like a curtain that tore open every now and then to reveal the forest, then sewed itself up again. All this and more.

They stayed, assuming that no one would come into those dark and dripping woods. They were right. He found a flat brass box with some tools and a few tin boxes of screws and moved the hinge up into harder wood. They made love whenever the moment found them; almost any task could suddenly take a detour of an hour or more and did, often. "Can I borrow your spoon?" she'd say, walking her fingers under the bowl on his lap as they sat cross-legged in the morning with the watershadows moving up the walls, and he'd look at her with that half-smile, so very confident, so beautiful, so *hers,* and say "Be my guest," trying not to move as she helped herself for a minute, then two, smiling at him — "And some cream, please, sir?" — and by the time they got back the tea would be cold and he'd take it out on the porch and toss it in the long grass and walk out after it as naked as the day and then talk her out as well and she'd run laughing, still sticky and warm with him into the sodden field and hold him as the wind raked the world around them. When they weren't making love they'd busy themselves by gathering what they could into meals and by sitting next to each other on the porch with their backs against the wall and their feet drawn up, watching the pine branches dip and wave and the wind comb the tall grasses, talking. She told him things: about her village and her parents and her summers with her mother on the Bečva River and the dog she had lost when she was eight. And she told him about the man she had met in Brno the year before and what he was like and that they had talked about getting married once.

Days of small rituals. Three times a day they would move aside the floorboards and pull out the basket with the shrinking bit of cheese and the quarter loaf of bread she had bought in town with the last of their money, then lower it back down and cover the hole with the boards like a secret. Twice a day they would walk out into the rain to collect whatever half-dry wood they could find, snapping the small branches from inside the prickly hearts of pines, searching under overhangs for pine cones. One day they came across a door lying flat on the grass in a meadow, then a broken window, and realized they'd come across an old shack that had fallen years ago. Some of the wood that was off the ground looked burnable. They picked up the window and pretended to look through it to see what the weather was like outside and propped up the door because it looked so strange standing in the middle of that meadow like a memory of something, then dragged it back through the soaking woods to their shack, where he broke it up with an ax he'd found leaning against the wall by the stove. The helve was loose but someone had driven a nail through the top to keep the ax head from sliding off, and they started a small pile of boards and sticks to the left of the door and every night they made a fire in the stove and the wood cracked and spit and before she fell asleep she would look at the orange light coming through the crack around the stove door, like a thin, crude circle in the dark.

It was on the fifth day, as they sat on the floor of the porch sipping tea they had made from chamomile buds and strained through a piece of burlap, that she told him about the morning she had walked with her father to bury her brother. Her brother, she said, had lived only a few hours in this world, like a moth, and been buried in a coffin the size of a loaf of bread. She'd never known him, and perhaps it was for this reason that she remembered that morning not for its grief but for its warmth.

A magical morning. On the way to the cemetery her father had held her hand and told her a wonderful story about a *trpaslík,* an elf, who knew of a door in a hillside — a door no larger than a hammer, he said, with a wig of grass hanging over its sill — which led to another world, the world below the pond.

The people who lived there, her father told her, spent their days looking up like astronomers, watching the signs of the upper world, mourning what they had lost. A fisherman's red bobber touching the sky, a dog's pink tongue lapping at the horizon, children clothed in silver bubbles, like frogs' eggs, which would unpeel and follow them as they kicked to the surface . . . These were the things they lived for, and in the long winters they would sit in the icy dark by their watery green candles and spin fantastic tales from the bits of misunderstood things they had seen.

But the *trpaslík,* her father said, who knew the upper world for what it was, in all its beauty and corruption, felt sorry for them. Not realizing that they loved their sadness, that the truth would be as poison to them, he resolved to tell them what he knew. One day, taking an especially deep breath — for *trpaslíks* could hold their breath for almost an hour, her father said — he opened the secret door and walked down the long narrow stairs until the clay began to get soft under his feet and he saw, far ahead, the dim circle, rimmed with roots, that marked the entrance to the pond.

He found them, as always, swaying like water weeds in a gentle current, looking up at their watery sky with tears in their eyes. He would save them, he thought. And he began to speak, but as he did, a look of even greater sadness came over their faces, a sadness different from the one he knew, and they bent as if in pain and tried to stop up their ears with their soft green hands and when they found they couldn't block out the sound of his voice telling them the truth they wrapped those hands around his throat and held him until he stopped speaking. And the *trpaslík* woke, her father said, and in his heart was a pain and a love he'd never known, and he looked up at the sky toward a watery light he didn't understand and thought if he could only look at it forever he would never want for anything more.

She didn't know why she loved that story so much, she said, looking out over the soaking meadow, or what it was about the memory of that morning that meant so much to her, but she had wanted to tell him about it. She wanted to tell him everything, she said, even the things she didn't know.

And Tomáš Bém, who did not yet carry an ampoule of fast-acting strychnine around his neck, sat on the floor of the porch with his feet out of the rain and nodded. "Tell me, then," he said. "Tell me everything."

And he fixed some things and told her what he could of his life and memorized what he could of hers and when the rain had stopped and their time was up they put the nails back in the can and made the bed and locked the door behind them and re-placed the key on the sill and left. And yes, my mother turned around at the edge of the meadow and looked back, and once more after they had parted at the turnoff to Mělkovice having agreed to meet at the same place a year later at dawn if the war had ended and he had not yet come for her, and on the first of each month after that. Not quite the year-and-a-day of the fairy tales, but close enough.

And he turned at the bend of the road as she knew he would, the rucksack on his back, and stood there for a moment, looking at her across all that space, then raised his right hand as though taking a pledge, and was gone.

HE DIDN'T TALK ABOUT IT WITH THE OTHERS, NOT BE-
cause he didn't know or trust them, but because he knew —
from their silences, from the absurd ways they tried to keep
themselves busy, from their small hard flashes of anger — that
they were all fighting the same enemy, an enemy they were
uniquely unsuited to fighting, an enemy that grew stronger by
the day. When they talked, they talked about other things: the
stove, the cold, whether the schoolteacher was coming too often. They talked about whether it would be possible for them to
leave the church for a few hours at a time to break the monotony
and get some hard information about what was happening outside. They talked, in bits and pieces, about the places they'd
known in Poland and France (Gabčík had joined up with the
Czecho-Slovak Legions in Agde, Kubiš in Sidi Bel Abbes; both
had been in the fighting along the Marne), about the Egyptian
ships that had taken most of them to England after France had
fallen, about the men they remembered from Manchester and
Ringway.

He liked them all, if not equally, recognized the value of their
hardness, their stubbornness, admired their capacity for pain,
but of all of them he liked Gabčík best. Trained as a metal-
worker and a machinist, he seemed an unheroic character at

first glance; with his sloping forehead and his pointy features and his small, almost womanly lips he reminded Bém of the wooden, swivel-headed puppets parents liked but children never played with, the ones whose cone noses always fell off before the day was done. And yet there was something about the man: his eyes, maybe, which seemed almost sleepy but weren't, or the unselfconscious way he would lie on his side propped up on an elbow, smoking. Unlike the others, who seemed to be pacing even when they were still, Gabčík alone seemed willing to wait, to lie on his elbow and smoke, watching the others in that slow way of his, until something came up that required movement. He and Kubiš made a good team; the one shorter, quicker, more volatile, the other tall and slow and quiet, his eyes always one step from a small, sad smile, his big body storing energy like a cat in the sun.

Strangely, instead of irritating Kubiš, Gabčík's silence provided an outlet for jokes and insults, which helped calm him to a degree. "Look at him," Kubiš would complain to no one in particular, "just lying there by his bowl," and Gabčík, ignoring him, would move the cigarette over to his left hand and slowly reach over to the pot and dip a ladle in the soup without rising from his elbow. "You have no idea what it was like living with him in that goddamned cellar in Poděbrady," Kubiš continued. "He ate everything. At night he'd creep out and graze on berries in the moonlight. You're going to get us both killed, you fool, I'd tell him. I'm hungry, he'd say."

Gabčík put the ladle back in the pot, stirred once, then moved the cigarette back to his right hand.

"He didn't stop eating for three days," said Kubiš. "When we ran out of food I started getting nervous. I thought I'd have to shoot him, like in that Jack London story."

"What Jack London story?" said Gabčík.

"The one where he shoots the dog."

Transferring the cigarette again, Gabčík reached over the pot, moved the ladle this way and that, as though clearing a space, then delicately dipped some soup and brought it to his mouth. Replacing the ladle, he moved the cigarette back to his right hand and took a long, thoughtful drag. "Don't think I know that one," he said.

And Bém, watching from the side, appreciating their gesture, as the others did, thought again that if it came to it, Gabčík would be the one he'd want next to him. More than Opálka, their commanding officer; more than blond, stoic Valčík, who looked like a spellbound shepherd when he slept; more than any of them. Two days earlier, in the middle of the morning, a sudden shouting from the street followed by three quick shots had sent a surge of fear and adrenaline through them all. It had had nothing to do with them, they learned eventually, but in the first ten seconds they had all reacted in their own way: he himself had stayed precisely where he was, behind the column next to which he had been standing; Opálka, gun drawn, had run to his predetermined position by the sleeping wall; Kubiš, as though some catch had been released inside him, had sprung to the wall under the small high window that looked out on the bricks of the building opposite. Gabčík, seemingly without haste, had taken three long strides to the central column midway between the stairs and the west wall, put his back against the stone, and stopped, his gun pointed at the ground and his head bowed as though listening to someone explaining something important. On his homely, wooden-puppet face was the same expression he'd had while stirring the soup: calm, inward, attentive but removed. It was only later, after everything had passed, after the trembling in their leg muscles had stopped and the taste had gone from their mouths, that Bém realized that Gabčík had moved instinctively to the one place in the crypt with a clear view of both possible entrances, the covered stairwell and the high window.

On June 8, shortly after the bells had rung noon, Opálka left the church for three hours. He returned visibly shaken. The reprisals were getting worse: hundreds dead, thousands more arrested or tortured, the Resistance under siege all through the Protectorate. Rumor had it that on hearing of Heydrich's death, the Führer had demanded the immediate execution of ten thousand Czechs, chosen at random, and had only been dissuaded by Karl Hermann Frank's argument that a reprisal of such magnitude and visibility would hurt morale among Czech factory workers and lower output from the munitions plants.

The new way was no less bloody, Opálka said. The net was tight: intellectuals, writers, former government officials, sympathizers, anyone suspected of harboring pro-Resistance sentiments, all were being arrested. Some had escaped. Others were apparently hoping to somehow slip through. Many, especially those with children, seemed frozen in place, unsure of where to run. The reward for any information leading to their arrest, Opálka said, had been raised to twenty million reichsmarks.

At times he wondered if it seemed as unreal to the rest of them. If they too found it hard to believe that just over their heads, not ten meters away, a hot June day had begun and that men waiting for the tram on the corner of Řesslova were taking off their hats to wipe their foreheads, or that two hours from now, schoolgirls lying out in their gardens listening to the big-band sound of Karel Vlach on the radio would be moving their towels into the shade. How amazing that life should continue on as it did, that the trams should come and go and people should shop for food and fall in love and complain of indigestion. It seemed absurd, like cooking a meal in the kitchen while a fire raged in the living room. And yet for most, that was how it was. Children who had been born when the tanks pulled into Prague were almost four years old. Time had done its work; the fire in the living room, though roaring now, was nothing new.

It was getting harder not to think about her — to guess where she was or what she was doing. He tried not to remember her walk or her smile, the way she would look at him sometimes. He tried not to remember her spontaneity, the sudden glimpses she gave him of the child she'd once been. He tried not to think that she was out there, a five-minute tram ride away. It didn't work. It made no sense to exclude her. How much easier the whole thing would be, he admitted to himself now, if he could only talk with her for an hour — one hour — absorb a bit of her strength.

They were to be taken out of the church on the nineteenth, Opálka had told them. Bém tried not to think about that either, about the eleven days still ahead of them, about the coffins they would have to lie down in with their guns at their sides, listening to every noise coming in from the outside world, and yet there was nothing else to do but think about the coffins, the days still ahead, that date interminably crawling down to them like a glacier in the sun.

That his life could end on the nineteenth, or any day before that, he simply did not consider. Over the past two years he'd grown as used to the idea of dying as any man could — he'd tried to think about it clearly and rationally, but the thought of not hearing her voice again was not possible. He would not permit it. He would survive. He knew this. He would find her again. He would make it to the other side through sheer force of will.

The others, he felt, believed much the same thing. A new kind of strength was taking over now that they had a fixed date toward which to aim. They would survive this frozen crapper and the goddamned sleeping holes, and they would survive this war, and Gabčík would marry Líba Fafek, who had been with them at the hit, and Opálka would return to his family, and Valčík would work on his motorcycle until the Second Coming of Christ, and someday when the war was over they would get together and bore everyone around them silly recalling the stove and the cans and the goddamned window and the missing bricks, arguing over how many columns there had been between the beds and the wall or whether Petřek, the priest who looked like an aging goat, had actually had a goatee or not.

At times it all seemed possible. The day would come. They would get in the coffins. The plan would work. At other times they would suddenly remember what they had done, and the enormity of it would flood over them as if for the first time and they would see it as if from the outside — as if someone else had been responsible, not them — and they would know that it could never be that easy.

They had done the unthinkable, and in their own hearts they did not quite believe it. It had seemed strangely unreal to him even on the morning of May 27. He'd woken early, instantly conscious, and quickly gone to the living room and removed the gun from the hole under the sofa cushion. The ammunition was where he'd left it. The family he was staying with was still asleep. He'd told them the night before as they were eating dinner not to worry if he didn't come home the following night, that he might be staying over with a friend in Židenice for a while.

"For how long?" the father had asked, tearing off a piece of bread.

It was hard to say.

Was he taking everything?

It seemed best, he said.

"I'll get up and make you something for breakfast," the mother said.

He shook his head, pierced yet again by their courage, by the plain-faced little girl across the table with her straw-blond hair and her raw, bitten nails, by the plastic yellow tablecloth with its smiling, semicircle burn mark. He'd be leaving very early, he said.

The father broke off another piece of bread. "You'll be careful, yes?"

"Of course," he said.

"You take care of yourself, Tomáš," the mother said.

"I will," he said.

Sitting at the kitchen table, he loaded the gun, put the rest of the ammunition in his pocket, then forced himself to eat a piece of bread and drink a half cup of coffee. He hadn't noticed the vase, the jasmine cuttings. It didn't seem possible that this was it — that after five months of waiting and planning, the day had come. Leaning over, he moved aside the heavy blue curtains. The sky was lightening. It would be a beautiful day. Four hours. He could picture the turn in Líbeň, the tram stop, the row of stores. The spot by the wall where he would stand — 110 meters from the turn, 40 to the nearest side street. He stood up, feeling the pressure of the gun under his left arm. All right. He slipped the money under the vase, swept the bread crumbs into his cup and saucer, and brought the dishes to the sink. He'd never prayed in his life. It seemed ridiculous to begin now. On a whim he clipped off a cluster of jasmine with his fingernail and slipped it in the buttonhole of his lapel.

By the time he walked out of the building to catch the tram to Vysočany where he was to meet the others it was morning. A pale, buttery light was already spreading from the east. There were few cars. The trip was uneventful, the tram nearly empty. Three and a half hours. The sudden rise of nausea, to be expected. He looked out the window. Wet pavements. Street sweepers. Here and there a uniform. The suit they'd gotten him was too hot. Three and a half hours. It didn't seem real. It occurred to him that it might never seem real, and that it didn't matter if it did or not.

He could see them now, again, standing by the corner of that little park that smelled like smoke, Gabčík carrying the battered suitcase with the sten gun and Líba Fafek making jokes about the bonnet she was to wear to signal to them whether Heydrich's car had an escort or not, tilting it down, then back, like a girl preparing to pose for her portrait. They were just a group of friends: university students perhaps, now that the universities were closed, or musicians after a long night. The tall one carried a suitcase stuffed with grass for his rabbits, which were legal to raise in the Protectorate. Prague was full of back-alley hutches and suitcases of grass; entire fields were being moved this way and that.

Opálka went over the plan one last time. Everyone knew his station. Heydrich's schedule had been confirmed the previous afternoon by a watchmaker named Novotný who had been called in to fix an antique clock and had seen a document left open on the desk. The Reichsprotektor was being summoned to Berlin that afternoon. He would depart his castle at Panenske Břežany between nine-thirty and ten. His car would take the usual route. Since it was a beautiful day, he would demand that the Mercedes be open to the weather.

Bém knew it by heart. They all did. Líba Fafek was still playing with the hat. Kubiš, who along with Gabčík had been chosen to carry out the assassination, stood off to the side, nodding his head as though listening to fast music. Líba Fafek was to turn onto the road in front of Heydrich's car. Valčík would be stationed above the curve; he would signal Heydrich's approach with a pocket mirror. At the turn in Líbeň, Líba would step on the brakes, forcing the Heydrich car to slow. Kubiš and Gabčík would be waiting by the side of the road. Kubiš would kill both Heydrich and his driver with the sten gun; should anything go wrong, Gabčík would back him up with a grenade. The others would be stationed above and below the turn to distract any police. After the hit, Gabčík and Kubiš would make their escape on bicycles. Was everybody clear on their destinations after the hit? Opálka asked.

A wave of sweetness came to Bém from the flowering lindens growing in the park. For a moment or two he thought he would be sick. A schoolboy with a boxer on a leash was walking the dog around an empty fountain. And suddenly it was as if he were outside the group, as though he were the boy with the dog, seeing them standing there at the corner — the man with the suitcase, the woman with the hat — feeling the tug of the leash in his hand. And then it passed and he knew he would be all right.

Gabčík had put his big arm around Líba Fafek, who wasn't smiling anymore. She had taken off the hat and was holding it over her stomach.

They had a little over ninety minutes to be at their positions, Opálka said. No more waiting. He looked at Kubiš and Gabčík. The bicycles were waiting for them in the schoolteacher's garage as arranged, he said. They were women's bicycles, but since bicycles were in short supply, no one would notice.

Valčík abruptly leaned over and vomited into the bushes. "It's fine," he said.

"You're all right?" Opálka said.

Valčík took a white handkerchief out of his pocket and neatly wiped his mouth. "I'll be fine," he said.

"You're sure? If not, I have to know now."

"Quite sure."

Kubiš shook his head. "Women's bicycles," he said. "As a kid I wouldn't have been caught dead."

Gabčík, next to him, smiled that small, sad smile of his.

"I'm sorry," said Opálka.

"When this is over, I'm going to put in a complaint with London," said Kubiš.

"I understand."

"Yes, well." Kubiš looked around at the group. "Maybe we should go, don't you think?" He turned to Gabčík. "Wouldn't want to keep the goddamned rabbits waiting."

They shook hands all around, feeling awkward, then turned to go. Gabčík kissed Líba quickly and picked up his suitcase.

"I just wanted to say that it's been a pleasure," said Opálka suddenly, but though Valčík nodded and wished him luck, the others were already walking away, and didn't hear him.

And then it was just him and Opálka. A trolley went by. He could feel the fear now, like a physical thing, like a train in his body, one valley over. It was time. The boy with the dog had disappeared. He hadn't noticed him go.

THAT SAME AFTERNOON, LESS THAN SIX HOURS AFTER she saw him turn and disappear around the bend of the road to Mělkovice, my mother stood waiting outside the Škoda factory in Adamov.

A darkening day. The women with the bowls of vitamin pills were already in place inside the steel-and-barbed-wire gates, waiting for the night shift. She heard the whistle and soon they were streaming out, thick with fatigue. She recognized him in the crowd, and she watched him walk up the broad avenue between the black, hangar-like buildings that seemed to fill that valley, then turn toward the security gate. He walked alone. He was wearing a blue factory uniform and a short jacket and carrying a lunch pail.

My father saw her standing across the road on the root-cracked sidewalk, and simply stopped. The crowd bumped and ground around him. She saw his shoulder jerk forward when someone shoved him and then he was walking across the cobbled road on which a line of canvas-covered trucks waited, halted by the river of men headed for the train station.

He stopped a few meters away. My mother saw him glance at the sandy patch of grass by the sidewalk, then up the valley. He nodded slightly, as though remembering something someone once said. She hadn't realized until that moment how much he loved her.

"Are you all right?" he said finally.

She nodded. "I need to talk to you," she said.

"No need."

"I know. Still."

He nodded again. She knew him. There would be no scene, no cinder-in-the-eye. He had his pride. He would make it easy for her.

"When did you get home?" he asked.

"Yesterday."

"I love you," he said. "Does that matter?"

"It matters," she said.

He smiled. A smile like a spasm. "But not enough."

"No."

My father nodded and then, setting his lunch pail gently on the sidewalk, unpeeled his glasses from around his ears and began wiping the lenses with his handkerchief. There was nothing in his eye. She looked away. One of the women holding the bowl of pills by the gate was checking the heel of her shoe.

"We still have to work together," he said.

"I know."

"Can you do that?"

"Yes," she said. "Can you?"

He picked up his lunch pail. "Is this what you want, Ivana?"

"Yes," she said, looking at him. "It is."

"You love him that much?"

"Yes."

"I see." My father put his glasses back on, winding them carefully around his ears. "I should go," he said. "You'll be all right?"

"I'll be fine," said my mother.

"Well . . ." He smiled, the way a man might smile while pulling a long splinter out of his arm. "I keep thinking I should kiss you goodbye."

She was well down the sidewalk when she heard him call her name. He was standing by a bench with two slats missing from the back. She'd known him well. "There's something you should know," he said.

She waited.

"I want you to know that I'll be here," he said.

"Don't . . . ," she began. "I don't . . ."

"I know you don't," my father said. "But I'll be here when he's gone." And he turned and walked away down the sidewalk.

That evening my father walked out of the Brno railroad station. He crossed the avenue to the trolley stop and took the trolley home to the corner by the butcher's, closed now, then walked up the hill to his parents' apartment overlooking the courtyard. And he woke at four in the morning and did it all again, backward: the unlit streets, the blacked-out train, the passengers groping for seats like the blind. And that evening when he walked out through the post and barbed-wire gate past the guards and the women with the vitamin pills he looked across the street, in spite of himself, to see if she was there, then turned toward the railway station with the others.

He couldn't stop the thinking and he didn't try. He thought about her when he walked up the square, where they used to walk together, or past the little tilting street that led to the Špilberk Castle gardens where they had planned their lives together. All that fall and well into the winter he worked his way through the briars that spring up in the foundations of love. He expected them. Rage? What was there to rage against? How do you fight for love? Or against it?

He saw her every few weeks. At meetings, on the street. They didn't talk much. It didn't matter. He could tell that this man, whoever he was, wasn't with her — that he was gone and that she was waiting for him.

My father didn't wish him ill. Anything but that. No, to kill the beast he needed it alive. Alive and well and living in boredom. Sitting on the side of the bed, pulling on its slippers; arguing at dinner over the price of the new furniture. Just let him live, he thought, and die on the field of days as other men do. He could wait.

In any case, it wasn't as though there were no distractions — the occupation made sure of that. The work in the factory was unpleasant, the daily ritual of seeding the bearings with steel dust bad on the nerves. The older factory workers — dutiful men, law-abiding traitors — hated him and his few comrades on principle: for being students, for being new, for interfering.

The world outside the factory was hardly better. Nothing was sure. No one knew how far things would go, or when they would be over. Some things stayed the same; others changed. The diktats printed in the newspaper or announced over the loudspeakers seemed to bring something new every day. The schools were to be closed on such and such a date. All radios were to be registered with the authorities between the hours of ten and four. All persons of Jewish descent were henceforth forbidden from entering public spaces: theaters, movie houses, restaurants . . . Listening to foreign frequencies was a crime punishable by death. Absurd. This wasn't war. This was disease. They were everywhere you looked now: in cars, on corners, striding down the cobbles, like an infection in the body.

Appropriately enough, symptoms had begun to appear, like yellowed nails or brittle hair. To amuse himself, he noted their progression. In answer to the command form, for example, a forest of gestures had appeared, gestures signaling not merely a recognition of the status quo — for who could help but recognize it? — but agreement, willingness, above all, subordination: the dropped glance, the slightly bowed head, the careful smile. A bag or briefcase clasped like a child to the chest.

It was fascinating in its way. Faced with an individual who had complete power over them, most people would find themselves, almost unconsciously, wanting to please him. You could see them seeking out the right facial expression, the correct stance; like animals in the open, they would instinctively find the place between dignity and cowardice — and stay there. Not move. Draw their neutrality around them like camouflage. It was a kind of game. Validate the other's disgust for you without encouraging it; play the mongrel without incurring a kick.

Of course, this was the easy part. The challenge was in keeping public behavior from bleeding into private life, in keeping the two selves apart. And this was impossible. No one could accomplish it entirely. No one. Every hour you lived, from the moment you woke in the dark, you were reshaping yourself to survive.

It made for an interesting problem: the better you were at the role, the more talent you had for it, the more likely it was that you'd live — and the more likely that you'd lose yourself along the way.

Hate helped. In keeping things clear. But hate was a hammer anyone could use, and it served the others as well, and in precisely the same way.

And so he waited, and survived, seeing every side. Amused and appalled at the spectacle of men's predictability: at the shopkeepers who now refused to sell bread to Jews, at the children who made good money shopping for them.

That June, tired of his friend's constant questions, he told Mirek what had happened. He was sitting at the kitchen table, facing the window that looked out on the garden and the apricot tree, heavy with unpicked fruit. The whole south side of the house was overgrown with a layer of green vines, half a meter thick. When they bloomed once a year, as they were blooming now, the air inside the house seemed to vibrate as though it were alive. He looked down at the table: gray bees were landing on the small gray blossoms that waved and dipped over the napkin and the fork and the empty plate. "She'll come back," said Mirek. "She'll grow tired of him after they're together for a while."

"Maybe," said my father. And because he loved her as much as he did, he almost wished it could be otherwise.

HE AND OPÁLKA WERE THE LAST TO LEAVE. THEY STOOD next to each other watching Gabčík and Kubiš walk down the cracked sidewalk toward the avenue, passing through the long morning shade. Líba Fafek had disappeared up a side street. Valčík was already walking around the empty fountain, one hand trailing along the stone.

The air moved, a breeze bringing a breath of coolness. It seemed to come from the buildings above them: a deep, musty sigh, smelling of cellars and hallways.

Opálka picked up the battered leather briefcase which no longer contained the student papers and music sheets he had carried in it for fifteen years but a length of sausage in newspaper and three hand grenades, nestled in the dark like hard green eggs.

"So . . . ," he said.

"So," said Bém.

"We have a few minutes yet, we may as well wait here."

"All right."

"It's going to be a hot day."

"Yes, it is."

Opálka took off his hat and looked inside it, then placed it back on his head. "Are you all right?"

"I think so."

"Nervous?"

"Of course."

Opálka tried to smile. "For a few seconds this morning I couldn't remember the number of the tram to Vysočany. I've taken it all my life."

They turned back to look at the others. Kubiš and Gabčík were nearly at the avenue now. As they came to what appeared to be a stretch of broken cobbles, Kubiš gave his friend a small shove with his shoulder. When the other shoved back, he stepped neatly aside, making Gabčík stumble slightly.

"Boys," said Opálka.

"He seemed almost happy this morning."

"Kubiš? He's in his element. They both are, in their way. I've never been like that. I think too much."

"Most do," said Bém.

"A curse. I have to keep it leashed all the time."

"It's not all bad if it helps you see things."

"Think so?"

"Not really."

Opálka paused uncomfortably. "I should have asked you this before, but is there someone . . ."

"You mean in case . . ."

That's right.

"No. Not in the way you mean. Thank you."

"Absurd, isn't it?"

"What?"

"Thinking this way."

"Not as absurd as it should be."

"True."

"And you? You've made arrangements? For your family, I mean?"

"I have. Thank you."

Opálka pushed up the sleeve of his jacket to check his watch. "It's time, I'm afraid," he said.

"I don't mind," said Bém.

Bém had gone only a few steps when he heard him call. "Tomáš?"

He turned.

"One more thing . . . Do you like beer?"

Bém paused. Opálka was a brave man.

"I do," he said, though he didn't, particularly.

"We should get a beer sometime . . . when this is over?"

"I'd like that."

Opálka nodded. "All right," he said. "All right. We'll do that, then." And picking up his briefcase, he walked away.

By the time he got to the tram stop, walking in the shadow of the buildings, he was sweating freely. The suit they had gotten for him was too heavy. It was much too heavy. He would sweat like a pig. It didn't matter.

He waited in the shade, his back against the façade of a three-story building like a soiled cake. The crowds were increasing. Men carrying briefcases stood on the island, holding their hats in one hand, with the other wiping their heads with handkerchiefs. Boys in shorts dodged through the crowd. He couldn't help but look for her, even now. The thought that he might actually see her terrified him.

A sweet-faced matronly woman with calves like bowling pins walked next to a dark-haired young woman pushing a baby carriage. He knew these faces. Two workers in overalls passed by, one leaning in toward the other, the other listening intently until suddenly he exploded with laughter, throwing back his head as if shot. They knew nothing. None of them.

A tram. Not his. One hour and fifteen minutes.

What would the woman and her daughter say, he wondered, if he walked over and told them what was going to happen in Líbeň in just over an hour? Would they believe him? Would they turn around and go home and wait by the radio? Would they start screaming to the two soldiers looking in a shop window on the opposite side of the avenue?

He could feel the weakness rising in him like a wave: that familiar inner trembling, that doubt. He recognized it for what it was — fear, not of the leap itself, but of the seconds before the leap, of those moments on the cliff when everything could still be otherwise. And leaning against the building, feeling his legs going weak under him, he did what he had done with that fear ever since they were children together and quickly killed it, opening the tap of rage in his heart and feeling it flood through his veins like adrenaline, thinking of his mother's laugh coming up from the courtyard and the look on his sister's face the morning she came upon the jar of yellow butterflies dead in the sun and the winter morning two years ago when he had watched an old man kicked to death in a square in Brno because he had tried to board a tram without seeing them waiting. It had taken a long time. He'd watched through the frame of the tram window as one of them whipped the old man's face and back with a black riding crop in a fury so profound it seemed like a crack in the order of things. The old man had crawled about in the melting snow, first trying to pull himself up a lamppost, then grabbing onto the boots of his attacker, then toward the crowd which moved back like a respectful audience, and from somewhere in the tram a woman's voice had said, perfectly clearly, "For the love of God, someone do something," not because she expected it, but because she had to say it. No one moved. Bém noticed that the man next to him, a laborer dressed in overalls and a heavy black sweater, had bitten his lower lip; a thin stream of blood was running into the stubble on his chin. There was nothing to do. And remembering all this, Bém felt the sickness leave him, and when the tram came he walked across to the island and swung himself on and the doors closed behind him.

He could see them there, just before the road turned into itself and disappeared: Gabčík, his suitcase next to him, pretending to do something with the chain on his bicycle; Kubiš leaning against a telephone pole a few meters away, smoking. Even from that distance he seemed both alive and nonchalant, like a man waiting for a date while pretending not to care.

The fact of it flashed through his brain like a jolt of electricity and was gone. They were waiting for Reinhard Heydrich. Reichsprotektor. Obergruppenführer.

Forty minutes. The usual crowd. Heydrich's car would be leaving Panenské Břežany any minute. It could have left already. A tram pulled up to the stop before the turn and three people got off. If a tram stopped there during the hit, Kubiš had pointed out, it would be directly behind Heydrich's car. They had considered that fact. There was nothing to be done.

The scene was strangely peaceful. The trees on the hill above the turn moved tentatively in the breeze and were still. A car went by. Then another, the other way. Then two more. To the south, dimly, he could see the city. The air above the Vltava, or where he knew the Vltava to be, seemed softer, shot through with mist. A sort of calm had settled over things. A distance. The world seemed drugged, slowed.

No police to be seen. Nothing unusual. No sign. Gabčík picked up the bicycle and leaned it against a pole. A blue summer sky. Two small clouds.

He turned to look behind him. Through the shrubs that grew along the top of the retaining wall at his back he could see a row of small houses, their yards a clutter of fences and gardens and half-successful trellises and piles of brick. A woman was hoeing, working the ground with short, choppy strokes. An older, shirtless man was pushing a wheelbarrow. He noticed that the wall to his left was bulging a bit, the stones tilting out from the face, as if forced by the weight of earth above it. Someone would have to repair it.

Nothing. What would happen would happen. It was all right. He thought of her for a moment and she seemed very fine to him and very far off. He couldn't bring her closer.

He could feel himself sweating, the cold rivulets trickling down his back and sides. He took off his hat and wiped his forehead with his sleeve and looked toward the hill. Nothing. He felt the gun under his arm. Kubiš was still leaning against the pole. He'd wanted to be the one to look him in the face and pull the trigger. Didn't matter.

Another tram arrived. An old woman got off — he could tell by the way she walked, bent under the weight of the bags in each hand, by the blue kerchief on her head. It was half an hour from Panenskě Břežany. He looked toward the hill. Nothing.

Sweat. Blooms. The smell of grass. No police. A man holding a little boy by the hand was crossing the street. Another tram was . . .

A flash like a spark of mica on the hill. For an instant he didn't realize what he'd seen. He glanced down toward the curve. Gabčík was kneeling on the sidewalk by the open suitcase. He stood and slipped something into his coat and kicked the suitcase shut with his foot and strode toward the curb as Liba Fafek's car appeared around the curve, a black open Mercedes, like a premonition of something, right behind her, both cars already slowing until the Mercedes seemed to have stopped altogether and there was Gabčík standing in the road ten meters away, throwing open his coat.

Nothing happened. There was no sound. Everything seemed to have stopped. He could see the gun in Gabčík's hands. He could see the driver, suspended, staring at the big man in the raincoat as though he didn't understand who he might be or what he could want. He could see the man seated behind him: the visored cap, the long, white face . . .

Suddenly everything accelerated. He could see Gabčík moving and jerking about strangely, bent over the gun in his hands as though talking to it. The gun! The gun had jammed! It was impossible. The limousine was picking up speed. It was simply going around him. Instinctively, helplessly, Bém began to run toward the scene even as he saw Kubiš sprinting up from the side and then a flash and a burst of black smoke and the limousine skidded to a stop. Two popping sounds. Another. Gabčík fell and was up, staggering toward the bicycle leaning against the wall. The man was standing up in the back of the car as though it were a chariot, pointing at him. Bém could see Kubiš running down the avenue. The driver was firing at him. Gabčík was on the bicycle now, pedaling madly down the sidewalk. People were jumping out of his way.

Bém slowed, then stopped. The man climbed out of the smashed end of the limousine as if stepping over a fence. He was alive. It was over. They had failed. The suitcase lay ten meters away. Kubiš's bicycle was still standing by the wall.

He recognized him. Even from this distance, he recognized him. That face. That long, curved talon of a nose. He was gesticulating with his right hand, ordering something.

A delivery van had stopped. The man took two strides toward it, raised his right hand as though snatching something off a high shelf, and fell to the pavement.

Bém began to walk in the other direction. Quickly, not hurrying. He walked past the bulging stones where he had waited. The shirtless man he had seen pushing the wheelbarrow had come down to the edge of his yard. There was no avoiding him. "Viděl jste co se tam stalo?" he called down to Bém from the top of the wall. Did you see what happened there? Bém said he thought the tram had hit someone, and walked on. Don't look back. He was grateful he'd put on the hat. Still, his abruptness had made him worth noticing. He should have stopped, gossiped a bit. Erased himself.

He came to the next road and took a right, walking up the quiet sidewalks, then down the hill past the school to another avenue. A tram was coming. He got on it.

"WE MUST THANK GOD FOR BLOOD POISONING," THE priest, Dr. Petřek, had said. He was standing at the bottom of the steps wearing a long coat with a fur collar. No, no, he wouldn't have any, thank you. Heydrich's wound, he said, had not been considered particularly dangerous. No vital organs had been affected; the bleeding had been contained. The German surgeon who had been rushed in had assured the authorities that the ten-centimeter-deep gouge was not fatal, that the Obergruppen-führer's life was not in danger. Petřek stroked his white, goat-like beard. The swine had counted their cards early, he said; the good Lord had yet to play his hand. The wound, it turned out, had been full of debris — bits of metal and upholstery from the car seats, leather and horsehair . . . But perhaps he would have just a little, no more than a finger's width — it *was* cold down here. In any case, a week later septicemia had developed and quickly finished the job, which proved once again that even when we thought we were free and clear and seemingly out of danger, the hand of the Almighty could smite us. And he drained his glass in a way that showed he was not entirely unfamiliar with slivovitz, and left them.

"That was a nice coat," Gabčík said. He was sitting cross-legged, cutting carrots into a can. No one had said anything.

"We must thank God for blood poisoning," Kubiš said, and farted.

On the evening of June 10 Petřek was back. Bém had slept badly the night before, struggling through dreams in which his father appeared to him in a threadbare suit and he saw his mother sitting on a small stone bench against a wall with his sister on her lap. Then it was dark, and in the dream he knew he had to meet her somewhere, that she was waiting for him, and he rushed through endless, unfamiliar cities, running up stairwells and down badly lit hallways, looking for rooms whose numbers were always out of sequence or missing, all the while knowing that the whole thing was absurd, that he was years too late but unable to bring himself to stop. He was in an industrial district filled with low brick factory buildings surrounded by high fences. Tilting cement embankments, pale and high as Sahara dunes, rose in his path, and he scrambled up them on all fours, like a dog. At some point he found himself standing on the shore of a vast river, and realizing that he would have to cross it, he bent to take off his shoes, and woke. The stone ceiling of the niche was inches above his face.

He rolled over to look into the main room of the crypt. A white square was shining on the stone floor. For a second he didn't know what it was, then realized that the moon's pitch had somehow caught the tiny window high on the north wall, that he had woken at the precise moment — perhaps the only such moment for a month, or a year — when everything met. Then again, maybe it had been the moonlight itself that had woken him, like a visitor moving about the room. He watched it narrow, parallelogram, rectangle, square. How beautiful it was. Ten minutes later it was gone.

The next evening, Petřek came down to talk to them, and nothing was quite the same afterward. He came without his coat, and they all knew from this that something had happened

— or told themselves later that they'd known — and they left what they were doing and gathered by the bottom of the steps. He didn't hesitate. At ten the night before, Petřek told them, the village of Lidice, about twenty kilometers west of Prague, had been destroyed. An act of retaliation. The inhabitants were registered; movable property was evacuated. At dawn, the male population of the town — 150 men and boys at least — had been herded into a barn and executed. Another 190 women and children had been deported, presumably to Ravensbrück. The town itself had been razed. Obergruppenführer Frank's orders, supposedly given to him personally by the Führer, had been to erase all evidence that the town had existed, all coordinates, all markers. Rumor had it that the stream that ran through the town was to be rerouted in its bed. It appeared the town had been selected at random.

He had thought about whether he should tell them, Petřek said, and had decided it was only right. He was terribly sorry.

Bém watched them as he spoke. Kubiš, who had been cleaning his gun, looked down at it for a moment, then brought it up to his face and blew on it as though blowing away some dust. Gabčík, who had been leaning against the wall eating a piece of bread, kept chewing. Valčík smiled and looked down.

He was sorry, the priest said again.

"Well . . . ," Opálka said. He shook his head.

"An inhuman thing," the priest said. "God will not be merciful . . ."

"Yes," Opálka said.

"None of you must think . . ."

"No . . . of course not."

"No one could have foreseen this."

"No," Opálka said. "You're right."

"We must pray . . ."

"Yes," Opálka said. "Thank you."

• • •

There were no rages, no tears, no flashes of anger. They didn't talk about it. They didn't know how. They took the blow like a short, hard kick to the stomach from an invisible opponent — from God, say — and went on. It was the only thing they knew how to do. They'd been chosen precisely because they could.

But he could feel it there nonetheless — a kind of sickness, a rot. These men — Gabčík, Kubiš, Valčík, and the rest — were still dangerous, they would always be dangerous, but now something had changed in them. Something essential. And because they sensed this, they grew still, careful. They didn't fight with each other, or even argue. A simple, instinctive civility became the order of their days. There was nothing false or forced about it. "I'll need those potatoes when you have them." "You want some more soup?" "No, I'm fine." It was pure instinct. Something was hunting them. Something they couldn't see, or fight. If they stayed still, stayed together, it might pass them by.

He tried to keep them numbers: 150 men and boys, 190 women and children. Numbers. Not unaware that this was exactly what the others had done in order to be able to do what they did. He didn't care. He had been to Kladno, only a few kilometers away from Lidice. He knew these towns. If he allowed himself to see the faces blinking in the lights, the marks of the sheets showing on their faces like scars, the men — enemies, perhaps, who had not spoken for years — now suddenly talking, asking each other what was happening, where they were going, as if nothing before had ever really mattered but had only been a long, elaborate game . . . If he heard them giving quick instructions to their wives or assuring their sons that everything would be all right even as the village dogs, barking, were being shot down one by one in the street, in the chicken yards . . . If he allowed this, something might give. And that could not be. Ever. They were numbers. To hell with them.

But some things could not be fenced off. They came through the walls. They were like a chemical change in the brain. Day by day he could feel it coming over him, a kind of slow, undramatic numbness, as though some invisible spigot had been turned the night Petřek had come down to tell them the news. It was like falling out of love: one moment she was still the woman you knew and thought you wanted, the next something had shifted imperceptibly and it was over. The world outside was receding. Or maybe he was the one falling away from it. Either way, he was unable to care in the same way he had before. The Beneš government in exile, the Resistance, the Wehrmacht and security police even now combing the city for them — all these seemed far away from him, strangely abstract. He told himself how he should feel, why these things mattered, and mattered supremely, but it was no good. He could remember how he had once felt, but that time had passed.

Hour by hour, day by day, as they made their meals or did their exercises or wrapped themselves up in blankets before crawling into their niches, he could feel the circle drawing tighter around them. Around him. Two things mattered now. The men around him mattered, because they alone, of all the people on the earth, carried the same burden. Because they understood. And she mattered. Because she didn't. Because she was free of it. Because he loved her.

She would be the rope into the well in which he was drowning. He knew this as surely as anything he had ever known in his life. There was nothing sentimental about it. It was simply a fact. Paper would burn. Day would bring light. What lived would eventually die. She would save him, and she would be able to do this because she was who she was. Because the gods of the arbitrary world had decided it should be so. Because her voice, her body — her very soul, if you like — spoke to him.

When he was twelve he'd spent two weeks on his uncle's farm near Jindřichův Hradec. One night he'd woken up to a sound — a kind of rhythmic barking, a forced *aark aark aark* — unlike anything he had ever heard before. The sound was coming from somewhere behind his uncle's barn. He tried to go back to sleep but couldn't, so he pulled on his pants and woke his uncle, and together the two of them went out to see what it was and found an old water cistern with the neighbor's cat drowning at the bottom of it. His uncle pulled it out with a rake, still making that awful barking sound — a sound he wouldn't hear again until he visited the seals at the London Zoo — and wrapped it in a shirt to keep it warm but it didn't seem to know where it was and it just kept barking until it died. If they'd fished it out a half hour earlier, his uncle had said, the thing might have made it.

Well, here he was. The analogy, and the image at the heart of it, gave him pleasure — he didn't know why. The absurdity of it. The stick-in-the-wound absurdity of it. It was the first thing that had given him pleasure in days. Here he was. Here they *all* were, swimming in circles in their own little cistern — God's little cistern — barking like cats. Eight cats drowning in a well. It sounded like a nursery rhyme.

She would save him. She was the rope, the rake, the steps appearing in the stone, leading up from the water.

THE MORNINGS ON THE TRAM ON THE WAY TO THE Language Institute in Líbeň were difficult for my mother. By late afternoon she would be tired and so less likely to think about things. She tried reading, but the movement of the car gave her headaches, so she spent the forty minutes simply staring out the window at the people coming out of stores or waiting at the stops, some hurrying by with bags or briefcases — businessmen, lovers, a little boy in blue pants holding on to his mother's dress with one hand while bouncing some kind of stringed puppet-like thing with the other . . .

In the first half of May, as the weather warmed, the half-windows in the tram would be pushed down and the air would come in — pillowy gusts smelling of petrol and leaves — until some idiot worried about her hair would lean over and ask the person under it if he could close the window a bit, and then May 27 came and human beings were lined up against walls and shot, and yet nothing changed somehow. People still went to work, if they had work to go to, and when the weather was warm, the half-windows were pushed down and the air still felt good in her hair. At times this seemed natural and right — what else did she expect? At other times — brief moments, usually — it seemed both heartbreaking and utterly mad as if, looking out the tram window one day, she had glimpsed a woman burning on a street corner, her dress going up in great black billows as she waited patiently for her tram.

She didn't bother trying not to look for him. Twice she thought she saw him — the hat, the glasses, that smooth, deceptively easy walk — and rushed out at the next stop, to the predictable disappointment. It didn't matter. On July 16, only six weeks later, she would take the train out to Žd'ár. She'd already arranged to take the day off. She would get out at the familiar train station and walk along the wall and the trees, past the little *hospoda* where she and her father had once seen the dwarf sitting on the bench, then take the number 9 bus to the bridge. From there it would be less than five kilometers to the crossroads. One year. He might not be there; she knew that. It didn't matter. He would be there eventually. And the forest — the mushrooms, the mossy icons, all the things they had known — would help. They'd make him real.

She didn't let herself think, after May 27, that he might have been involved. It was not something she could think about. There were many things that my mother could not think about. That he was dead. That she would not see him again. That she would not hear his voice again in this life. When she heard the descriptions of the attackers being read over the loudspeakers in Václavské náměstí that outrageously blue Sunday morning, the phrases echoing off the façades of the buildings, overlapping each other, she had simply stopped breathing. All around her the streams of people hurrying up the sidewalks or crossing the avenue had shuffled to a stop and frozen. Pantomimes of listening — the hand to the ear like a timid greeting, the slight tilt of the head: *At half past ten this morning, a failed attempt . . . anyone with information . . . two have escaped, one on foot, the other on a bicycle.* It was not him. It was not him. Nothing else mattered.

Every day she checked the newspapers for the lists of names of those arrested or shot for crimes against the Reich. Nothing. He had disappeared. It did not surprise her. If anyone could slide through, he could. She'd seen his way with the world — his competence, his carefulness. He had that aura about him, the aura of luck. When the bullet came, he'd be the one who bent to tie his shoe. She believed this.

These days she found it easier to think about the other one. He was safer somehow. She hadn't heard from my father, hadn't expected to. It was strange sometimes to think of him only hours away, going about his daily business. Getting on the 4:40 train to the factory, waiting at the stop in the evening for the tram to Žabovřesky . . .

Odd to think how different her life had been then, and how quickly it had passed. One moment you were taking the train to Vysočina or sitting in someone's living room passing around a tray of *koláče,* and the next someone had licked a finger and turned a page and everything had changed. You could leaf back and see yourself taking the train, sitting on the sofa, passing the tray, but now it was as if you were reading about a character in a book, a character who resembled you in every way, whose thoughts were familiar, who *was* you — but a character in a book nonetheless.

They'd talked endlessly. They'd made love. It was easy to think about — had always been easy. It didn't matter. Page after page. For a week or so that September they'd worried that she might be pregnant, but it was a false alarm. They'd talked about marriage. They could live with his parents until the war was over, he'd said, then move into a place of their own. He had been doing well at the newspaper before the war began; he could pick up again where he had left off. Nothing was certain, of course, he realized that, but Soukup himself had told him more than once that he could make editor by the time he was thirty. They could do worse.

His good-humored understanding of her had annoyed her those first few months, as did his failure to notice the men's names she dropped into their conversation like tacks, hoping to get the reaction she'd always gotten from men before. Eventually, as she had come to see that his humor lacked condescension, that his confidence was not really presumption, it bothered her less. Touched by his decency, by his obvious regard for her, unable, in short, to find a good reason *not* to love him, she listened to his plans for them. She wondered now what she could have been thinking. It would all be over soon, he would say, stroking her hair as they lay in some grassy corner of the Špilberk gardens, and then they'd share the bit of food they had brought with them — generally a slice of bread and a small green kohlrabi — and start back down toward the city.

She'd thought she'd been in love with him then. Which was not surprising. Good to look at, intelligent, funny, he'd seemed to be liked (or at least respected) by everyone who knew him, and when she let him take her virginity that night in the garden behind the second wall, it was not only because she liked his lank, dark blond hair and his thin, aristocratic nose but because she had begun to sense that his decency had little to do with weakness and a good deal to do with strength. It was not her fault. How was she to have known that love is not something to be measured out in spoonfuls, that decency has its limits.

There had been a calm about him that she'd liked at first, a refusal to be drawn in by the world, an understanding of things that was rooted in pain but rose above it. It was a quality she hadn't known in a young man before — most of the men she knew were children, forever preening or pouting, throwing themselves this way or that without knowing why — and if truth be told she hadn't minded living within the still circle it made. He wasn't dispassionate. When they'd rolled over his rimless glasses that very first night, crushing both lenses with a hollow pop like the sound of a flashbulb going off, he'd chuckled and shook his head, and then, pausing only to see if she had been cut, rolled her over him and back to the grass, his fingers tangled gently in her hair, and finished making love to her.

Afterward they'd found what was left of the mangled frame and he'd put it in his pocket and she'd led him out of the garden and down the barely lit walks, and he had joked about the vague shapes he saw ahead of them and tapped the path in front of him with a crooked tree limb as though he were blind. She could tell he didn't like this business of having to walk back down the sloping flights of stairs and through the half-deserted streets with his arm hooked into hers as if he had aged suddenly, inexplicably, but these things happened.

He'd taken it well. As he took everything. She'd expected it — and both admired and slightly despised him for it. A good man. She could think of nothing to dislike about him. And yet, if just once she had sensed some anger beneath his decency, his irony. If just once she had sensed the place in him where all his negotiations with the world ended, and the man began.

It was unfair, really. He'd loved her — possibly loved her still. She could list his qualities, and these qualities were substantial and real. Anyone could see them. In fact, if the two of them had been houses or cars instead of men, he might well have been the better of the two. And none of it mattered, because for all the things he was, there was one thing my father wasn't: he wasn't the other one. For this she couldn't forgive him. Fairness had nothing to do with it.

MY FATHER HEARD ABOUT HER OCCASIONALLY — FROM friends, from former schoolmates, even from her mother, whom he ran into one chilly April morning as she was crossing the street to the greenmarket. It was to be expected — Brno was a village of three hundred thousand souls, people always said, and it was true.

It had rained that morning, and low, fast clouds were rushing over the buildings, thinning to a clear, piercing blue one moment, thickening to rain the next. He saw her flinch when she saw him, saw first the quick, unpremeditated smile — she'd always liked him — then the quick desire to pass without having to speak to him, then the realization that it was too late. That it couldn't be helped.

It was good to see him, she said; he was looking well for these times. She was just hurrying to the greenmarket — not that there would be anything to buy. For two weeks now there had been nothing, just potatoes full of eyes, some garlic . . . Everything was so overpriced . . . She didn't know how people did it — well, that was not true, she did know, in some cases she knew very well, but this was not the time or place . . . And you, she asked him, your parents are well? He told her they were. And was he still at the factory as before? He was, he said. Everything was pretty much the same as it had been, he said.

Ivana was in Prague, she said, living with her uncle Ruda's family. She was working at the Language Institute they had there. "You should write to her sometime," she said, patting the sleeve of his coat, and for a moment he hated her for her stupidity and her kindness. My mother was young, she said. These things took time sometimes. She had cared for him very much, she said. And he smiled because he knew these things were true and because this was the joke of it, and he wished her well and continued on his way.

The world was full of jokes. My father appreciated them all. That he should have written that letter for Honza Kolařik that day was a joke. That he should have seen my mother's face as if for the first time that afternoon, though he had seen it a hundred times before . . . that was a joke too. That he should love her still, that he should realize only after she'd left him that he'd made a space for her — a space that he now carried around with him everywhere he went, like a cored apple . . . that was yet another joke, and a good one. And he was the punch line. She loved another — she'd told him so to his face — and yet he continued to love her anyway, to think about her, to worry about her, and there didn't seem to be any way out of it. That was the biggest joke of all.

In the first month or so he'd been just miserable and angry enough to let himself be talked into trying the usual schoolboy remedies: the bottle of slivovitz, the circle of friends, the long diatribes against women in general. For the better part of half an hour he'd sweated over a fifty-crown whore who had cried out in perfect time to the creaking of the metal bed as though she and the bed together made up some kind of mechanism, speeding and slowing down with his thrusts . . . ridiculous. Witchcraft. One thing had nothing to do with another. His friends might as well have recommended that he drink tea or eat a clove of garlic at midnight. It would have been no more absurd than anything else these days.

There were distractions, of course, some of them quite humorous. The factory was a distraction. They were hated there, ironically enough not by their enemies, the soldiers charged to protect the Reich's armament industry, but by the factory workers who had been there before the war, good Czech citizens like themselves. These hated them for being intellectuals, troublemakers, for interfering in things, for disrupting things. Carburetors or shell casings, it was all the same to them. Making the quota meant a Christmas bonus, an eighth of a liter of rum — everything else was politics. Idiots. They could be told they'd all be shot on Saturday, and they'd work like dogs to get out the required number of bullets by Friday. And betray anyone who tried to slow them down.

He was liked a bit more than the others, he wasn't sure why. Perhaps because his father had been a janitor, or because he knew one end of a screwdriver from the other, or because he didn't try to ingratiate himself. "You're all right, Sedlák," one of them had said to him a few weeks after he'd started there, "not like all these others with their Latin grammars jammed up their asses."

"Is that right?" he'd said.

"I can tell," said the man, whose name was Tonda Králíček, and who worked the lathe two stations down from him, his stomach in his blue worker's overalls pushed against the steel. "You know how to work."

And work he did, he and four of the others, adding steel dust to the oil while pretending to correct some small malfunction or measuring the gap of the blade with the micrometer, resisting the temptation to do more, to go faster. One broken machine could knock out the line for a day, a week . . . One tenth of a centimeter difference in the depth of the holding groove could make the casing too tight, and somewhere on the Russian front a shell would explode while still in the cannon. It had to be enough. Get too greedy, go too fast, and you'd make a mistake. Someone

— likely as not one of your fellow citizens — would notice something and then the process, unencumbered by any need for evidence or courts, would accomplish the rest with great efficiency. You'd be led out to the courtyard between buildings B and C, near where the bicycles were parked, and shot in the back of the neck. It had happened twice in the past month — a man taken out, a bicycle orphaned.

It was a peculiar game. You had to dance just right, though you couldn't hear the music and the steps themselves were unmarked, and every now and then, just to keep things interesting, your leg or arm would be jerked by a string you hadn't known was there. That February, for example, Králíček had joined him as he sat eating his piece of bread with preserves in the second courtyard, rotting his teeth, and they'd talked a bit. He lived near Blansko, Králíček said. He had two daughters and a son. He didn't give a damn about politics. If there was one thing he hated, it was these little interferers, snuffling their wet noses into everybody's business. That breakdown in the drill press in the second sector had not been an accident — he knew that — and they'd all lost three days of work. And for what? It was not as though they were treated all that badly . . . they should be grateful for having work at all. He had a sense the breakdown had something to do with the oil.

He had a *chata* in the woods not far from Blansko, Králíček said, just a little place near a pond. Not much, really, but he loved it like a baby loves its nipple, counted the days till the warm weather returned and he could start going up. "You like to fish, Sedlák?"

He told him he'd never been. It wasn't true, but he sensed that this was what he needed to say in order to keep up the terms of the relationship — a relationship based on the illusion of his directness, his unwillingness to pretend to anything. "You'll have to come up sometime, then," Králíček had said, "I'll take you," and in spite of himself, he had felt moved. Králíček, he realized, was not a bad man, and most of the horrors of this world were committed by men just like him.

It became this thing between them: he would take the bus up to Blansko and they would go fishing. His son hated fishing, Králíček told him, had never been much interested in anything besides playing with himself.

He shrugged. "Maybe I'll hate it too," he said.

"Maybe you will," Králíček said, and smiled.

He discussed it with the others, and it was agreed they would ease off for a time. Adjusting the settings of the carborundum bits was simply too dangerous; quality control could catch the discrepancy at any time, and the authorities made no allowance for accidents. The dust in the oil was better; it worked flawlessly, if slowly. And the dust was already everywhere — in their mouths and ears and shit; sitting in the latrine, he could see it glistening in the light coming through the hole in the pane, a fine steel rain. Králíček was a problem; they'd have to watch him carefully.

Nothing happened. The dance went on — the grand distraction, from which he couldn't allow himself to be distracted. None of them knew what to do about Králíček or the others, and a week later they began to seed the oil again, a fraction of a gram a day. And then one morning during the first break, Králíček waved him over to where he sat on his stool two stations down, his short legs in their blue overalls crossed at the ankles, and pulled an envelope from his chest pocket. "Take a look at this, Sedlák," he said, taking out a small stack of photographs. One photograph was of a one-room cabin with a metal pipe for a chimney; another showed Králíček sitting on a stool by the edge of a small pond holding a long fishing rod, his legs crossed at the ankle. Very nice, my father said. A third was of a big carp; the fish had been knocked on the head, and one of its eyeballs had bulged and swiveled upward, giving it a comical look. Králíček, who was holding it forward, had drifted out of focus; only his fingers, made huge by proximity, stood out clearly, pressing into the fish's scales.

"That's a big fish," my father said.

"There are bigger," Králíček said.

A week later, he was as dead as the carp in his picture. Rumor had it that he'd been caught smuggling food. And this too was funny, in its way — the way opening a vein with a pair of manicure scissors was funny.

The next Sunday, without knowing he was going to, my father went to the train station and took the train to Prague, where he walked around the streets for an hour, slapping his hands against his legs to keep them warm, then returned to the station and took another train back to Brno. There was no point in trying to find her. Let the comedy play itself out. If she returned, it meant that the other one was dead, and he'd take her back. He had no choice in the matter.

AFTER LIDICE, TIME CHANGED FOR BÉM. IT SMOOTHED out, unwound more easily. As if pain were a lubricant. He barely minded waiting now. It seemed to be the same for the others. A terrible patience had settled in, and if he recognized in it at times the resignation of snowed-in mountaineers who, having gone beyond their altitude, have quietly begun to die, he knew as well their reserves, what a moment's need could loose in them.

The coffins were ready. Everything was set. On the morning of June 19 they would be driven to a storeroom in Kladno in two funeral cars. The coffins would be uncomfortable, Petřek had said — after all, they hadn't been built for the living — but breathing, at least, would not be a problem. He and the others, he said, had discussed various possibilities, then settled on drilling small holes precisely every two centimeters along the edges of the lids. It had taken them the better part of an afternoon. The holes looked like some kind of decoration in the wood; touched up with paint to hide the work of the drill bit, they were almost imperceptible.

They would have to be ready by six, he told them. If all went well, they would be moved from Kladno to a gamekeeper's cabin in the forests of Moravia that same evening. If any complications delayed the transfer, there were provisions enough in the store-room to last them a week.

It was convenient to know the exact hour when you would be placed in your coffin, Opálka had said afterward, and the others, who would normally have been the ones to carry that burden, and who appreciated his effort, smiled politely and nodded. Not everyone had that luxury, they said. St. Peter by appointment.

He didn't think about my mother. Or rather, he thought about her incessantly but held her back, didn't look at her directly. She was his secret, the thing he had in reserve. If he indulged it, he'd use up its power; it was enough that she was there.

On the fourteenth the schoolteacher brought them kerosene and candles. The writer Vladislav Vančura had been shot, he told them. Others as well. The Germans were flailing, he said. The twenty-million-reichsmark reward had gotten them nothing; the bicycle was still in the display window of the Bata shoe store on Václavské náměstí. It would rust there. He could see no problem with their going out one at a time every few days for air. Kubiš and Gabčík, of course, were out of the question.

It rained that day, and they watched the clouds through the window on the north wall.

On the fifteenth Valčík put on his hat and went out for five hours with a gun in his pocket and a strychnine ampoule around his neck and sat in the sun on a bench in the Children's Park.

On the sixteenth they cleaned their guns and went over the procedure one last time: The signal if the cars were being stopped; the signal to shoot. Where to keep the strychnine so that it could be found quickly and administered by someone else in case one were unable to get to it oneself. And that evening Kubiš, while slurping his soup, looked up at them and laughed and said, "Christ, boys, less than two days," and the rest of them had shaken their heads and nodded. They were afraid, all of them, but that was all right. Fear they knew.

On the morning of the seventeenth, hoping to quiet the muscles in his legs, Bém went for a walk across the square and up Francouská Street and she walked out of a grocery store directly in front of him. It was absurdly hot for June, still and white, and he looked at her, at her hair, at the side of her face . . . She was looking into her wallet, counting her change, the net bag hanging from her arm, and he watched her tilt her head impatiently and push a strand of hair behind her ear with her left hand and then she stopped and looked up and stared at him for a few moments, and then, not even knowing that she'd begun to cry, the wallet still open and the bag swinging awkwardly against her side, walked straight into his arms. He hadn't been looking for her. Or maybe he had.

They walked everywhere that long morning as the heat built up in the squares and the leaves began to droop, at first following the busier avenues, her arm through his and her head on his shoulder, an atom of life in the crowd, then drifting north through the Vinohrady district along crumbling retaining walls and up endless cascading flights of stairs that seemed to sweat some kind of stone moisture in the heat, until they came to the huge Olšany Cemetery, where they passed through the wrought-iron gates and down the four worn steps and disappeared into the vast shade of that place, a forest of ivy and stone. And when they came to the end of a long path they stood very still and she felt the same arms, the same chest pressed against her breasts, smelled the same particular smell of him. "I didn't know if you were alive," she said.

"I am," he said.

She sensed it immediately, I think, in the paleness of his skin and the bones of his back and in the way he tried now when before he would not have had to try. There was a need in him now — they both knew this — and she wanted to tell him that she would fill that need, that he could draw from her for as long as he needed to. She didn't ask where he'd been or how long he could stay; all she wanted to know was how long it would be until it was over. They were sitting together on a white stone bench at the end of a row of garish marble slabs that gave the impression of doors whose houses had disappeared. He had taken off his jacket and loosened his tie in the heat.

"A while," he said. "A few weeks." Dusty-looking sparrows kept spearing into the greenery, then flying out. "It's not quite done," he said.

"And the sixteenth?" she asked.

"I don't know," he said, "I don't know if . . . ," then looked at her and said, "I'll be there."

"Can you walk with me for a while?" my mother asked him.

"Anywhere," he said.

And so they did, down street after street, avenue after avenue, through deserted districts filled with warehouses and across a little bridge that spanned railroad tracks on which no trains could be seen in either direction, then up through the dusty vineyards and down again toward the river, burning in the midday sun. Just before two o'clock they stopped in a small *potraviny* store and bought a quarter loaf of bread and some soft cheese and she reached up and took a jar of preserved apricots off a shelf and they paid and carried them a kilometer or so to a small park near a building that looked as if it might once have been a museum of some sort and sat down in the shade to eat, but the cheese had begun to go bad, and even though he tried to cut off the bad parts with his pocketknife it was no good — the mold had gone through. He wasn't really hungry anyway, he said. My God, it was hot.

"Not quite the same, is it?" she said, smiling.

"No." He was lying on his back in the grass, the bits of pared-away cheese and the open knife next to him, and he leaned up on an elbow and looked at her. "It doesn't matter." She watched him tear off a blade of grass and begin twisting it around his finger. "There's something I have to tell you," he said. And he told her about the gun, feeling as if he were making it up to make himself more interesting, and she said it was all right, though in fact the word "gun," like a single clap, had set a flock of panicked thoughts wheeling through her mind, first this way, then that, and then he said, "So, should we go?" and he was suddenly standing in that way he had, just as he had that first night after they had come out of the wheat field with Svíčka and she'd seen him sitting back against the pine with his rucksack. He reached down his hand to her. "It'll be the same," he said, pulling her up to him. "It may take a while, I don't know how long — a few weeks, maybe longer — but it'll be the same again. Trust me."

"I know that," she said. "I do."

He indicated the little park they were standing in, the vacant lot next to it, the reedy weeds, the white, hot sky. "This doesn't matter."

"I know," she said.

But it did matter. The gun in the coat over his shoulder mattered. Their presence on every street or sitting in the cafés with their black boots thrown over their legs mattered. The heat mattered. Yet she knew there was nothing to be done. They had to walk. The red shoes were on — there was nothing else to do.

Just after three they crossed Libeňský Bridge, the Vltava flowing small and discolored below them, walked up a broad avenue with rows of small buildings on either side to a park with a stagnant fountain, and shared a lemonade. They sat on a stone bench and my mother told him about her uncle's apartment and her morning ride to work and how she thought she had seen him, and he listened and smiled when she said something funny and looked at her face as she talked, and she knew that he loved her, and that it would be just enough. She could feel it slowly bearing them down, and she could hear herself talking, talking simply to drown out its presence. They walked on, though they had nowhere to go, exhausted now, first left, then right, then left again, staying to the shade, wiping the sweat . . .

There was no shade along the bank of the Vltava, and as they hurried along the deserted cinder walkway they could see him, far ahead, sitting shirtless on a little stool between the shoreline bushes, the telltale rod sticking up like a scratch in the air. He was leaning forward, his elbows on his knees, motionless — a man fishing in an oven. They walked on, not talking now, bent on the shade of a stand of willows half a kilometer ahead, and as they approached she could see the fleshy shelves of his back, coated with sweat, the black rod protruding from a holder pushed into the bank. The river was narrower here, filthier. Pieces of what looked like furniture or bits of carpeting bobbed in the current; an automobile tire was wedged in the crotch of a tree.

It was as they were passing him, the sweat stinging her eyes, that my mother saw the yellow carp, the milk-white streak of its belly rising above the foam, its scales like rows of yellow coins or rotting armor, like a detail out of a dream of dying. Or so it would seem to her afterward. It floated just beyond the reach of his rod like an affront, and there was something terrible and funny about this. When she looked back from the shade of the willows she could still see him sitting there, his elbows on his knees, and she imagined she could see the fish, a spot of yellow in the shoreline foam, but knew she couldn't.

They went on. The sun had stopped in the sky. The fountains were dead. How long could he stay, my mother asked, though she hadn't meant to, and he looked away and said not long, a while, and for one miserable moment she wished he had to go so that they could stop this day, then knew it was the one thing in this world she wanted least, and that he felt exactly the same way. There was no help for it.

By seven they had made their way back to Vinohrady and the sun had gone behind Petřín Hill. A sluggish breeze moved down the avenues, then died. At a butcher shop they bought a bit of chicken, then a few stale *rohlíks* at a bakery that was closing, and walked on. On Žitná Street a group of four came down the middle of the sidewalk, and she and Bém stepped toward the buildings and let them pass. Two hours before the curfew, she asked him again how much longer they had before he had to go, and he looked at her and smiled a strange, pained smile. "I can't seem to leave you, can I?" he said. "Then don't," she said.

And she took him by the hand and led him back to Olšany Cemetery, carrying her shoes to save her blistered feet, and they found a gate that was open and a dark, overgrown place by the long back wall where the scraggy grass and dirt behind the row of trees and ivy were cool against her skin and he unbuttoned her clinging blouse and pushed up her sweaty skirt and entered her without saying a word, and the familiar shock of it, the desperate, unapologetic, hand-over-the-mouth ferocity of it, was enough to tell her that it would be enough. That she could save him. That she could save them both.

They stayed together that night, first moving even farther back into the dark of a small crawl space behind a row of overgrown monuments, then rolling her skirt for a long, thin pillow. It was very dark and they lay together, not touching because of the heat, talking as they hadn't been able to talk all day, and as she drifted toward sleep his voice would begin to fade, then suddenly grow louder, then fade again. Breaking the curfew was madness, they knew that. But it was done, and this place was as safe as any place could be; a patrol might come through, but there would be no dogs, and there were probably twenty kilometers of paths, thousands of monuments . . . No one would think to look behind precisely this set of stones, to crash through this particular thicket of vines.

At one point, it must have been well after midnight, she felt him jerk to attention and they lay very still as footsteps passed some distance away — a sound like knuckles tapping slowly on a bone — then disappeared, and sometime during those hours, reckless from fatigue, or love, he told her everything there was to know, where he had been and where he had to return in the morning and how it would go, and she felt, listening to him, that she'd somehow known it all along. She must give her notice at the Language Institute, he said — leave Prague. He knew someone who could get them over the border. They would meet on the sixteenth in the forest, just as they had planned.

And because they were young they made love again, just before the first leaves began to stand out from the dark, then dressed quickly, took a drink from the tap at the end of the row where visitors drew water for the flowers, and hurried out toward the gate.

The avenue was still nearly empty. She would walk him, my mother said.

It was a bit earlier than they'd thought. They waited for the tram for a while but none came, so they started walking down Vinohradská — walking tired, thinking about how they would manage it when the time came — then up Italská to Náměstí Míru, where a small knot of people stood talking on the corner, then finally down Anglická, past the shuttered stores toward Karlovo náměstí. There was some kind of commotion down by the square. An accident. They could see the barricades.

Bém had stopped. What is it? my mother said. A young woman was walking toward them, away from the square. Some kind of police action, she said. Something having to do with the church on Řesslova. The whole square was cordoned off.

She couldn't get him to move. She noticed they were beginning to attract attention. "Now," she said, taking his arm and whispering into his ear like a lover, "we have to go — now," and then he was walking fast, his head down, and as they passed each street like the spoke on a wheel she could see the barricades, the sentries, the security police with their black helmets standing in the low morning sun, and along with the nauseating throb of fear came the realization that he should have been one of them but wasn't, that he was here, with her, that he had escaped, that when the shot had come he had bent to tie his shoe, and they ducked into a small courtyard and my mother led him to a bench hidden behind the gate and held him as he sobbed, racked like a child, even as she noticed, over his shoulder, a father and a small boy with a white dog walk past them and out the gate, even as she heard the *pop pop pop* of gunfire, and realized with a kind of stunned gratitude that it was his love for her that had saved him.

IT WOULD TAKE TIME, MY MOTHER KNEW, PERHAPS A lot of time, but they would make it through — had made it through. The worst thing, the unsurvivable thing, had passed them by; now they could run. There would be no more waiting. He had said he knew someone who could get them out. And eventually, of course, the war would end, as all wars did. It had to end. The dead would be buried, the wounds would heal — or they'd learn to live with them.

She did everything. She managed to get them out of Prague to Jindřichův Hradec, from Jindřichův Hradec to Brno. She borrowed some money from her parents, found them a place, a two-room flat on the third floor of a building next to a printer's shop. It had an alcove for a kitchen and a window that looked out over the street, and there were a few pieces of furniture — a bed, a small table, a long white bookshelf with a few books in German and a Hebrew grammar . . . They had had to say they were married, of course, and when the landlady unlocked the door and showed them in, my mother had walked ahead, taking in the size of the rooms, the light, the bucket-sized sink, and she saw him watching her, and he understood what it meant to her and even tried to go along, turning a light switch on, then off . . . and when she had asked him if he thought it would be all right, he had smiled and said it seemed fine to him, a distinct improvement over their last place. A few minutes later, while checking the stove with the landlady, she looked up and saw him leaning against the wall by the open window, looking out on the street.

There was little meat to be had in the stores, but she managed anyway, making apricot dumplings one evening, bread and lentil soup the next, and they ate at the table by the window as the city grew dark around them. The evening breeze lifted the corner of the tablecloth now and then, and they talked about where they would go, what they would do. He had said he knew someone, she said, someone who could get them out. He would look into it, he said. They could stay here in the meantime, she said, until everything was ready. Yes, he said, it was the best idea. It was a very comfortable flat, he said — he liked it.

One evening as they ate, my mother turned to look out the half-closed window and saw the two of them reflected in the glass. He was looking at her. The light was almost gone but she could still make them out, sharing a table out there in the near dark, and even in the reflection she could see how much he loved her, the tenderness he had for her. He seemed to be memorizing her — and moved by this she turned from the image in the glass to the man sitting just across from her, but he had already looked away and was reaching for a piece of bread.

Three had died almost immediately. The remaining four had saved their last bullets for themselves. They'd tried to dig through the meter-thick wall to the sewers using knives and pieces of brick. When the fire hose was pushed through the small window on the north wall, they'd managed to find a ladder and shove it back out on the street. They had been betrayed by an informer, a partisan named Čurda, who later helped identify the bodies. The underground was being pulled up by the roots — men, women, entire families. Everyone they'd known. Everyone who had helped them.

My mother saw him looking at the pictures in the newspaper that morning — at the wet bodies on the pavement outside the church, at the close-ups of Kubiš and Gabčík. She was sorry, she said. On the roof she could hear pigeons cooing and then a quick flurry of wings. It was all right, he said. And for just that one moment, it was. And then he looked up at her with an odd half-smile on his face, as though he had lifted the paper to find he had no legs, and she said, "What? What is it?" and he said, "How would they have known it wasn't me? They didn't know it was Čurda when they died. They thought it was me."

She talked. She explained. They knew him, she said. He seemed to agree. She found work at a bookseller's and returned in the evenings and he was fine and she loved him and they ate their dinners together and he asked her about work and even smiled at the things that required smiling and day by day he slipped away — not willfully, not cruelly, but slipped away nonetheless. And she talked and cooked and held him at night and he did everything he could to help her and she said everything right and the reason it didn't matter was not because the others had died and he had not, but because he had been gone for sixteen hours when it began and because he would never know whether, as the water rose up their legs and the stairs began to disappear one by one, they didn't believe it was him.

And so together they staggered on, locked in love, until the morning my mother turned around at the tram stop for no apparent reason and made her way back to the flat next to the printer's and found the note on the table under the salt shaker and read the name and contact information of the man who was to have gotten them out of Czechoslovakia and underneath it, in the tall, disordered handwriting she had only lately come to know: Please don't look for me — I didn't have the strength to say goodbye. I love you will always love you. Forgive me.

And my mother refolded the note and put it back under the salt shaker and began the rest of her life.

IT WAS RAINING THE MORNING HE PARKED THE CAR BY
the old town wall, unwound the stems of his glasses from around
his ears, hooked them on the rear-view mirror, and started walking up the road from Žd'ár. No one had stopped him. He walked
easily despite the rain, one hand in his trouser pocket, his head
tilted slightly as though skeptical of the world ahead of him.
Through the archers' clefts in the wall he could see the river,
solid as pewter, a sooted steeple, a wooded hill, and for an
instant he saw them there — bows tensed, fletching brushing
their cheeks. Like children's figurines arrayed along the edge of a
dresser.

At the wrought-iron gate he called to an old man dragging a
tarp over an open grave, then pointed to some distant spot behind the bars and waited, his hand making a roof over the cigarette pinched between his fingers, calmly ducking his head every
now and then for a drag, watching as the old man finished
weighing down the four corners of the tarp with small heaps of
brick, then shuffled, still partly bent over, past the cart half full
of broken stems and small, muddy wreaths, and opened the
gate, and he thanked him and walked on up the path — left,
then right, then left again, putting as much distance between
himself and the gate as he could — then stopped by a new grave

and sank the knees of his trousers into the soft doughy soil. He brought the cigarette to his mouth in a big arc, sizzled it out carefully in the mud, then reached into his raincoat pocket and did what he would have done, had love and luck not interfered, twelve days before.

HE'D BEEN TRYING TO READ THAT MORNING, I'M SURE of it — first Sova's poems, then Horace, then Heine — fascinated by the way the fever seemed to charge certain words and phrases with a significance he couldn't quite grasp and suspected probably wasn't there. A warm, cloudy morning. Rain. His parents had both gone out. When the wind swung the window partly open my father wrapped the blanket around himself and went to shut it, and when his hand touched the wet metal of the latch, he shuddered.

He had hardly opened the new book when the frontispiece came out in his hand, and, irritated, he got up again and rummaged through the drawer of a desk that stood next to a tall black piano, then walked over to the dining room table with a squat brown jar and a pencil. He might be able to glue it back in. He wondered when they would return. The brush was too fat; it would glue half the page to the one after it. Dipping the point of the pencil just past the lead, he placed it across the mouth of the jar, opened the book to the missing page, then touched the gluey tip to the crease. A tricky business. Twice the book closed accidentally. Once he dropped the pencil on the table. He hated being sick. Heine had been sick for seven years, had written his greatest poems from the bed he would die in. It didn't make him feel any better.

The page went in badly. He pulled it out, dabbed at the glue in the crease with the tip of a napkin, then tipped it in again. Who knew when they'd be back. Everything took forever these days. He closed the book carefully, placed the Horace on top of it for weight.

Miserable weather.

He looked out the window and there she was. She was walking up the sidewalk, leaning slightly toward the suitcase in her right hand. She was wearing a long gray coat. For one nightmarish instant — perhaps it was the fever — my father thought that she was blind.

He wouldn't make her open the gate, walk up the path, knock on the door. He met her on the sidewalk in his slippers, in the rain, and even before he saw her face, before she collapsed in his arms and he half carried her down the rickety bricks that he and his father had put down when he was twelve, before he even got up from the table, in fact, he understood.

He saw it all, the arc and fall of his life — the sad carnival tune to which it would play — illuminated as clearly, as incontrovertibly, as if he had been hit by that hackneyed bolt experienced by characters in novels. He saw the gift, and the loss in that gift, and he rose from the table without hesitation or regret to shoulder the burden of his love.

ONE NIGHT WHEN I WAS FIVE OR SIX MY MOTHER WALKED out of the country bungalow we were staying in at the time. I woke to hear my father pulling on his pants in the dark. It was very late, and the windows were open. The night was everywhere. Where was he going? I asked. Go back to sleep, he said. Mommy had gone for a walk. He would be right back, he said.

But I started to cry because Mommy had never gone for a walk in the forest before, and I had never woken to find my father pulling on his pants in the dark. I did not know this place, and the big, square windows of moonlight on the floor frightened me. In the end he told me to be brave and that he would be back before I knew it and pulled on his shoes and went after his wife. And found her, eventually, sitting against a tree or by the side of a pond in her tight-around-the-calf slacks and frayed tennis shoes, fifteen years too late.

And I wonder if it was something in particular, the moon that night or the smell of the fields, that sent her out of my father's bed and into the forest, as though by simply walking far enough, deep enough, she might find him there, and herself as well, asleep in the moss, covered by a single blanket. I imagine my father closing the white-painted door of the bungalow and walking into the dark. Calling her name after he'd walked a bit farther from the other cabins. Listening to the far-off thrum of the freeway, two valleys over.

I wonder how he found her in all that darkness. And if he didn't say anything at all but simply took her back — for what else could he do? — holding her arm along the wood-chip path like an invalid crippled by grief. And if there was any way on this earth, in this life, she could not have hated him for it.

But I would wish it for her now — an endless forest, and twenty years till dawn.